DARK
HARVEST

KAREN HARPER

DARK HARVEST

MIRA®

ISBN 0-7394-4356-9

DARK HARVEST

Copyright © 2004 by Karen Harper.

Printed in U.S.A.

This book is dedicated to the talented MIRA team,
especially the sales force,
and, as ever, Don.

"For they do not speak peace,
But they devise deceitful manners
Against the quiet ones in the land."

—Psalm 35:20

Prologue

Columbus, Ohio
September 5, 2001

The kids were always the best and worst parts of Kat's job as a cop. Mike Morelli, her veteran partner who was always full of advice, insisted she cared too much and tried too hard to help them, as if she were some sort of social worker with a gun. "In the long run, you can't do jack about how bad some kids get treated today," he'd said.

Still, in her two years on the job, when she wasn't putting in eight hours on the streets, twenty-six-year-old Officer Kat Lindley volunteered to do elementary school talks about traffic safety and stranger danger. However strung out she was from working nights or overtime, it always helped her feel she was making a difference in a dark world.

"I'm glad to see all of you in Miss Noll's and Mrs. McGirty's classes again this afternoon," she said, smiling at the group of nearly sixty second graders seated cross-legged on the gym floor in a circle around her. The students had been in school since the week before Labor Day, so they were pretty antsy already. She'd come in full uniform, though it was so warm she'd left her hot Kevlar vest in the squad car. Sweat dampened her upper lip and brow and made her white shirt cling to her back. Her seventeen-pound equipment belt seemed especially heavy.

"First, we're going to review some of the things we went over last week," she told the kids. "Who can tell me what a circle of safety means? Raise your hands if you remember."

A boy she especially recalled had moved much closer to her today. Thin and blond, with ragged-cut hair, he wore the same faded Batman long-sleeved pullover shirt as last week. Though he sat in the crunch of kids, he seemed so alone. She'd asked that the children wear name tags, and his said, JOHN. Kat silently named him John Doe, not only because he seemed anonymous, but because his expression reminded her of a deer caught in headlights.

"A circle of safety is what we have to keep around us!" Tiffany, a cute girl with cornrows in her hair, shouted out when Kat called her name. "And we role-played to say 'No!' and walk or run away from strangers. Not to be afraid, but be con-fi-dent," she added as she drew out the last word.

"Very good, Tiffany," Kat said, still smiling at her little audience as she swung around to scan the gym. The Police Academy courses, as well as nights on the streets in this precinct, had taught her to watch her back. She didn't even like the kids sitting in a circle around her, but it allowed them to hear and see better.

"We'll do some more role-playing in a few minutes," Kat said, "but first I have a couple more questions."

Why, she wondered, was John wearing a long-sleeved shirt on such a warm day? Long pants, too, when the other kids were mostly in shorts. When he wasn't biting his fingernails, he kept fooling with the cuffs of his shirt, tugging them over his bony wrists.

Frowning but watching her intently, he scooted even closer.

A jagged, broken memory of her younger brother Jay flashed at her. He used to cling to Kat at night, after one of Daddy's bad spells where he'd been drinking and had taken it out on both of them. Jay cried real tears, but Kat always sat there dry-eyed, holding him in the dark, just waiting for the chance to get them away. In her dreams she was always knocking on tall doors, trying to find someone to take them in and love them like moms and dads should. She'd seen it on TV, she'd heard about it in school—families who hung together and took care of each other. And smiled and laughed, too.

"Boys and girls—" she went on with her lesson, trying to shut out the waking nightmare. "You can all answer these questions out loud together. Let's think about who really is a stranger. If someone knows your name, is he okay to trust?"

"No!" they chorused.

"That's right!"

John had shaken his head no, but had not called out with the others.

"Can you trust someone who even knows your street address and your brother's name and says he's friends with your mom?"

"No!"

"That's right, because he—or she—could just be hanging around and could have learned those things without really being a friend to you or to your family. Even though we're supposed to tell the truth, some people don't. But what if the person says he loves dogs and his is lost and he just needs some help to find it?"

"No-o-o!"

A lost dog. Little John looked like a lost dog. She

felt better when she saw he was answering the questions now, at least moving his lips to say "No, no."

She admitted the truth to herself then. John resembled her brother Jay as he'd looked those years ago, before she'd lost him, before she'd caused their separation and, in a way, his death.

Kat led the classes through a repeat of last week's role-playing about running away from a stranger encroaching on their circle of safety. "Remember," she said again, "if you get butterflies in your stomach, something isn't right, so it's best to run."

Butterflies in her stomach. That's how she felt about John Doe, despite the numerous times she'd been told—damn, she'd told *herself*—to keep her emotional distance for her own good. She'd learned even as a child to stay detached, but this boy was pushing her emotional buttons. Surely his teacher would have spotted any real problems and acted on them. Still, it was early in the school year, and these classes were large.

"If someone who is a stranger gets into your circle of safety," she told her audience as she gestured broadly, "and tries to grab you, don't be afraid. Not afraid, but angry. You have to make noise and fight. In this case, it is okay to fall to the ground, kick, scream and bite, all those things you've been told not to do. It's like when you were a little kid and threw a temper tantrum, or maybe like your younger brothers and sisters do now. But in this case, it's what you *should* do to get attention and scare the bad person away. And run as soon as you can."

After two boys happily demonstrated falling, kicking and yelling, Kat said they would go over everything again next week. She urged them to tell their parents about what they were learning and to talk at home about circles of safety and stranger danger.

When the kids began to file out, John lingered at the back of the group. Was he just straggling, or did he want to talk to her?

"Hi, John," she said, smiling and stooping to get to his height. "Did you have a question, or can I help you?"

"I was just wondering," he said, looking at her with pale blue eyes that were what she'd learned to think of as ancient, the eyes of scared kids she sometimes saw on the street. Eyes like Jay's, like her own in the mirror, years before she seized hold of her life. Her insides lurched, and she felt instantly, completely protective of this boy. Her own warning to the kids hit her with stunning impact: *If you get butterflies in your stomach, something isn't right.*

"Yeah, I got a question," the boy whispered, his voice reedy. "Can a stranger be your own dad?"

Though—or perhaps because—Kat couldn't get the boy to explain what he meant, she privately conferred with his teacher. Then Kat chatted with John Seyjack, Jr., again. "It's a pretty hot day, isn't it," she remarked, out in the hall by his classroom door. "I was sweating earlier. Why don't you roll up your sleeves to get a bit cooler?"

"No," he told her, "I'm okay. I like this shirt like it is."

Kat knew she shouldn't legally push it any further. His teacher had told Kat she'd seen no signs of abuse but promised to have a conference with John's father; school records showed the mother was dead. John was new to the district this year, so there was no one else in the building to consult about his past. Kat decided to take the boy home so she could assess his family situation.

She was convinced something was wrong. She'd seen it in her own brother in the first foster home they'd shared, after their mother had taken off to God-knows-where and Kat had told the neighborhood cop about Daddy's beatings. But that first foster home hadn't worked out, so Kat took Jay and ran away. She had been nine and he six.

"You don't need to take me home," little John Seyjack protested again, his voice almost inaudible over the crackle of the police car radio. "Usually, I walk all by myself. You got great wheels though. I always thought the lights and siren were, like, way bad."

"Would you like to turn on the lights and beep the siren?"

"Oh, yeah? Could I?"

She showed him how and smiled when he did. His eyes lit and, excited as he seemed, he also relaxed a bit. She had considered making a deal with him: you roll up your shirtsleeves first. But she was hoping to establish some trust with this little loner.

"You can let me out here," he said, pointing. "I'll walk the rest of the way home—just down there."

But she found a spot to parallel park the cruiser. The boy had said his dad would be home but seemed hesitant to confide anything else about him. She told herself she was just giving the kid a ride and would merely meet John, Sr., to assess the situation. She'd explain she was off duty—as if a cop was ever off duty.

The houses were crammed together in this neighborhood near Cleveland Avenue, old enough and cheap enough that they had no garages and everyone parked on the street. The Seyjack home was a side-by-side duplex with peeling gray paint and the curtains all drawn. An air conditioner propped up on slanted wooden stilts hummed in an upstairs window. The yard was crowded by a bent wire fence and cluttered with unplanted and untended brick-lined flower beds of dirt and weeds.

"He works nights," John said, as if he'd explained the closed house to others. She was going to ask who stayed in the house with him at night when he blurted, "Are you going to tell him about a circle of safety?"

The house door swung open before she could answer. On the other side of the snagged screen door stood a short, clean-shaved, thin man in cutoff jeans and a black T-shirt, a can of cola in his hand. He wore thick glasses, and his brown hair was slicked down as if he'd just taken a shower.

Kat breathed easier when she saw the house was lighted inside. No smell or sign of alcohol or even tobacco.

"What's wrong?" he asked, frowning at his son. "You get hurt, boy, or done something wrong?"

"Everything's fine, Mr. Seyjack," she assured him, forcing a smile. The man was about five foot six, her height. As wiry as he was, she might outweigh him. She saw where John, Jr., had gotten his ashen appearance and nervous demeanor.

"I was just heading this way and thought I'd drop John off," she explained, one hand on the boy's bony shoulder and the other casually gesturing. "We've been doing traffic safety and stranger danger lessons in school. Absolutely no problem, Mr. Seyjack."

"Better not be." He opened the door and reached past her to put his hand on John's head and pull him into the house. Like any good cop would, Kat took the opportunity to step into the doorway and assess the scene. The boy scooted inside past her. The front room looked shabby but neatly kept—normal.

"You the school cop?" the man asked.

"No, sir, I just volunteer there. I'm off duty today."

"The boy's not been talking out of turn, has he?" the man asked with a glance back at the child.

The hair on the back of Kat's neck prickled. The slightest undertone of coercion or threat etched the man's voice. But it was his narrow-eyed look and the way the child froze that told her she'd been right. Whether physically or emotionally, John, Jr. was being abused and was as endangered as if some stranger had crashed into his circle of safety. *"Can a stranger be your dad?"*

Kat tried to keep her usual calm as she dropped her right hand to her holstered gun. She knew she was good at defusing tense situations on the street, or listening to problems—times when a male officer might have jumped in with both feet. The truth was that a female officer's best weapon was her brain. The part of Kat's career she loved most was getting and staying in control of a situation, setting something right. She had learned, as little Tiffany had said today, "con-fidence." Damn, maybe she was overreacting here, just because of her own wretched childhood. This kid was all right, and she was overstepping.

But then—whether it was a silent cry for help or little John just needed to scratch an itch—the boy pulled up his shirt, revealing a stark white belly and a prominent rib cage. Her first thought was that he was awfully pale for the end of the summer, when other kids looked so healthy and tanned. Her second was that the livid, crescent-shaped scars crisscrossing his flesh were from a series of whippings with some kind of cord.

Before Kat could react, the man glanced again at

his son. Then he slammed the door and hit her in the face with his fist and the pop can in a blur of motion.

The pain was incredible. Hot streaks of fire radiated through her face, her head, her neck, down her spine. She crashed to her rear and her back, sprawled at first, hitting her head again on the floor. But somehow she instinctively reached for her flashlight. She needed a club, and fast.

But gut instinct, as much as her watering eyes, told her *gun!*

The small weapon her attacker pointed at her must have been stuck in the back of his pants. The tiny bore of the pistol seemed as big as a planet.

She went for her pistol with her right hand and her walkie-talkie with her left.

"He been talking, ain't he?" he demanded. "You got other cops outside?"

Kat went on sensory overload as adrenaline and panic poured through her. She acted instinctively, twisting away as she went for her .45. She had the safety on, too, because of being in the school. Should have worn her vest. Didn't have her ankle holster gun today. In that split second, she imagined she heard Morelli's voice: *"Nothing is routine. Expect the unexpected."*

Everything happened so fast and yet dragged by in slow motion too. "No, Dad!" the boy cried, his voice loud. "I didn't tell her nothing 'bout the extra money!"

The extra money?

The boy screamed as the man shot Kat. The bullet blasted her in the hip. Searing, red pain, then an icy coldness. But no gush of blood. Had it hit her, or had she just fallen awkwardly?

Instead of cowering or scooting away, she rolled toward the man, into him, knocking him over her.

The boy was shrieking, "No, Dad. No! I didn't tell her nothing!"

Kick, scream, bite. Her own advice flew at her as if someone had shouted it. *Gun. Gun! Get his gun.*

On the floor, the shooter lunged at her. They struggled for his weapon, even as she managed to hit the red 10-3 officer-down button on her radio. The dispatcher would not know the address. She screamed into it, "316 Creigo Street, 33, 33!"

The gun they fought for—the 33 code—was a 9-mm semiautomatic. Kat tried to keep the muzzle from pointing at her or the boy.

"Run for help, John!" she shouted. "Go! Go!"

But the child seemed frozen where he stood.

As if from a great distance she heard the scratchy voice of the police dispatcher, but the grunts and noise of their struggle obscured the words, and she couldn't even see the radio now. Kat was good at projecting an authoritarian voice, cracking out orders to *Freeze! Drop the gun!* But too late for that. This man fought like one demented, and she did too. She ripped his glasses from his face.

When they rolled over again, through the haze of pain and fear she managed to draw her gun. Had to squeeze the trigger…before this bastard squeezed…or shot the life out of her…

But he shoved her away and jumped up to grab his son, pinning him against his adult body like a thin shield with the gun pointed past the boy's ear at her. She lifted her gun, too, ready to shoot. All the air seemed to suck out of her lungs but she had to speak.

"Drop that gun, Mr. Seyjack—before it accidentally goes off again," she said through gritted teeth, though her own pain screeched loud enough to drown out her words. Panting hard, she tried to get some mobility back. But her whole left leg was now wet with hot, sticky blood and wouldn't obey her. She held her gun as steady as she could, both arms extended.

"Drop that weapon!" She tried a command again, but her voice trembled like her muscles. At least she'd never been one of the female officers who cried when things went wrong. She hadn't cried since they'd taken Jay away from her. "Mr. Seyjack, release your son and drop the weapon!"

She was afraid to shoot. Even if she aimed for the man's head and upper torso, her vision was starting to blur and she might hit the boy from this low angle. She was suddenly certain she was going to black out.

"Remember the circle—of safety, John?" she rasped. The pain clawed not only at her hip but at her belly and back. "You know—what to do…"

The boy tried to drop to the ground, kicking and screaming, throwing his father off balance. Maybe she could get a clear shot, but another blast was deafening. Her shooting hand exploded. Her gun flew away.

Kat heard a man's voice yell, "Traitor! My own flesh and blood—you little traitor!"

Then the world went black.

1

Maplecreek, Ohio
September 6, 2002

"For someone who'll never shoot again," Kat Lindley muttered as she strode up the walk of the only new building this little town had evidently seen for years, "whatcha gonna do?"

Kat really wanted this interview to go well, even though it was for what her buddies in the CPD would call a "rubber gun job"—desk work. She could feel the cool morning breeze in the ache of her reconstructed hip and wrist as well as on her sweaty palms. Imagine, metal screws holding together bones in a woman her age. At least now she could sympathize with Morelli's early arthritis.

But Kat was relieved she'd never have to work the city streets again. The reality of little John Seyjack's murder at the hands of his berserk father and then Seyjack Senior's death during the ensuing SWAT team response had shaken her to her core, even though she had been unconscious during all that.

She wasn't sure she could face the unknowns of being a cop again. She'd been through hell this past year, almost bleeding to death, then a lengthy hospital stay, hip and wrist surgery, and walking on crutches, then a cane. Rehab had been grueling to regain her

ADL's, activities of daily living, which did *not* include ever shooting a gun again. That was a necessity for an active duty cop, so her dream career was as fractured as her bones.

Kat had been through counseling, too, though she hardly needed a shrink to realize she blamed herself for causing the child's death. She knew it had ripped open her wound of festering guilt from losing her little brother years ago. But she still felt she was to blame for taking Jay away from their first foster home. The result was their separation when placed in their second homes. Jay had died of a burst appendix because his foster family believed in prayer more than in doctors. If she hadn't rebelled in the first foster home, however rough it was, they would have been together. She'd have gotten him help when he became sick. No psychiatrist could really help her, because she could never make up for it, never forgive herself for the deaths of Jay and John.

Two months ago, Kat had pulled herself out of her depression and had taken training to become a police dispatcher, though she'd probably die of boredom doing it. And it would be a real downer not to be on the streets anymore. Since she had no ties in Columbus beyond a few friends on the force, and she had less in common with them every day, she'd chosen a clean break with her past.

Last month she had moved here to northeast Ohio, which she'd always thought of as peaceful Amish country. She'd rented an upstairs apartment from a widow in the town of Pleasant, near Maplecreek, the county seat. At first she spent her time hitting the antique sales she'd always loved, carefully bargaining for pieces she could use or resell. But her nest egg had dwindled, so she'd applied for the job of the Roscoe County Sheriff's Police and Emergency Vehicle Dispatcher. If she didn't get it, she'd surely find something else to tide her over until she could get an antiques resale business going. That was her new goal in life.

"Katherine Anne Lindley, go get 'em," she whispered as she went in the double doors of the new civic center, which served as police station, volunteer fire department and mayor's office.

The current day dispatcher, a pregnant young woman who explained she was also filling in for the receptionist, who was at a dentist's appointment, greeted her warmly and took her right in to meet Sheriff Ray Martin in his large, glass-walled office.

"Katherine, real glad to meet you," he said, shaking her hand. He indicated a maple colonial chair and held it for her as if seating her at a table. The chair's padded cushion was covered in quilted calico with a ruffle.

"It's a real pleasure," he added as he sat in his own chair across his cluttered desk. The handsome wood console behind him held the expected fax machine, PC screen and keyboard, but also ceramic planters full of sprawling ivy and a slew of what must be his kids' photos.

"Please, call me Kat. I haven't been Katherine for years," she told him, returning his bright smile. The man and his office fit the area. Maplecreek's large farms, mostly Amish-owned, the gift shops, bed-and-breakfasts, "Dutch" restaurants, and small commercial ventures made a real stew-pot of past and present. The town could have been straight out of a Currier and Ives print, but for the continual onslaught of tourists who came to gawk, eat and buy, just as Kat often had.

Sheriff Martin was about fifty, five foot eleven, a sturdy-looking man with military-cut, silvering hair and the hint of an incipient potbelly, though he wore his crisp-looking brown and tan uniform well. His hazel eyes were alert and interested as he led her through initial small talk. Their conversation showed Kat he loved his job and his jurisdiction. His youngest son, Mark—the sheriff showed her a picture of himself with a plump, smiling wife and three kids—was currently quarterbacking the consolidated high school team, and they had a big game tonight. It was homecoming, so they were going to have fireworks at halftime.

Maplecreek was the place he had grown up in and returned to after military service, Ray Martin told her, putting her even more at ease by almost letting her interview *him*. He rocked slightly in his swivel chair as they chatted. She felt she could trust him, though she'd learned the hard way that she stunk at quick character assessments.

"Before we discuss the specific duties of this job," Sheriff Martin went on, "I just want us to be clear about your move here. It's a long-term thing, that right?"

"Yes, I've pulled up stakes in Columbus. And I don't want you to have any questions about all I've been through lately. After an incident went—" Her voice snagged and she took a deep breath. "After it went very bad last year, I was shot. I was investigated by Internal Affairs for the way I handled a situation. But I was cleared. Actually, the man who shot me had not only abused his son but robbed several banks in the Columbus suburbs."

He nodded. "Gotta admit I read all about you online, Kat. Besides the IA guys clearing you, I see you got a string of awards, American Legion of Valor, all that. Listen, I understand about needing life changes and that it can be tough to readjust. For years, Roscoe County had one sheriff. Like a king around here, Sheriff Barnes was—did things his own way, so folks come to expect business as usual from me. But we got us this new civic center, new leadership, new ways of doing things. This area's growing and changing, with even some residential developments creeping in. It looks real idyllic and peaceful here'bouts, but it's full of folks who don't always see eye-to-eye, which you'll learn soon enough working in this office.''

"If you're offering me the job, Sheriff, I'm ready to accept.''

"Good,'' he said, getting up to shake her hand again, as if that sealed it. "Tell you what. How about I let you meet the office staff and spend an hour or so with the day dispatcher today, 'cause she can explain what she does better'n me. If it's fine by you, you can start on Monday. I'm real shorthanded, and it'll be good to have a dispatcher who knows the ropes about enforcement, too, know what I mean?''

If she didn't know, Kat figured, in a town this tiny and an area this rural, she would soon.

"Eli,'' Luke Brand told his nine-year-old son in the low German dialect the Amish always used among themselves. "I told you to cut *green* branches for roasting those sausages.''

"But *Daad*,'' the boy protested with a gap-toothed grin as he thrust his dried, burning stick over the flames among those of the older kids, "it gets done fast this way, and I like it crusty. The sticks I cut for Sarah and Melly were green, *ja*, see? For the marshmallows later I'll get me a new one.''

Luke just shook his head. Little Eli always liked to turn his marshmallows into flaming torches, too. This Friday night bonfire, which drew so many of the Amish young people, was at the back lot line of the Brand farm this week, so Luke had volunteered to oversee it. Since he was a widower, the teenagers during their running-around period seemed to accept his watchful eye easier than they did that of someone with a fussing woman in tow. And the courting couples didn't mind if he brought his two kids and his brother Dan's nine-year-old daughter Melanie along. To keep out of their way as best he could, he took his sizzling sausage, thrust it into a bun smothered with onions, mustard and homemade cucumber dill pickles and went off to eat it near the edge of the cornfield where the boys had left their courting buggies.

It was a beautiful, moonlit autumn night, and Luke was glad to be doing something to keep from feeling lonely. In the five years since he'd been widowed, the nights were the hardest to get through. His family and friends had tried to pair him with some of the younger girls, since most Amish women his age were wed, but things just hadn't clicked for him, although he wasn't mourning Anna anymore.

He sighed and his shoulders slumped before he got hold of himself and remembered to stay grateful for his many blessings. The coming autumn was his favorite time of year, with warm, sunny days, cool nights, and the trees turning rich reds and golds. The vast cornfields that surrounded the farm would be ready for harvest soon, for the growing season was late this year. He could feel the first hints of crisp air clear down in his lungs when he inhaled.

But he admitted to himself that he'd like to share all that, take a walk in the woods with someone special. At least at night he was usually exhausted enough to sleep long and hard from all the work around the farm and his windmill shop.

Out here, away from big-city lights, as his brother Dan always said, the stars stood out like scattered diamonds, not that Luke, even at age thirty-two, had seen either scattered diamonds or big-city lights. Unlike Dan and others who took off for a taste of worldly life among the English in their *rumspringa* years, Luke had stayed home. He'd been happy here in Roscoe County, sure of what he wanted.

The only unexpected thing he'd ever done was start a shop, where he and a small staff made decorative windmills, as well as full-size functional ones. The church elders had held a meeting to decide about the propriety of the decorative windmills—"just for pretty," as his wife had said. That very month, Luke had won his argument but lost his Anna in childbirth complications when she bore Sarah. Despite the fact she'd done all the prenatal visits with her doctor, her blood pressure had shot up and she'd developed eclampsia.

Luke looked at his five-year-old, blond daughter, giggling with Melanie, both of them wide-eyed over the way the courting couples held hands, stole *smootchs,* or whispered together. Sarah wore her black bonnet over her *kapp,* but Melanie, free spirit that she was, wore a Cleveland Indians baseball cap backward over her curly auburn hair. Covering her head around her father's people was some concession, Luke supposed, to her half-Amish roots, for his brother Dan had left the faith ten years ago to wed a worldly woman.

Luke heard a strange hum, a dissonant, distant sound. Even over the kids' happy voices as someone started a song, it caught his attention, like the buzzing of a wasp. Not an airplane, he assured himself, glancing skyward and walking farther from the circle of firelight. Surely not a car on the road, for the lanes to the Brand acreage, which he farmed with his brother Moses, were far enough away that the wide cornfields would mute the noise.

But the strange sound kept coming closer.

Pricking up their ears, the horses hitched to the courting buggies sidestepped and whinnied. Some sort of small motor, Luke decided, as he walked farther away from the kids to gaze down the twelve-foot-wide lane they'd left unplanted between two cornfields so they could get the combine and wagons in. Yes, he saw a single, small light coming at him down the lane, bumping through the ruts.

He shook his head. A motorbike. No doubt one of the Amish kids had rented it. Cars, motorcycles, drinking, smoking, movies, rock music and dances, even drugs on occasion—some Amish teens tried everything before they finally committed to the church and things Amish. But he didn't need some kid full of beer turning the corner and hitting those around the fire.

Luke stepped into the middle of the lane and waved his arms, crisscrossing them slowly before his face. Like his brothers, he was tall for an Amish man, nearly six feet, but he was wearing all black and the rider evidently didn't see him.

Then he realized the biker saw him but wasn't going to stop. He wore a dark visor, like on a space helmet or one worn by some football players on TV Luke had watched in English homes or shops. And gloves—he wore gloves.

At the last minute, Luke leaped out of the way. As the motorbike made the turn, the rider, in jeans and black leather jacket, dragged his booted foot to keep from taking a spill, then accelerated again.

Luke lunged after the bike, around the corner of the cornfield, screaming at the kids, "Look out! Look out!"

Nine-year-old Eli Brand spent a lot of his time watching his dad. He lost his mother when he was four, and he was scared he'd lose his dad, too. He watched him real careful, every time he could, especially when Dad climbed those high windmills.

Now the motorbike—the one his dad was yelling about—came real fast around the corner of the field.

"Look out! Look out!" Eli repeated his father's shout.

Despite being absorbed in their singing, by now the older kids had seen the bike and stood gaping at it. Eli was grateful the driver steered easily around them. But he threw something into the bonfire, right past Eli's head—a package that exploded with noise and flames. Shrieking rockets and a blaze of color blasted sideways and skyward.

Horses shied, reared and dragged their buggies, bumping into cornstalks or each other. Kids dove for cover, running, screaming, scattering into the rows of tall corn or toward the nearby ravine.

Eli wanted to run to his dad like his little sister did, but his legs wouldn't move. Stars kept banging like real loud popcorn. Beside him, his cousin Melly looked frozen in fear. He took her hand and ran from the heat, from the noise, toward the shelter of the trees.

Others ran that way, too, and Eli and Melly got caught up in the rush and push. He knew the ravine was steep and thick with trees, so they could hide there in case the man on the bike came back, in case the fireworks caught the field on fire.

The ravine was black to their eyes, which were used to the lights of the bonfire and the booming flares. He couldn't see, and Melly was running really fast, yanking his hand. Then Melly was gone into the darkness, screaming.

Something whipped Eli in the face, right across his eyes. Stabbed by pain, he grabbed a tree and held on tight, so tight.

In his hurt and fear, he saw again in his head that night his mother died. He was holding tight to Grandma Ida's hand as she took him into the hospital room to see his mother—to say goodbye, they said. Something went bad when she had Sarah—"in clamps seesaw" and too much high blood pressure. This scene in his head was the first thing he could remember in his whole life.

"Anna, are you in pain, my love?" Dad had said to Mother as he sat by her hospital bed with baby Sarah in a tiny bed on wheels right by hers. Mother looked too big, like she ate too much and was all swollen.

"Yes, but I'm not afraid. Everyone will help you, my Luke, especially with the baby. You and Eli take care of each other...."

That was what Eli remembered—not saying goodbye to her, not even much of the funeral. Only that he had to take care of his father, but his eye hurt so bad he couldn't even see to find him.

Luke was stunned by how deathly quiet it had become, but for the scuffing sounds of some older boys stomping out an errant grass fire. He heard the whine of the motorbike fading into the distance. Whoever had been on it knew the lanes between the fields and the way back to Ridge Road. And he knew where the Amish kids would be and when. Yet, surely that had not been one of their own. "Come on back!" Luke shouted, still hugging Sarah. "It's over now."

But he knew it wasn't over. For months someone had been harassing the Plain People of Maplecreek in ways that could no longer be passed off as mere pranks. And now, children had become the targets. He had discussed with his father, the bishop, about whether something should be done. With this outrage, Luke intended to insist on it, however much Christian doctrine said to "turn the other cheek."

But his fury segued to frenzy when he realized two kids were missing, his own Eli and Dan's Melanie.

"Did anybody see Eli and Melanie?" he shouted, prying Sarah loose and handing her to Mattie Wengerd, who seemed the calmest of the girls. "Who else isn't here?"

"They ran down there, Eli and Melly, holding hands, toward the ravine, Mr. Brand," a boy called. Silas Yoder emerged from the darkness, helping Eli walk, for Eli was holding his hands over his face. Blood coursed down the boy's cheeks and neck.

"Eli got whipped in the face with a branch and he lost Melly," Silas cried, as Luke tried to get a look at how badly his son's face was cut.

There was so much blood, Luke couldn't tell. He ripped his jacket off and tied its arms around the boy's forehead above his already swollen eye. With regret, he let Silas tend his son again and turned away.

If anything happened to his niece, it would kill Dan and his wife, Brooke. The girl was their only child, though she'd been raised with Brooke's niece, Jennifer.

"Two of you go for help and bring back lanterns," Luke ordered the boys. "I know you're hurting and scared, son," he told Eli, squeezing his shoulders, "but do you know where Melanie is?"

"She was with me—we fell," the boy choked out. "I don't know. I couldn't see... Dad, it hurts but I'm not scared."

Luke blinked back tears. "Silas, find your buggy and take Eli to his grandparents at the *daadi haus,* and have them tend him and get him to a doctor. Eli, I'll be there as fast as I can, but I've got to look for Melanie. Silas, have someone get her parents and send help."

"Amish help or English?" Silas asked. The Amish handled their own problems and traditionally did not trust worldly law enforcement.

"Get all the help you can!" Luke shouted over his shoulder as he grabbed and lit a lantern. Holding to trees when the way got too steep, he started down into the black ravine, crying, "Melanie? *Wo bist du?* Where are you? Melanie!"

Brooke Brand felt trapped in a double nightmare, remembering that awful night Dan's niece Katie died and the time she'd almost lost her own niece Jennifer in an attempted abduction. Now, with her arm tight around the seventeen-year-old Jen as if to assure herself things would be all right, Brooke stood, helpless and distraught, as the Amish searched a dark ravine for her only child.

"Melly will be all right, Aunt Brooke," Jen, still bare-legged and dressed in her cheerleading outfit and Eagles jacket from the homecoming game tonight, told her. "I just wish she'd come to the game with you and Dan, but you know how she loves to be with Eli and the Amish kids.''

''I'm going down into that ravine myself,'' Brooke insisted, but she was shaking too hard to even move. Her unspoken fear was that the man on that bike had somehow abducted Melly, the way Jen had been taken once. ''I can't lose her, Jen, I can't!''

''They'll find her, and she'll be okay. Nothing can hurt a tough little tomboy like Melly.''

The night was pierced by occasional shouts of the searchers—at least ten Amish men, the county sheriff, both his deputies—and by the fierce pulsing of the strobe lights of the two police cars and the volunteer rescue squad that stood ready.

''Stretcher!'' Brooke heard the word passed along. ''We've got her!''

Stretcher, Brooke thought. They were calling for a stretcher, so that meant she must be hurt, didn't it? Hurt, that was all.

Holding hands, she and Jen tore toward the trees edging the ravine.

''We're gonna bring her up, ma'am, so just wait there,'' Sheriff Martin told her. Through the thick screen of trees she could see the searchers' lanterns and flashlights below. ''She's breathing, Mrs. Brand. Just seems to have knocked herself out on a tree trunk or rock—big bump on her head. Rolled into a deep pile of leaves where she was hard to spot, but Luke Brand found her.''

Her brother-in-law. ''Oh, thank God. Thank God!'' Brooke sobbed, hugging Jen.

The EMR volunteers with the stretcher moved past her into the depths of the ravine, even as Luke trudged up toward her. He was the same height as her Dan but didn't have the same laid-back nature and lankiness.

Luke was all taut muscles and even tauter emotions, like a coiled spring. Brooke hugged him hard. His body felt as chiseled as Dan's handmade furniture.

"Thank you, Luke! Thank you!"

Luke hugged Brooke, then set her back. "I think she's really out, Brooke, out cold."

"A concussion? Can she can move her legs or—"

"They can't tell yet. You hear what happened? Why she ran?"

"Yes. Luke, I know the Amish forgive and forget, but someone's to blame for this, and they've got to be stopped."

"I wish I had done more, handled it different. I'm having lots of trouble accepting these attacks on us as the Lord's will. And I'm going to do something about it, whatever the bishop says." He muttered the last words under his breath.

His voice held more than determination. There was anger, though the Amish always tried to stay on an even keel, these peaceful Plain People she'd come to love and admire so deeply in the ten years she'd lived among them.

"I gotta go find out how Eli's cut face is," Luke told her. "I bet he needed stitches."

But Brooke didn't hear anything else Luke said. They were carrying Melly's small, still form, strapped on a stretcher, up from the dark chasm. Dan came behind, his hand on their daughter's foot as if his strength could will her to awake. Melly's head was taped to a backboard and a foam collar supported her neck. Brooke gasped. Katie had looked like that the night she died.

"Is she—paralyzed?" she demanded of them all, taking Melly's cold hand in both her trembling ones.

"Can't tell yet, ma'am," the medic holding the

front of the stretcher told her. "She's comatose. And unless she regains consciousness soon, they may MediVac her to a bigger hospital than the county one."

Brooke nodded. She hated that place in nearby Pleasant. It was where Katie died after a hit-and-run. No, her daughter was not going to that hospital.

"Sheriff," Brooke cried, running over to his car where Ray Martin was just getting off his radio, "I want you to call for a chopper to airlift her right now, from here. To the Cleveland Clinic, to Children's Hospital in Columbus…somewhere she can get the best treatment immediately. I can call on my cell phone, but I'll bet you could get it done faster."

The man actually looked as if he'd argue. But he knew Brooke was one of the only two lawyers in town—or else he knew a rabid mother of a hurt child when he saw one. He immediately got back on the radio.

Praying, whispering, Dan, Brooke and Jen huddled at the back of the rescue vehicle while the medics worked inside to stabilize Melanie for the coming helicopter flight.

"Luke's going to do something this time about these attacks," Brooke told Dan. "He's the real leader of the Amish community now that your father's ill. I don't care what they say about the church elders taking more control."

"Dad will calm Luke down," Dan muttered, wiping tears away with the palm of his hand. "God's will, the martyrs' heritage, acceptance and inner strength, all that."

"Not this time," Brooke insisted, gripping him so hard he winced. "Not this time."

2

"Is your stomach still bothering you, Dad?" Luke asked as he sat down next to his elderly father, Jacob Brand, the next evening on the porch of his parents' home. The weather or one's ailments, Luke figured, was a safe way to begin this potentially volatile conversation.

He'd finally found a place to get some privacy for the two of them on this busy Saturday. The traditional grandparents' house on the Brand farm was just across the lane from the farmhouse where Luke lived with his children and past Luke's windmill shop. It was customary for the grandparents to move into the retirement *daadi haus* close by, when the eldest son assumed the main farming duties and had several children of his own. Luke was the third son, after Moses and Dan, a furniture maker who lived in town with his non-Amish family. Gid and Mahlon, their younger brothers, had moved their families to western Ohio.

"Feeling some better." The man the Amish community called Bishop Brand gave his usual reply. "But it's not my stomach we must speak of, my son. You know vengeance is not our way, but must be left in the Lord's hands."

So the sage old man did know what he wanted to discuss. "I'm not talking vengeance," Luke insisted, rising from his mother's rocking chair to pace the porch, but he got hold of himself and sat on the railing, leaning toward his father. "I'm talking earthly justice, just good, commonsense protection for our people. Now that someone's evidently targeting our children, I'm even talking survival. This isn't just someone running buggies off the road or ruining quilts hanging on a line anymore. Dan's Melanie is in a coma, and Eli may have permanently lost the sight in his left eye. What's next?"

"Luke, sit. Sit and consider what I have to say."

Luke thumped down in the chair again so hard it rocked back to hit the wall before he hunched forward in it. Still seething, he regarded his father silently. Whatever the bishop said, he was going to get outside help on this. He knew Dan and Brooke would back him, but they were at Children's Hospital in Columbus, over a hundred miles away, at the bedside of their daughter. And Dan and Brooke weren't Amish.

"Go ahead, Dad," he said when he realized his white-bearded father was waiting for him to calm down enough to listen.

"You have been my rock these past years, Luke. So God-gifted with words, so dedicated to our people, *you* should be the bishop, but the Lord knows best. Dan left us for a different life, and Mose is busy with his big family. Gid, Mahlon, Ruth and their families had to leave to afford land for their sons. But even when you lost Anna, you stayed strong and sure that this was your home, your place in life."

"I'm strong and sure now."

"*Ach,*" he said, throwing up his mottled hands. "It takes a strong man to bear up under persecution and still go the extra mile, to turn the cheek. My son, 'the wicked watches the righteous and seeks to slay him,' but the Lord will protect his people in the land."

"The earlier pranks—that sort of petty cruelty, I can take, Dad. But I respectfully tell you I can't accept it when our children are harmed and endangered. It has to stop here and now, even if God will avenge it on His judgment day. I'm going to the sheriff to tell him I will swear out a complaint if he finds who's to blame for tossing those fireworks in the bonfire last night. Dan and Brook's Melanie may never wake up for all we know, and Eli's eye..."

He sniffed hard and blinked back the sting of unshed tears.

"Luke." Bishop Brand began again, putting his hand on the arm of Luke's chair. "In a court of worldly law, even if they caught the evildoers, a judge or jury would say the children chose to run into the ravine. Accidents do happen, they would say. It would be judged some sort of—what is that Brooke called it?—misdemeaning."

"Misdemeanor," Luke said. "But the truth is, Dad, that's what they call hate crimes now."

"So what is new for our people? And our fighting it could only make things worse. You know the sheriff has looked into the incidents before."

"He only knew of a few minor incidents because Brooke reported what she heard, not because our people did. The sheriff has no idea of the extent of things. So here's my idea."

"I am listening, *ja.* Do I have a choice?"

Luke turned his chair sideways to look directly into his father's flinty stare. "The cowards who are harassing us think they're safe, so things are escalating. We need someone living within our community to look into it, someone our enemies will not recognize or suspect is trying to learn who they are. Someone to gather evidence, someone the evildoers do not see as a threat, someone who could spot who they might be."

"*Ach,* you know who they could be, and I do too. Those so-called Patriot Knights, who cannot accept anyone different from themselves. Or the carpenter's union, angry with our men for under-bidding them on jobs. Or maybe someone who resents we do not pay taxes or send our *kinder* to their schools. But—you don't mean,'' he said, reaching out to grip Luke's wrist, "bring in some outsider, an *auslander?*''

Before he could get cut off, Luke plunged on. "Harvest time will soon be here. We could ask Sheriff Martin to arrange for a deputy from some nearby community to come in, someone who could dress Amish, pass for one of our Pennsylvania or Western Ohio relatives here on a visit, just for a few weeks. We've brought in cousins to help with the harvest before. I'm asking you for permission not only to request that but to house him here.''

"Here? On our farm, this deceit?''

"Here, in the back room you and *Mamm* have in this house. That way you could keep an eye on what he learns, and I'd be nearby to help him to get this all cleared up.''

"All this, are you asking me or telling me, my son and my brother in the faith?'' Jacob asked, as his white eyebrows shot up so high they disappeared under the black brim of his hat.

He sat back in his rocker and folded his hands across his belly, though whether in defiance or in pain, Luke wasn't sure.

"I know you'll want to pray on it and consult the elders too,'' Luke said, grateful he'd gotten it all out. But God's truth, he'd just explained what he was *going* to do, not asked for what he'd *like* to do. "I heard you tell Mother just last week, you don't want to leave your people in danger,'' he added in the sudden silence between them.

"With my bouts of stomach pains, I might die, you

mean? Maybe I have ulcers after all, and it would be no surprise they are acting up right now.''

''Surely you'll be more upset if this attempted intimidation continues. And I didn't mean you were going to die but that you didn't want your people to go on fearing for their safety—maybe their lives. Our ancestors came to America to put a stop to all that.''

''To me, it sounds like you are trusting yourself, not the Lord,'' his father accused, jabbing the air between them with a bony finger.

''Only trusting myself to do what I believe He commands of me, to help protect his flock.''

''And He cannot do such Himself?''

''Yes, He can, but He uses us as his workmen here on earth. Dad—Bishop Brand—I cannot look into the eyes—the eye—of my only son and tell him I didn't try my best to stop this, or worse, from happening to another Amish child or to our way of life we so cherish.''

To Luke's amazement, his father slowly nodded. ''If you find the right man, one you believe God has sent for this task to help preserve our way and our children,'' he said, ''your mother and I will take him in here and help him at least look and act Amish.''

On the Sabbath the next day, at the end of his sermon, Bishop Brand presented the plan to the Maplecreek-area Amish congregation, meeting this week in the Wengerds' barn on Sawmill Road. There was some murmuring, some discussion, but then consensus. As ever, the Amish would act as a community, in this case accepting and protecting the *auslander* who would come to help them. If anyone worldly asked about the newcomer, they were to say simply that he was a distant cousin of Bishop Brand.

''And since we're all descended from Adam and

Eve in the first garden,'' Luke had overheard his mother whisper to his sister Emma, '''distant cousin' is a truthful way to put it. All this must stop and now!''

On Monday morning, Luke left his windmill shop and farm chores and drove his buggy into town to talk to the sheriff. He tied his horse behind the hardware store and went in the back door of the new civic building, feeling as if he were undercover himself. He didn't want word around the English community that he was going to the sheriff. It had been his people's custom since they were persecuted and martyred by the authorities in Europe years ago to have no truck with worldly law enforcement. If he'd thought of it, he would have sent word for the sheriff to meet him somewhere on neutral ground, but it was too late for that. Still, he and all the Plain People must learn to keep secrets now.

Walking down the back hall, Luke saw Sheriff Martin sitting in his office. The door was open and the top half of the walls were glass. Luke glanced through to see three women in the large, front room: an elderly one sat at the reception desk, a pregnant one stared at a computer screen, and a blonde with a trim bottom bent over the shoulder of the pregnant one.

He rapped his knuckles quietly on the sheriff's door.

''Hey, Mr. Brand, come on in,'' Sheriff Martin said, rising and shaking his hand. ''Sorry to say I don't have anything yet to report about who trespassed and assaulted your young people on Friday. I hear your boy may lose an eye—the sight in it, I mean—and that your niece is still comatose.''

The man closed the door to the hall as he spoke. The three women looked their way. The white-haired receptionist and the pregnant woman showed surprise to see an Amish man there, but the blonde just studied him, her face alert with interest. Her wide-set eyes under arched brows, a pert nose and full mouth made her pretty in a natural way, especially since she wore little makeup. Though she had no covering on her head, she wore her shoulder-length hair in a simple way. Her sky-blue gaze locked with his before he looked away.

"I ran into a dead end," the sheriff was saying, "trying to see if the Boosters Club—that's the parents' group that supports athletics at the high school—had any of their halftime fireworks missing, but they said no. What can I do for you?"

He sat in the chair next to Luke, rather than retreating behind his desk. The sheriff was obviously trying to be accommodating, and he listened intently as Luke explained his idea to get some outside help.

"I wish I had someone to spare for that, Luke, but I'm really shorthanded here. We're underfunded from government cutbacks and facing the demands of a growing community, one which—obviously—has some real problems lately. I wish like heck I could afford someone to loan you for a few weeks to work undercover, but I'm stretched to the limit lately."

Luke's hopes fell. Perhaps this wasn't God's plan. Did that mean he had to find a way to do the detecting himself? With the harvest season, the shop and his family, he could never spread himself that thin.

Suddenly the sheriff turned in the direction of the women on the other side of the glass wall. "I really want to help your people any way I can, Luke," he said, now looking back at him again. "I know some folks around here have various beefs with the Amish, but I consider your people to be fine, upstanding citizens. You're always willing to help your neighbors, whether it's a barn raising, charity sale, or just plain obeying the law."

Feeling deflated, Luke started to rise.

''Now, I'm not saying no,'' the sheriff said, holding up both hands as if to keep him in his seat. ''Look, if I could swing it on my end, is there any way that, instead of a man, you could take in a woman with cop experience and make her look Amish?''

''What?'' Kat cried, sitting in the sheriff's office as he explained a possible assignment. That tall, striking Amish man had disappeared, but he must have been the one who'd made this outrageous request. She lowered her voice. ''Undercover among the Amish? But I hardly know my way around here, and I certain don't know the Amish.''

''That's the point, Kat. Hardly anyone knows you, either, and you'd be coming in with an objective mind. That's what it's going to take—that and the investigative skills you've learned. The story is that you'll be a visiting Amish cousin from Pennsylvania. The Amish will take you in and—uh, train you, help you. And you, in turn, will try to get me some leads to follow up on these hate crimes. I'm not asking you to arrest anyone yourself, but it's pretty obvious that if I go sniffing around, I'm gonna hit nothing but brick walls.''

''I'd be in touch with you? Take a cell phone in or—''

''No cell phone, in case we're dealing with someone who could monitor calls. The Amish have access to phones, though usually not on their property. No, I think you should go in without the usual gear. We'll make plans to meet at night on a regular basis, somewhere near the Brand farm.''

''The Brand farm?''

''That was Luke Brand in here, the bishop's son. He's become a sort of Amish community leader, since his dad's recent bouts with stomach flu or something. He and his brother Dan have built some bridges between the two different cultures around here, made it possible for Amish to work the worldly shops, open small but thriving businesses. Only about half the Amish can make a living off the farms anymore."

"Luke Brand."

"Right. You'd pass as his cousin or something like that."

"Sheriff, I really want to help, but I came here to be your dispatcher, and, with her baby coming, Patty's eager to leave her post."

"I'll finagle it so she can stay an extra week or two, or I'll get our night dispatcher to take extra hours. Believe me, both of them will be grateful for the extra income, and of course you'll be on payroll. I don't know who else I could possibly use, and you're a new face around here. The thing is, I think you'll suit this assignment to a tee. The Amish are asking for our help, and they usually don't, see? But since their kids got hurt—even Luke's son—"

Kat's insides cartwheeled. "It was Luke Brand's boy who was hurt?"

"Right, and his young niece too, still in a coma. And I'd count it a personal favor to me and this town if…"

But Kat hardly heard him now. The dispatcher had told her about the two nine-year-olds who'd been hurt when they'd panicked and run from the fireworks— the boy who might lose his sight in one eye and the half-Amish girl who was on life support at Children's Hospital in Columbus. From her days on the force, Kat knew the hospitals there only too well—

"Kat?" The sheriff interrupted her thoughts. "Look, if you need some time to think it over, I'll tell

Luke I'll let him know later and send him on his way now."

"No—I...I'd like to talk to him."

"The deputies are all out, so why don't you two use the locker room. He's waiting there. I'll come along and see if we can strike a bargain then. And, Kat, I can't think of a better way for you to start to put down roots around here."

"Roots just aren't my thing, Sheriff. But trying to help people, kids—" Her voice broke. "I might give it a try," she said, "at least for a little while, just to give you something to go on."

"I'm real grateful and I know the Amish will be too, even though it's not their way to throw in a bunch of please's and thank-you's, since that's considered prideful talk."

What had she gotten herself into? Kat asked herself. The truth was, she'd hoped to find peace and quiet here, not a new challenge. And certainly not an Amish man whose eyes seemed to assess her as if she were standing at roll call again with the toughest sergeant she'd ever seen, ready to ream her out.

As Sheriff Martin introduced them, the impact of Luke Brand stunned Kat anew. He was tall, deep-voiced and amazingly well-spoken, although the unique cadence of his speech and his clothing made her feel she'd stepped back into another century. She asked immediately about how his son was doing.

"We won't really know if he'll lose the sight in that eye until its lacerations heal some," Luke explained. "He's in pain but not letting on, so we can't tell how to dose him with the medicine."

"I'm glad you were able to get him immediate care," she added, grateful she wasn't dealing with a religious group that could let a boy die of appendicitis when getting him to a doctor would save his life. Obviously the Amish had compromised with necessities like phones and modern medicine. She felt better about this already. "Is he in the hospital like the injured girl?" she asked.

"He's home and insisting on doing his share of chores. His grandmother—she and my sister Emma have helped tend to him and my girl Sarah since their mother's passed on—always says he's nine going on sixteen."

Kat's eyes flitted from Luke's firm mouth to his eyes as he spoke. Their color was almost indigo, the deep hue enhanced by his light-blue shirt under his black denim jacket. Somehow this very different man's mere presence bombarded her senses; her nostrils flared in the clean scent of pine soap mingled with—was it cloves?—which emanated from him.

He had removed his black, broad-brimmed hat and now held it in his hands as he explained the situation to her. As he turned a certain way, thick chestnut hair, covering his ears and touching his collar, gleamed gold in the window light. His beard was barely etched with silver. His face was square-jawed, rugged and sun-browned with white crow's-feet at the edges of his heavily lashed eyes. His hands were tanned too— big hands with clean, blunt fingers.

Luke Brand was a very muscular man—but what did she expect of an Amish farmer who must still work mostly by hand? His broad shoulders tapered to a narrow waist and hips above the thrust of his thighs against the black denim, broadfall trousers.

His voice bore a rough-edged burr, and she thought absently that he could be an announcer on TV or do voice-overs for ads.

"We were expecting a man," he was saying, "but a woman will be even less suspected by whoever is doing these things to my people." The three of them sat over coffee and glazed doughnuts that only Sheriff Martin seemed to partake of. Kat cradled the hot mug against her palms, while Luke too, let his coffee get cold.

"I have to tell you, I've been away from police work for a year because of injuries," she said, forcing herself to stare down into her black coffee instead of continually at him. "And I'm used to working city streets, not a rural area. Which reminds me," she added, looking up again, "I hear your niece is in Children's Hospital in Columbus. I know it well, if you'd like me to drive you or your family in to see her."

"That's a kind offer. I'll talk to some others about it. As for making you *look* Amish," he told her, and she saw that a hint of a smile crimped those taut lips, "that won't be too hard. The challenge will be your acting Amish and blending in. I'll bring my niece, Leah Kurtz, with me to meet you. She can get you some proper clothes and explain a few things you'll need to know before you arrive in our midst. She's the teacher of our school, and it might make sense to say you've come to help her for a while, keep you close to the *kinder*—the kids."

"Yes, that's a good idea," she said, though it brought back the raw memory of visiting the elementary school where she'd met little John Seyjack. She had to admit that hearing kids were hurt was what had made her agree to this wild proposal. Surely that was the only thing...

"I'll need to change my name, right?" she asked. "Something German? My last name, Lindley, is Swedish."

He nodded, started to speak, then evidently thought better of it.

"I did take two years of German in high school,"

she told him in the sudden silence. "I wasn't a very good student, but maybe some of it will come back to me." The truth was, she had signed up for the class because the young male teacher was cute and supposedly graded easy. Back then, she couldn't have cared less about school and learning, though she wished she'd paid more attention now.

"Our young people and adults can speak English with you," Luke assured her. "And the kids are partly in school to learn English, so you'll be a big help there, too."

He took a gulp of his coffee and rose. "I'd best be going now, to clear some things up at home and prepare a background for you."

"In other words, a cover story," she said as she stood too. Their eyes met and held again.

"You ever worked undercover, Kat?" Sheriff Martin asked.

Kat jumped, slopping coffee on her wrist. She'd forgotten he was there.

"Nothing like this," she said, because damned if she was going to tell Luke Brand that she'd posed twice as a hooker in stings to snag pimps and johns. In a way, she thought, she was venturing into another world now, one filled with people alien to her. She might as well be setting out on a *Star Trek* spaceship where no female cop had ever gone before.

3

"We'll be at the hospital in less than ten minutes," Kat told her passengers as she drove along the busy I-71 South past downtown Columbus.

Her thoughts were as crowded as the freeway. Looking in her rearview mirror when she changed lanes, she could see Luke staring at the city skyline. She'd been noting the numbers on squad cars, thinking each would carry someone she knew, though this had never been her patrol area. Her right hand was starting to ache from gripping the steering wheel for over two hours, and she regretted not keeping up with her isometric wrist exercises. She'd forgotten how tense she could get here, she admitted to herself, as she jockeyed another lane to the left to take I-70 East.

Luke and two Amish women had taken her up on her offer to "taxi" them, as the Plain People put it, into Columbus to visit with the parents of the female victim, Luke's niece Melanie Brand. The two women passengers, one elderly and nervous, the other young and eager to please, were Ida Brand, the victim's paternal grandmother and Luke's mother, and Leah Kurtz, the victim's cousin and the Amish community's schoolteacher.

"I'd like it if you'd call me Lee," Leah told her, and Kat wondered why she hadn't said that before. Kat always told people up front that she wanted to be called Kat instead of Katherine. At age twenty-five, this young Amish woman was something of an old-maid already, Kat had learned, a *maidal,* the German word evidently was. Kat wondered what that made her, at age twenty-seven, in Amish eyes.

She glanced in her rearview mirror again. Luke was still looking out the window, frowning.

"Lots of the Amish have nicknames," Lee explained when Kat nodded. "*Ja,* and that reminds me, we want to know if you think Katie's the nickname best for you, close to your own and all."

"No Amish we ever heard of named Kat," Ida Brand put in. "In Amish country, cats live in the barn. Katie, *ja,* Katie Kurtz."

"We think that name would be best," Luke said quickly, probably trying to distract Kat from his mother's comments.

He'd done a lot of the talking earlier from the back seat. Kat supposed they thought it was unsuitable for an Amish man to sit beside her. It scared her to realize how little she knew about the ways of the people she hoped to help.

"Katie Kurtz?" Kat said. "Would that mean I'm supposedly related to your family, Lee?"

"Right," she said.

Kat sensed something was wrong. She glanced at Lee, but decided she'd try to get it out of her when they were alone later. Kat had observed that Lee was an interesting blend of order and disorder. Tendrils of curly, brown-gold hair escaped from beneath her black bonnet and starched cap. However calmly she spoke, an explosion of expressions flitted across her heart-shaped face. Her sense of good humor obviously warred with a disciplined demeanor. At first glance, Lee looked plain, but her eyes were emerald and

framed by lush, dark lashes. The effect was both sur-
prising and stunning.

The bishop's wife, Ida Brand, seemed stoic and kept
mostly silent, though when she did speak, the others
listened. Her face was dignified and handsome, even
with the lines of her years and hard work etching her
skin. Kat guessed she didn't approve of Luke's scheme
to bring an outsider—a female former cop—to live in
her house, but other than that, she wasn't yet sure how
to read the tall, wiry woman.

Kat drove into the large, busy parking lot, found a
space as close as she could to the entrance, then led
her charges toward the hospital. Lee lagged behind
with her as Luke escorted his mother.

"I understood I'd be passed off as a Brand cousin
on a visit from Pennsylvania," Kat, almost whispering, said to Lee. "Don't Mrs. Brand and the bishop
want to take me in? So now I'm Katie Kurtz?"

"Oh, no, though really pleased I am to have you
become one of my distant Pennsylvania cousins for a
while," Lee said, keeping her voice quiet. "So that
means you're visiting from Inter—"

Luke turned back and gave Lee a look that made
her stop in mid-word. "I'd best explain it all to you,"
he told Kat. "Lee, you take your *grossmutter* ahead
of us. We will join you to see Brooke and Dan in
intensive care in a few minutes. Don't forget to tell
them you want neuro intensive care."

A look passed between Ida Brand and Lee again,
but both did as he'd said. Something *was* wrong, Kat
thought. And this was the first time she and Luke
would be alone.

"Let's step over here a minute," he said, and they
walked to a corner of the parking lot. The breeze was
cool and quite strong. Kat's hair blew in her eyes and

her mouth, so she held it back with one hand as she looked up into Luke's rugged, intense face.

"I was going to explain this later, but there would be little reason for an unwed female cousin to make a visit so far from her Pennsylvania home to help with the harvest."

"Also, at my age, I'd probably be married if I were Amish, so why would I be visiting with no husband—or kids?"

He looked surprised. "True. There have been some Ohio-Pennsylvania marriages...but I'm jumping ahead. My father, the bishop, invites you to live in his and my mother's house while you are among us, so that he—as well as I—can keep an eye on this dangerous thing we ask you to do."

"In other words, keep an eye on me? Luke, I'm a former cop. I'm trained in investigation and self-defense. I don't use a gun anymore because of a wrist wound, and wouldn't bring one into your midst anyway, but my own safety is the last of my worries."

"Let me explain the rest," he said, holding up both hands. "So that no outsiders are suspicious of your sudden presence, we hope you will be willing to pass as my betrothed for the few weeks you are among us."

Her insides flip-flopped. "Your betrothed?"

He nodded calmly, but his voice held a note of agitation. "That would be the reason you are staying with my parents instead of with the Kurtzes, although you are supposedly related to them—to Lee's father's people from Pennsylvania. That would be the excuse if you and I are seen together, if we go out to look into someone's behavior. That would be the reason we could be seen riding out some evening when we meet the sheriff to tell him of our progress. Courting couples, especially those betrothed, often go about to-gether.''

She was speechless for a moment, then managed to say, ''The bishop agreed to this—a phony engagement?''

''As a protection to you. We can break it off—we can say we did—when you leave.''

''Honestly, Luke, things will work best if you and your father don't think you have to protect me.''

''Whatever we think, others would notice if you were on your own, asking questions, following someone, if you are to pass as an Amish woman. I know you are used to different methods in this big city, but that just isn't our way.''

''I understand that, and I'll be careful. I'll be certain I have a good excuse for wherever I go, or even work at night, if I must. Believe me, I'm used to that.''

A frown crushed his strong features. ''So you won't go along with our idea?''

''I didn't say that. No doubt you and your people know what's the best ruse for me. But I'm going to need to get out into the community, the worldly one, not just stay within the circle of Amish safety...''

Her voice trailed off, and she bit her lower lip. Little John Seyjack had asked her if she'd tell his father about the circle of safety. The child's own father had been his betrayer. She could only pray that the culprit behind these Amish hate crimes was not one of their own, but she meant to keep her options open. She cleared her throat, aware Luke was staring at her.

''I'll become Katie Kurtz, then,'' she said, ''but from now on I want to be partners in future decisions that affect me. I can't work confidently if you or your people keep things secret, something unsaid. Agreed?''

"Agreed, at least on my part."

"Okay," she said, as they started toward the hospital. "Then, starting tomorrow I'll try my best to be Katie, Lee's cousin and your fiancée—"

"Betrothed."

"Yes—visiting from where in Pennsylvania?"

"From Intercourse," he said and obviously tried to bite back a grin.

"Really?"

"Yeah," he said, smiling openly now as she smiled back.

He had a slightly crooked smile that flaunted strong, white teeth, and it dazzled her before it quickly disappeared.

"The Kurtzes," he explained, "my sister Emma's husband's folks, almost all came from Intercourse. The word just used to mean human interaction, trade and such."

"I realized that, of course," she clipped out and headed for the hospital before he could see she was blushing. Ridiculous—she never blushed.

"But one more thing," Luke said, stretching his long strides to catch up. "Katie's the perfect name for you, since yours is really Katherine or Kat. I just want you to know Levi and Emma Kurtz had a daughter Katie once, another Katie Kurtz."

"Had? What happened to her?" Kat asked as she saw Luke startle when the doors of the hospital reception area whooshed open.

"She died," he said. "I'll tell you all about it later."

Kat gave him credit for covering his surprise about the automatic doors. She only hoped she would be able to carry off so smoothly the surprises she would no doubt face in his world.

* * *

"Would you like to go in for a moment, too?" Brooke, the injured girl's mother, asked Kat as they stood in the corridor outside Melanie Brand's room in the neuro intensive care unit.

"That's all right," Kat said as she watched Daniel, Luke's older brother, put his arm around Ida Brand and lead her into the hospital room. "It's more important that they have the time with Melanie. I'll just go back to the waiting area."

"I'd like you to see Melly, though God knows she doesn't look like herself with all those tubes and the trach," Brooke said as she took Kat's hand to keep her there. The thirty-something-looking lawyer, who also owned a former bed-and-breakfast in town, was an attractive woman with classic features softened by honey-hued, chin-length hair. She looked washed-out and exhausted, but strength and vitality animated her voice. "I've found it helps," she continued, "to see what you're fighting for—to keep it from happening again."

"All right," Kat said, amazed to hear herself agree. This sort of thing—hospitals, pain, long roads to recovery—really shook her. Worse, she was already sabotaging her attempt to remain objective. But when Ida Brand came out with Daniel, she let Brooke draw her into the room.

Screens with electronic readouts and moving lines, rhythmic sounds, that familiar antiseptic smell—all jolted Kat. Her own ordeal came crashing back, but she shuffled to the bedside where the girl lay, pale as the sheets, with machines breathing for her, monitoring her very life.

"She thrashes about sometimes," Brooke whispered. The pediatric neurology nurse had explained that they should watch what they said, since coma patients could often hear, though not respond.

"We love you, Melly," Brooke said, stroking her daughter's arm. "You just rest now, but come back to us as soon as you can."

They tiptoed out. Kat was shaking; she could feel her heart pounding as if she'd done a five-mile run.

"We may be in this for a long haul here," Brooke was saying, hunching her shoulders and hugging herself. "I wish I could be in Maplecreek to help you find the bastards who did this." She wiped tears from under her eyes.

"I could use the help—and the support."

"But then," Brooke said with a sigh, "if I started poking around, whoever's doing this would probably go back in their holes for a while, and they need to be flushed out and caught. The last time I reported one of their vicious pranks to the sheriff, they lay low for a couple of weeks."

"What was it you reported?"

"Some jackass—actually, maybe more than one— filled fire extinguishers with a combination of chicken manure and water and sprayed it all over the quilts hanging on lines for a charity auction. Luke can fill you in on that."

"He did mention it. It was on the edge of town at a farmhouse where the proceeds were going for Amish relief."

Brooke nodded. "Because the Amish don't believe in insurance, they have a fund for those with special needs. Anyway, vandals sneaked out of the woods behind the house, let loose with one or more fire extinguishers, and managed to run back into the trees before anyone could stop them. Young kids were watching over the quilts just then, and they got doused too—including Luke's little Eli.''

"I didn't mean to interrogate you about this now," Kat told her, touching her shoulder. "The only child who really matters right now to you is in there."

"Thanks for understanding," she said with a sharp sniff and blew her nose. "I've got to level with you, Kat. The Columbus police really let me down once, and that was one of the reasons I fled to Amish country. But that also meant I found Dan and a new life—and had my Melly.''

"I didn't know…" Kat began, surprised by what they had in common, even if it sounded like Brooke resented the CPD.

"Of course you didn't," Brooke rushed on. "I only wanted to say I'm trusting you to handle this, and if I can help—even from here—let me know."

Brooke's husband came up to put his arm around her, and the Amish joined them in a tight circle. Kat had noted how people had stared at their black capes and bonnets, at Luke's hat, how the family had turned heads coming in, yet kept going with great poise and grace. She sympathized with them for the way everyone watched them, because it reminded her of how people gave a wide berth to cops.

Kat knew the Amish would go on through these trials, and perhaps worse to come, unless she could somehow help them. And she wanted that more than anything, especially now that she knew these people of prayer were not like those who had let her brother die. These people might have one foot in the past but they knew how to make bargains with the present.

"I'll do everything I can," Kat promised, speaking directly to Brooke. Tears pooled in Kat's eyes to blur her vision as Brooke bit her lower lip and nodded almost fiercely. In that moment, Kat thought, here among these Amish, the two of them, worldly women and strangers, understood something unsaid and felt like sisters.

Mission impossible, Kat thought, as Lee laid out Amish garments for her on the bed in Kat's apartment the next morning. She must begin to dress and look Amish because she was going by buggy with Luke to the Brand farm to begin her assignment today. Looking at the garments, she thought this was like the Police Academy all over again, only with different clothes and posture. And this time, her instructor and inspector was a soft-voiced young woman rather than an academy sergeant shouting about polished shoes, trouser creases and a shined visor, not to mention a stiff spine, with stomach in and shoulders back.

Kat had noted the way Amish women walked was a far cry from the wide stride and take-charge stance she'd learned to use as a cop. The Amish walked easily, casually, without looking all around to assess a situation, though, given this mess they were in, they'd better start doing that—and she'd tell them so. In general, unless they were chattering or laughing among themselves, Amish women seemed more inside themselves instead of "out there." And they seldom raised their voices. She tried to emulate what she saw in Lee and Mrs. Brand, but she so easily slipped back into her old habits.

In short, this was going to be one hell of a lot harder than she'd imagined. Including watching her mouth. She was used to cops swearing. She had known some who would earn a gold medal in the obscenity olympics. But the Lord's name was never abused for petty things among the Amish she'd observed so far. When one of them said "Oh, my God," it was a plea or prayer.

"Well, I'll be," Lee said, staring at Kat's crimson toenails when she kicked her loafers off. "I knew English women painted their fingernails, but not the toenails too."

"You mean, toe bad?" Kat said, and she grinned while Lee giggled. "I think we both have a lot to learn. I'll take it off later."

"The only thing is, on warm days, almost till the snow flies, a lot of us like to go barefoot, at least around the house."

"Is there some kind of special bra?" Kat asked after Lee had pointed out the garments on Kat's bed and pronounced each of their names in German. She saw a plain white, store-bought slip and panties with little legs on them. Kat told herself then and there that she'd just wear her own. No one was going to see up under those mid-length dresses and aprons they wore, anyway.

"We don't wear bras," Lee told her matter-of-factly.

That, at least, seemed not only comfortable but sexy, Kat thought. It was a good thing she wasn't a fashion maven and didn't have big breasts that needed support. At least the dresses of single women were solid, bright colors, not black, and the aprons matched so they didn't stand out much. Lee had brought her a dress-apron duo in royal blue, which she selected, and a spare in grass green. As she donned the garments, she wasn't sure she felt Amish so much as like an actress in *Little House on the Prairie,* a TV show she used to like as a kid.

"Someone left the snaps off this dress," she told Lee.

"No, we pin them, see, with straight pins," she said, fishing some out of her big, black purse. "They're done so carefully, seven of them, you can hardly tell, but it takes a while to get the knock of it."

The knock of it? Even Lee, as well-spoken as she was from teaching English, occasionally misused a word, sometimes in a hilarious way. But Kat could just imagine what her own jabs at relearning even basic German would sound like. Actually, what she planned to concentrate on was trying to speak English as they did with that distinctive up-down cadence, calm tone and occasional inverted word order. "That I like," Luke had said. "This I don't want to hear," she had overheard Ida say yesterday to Brooke.

"Ouch!" Kat cried as she stuck her finger on a pin.

"See, I told you. I'll do it for now, and you can practice later. If there's a problem, Mrs. Brand will be there in the house to help when you get dressed."

At least the black stockings were warm, Kat thought, as she thrust her feet into her running shoes, the only items she'd wear that were her own. No wristwatches, certainly no jewelry. It was all prideful and individualistic, she had learned that much. The Amish had done away with anything that called attention to self, for it was cooperation, not competition they valued. She rather liked the idea that people weren't judged by such things as the style or expense of what they wore.

"Okay, now the hair, *kapp* and bonnet," Lee said. "We'll have to part your hair in the middle and pull it up into a knot to hide under your *kapp*."

That, Kat managed mostly by herself. She gazed in the big bureau mirror, amazed at the way she looked in the starched white cap with its graceful, tiny pleats. Lee pinned it in place.

"There!" she cried, sounding pleased with herself. "I think you'll pass for Amish."

Kat couldn't care less if she didn't wear makeup or fuss with her hair, though she'd rather wear it down. She studied herself in the mirror again. She'd better take a last, good look, since Lee had said the Amish only used hand mirrors, and seldom those. Kat had to admit the clothing had gone a long way in aiding her transformation.

"There you go, Katie!" Lee cried, patting her on the back. "I see an Amish woman, not a lady policeman."

Kat shook her head to clear her tangled thoughts. It was time. She was going to Maplecreek with Luke in his courting buggy to move into his parents' place, while Lee drove herself home in another buggy.

At the Brand farm, which she hadn't even laid eyes on yet, she'd be instructed some more, including Luke's teaching her to drive a buggy. Since her landlady was not home right now, Luke was out in her rented garage, covering her car with a tarp. Saying she was going to Florida with a friend for three weeks, Kat had already made arrangements for her mail to be held here.

But this *was* going to be a real trip, she thought as she hefted the plain black suitcase Lee had loaned her, now packed with personal items. But there were no cosmetics, no worldly clothes, no cell phone, no laptop. The only thing she had from her police past was the big, black flashlight she used to carry on her gun belt. However dedicated she was to this, and however much support she had been promised from Sheriff Martin and the Amish, she felt suddenly alone.

"So...Katie!" Luke said when he saw her come down the stairs.

His deep blue eyes widened, then narrowed as he took her in, before he obviously forced himself to stop staring and lifted her bag for her. She almost told him she could handle it, before she remembered who she was now.

"We're off, then," Luke said.

"In more ways than one," Kat muttered to herself as she followed Luke and Lee out and locked the door.

4

Despite her bad case of nerves, Kat began to relax in Luke's buggy. Perhaps it was the rhythmic sway of its black fiberglass frame behind the horse, Sandy's, bouncing rump or the mesmerizing *clip-clop* of the mare's hooves. Luke and Kat had nodded or waved to a few folks in other buggies and moved over onto the berm for passing cars, vehicles that now seemed big, fast, threatening metallic hulks to her. Kat was relieved to leave them behind on the main road from Pleasant to Maplecreek. It was just plain peaceful as they skirted the town to take the rural roads, first Hill-farm, then Ridge.

Most of the Amish farms were large here, their houses, barns, corn cribs and silos set down dirt or gravel lanes away from the paved roads. Several of the farms had windmills, their metal paddles whirling in the breeze. Here and there in a yard or field sat an old, rusty oil-drilling derrick.

"This area isn't rich in oil, is it?" she asked, sitting up straight as a thought hit her.

He shook his head. "What little there was decades ago played out, but no one bothered to remove the reminders. We keep them on Amish farms as proof that modern mankind is vulnerable to all sorts of wells going dry if the land isn't cherished."

So little spoken, Kat thought, but so much said. She dismissed her first theory, no doubt of many to come, that someone did not just want to terrorize the Amish but drive them out. Even in these times of dwindling fossil fuels, they weren't being attacked for the oil under their land.

They passed occasional small wooden buildings on the road, which Luke told Kat were not outhouses but phone shanties. The Amish could use phones as long as they weren't in their homes. She soon learned to spot Amish houses as the ones with no phone, electrical or TV cable lines linking them to power poles. As for outside latrines, Luke assured her the Amish here had gone to indoor bathrooms, though the school still had his-and-hers outdoor facilities.

Along one road, next to vegetable booths or wagon beds piled with goods, hand-lettered signs touted quilts or garden-grown delights but noted, No Sunday Sales. Goose-necked squash, Indian corn and pots of purple or gold mums made splashes of color against the wooden stalls. The prices were posted so folks could leave the right amount in a jar. Such openness and trust, Kat thought, and yet some idiots were taking advantage of these people.

At this slow pace the earth seemed to open up, revealing itself with sounds and scents she'd never noted. The fields of corn rustled, and freshly planted winter wheat swayed past the buggy; an occasional pumpkin patch went by. Red-winged blackbirds twitted, frogs croaked in a pond, and an alarmed turtle splashed into the depths as they passed. Kat—no, she was Katie now—smelled freshly turned earth and, at one point, the manure a farmer was plowing into a newly cut field.

"Good country air!" Luke said and laughed when she twitched, then held, her nose. "Ever live in the country?" he asked, his deep voice as hypnotic as the ride. They had talked about a lot of things, but sometimes just let the silence seep into them with the warmth of the September sun.

"I was always a city girl," she told him. "This is lovely."

"I think so. Big family?"

"Just a brother—that is, after my dad died and my mother left."

"Left?"

"Let's just talk about this world here, okay, the one I need to know about."

"Sure. Fine. That's the schoolhouse we just passed."

"A one-room schoolhouse?"

"All of ours are. When you help Lee, you can either buggy there or cut-corner across the fields and meadows on your own two feet. My Eli and Sarah will show you the way, and others walk with them. Eight grades, one teacher," he explained. "I've taken tech courses and studied on my own since I left that school, but I have fond memories of my days there."

Kat bit her tongue. *Good for you,* she'd almost said, *because my childhood was pure crap.* Strangely, she envied this man for his happy memories, his family, his roots here in this beautiful place.

Though Kat tried to concentrate on the here and now, pieces of her past kept intruding. She'd been moved from school to school as a kid, each urban brick rectangle of classrooms overlooking an asphalt parking lot and playground. Each time she'd become attached to a friend or teacher, it seemed her parents had moved on. Even in the foster families, for whom she'd had high hopes, she felt only among them but not part of them.

She'd become sullen and sulky. She'd gone looking

for trouble, especially when Jay was sent to another foster home. More than once, she'd beaten up bullies who picked on her or other loner kids. Though she hated kids in cliques or gangs, she'd secretly longed to be one of them, to be part of something. Thank God a local cop had turned her life around: he'd let her go instead of arresting her for defacing buildings with graffiti, though he'd made her clean it up and helped her do it. He'd checked up on her that December and made sure she got some of the Toys for Tots that officers collected at Christmas. And best of all, he'd given her a glimpse of a group of people who covered each other's back, who dressed alike, talked their own slang—and wanted to help, not hurt, others.

Luke's voice jolted Kat from her memories.

"I'd always take rolling country over flat land."

"In a buggy this area seems so much hillier than in a car," she observed. "This poor horse."

"Amish buggy horses are all retired harness racers," he said with a quick sideways glance at her. In the small buggy their shoulders bounced companionably together, though that felt a little awkward. And it was hard on her arm, which she thought was pretty buff, but his muscles seemed solid steel. "I think they like their life here," he went on, when she'd nearly forgotten he was talking about the horse.

"You ever ride or drive a horse?" he asked. "You're gonna have to learn, and I'd like to give you a lesson today."

"The only horse I've ever been on was when I was a kid at the Ohio State Fair, where the ponies go in circles and they practically strap you on," she admitted.

"See there," he said, his voice strangely comforting, almost caressing. "A good memory. Here's our lane. I'm gonna give you a horse to use, named Dilly, that's as good as my Sandy. You ever get lost around here, you give Dilly her head, and she'll bring you right home—like this, see?''

He put a lot of slack in the reins, then handed them to her. She held them tightly but did not pull one way or the other as Sandy took them into, then up, the long lane toward a white farmhouse, big barn and double silo. A windmill—no, six of them—stood tall, as if guarding the place.

''Surely you don't have a problem with water here,'' she said.

''Only one's a working mill,'' he told her, pointing. ''The others are models I construct and sell.''

''Oh, you even sell little ones.''

''Very popular for yards and gardens among both the Amish and the English,'' he said without a trace of pride in his voice. ''That smaller building is my windmill shop, and beyond it, the *grossdaadi* or *daadi haus,* where you'll stay.''

''It's a huge farm,'' she said as he took the reins back. ''So much corn! Which reminds me, I want you to take me out to the scene where the biker threw the fireworks, so I can look around.''

''Will do, but you need that buggy lesson too. Let me help you down. Since we're supposedly betrothed, you'll have to let me open doors and lend you a hand, at least in town.''

He jumped down and wrapped the reins around a small hitching post in a yard with immaculately kept flower and vegetable gardens, next to his parents' small, one-story house. The hand he held up engulfed hers. As she stood to climb down, Kat saw a dark-blue curtain flutter from inside; perhaps someone had been watching for them.

It was a good thing Luke had her hand, because the longer skirts were as foreign to her as the iron buggy step she almost missed.

"Welcome, Katie Kurtz," Luke said. "And when it comes to the snakes who've been attacking our people and our kids, good hunting."

"You get enough to eat, then?" Ida Brand asked Kat for the fourth time. "Got to feed you up, for sure, if you want to pass for Amish."

"Yes, plenty, and everything was just delicious, Mrs. Brand."

"Now you got to call me Ida or Jacob Ida, the proper way for someone supposedly Luke's future wife," the woman said, her voice suddenly chilly. But again she held out the plate of rich butter cookies called Jumbles. Though after meat-loaf sandwiches, hot potato salad, pickled beets, sweet onion salad and applesauce, Kat could hardly budge, she figured it was a smart move to take another cookie. Luke's father hadn't joined them, since Ida said he wasn't feeling well and was "taking a little lie-down," but Kat wondered secretly if he hadn't just overeaten around here.

"I hope Bishop Brand's feeling better soon," Kat said.

"I don't want you to think he's boycotting you," Luke told her. "He has off-and-on stomach problems, that's all."

"Oh, *ja*, he wants to meet you, sure," Ida agreed.

She got up to answer a knock on the back door. "Your mother is a great cook," Kat told Luke. "Since personal praise isn't welcome, I'm telling you, not her. For someone who used to live on fast food and is a disaster in the kitchen, I think I've died and gone to heaven."

For some reason Luke laughed out loud. She wished she understood these people better, especially him.

"It's a perk of being Amish," he said. "Almost all our women are great cooks. It kind of comes with the territory." He got up as his mother brought in a plump, non-Amish woman carrying a picnic basket, so Kat rose, too.

Her first test, she thought. Ida and this woman were all smiles, so the guest had to be local and know who looked Amish and who didn't.

"Marnie," Ida said, "this is Luke's betrothed from Pennsylvania, Katie Kurtz, just came today." As she spoke, Ida's smile faded, and she looked almost pained. That was another thing she had to get used to, Kat thought. Patrolling the mean streets, she'd learned to think of everyone as a potential liar, but here—at least among the Amish—it hurt them not to tell the truth.

"And Katie," Ida went on, "this is our English friend, Marnie Girkins. She owns a shop, a bed-and-breakfast and restaurant in town, *ja,* and hires a lot of our Amish women and young people too. A widow many years, reared her children by herself and a hard worker, too."

Kat mimicked the way Lee had greeted her yesterday. "Good to see you," she said with a nod and a smile.

"I think it's lovely, just lovely that Luke has found a wife for himself and a mother for his two children," Marnie said and reached out to pat Kat's shoulder. "I hope you'll be happy here, very happy. And when is the special day?"

"Still under discussion," Kat said.

"After harvest, traditional wedding time," Luke added.

"Is it—well, kind of arranged?" Marnie asked. "I didn't know you've been gone courting to Pennsylvania, Luke."

"A mutual friend introduced us," he told the beaming woman. "But with Katie visiting here, this will be our real courting time."

"Wait until my daughters hear that. It's so much better than the way they've met men before, now that they are out on their own—one in Cleveland, one in Toledo—at a bar or even on the Internet—online, as they say." Marnie pretended to shudder and rolled her eyes. "As I said, my happiness to you, my dear, and welcome to Maplecreek."

"*Ja*, that's kind of you," Kat said instead of the worldly "thank you" she almost blurted out.

"Well, can't stay long, Ida," Marnie went on, opening her basket, "but I wanted to drop off some of that herbal chicken-noodle soup the bishop likes from the Dutch Table. Everyone misses him when he and the elders don't drop in for a few days."

"Some days it's all he'll eat, my Jacob," Ida said, accepting the Tupperware bowl with a nod. "He likes mine too, but your angel hair pasta and extra vegetables, it's his favorite."

"I'll bet he just likes it because that angel hair has a heavenly name," Marnie joked and poked Ida's elbow with hers.

Kat kept her expression calm but her attention keen. Marnie, as grandmotherly as she looked, was obviously a sharp business woman. Since she hired the Amish, she could be a helpful resource, someone who bridged both worlds and might have overheard something in her restaurant or shop that Kat could use. The Amish obviously trusted and admired her. Although Kat's plan was to trust no one but her host family, perhaps there would be a way to use Marnie Girkins without her catching on to the charade.

Kat had eaten at the Maplecreek Dutch Table Restaurant, which Marnie had mentioned, once or twice, but not since she'd moved to the area. The bustling place employed a large Amish staff of servers and cooks, and was filled with both English and Amish locals as well as tourists. Yes, Kat would have to find a way to visit it soon.

Marnie herself was an attractive, silver-haired lady of about fifty to fifty-five, and above-average height, maybe five-eight. Her jacket and ankle-length skirt looked new, both in blue denim worn over a long-sleeved, pale yellow blouse. As well as the woven-wood picnic basket with its painted silhouettes of an Amish man and woman, she was toting a big purse with a quilted cover.

"I've got to move on, as I'm dropping some soup off to Reuben Coblentz, too. And Luke, I'm glad you're here, because I brought some fudge for little Eli and Sarah. I'm so sorry...about what I heard, so sorry that had to happen."

"Very kind of you," Luke said, accepting the wrapped fudge. "Eli and Sarah always look forward to seeing you."

"Katie," she said, turning toward Kat again, "if I'd known you were here, I'd have brought a welcome and congratulations present for you, too. You just come in and see me in the restaurant or the shop." Her pert smile lit her face, clear to her brown eyes. "All right, Ida, got to run. Too much to do in one day."

Ida escorted Marnie to the door and went out with her.

"At least," Kat observed to Luke as she carried

dishes from the table to the kitchen counter, "there's someone who appreciates the Amish, and I'm sure there are many others. But I'd like you to give me a list of anyone, absolutely anyone, you think needs watching or investigating."

"Giving you that list is on my list," Luke said, "but I want to teach you to drive first. I've only got an hour or two before I'm going to have to get back to farm chores and talk to my crew in the windmill shop. Fortunately, it's our slowest sales season because our busiest farm time is coming up with harvest. And since you won't be here long, we have to make every minute count."

She nodded as their gazes snagged and held again. The moment was briefly awkward, yet laden with eternal impossibilities. Kat quickly went back to clearing the table and was surprised that Luke helped her. One of the things Lee had told her was that a strict division of labor was observed by the sexes. But whatever Luke thought might be man's work or women's work, Kat fully intended to make clear to him, once and for all, that she was not expecting his help, beyond initial advice, on this investigation.

"First, I'll show you around the barn," he told her, "in case you ever have to harness your new wheels as well as drive them. And I'd like you to meet Eli and Sarah when they get home. Eli's eye's patched over, but he wanted to go to school. They are the only reason I almost didn't agree to saying you're my betrothed."

She accidentally dropped a fork on the linoleum floor. "They surely know I'm not," she said, both asking and insisting.

"We had decided to tell the truth only to the children old enough to sit in church, twelve and up. But, yes, I did tell Eli and Sarah, though they are nine and five. They would know you're not Amish the minute you couldn't talk *Deutsche*, anyway. Sarah is just learning English at school."

"I hope...they understand."

"They understand they don't want to be scared or hurt again."

After Ida came back in, Kat followed Luke out the side door of the immaculately kept, grandparents' house. Her room, the only spare bedroom, was at the back of it, but it would suit her just fine. The only problem was that her two-window view was of nothing but a twenty-foot strip of grass, then corn. She felt hemmed in, as if someone could sneak up to spy on her and she wouldn't see them until too late.

"So who's this Reuben Coblentz that Marnie Girkins is also taking soup to?" Kat asked. "I've got to start learning people around here, Amish or not."

"Former Amish, shunned Amish," Luke said shortly, as they started across the lane toward the big barn.

"You're going to have to tell me more than that."

"Drank most of his money away, but still has his farm—barely. Won't sell it to the Amish, but isn't making a go of it, either. His few friends are English, and Marnie's just being kind."

"He's a bitter, angry man—is that what you're telling me?" she demanded, gesturing in the direction she thought was toward Coblentz's farm. "And he could hold a grudge against your people and has English friends? In that case, I'd better see his name high on that list of possible suspects."

He nodded, his expression grim. It was not like Luke to avoid responding, but he seemed suddenly as forthcoming as the stone watering trough outside the barn. Inside the big building, it was dim, vast, and warm. "Come on, Dilly," he said to the bay mare that nuzzled his hand over the top of her stall. "Meet your new best friend, Katie, and if anyone asks you, just neigh she's the woman I'm going to marry."

But Kat wasn't going to be cajoled, teased or deterred. Right then, she started making her own list of suspects.

By the time Kat learned to harness and hitch Dilly and drive Luke's courting buggy, her head was spinning. "I'll take you up and down the lane tonight after dark," Luke told her, "because we can't have worldly outsiders see you learning. Even the kids handle horses and buggies."

"Maybe I should ride a bike or scooter around," she said wryly, evidently pulling back too hard on the reins, because Dilly stopped dead in her tracks again.

"Only Amish men and boys ride bikes or use scooters, and all those just take foot power," he said, missing her joke. "Either just say 'giddap,' or, if you really want Dilly to put her shoulder to the traces for you, blow her a kiss."

"Really?"

He did it, an exaggerated double air-kiss. Kat laughed as the horse picked up her pace.

"How fast is it safe to go?" she asked.

"Flat out, Dilly will do about nine miles in thirty minutes," he said, jerking slightly in his seat as Kat tried the "whoa" with the pull-back on the reins again. "But a safe speed is three miles in a half hour at a regular clip. Don't worry, I'll try to have myself or someone else with you most of the time, but you need to know this in case of emergency."

"Luke, I repeat, I'm not afraid to go out alone, and

you have a farm and shop to run," she protested, bracing her foot on the splashboard as they bounced along on the steel-rimmed wheels back and forth between the barn and houses. Three Amish men, who must be employed at the windmill shop, took to looking out the windows, and Kat saw two faces watching from the *daadi haus.*

She wanted to do a good job at this; actually, she liked the horse and small, square buggy. It was protected on three sides under a vinyl roof but was open in the front above the splashboard. An unlit lantern bounced along in back, next to the fluorescent triangle and reflector lights, which were run at night, Luke said, by a battery under the seat—one that was turned on by an ignition key, no less. The interior had dark-green carpeting and soft upholstery and smelled like leather and the cloves she had found out Luke liked to chew.

"Let's say lesson one is done," she insisted, "because I want to take a look at the site of the fireworks, although it was probably contaminated by the emergency vehicle and the kids' buggies that night."

Luke let Dilly walk the buggy back into the barn and then steered Kat on foot toward the lane between the cornfields farthest from the road. Because the area was hilly, she could see now that the rows of corn were not necessarily straight, but followed the contour of the terrain.

"Was the motorbiker coming down the middle of the lane, as far as you could tell?" she asked. "It would seem logical, since the driver's visibility couldn't have been good with the darkness, especially inside that closed visor you mentioned. He'd want to avoid getting too close to the corn."

"Down the middle when I saw him, but that was only from about...uh, probably here."

"If he was keeping to the middle of this lane and the cars and buggies in and out pretty much did too," she reasoned aloud, "his single-tire tracks could have been missed by the double-axle wheels. It's mostly matted grass or ruts here—"

"From our draft horses, pulling wagons in and out."

"Even so, we might find a spot where the wheels and hooves missed his tire tracks so we can get a look at the treads of the motorbike. If we do, maybe I can make some sort of crude plaster cast, because I'm the only CSSU we're going to get around here, unless something worse happens. Oh, sorry about the jargon," she said when she looked up to see him frowning. "CSSU is Crime Scene Search Unit—the guys who collect physical evidence."

"I'll learn that, and you learn some German," he said. "By the way, I have plaster I use to patch walls that we can use to make casts." He went back to looking at the ground as they walked toward the back lot line, shoulder to shoulder. But they found no place where they were sure they had a definitive impression of the bike tires. Still, Kat spotted a small splatter of something black and shiny, which stood out in the sun.

"What's that?" she asked, pointing, and they both hunkered down by it.

Luke put a finger in it. "Oil," he said. "Maybe motor oil from when he tipped the bike to make the turn and it nearly spun out. Yeah, here's exactly where he went around the corner. He dragged his boot somewhere here."

"Boot? Do you recall anything about what kind of boot?"

"Not a worker's boot. Our carpenters wear one with a blunt steel toe, but this had a more pointed one."

"Maybe like a western boot—a cowboy boot?"

"Could be, for all I know. It's a big blur, but I can tell you his bike was black without any logo, icon or wording. Sad to say, his black leather jacket didn't have anything on the back of it."

"So who wears black leather jackets around here, besides the occasional stylish tourist?"

He shrugged as he stood. "No one in particular. Maybe the Patriot Knights, if you mean a group of people, but most of them have something on the back of their jackets."

"Like their own names, or the words *Patriot Knights*?"

"Mostly American flags or fierce eagles coming in for a landing, I think."

"The sheriff mentioned the Knights too, but evidently didn't consider them a problem. They're a far-right militia group?" she added before she realized it was ludicrous to ask Luke if the Knights were "far right." How much more far right than the Amish could anyone be?

"I'd say they've made patriotism their religion. They see enemies everywhere in what's going on in modern society." He shook his head. "The Amish see things wrong with the modern world, too, but we don't hoard weapons and play soldier. I guess most folks around try to ignore the Knights, except when they have their Fourth of July fireworks show. Lots of worldly folks, even some Amish, park along Roscoe Township Road or sit on blankets in a meadow there to see it."

"Which proves they use fireworks."

His head snapped around. Frowning, he said, "I

should have thought of that, but the Knights haven't bothered us. I guess people around here believe in 'live and let live' with them, that their secret meetings are just something like the Elks would hold. Far as I can tell, they're loners, and not dangerous, just misguided.''

It was, Kat thought, a place to start. However much the Amish accepted the Knights' philosophy as ''live and let live,'' she'd just check them out as well as the mysterious Reuben Coblentz. She surmised Luke might have had some sort of falling out with the man. She'd ask Lee about that tomorrow when she went to play teacher at school. Then she planned to scout around, as if she were just exploring her new home area, including driving by Roscoe Township Road.

''I just remembered something else,'' Luke told her. ''The driver wore gloves. I guess it might have been so he wouldn't get burned by the fireworks.''

''Or leave fingerprints on anything. It's certainly not been cold enough to wear gloves for warmth. Luke, why are there two burned spots here?'' she asked as she peered around the corner of the big cornfield.

''The fireworks went wild, and this irregular spot was a grass fire the kids put out. Over there's the ravine where Eli and Melly were hurt.''

They spent a half hour walking through rows of corn, looking for possible unexploded fireworks she could use to trace their purchase. Nothing. They again walked the site, then the grass lane on the other side of the field the biker had used to flee. Nothing. But where that lane met the paved road, they found another small slick of oil.

''Maybe he hesitated here before he turned out,'' Kat said, ''or tipped his bike again. For all the good it's probably going to do me, I think I'm looking for either a newly serviced motorbike or one that needs to be.''

"It isn't much," Luke said as they walked toward the *daadi haus* to greet his kids after school. "I hate the idea that we're going to have to wait for another attack to get some good—or bad—evidence."

Kat nodded grimly and stretched her strides to keep up with Luke's long legs. "Pardon the poor humor," she told him as they cut across the well-kept lawn, "but I promise you no grass will grow under my feet."

So much for staying objective, Kat told herself when she saw Luke's kids for the first time, as they made their way across the lawn toward their grand-parents' house after school. Even at a distance, they were Amish-country-postcard adorable. Eli, taller and older—and of course, the male—seemed to be guard-ing Sarah, but she, too, seemed to be leading him. They waved and shouted goodbye more than once to the cluster of kids who walked on without them down the road.

As they came closer, Kat saw that Eli wore a pirat-ical patch over his left eye. His black and blue face had stitches across his forehead, making him look as if he'd been beaten. Remembering Jay again—John Seyjack, too—Kat blinked back tears. Blond, blue-eyed little Sarah, despite the fact she was pouting for some reason, looked like a large doll, though not an Amish one, because those had no faces and this child had a very expressive one. Right now, Kat read like a book that Sarah didn't like having her here.

"I am very happy to meet you," Kat said, smiling at them both and shaking hands. Eli's was a firm shake and Sarah's like a limp fish. *"Wie geits?"* She used the greeting, one of the few things she recalled from German class.

That sent Sarah off into a spiel of German to Luke. Eli, too, chattered away in their dialect.

"They say," Luke told Kat, "that Teacher Leah has announced at school that you will be coming to help them learn English tomorrow and that at lunchtime there will be a special picnic in your honor. Students are bringing food to share and some of the mothers are coming too."

"That will be nice and a lot of fun," Kat said, nodding.

"And help you to catch the evildoers—we will do that too," Eli told her, while Sarah just stared.

Despite it all, Kat almost laughed. It was bad enough that Luke insisted on playing sidekick, and now little Eli, was too. These people might be pacifists, but they were brave. And whatever it took, she was going to help them.

5

Her first night in Amish country, Kat realized she'd never seen a place so vastly dark and deeply quiet. That was, dark but for the silver pinpoints of stars overhead, as if huge hands had stitched some sort of infinite quilt in the heavens. And quiet only if she didn't count the creak of crickets and the restless rustle of cornstalks outside her room. Even Amish homes were achingly quiet. No hum from electrical gadgets, no telephones, TV, radio or computers. She had heard only the purring of gas lanterns, but now that sound ceased as she turned hers down until it gutted out.

She was grateful to take off her *kapp* and literally let her hair down. Kneeling before her bedroom window that looked out the back of the *daadi haus,* she watched the tall, endless cornstalks rubbing shoulders. If there was going to be a moon tonight, it wasn't up yet.

At supper with Ida, Luke and the children in the big, amazingly modern kitchen of his farmhouse, Kat had shared a meal of leftovers she and Ida had fixed together. Afterward, Luke had gone out to his windmill shop to catch up on his work, so Kat had stayed with Eli and Sarah while Ida took a plate of food over to the *daadi haus* for Bishop Brand. Though Kat had tried to talk to Sarah, the child had only nodded and kept cutting out and crayoning autumn leaf decorations for the party at school tomorrow. At least that gave Kat a chance to carefully question Eli.

"How's your eye doing?" she'd asked as the three of them sat at the cleared kitchen table.

"Don't know yet, Doctor says. I won't let those evildoers scare me, though."

"I hear you were there when some quilts got sprayed."

"Phew, they smelled bad," he'd said, pinching his nose to demonstrate. "They got ruined." He'd stood and looked out the side door toward his father's windmill shop, then came back to sit down. "Didn't see who did it. All in black, they were, just like that guy on the motorbike."

"They? So more than one person ruined the quilts—the evildoers?"

"Must have been two. Quilts got sprayed from two sides 'bout the same time I got hit with the stuff, I guess."

It impressed Kat that he hadn't mentioned his own plight first. "What kind of black clothes did the two men wear?"

He'd looked at her with a sharp expression, as if it wasn't proper she should ask about men's clothes. "Not sure, but long sleeves and pants, I guess, 'cause they hid quick in the trees, just blended in."

"Did you actually see them run in or out, Eli?"

"It happened real fast, like a blur. Oh, *ja,* no skin showed, no faces, either."

"Could they have worn dark jeans and maybe a black leather jacket?" she prompted when he said no more.

"Sure, could have, a lot like the motorbike rider at the bonfire."

She realized she might be leading her little witness,

but this information was too good to pass up. Still, she held back from asking if the two men wore motorcycle helmets. "And no skin showed or faces, either?" she prompted.

The boy frowned as if in deep thought. His freckles suddenly stood out amidst his bruises. "It was kind of," he said, speaking slowly, "like in pictures of the English going on snow skis to keep their faces warm."

"Ski masks? Dark, knitted ski masks?"

"If that's what they're called, that might be it, I guess," he'd admitted, glancing out the door toward Luke's windmill shop where he obviously longed to be.

"You've helped me a lot, Eli. And if you think of anything else about how they looked, please tell me, will you?"

"For sure, 'cause like I said, just like Dad, I'm going to help you."

"I appreciate that. I think you'd like to learn to help your dad in his shop, too, wouldn't you?"

"He says I can when I'm bigger. I already did sometimes, but not with my eye hurt. If I can't see real good, I don't know. What I want to do most is climb the windmills when they get put up, like he does."

"Luke—your father—does the installations? Climbs clear up there?"

"*Ja,*" he said, flashing her a rare smile. "Way up to the blades and vanes above the platform. But he wears his safety harness, even if the Amish carpenters won't. People get real mad about that."

Her cop instincts set off alarm bells. "Who gets mad at the Amish for that?"

"The worldly carpenters' union over at Amish Acres. They don't like it that our carpenters don't wear safety harnesses or hard hats, but mostly don't like them 'cause they charge less.''

Kat didn't understand all the boy was saying, but it was another possibility she'd have to pursue. If Amish carpenters had underbid or bucked a union, surely that could mean retaliation. It was something else she'd have to ask Luke and Sheriff Martin about, and here, from the mouths of babes...

"Best of all, the windmills are pretty, too, like giant flowers, like daisies,'' Eli was saying, as if the conversation about carpenters had never happened. He'd gotten up from the table to look out toward Luke's shop again. "Dad told me that's what my mother said once. And Dad told me, using wind power for water and maybe someday making electricity for our people, that's modern Amish!''

Modern Amish, Kat thought, and even now, looking out her window, bit back a grin. How much she liked Eli—and wished Sarah liked her.

She continued to gaze into the blowing night so full of scents and sounds and sights, things she'd never noted before, as if her perceptions had now been jolted to life. From time to time, she heard a distant, irregular *click-click,* a metallic sound. It could be coming from one of Luke's windmills, but it sounded as if it were coming directly from the field behind her where the giant corn nodded and beckoned.

It bothered her again, as it had during the day, that the corn walls around the farm meant someone could sneak up close to the house to observe. The men in ski masks had run out of the woods, Eli said. She'd have to ask Luke how soon the harvest would be. This strange feeling of being enclosed and observed would be enough to make her shut her windows at night, however much she loved to sleep with them open. And that intermittent *click-click* might keep her awake, too.

An unearthly screech nearby shredded the night. Kat jerked so hard she bumped her head on the raised windowsill, then hit the floor, flat on her face, next to the lantern she'd turned off.

What in hell—who was that? Ida and Bishop Brand had been in bed for hours, so she couldn't ask them.

And then, in the house, she heard footsteps...in the hall, just outside her door, shuffling stealthily. Wishing she had a gun—even if she had to shoot left-handed—she scrambled to grab her flashlight from the bedside table. Not turning it on, since that might make her a target, she wielded it like a baton and tiptoed barefoot to her bedroom door, then opened it slowly.

In the unlighted hall, a dark figure stood between her and the dim kitchen—a man, evidently all in black.

"Who is it?" she demanded, crouched to spring.

A match flared to light a craggy face with a full white beard. "Jacob Brand, in my own home," a raspy voice said. "That raccoon shriek scare you, Katie?"

She felt like a fool, standing poised for fruitless battle as he lit a lantern hanging on a wall peg. At least she hadn't tackled the Amish community's elderly, ill bishop, whom she wanted to impress. A damn raccoon had spooked the city cop.

Dismayed to be meeting him while she was acting like an ignorant wimp, and a worldly one at that, with her hair wild and loose, Kat felt herself flush. She managed to say, "I'm pleased to meet you, Bishop Brand. I hope you're feeling better."

"Some better, but couldn't sleep," he said, turning away, putting the lamp on the kitchen table and bending slightly to open the refrigerator door. He took out a carton of milk and got two glasses from the cupboard. "Come sit, then," he told her. "Been wanting to talk to you, and sorry I am to have the stomach upset off and on."

"It couldn't be appendicitis, could it? My brother once—he had that bad."

"Ulcer or acid reflux, doctors think, but they're wishy-washy on it. But I don't care about myself, compared to Dan and Brooke's little Melanie in that coma."

"I know. That does put everything in perspective. I hear her condition is unchanged so far and no one knows what—"

"God knows," he whispered. "It's all in His hands."

He put two glasses on the table and poured milk into them. Kat was actually yearning for a beer, but she took a glass of milk and sat two seats down the large table, at what she considered a respectful distance from him.

Bishop Jacob Brand's weathered face only slightly suggested Luke's features. A thin, wiry man, the bishop wore trousers under a black wool robe, as if he were chilled, though the night was quite warm.

"Saw you out the window when you came in Luke's buggy," he said. "In looks, at least, you pass *ser gut* for Amish."

She took that both as a compliment and a caution. "I hope this works out. I very much want to get to the bottom of these outrages against your people, so the sheriff can make some arrests."

He nodded and sipped his milk. "Now that I'm better, Ida's sleeping over at Luke's since he's working late at the shop. He works too hard and she does, too, mothering Luke's brood at her age. Katie, I wanted to tell you some things, maybe so you understand better.''

Kat leaned forward, gripping her glass. "I'd appreciate any help you can give me—you most of all.''

"*Ach,* hard for me to accept the people going out from the farms and families, but they must to make a living these days. Very hard for the women, but the men, too. Starting what the English call our cottage industries. The women waiting tables, cleaning rooms in bed-and-breakfasts, working in shops that make money from selling our crafts and our culture. Our little treasures, meant just for useful things, too often turned to tourist trash, sad to say. Better for our way of life the Plain People farm and live close to home, not have such doings with the world. That breaks up families more ways than one.''

Not wanting to interrupt him, she nodded.

"But things have to change," he went on, "when land gets scarce for our sons, more than three thousand per acre. Farmers used to be one-fourth of us, now more like one-tenth. Three of my own children moved away to afford farmland, and we don't see them or those grandchildren much.'' He frowned, shaking his head, which moved his white beard back and forth across his chest as he stared down into his nearly empty glass. "Then more English move into this area, and something has to give—'' His voice caught.

"That doesn't excuse the things that have been happening.''

"*Ach,* no. But our heritage is to accept suffering, show forgiveness, move on if we must. Only, I do not think it is God's will that we leave this place. The tourists and the new housing construction, Amish Acres—'' He added those last two words with such contempt that she almost expected him to spit on the floor.

He hesitated, then began to speak again. "The coming of so many English here to live or visit is heating up this stew of different people. *Auslanders,* they bring business for us to survive but they change our ways and tempt our youth and try to drive us out so we may not survive after all."

He went as silent as the house and the night.

"I will do all I can," Kat said, "at least, to see that these hate crimes, these attacks on you and your children stop, so that you *can* survive here and continue to prosper. And I would appreciate any other background information or advice you can give me, especially in your honored position as bishop of the chur—"

"Let me tell you how it is to be a bishop, a leader," he told her, his voice going steely as he rapped the table with his knuckles. "Our people elect their bishops for life, not by ballot—a worldly popularity contest—but by lot."

"By lot?"

"All eligible men, married and of good repute, can be nominated by any church member. Each man picks a hymn book from a pile of them to see if they have the short straw, so to speak—a Bible verse tucked within."

"Then, it's totally by chance?"

"No. God chooses that way, you see. And there is no celebration, no congratulations as when the world picks a leader. The family mourns and all offer their sympathy, the burden is so great. And my burden has been great these many years, to bear the griefs and grave decisions for my beloved people. And at Luke's urging, I decided to allow you to try to learn who is out to scare us and scare us off!''

Kat found she couldn't speak, but she nodded. If the president of the United States had summoned her to the Oval Office and commissioned her to take on an undercover mission to save the entire nation, she could not have been more deeply moved.

Luke dropped Kat and his kids off early for school the next day, though they usually walked. He was heading out to look at a site for one of the seven-foot-high decorative windmills his shop made in addition to the full-size, functional ones. Despite Bishop Brand's attitude toward Amish Acres, Luke had told Kat the windmill was for the entrance to the site of that new housing development. She had not yet had the chance to talk to him about the problems with the carpenters' union, but she fully intended to.

"I wish I could go with you," she told him. She tried to help stubborn little Sarah out of the buggy, but the girl jumped down on her own. "I want to look around that area."

"I'll be going back shortly to set the windmill up, and you can go then," he said as he clucked Sandy away. Eli and Sarah waved goodbye to him, so Kat did too, though she was burdened with a sack of something called moonpies Ida had baked for the Welcome Teacher party today. Eli toted his books and a plastic jug canteen of lemonade while Sarah carried her crayoned decorations. They were early, but Kat needed to case the school before the other children arrived. Teacher Leah—Lee—was already there.

While Sarah and Eli thumbtacked the decorations to the two big bulletin boards, Lee showed Kat around.

A big, coal-burning stove sat in the center of the neat rows of wrought-iron and wood desks.

"This is the cloakroom," Lee said as they stood in the long, narrow side area lined with wall pegs.

"Lee, can I ask you something so the kids won't hear?"

"Sure. Ask away."

"Reuben Coblentz, who lives near the Brands— what's the deal with him? I asked Luke but he wasn't too helpful for once."

"Reuben has a bug in his bean."

"What? You mean he's off his rocker?" Kat demanded before she realized she too was speaking in her own culture's slang.

"Reuben acts weird. He drinks all the time so he's under the *meidung*—shunning." Lee stooped to straighten a notebook and crayons in a cardboard carton labeled Lost and Found.

"Luke did say that much. So that means everyone avoids him, right? He's an outcast?"

"The purpose of our rules, called the *ordnung,* and the shunning, is to encourage people to see the error of their ways and, hopefully, prayerfully, ask to be reinstated."

"To return to the Amish fold?"

"Right." She nodded vigorously, standing to face Kat again.

"But in Reuben's case," Kat went on, "he continues to drink and abuse his precious farmland. He won't sell it to the Amish when it's desperately needed and going to rack and ruin, and he's a bitter man, maybe even resentful toward your people?"

"True."

Kat gritted her teeth. It was pretty obvious the Amish were not to speak of someone who was shunned, let alone deal with them. Kat knew she was just going to have to go—perhaps even walk through the cornfield where she wouldn't be spotted—to get a good look at the infamous Reuben, who seemed to have a motive, at least, for disliking or resenting the Amish. And Luke had let slip that Reuben now had lots of English friends. If they were his drinking buddies, who knows what kind of stuff they could be convinced to pull against the Amish who had more or less thrown Reuben out.

"One more thing," Lee said, so quick and low that Kat had to strain to hear. "I'm glad you asked about him in private," she whispered, gesturing toward the other room where they could hear Eli and Sarah talking. "Reuben Coblentz is Eli and Sarah's other grandfather—Luke's dead wife's father."

Kat stood with her mouth open as Lee darted out. Hell, she was expecting surprises around here, so she'd just have to chalk that up to one of them, she thought, smacking both hands on her long green skirt. But she was going to put Grandpa Coblentz under surveillance, and soon.

"Good morning, scholars!" Lee greeted the assembled group of forty-four students.

"Good morning, Teacher Leah!" they chorused.

"And this is Teacher Katie Kurtz from Pennsylvania, come to help some of you get better English. She will be here most days at least for a while."

All heads swiveled to look at Kat. Eyes wide, some smiles. "Good morning, scholars," she said.

"Good morning, Teacher Katie!"

This could not be real. These wholesome, old-fashioned ways, these people, she thought, as Lee led everyone in the Lord's Prayer. Lee had explained that the Amish plea to keep control of their own schools had gone clear to the United States Supreme Court before being decided in their favor, though the suit had been brought not by the Amish but by others willing to fight to protect their rights. And Kat was going to do the same.

The morning blurred by as Lee taught the older kids math and geography, unrolling maps hanging above the chalkboards. Kat stood among the first and second graders, getting them to tell about their families in English, and gently correcting or teaching them English words they needed. A disciplined approach to learning ruled here, with much recitation and memory work. Most of these kids might not go past eighth grade before some of them headed to vocational classes, but they were going to have actual knowledge in their heads. No spelling checkers or calculators or spreadsheets needed here.

Kat could sense how excited the students were about the extended lunchtime for the picnic. Several mothers had appeared in buggies ready to help set things up. The morning had only been interrupted by restroom breaks to the two smartly painted outhouses behind the playground equipment at the back of the building.

"It's such a lovely day that we're going to have the picnic outside," Lee announced at eleven-fifteen. Kids clapped; a few cheered. "But we are all going to eat together first from food set up on a table, and then we'll have time to play games. And I do expect all of you to return to the classroom ready to learn when I ring the bell to tell you that our special time is over."

Kat had noted everything was run promptly by the battery clock on the teacher's desk. So orderly, so proper, all of it. The wall hanging above Lee's head, which vertically spelled out the word S-C-H-O-O-L, read: Study, Cooperation, Honesty, Obedience, Order, Love. This might all seem hokey and out-of-step with the rest of America, Kat thought, but it seemed so good and right to her here.

"Oh, that's just lovely!" Kat cried when she saw a sheet-cake with a schoolhouse on it and *Welcome, Teacher Katie* scrolled across it in bright green icing.

"Hope that's chocolate under all that fancy stuff," Eli put in as he hefted the lemonade jug up on the table.

Lee told Kat, "That came from the bakeshop in town my mother owns, though she doesn't really run it. It's called the Bread of Life, and you'll have to visit. It's sandwiched, if you'll excuse the pun, between two of Marnie Girkins's places. Boys and girls," she went on, speaking louder now, "Mrs. Girkins sent a whole sack of Tootsie Roll Pops for you, but no one is to take one before you eat. And if you are going to play a game or run, no suckers in your mouths!"

"Would you believe I used to be really heavy when I was growing up?" Lee whispered, speaking only to Kat again.

"With food like this around, I think I can believe that," Kat told her as they exchanged smiles.

"When I started teaching, it just all fell off one year," Lee explained. "Chasing all these kids around, that's why!"

Kat was starting to get the idea that every Amish meal was a feast. Even their leftovers last night had been bounteous. Now, on two sawhorses, the bigger boys set up a table made from an old door, and the women and girls covered it with cold chicken, sliced ham, breads, cheeses, potato and macaroni salads, molded jellies and jars of beverages. Kat's doctors, who had wanted her to gain some weight after her injuries, should have simply sent her to Amish country.

Despite the array of food, Kat noted kids were gobbling their lunches without paying much attention; she suspected they couldn't wait to have extra time to play. A volleyball net, jump ropes and a softball diamond awaited, not to mention swings, a slide and a jungle gym. Kat tried to eat, talk and answer questions, still keeping her ears alert for anything she could glean from the myriad conversations, most of which were in English. But she tried to stay aware of the surroundings, too. A heavily treed lot backed up to the rear yard of the school, though the sides of the property were open to fields of winter wheat and the rural road that ran past in front. She tried to watch the woods and fields as well as the road; few buggies or cars went by. She especially kept an eye out for motorbikes. With all the noise the kids were making, she probably wouldn't even hear the distinctive whine Luke had described.

Kat began to relax, to enjoy herself. It all seemed so sweet, so safe. But then she saw a pickup truck, not speeding past, but turning in, slowly. Someone with a camera, perhaps?

Kat shielded her eyes from the sun. Maybe the driver had made a wrong turn, was lost or turning around. No, the vehicle wasn't turning into the drive, but making a big loop before the school, partly on the drive, partly on the grass... It was a black truck with dark-tinted windows, a truck absolutely caked with mud.

Her insides plummeted as if she were riding a roller coaster. Both the driver and passenger sides, their dark windows about one-third down, sprouted black barrels, muzzles aimed at the crowd of kids.

They looked like submachine guns!

Behind one, a masked face with goggles…

"Gun!" Kat screamed. "Gun! Get down, down!"

It took a moment, an eternity, for anyone else to react.

Then some kids screamed, some ran. A few hit the ground. Kat grabbed Sarah and shoved her down, yanked Lee on top of her and, in the split second before the first shots sounded, pushed others at Lee to huddle there.

Five feet ahead of Kat, a young child shrieked as she was hit. Crimson blood blossomed on her pale blue dress over her chest. A boy bled lime green—

Green?

Paintballs, Kat thought, relieved but enraged. The thin shells broke on impact, splashing blotches of paint and terrifying the kids. Not bullets, thank God, but they could cause welts at the least and put out eyes at the most. Where was Eli?

One hit Kat's neck. It stung. Lime paint splattered over her dress and the side of her face. It even went up her nose. She tasted it, closed her eyes, momentarily on her knees, swiping madly at her face with her apron until she'd cleared her vision.

The truck's license plate was not visible. Caked mud covered it, although it hadn't rained for several days. Kat still hunkered down, shoving kids behind her, forcing herself to look at the truck rather than run as it looped back for another pass.

Adrenaline poured through her. She almost threw herself at the truck—a Ford?—to rip the shooters out by the muzzles of their guns. But she was Amish now, not English. A teacher, not a cop. She could not give away her real identity to these cowardly bastards behind the wheel and the paintball guns.

Kat forced herself to stand her ground and assess the scene. Some of the older kids had run for the schoolhouse but the younger ones milled around like frightened sheep. The next volley of shots exploded in stings and colors on white *kapps,* aprons, shirts, faces.

With a grunt, Kat tipped the table on its side, spilling food off it, including the cake, as yet uncut. Taking a hit on her shoulder and one in her hair that ripped her *kapp* and bonnet back, she leaned the old door on its side against the sawhorses.

"Here, get behind here!" she shouted, gesturing to kids who still stood in the open.

Lee repeated her words in German, *"Komm! Komm schnell!"* as the younger children dove behind the makeshift cover. Unwilling to get behind it herself, Kat saw that the jug of Ida's lemonade had not spilled but had just slid off the tipped table. She grabbed it, unscrewing the big lid. It was still more than half full of liquid.

Kat waited until the truck passed, then splashed the liquid at the back license plate, hoping to wash the mud off. She was wide of the mark, but the lemonade uncovered something on the bumper she couldn't read in the blur.

Kat was certain she heard a male laugh as the truck sped away. Dripping with paint, fists clenched at her sides, she hurried out to the road. The truck accelerated, disappearing over the hill almost immediately. The entire attack must have taken less than two minutes.

Behind her Kat could hear children sobbing, the three mothers calling for their own, and Lee's shaky voice giving orders.

But one good thing had come from this, Kat told herself. Though the bumper sticker on the truck had been partly scraped off, the liquid she'd flung had uncovered an eagle, talons extended, flying past what had appeared to be a flapping United States flag.

6

―――――――――――

Although they could have walked through the fields and past the ravine to get to the covered bridge for their first meeting with Sheriff Martin, Luke drove them in the buggy. A light, chill rain was falling, enough to slick the roads. He had snapped the plastic cover onto the front of the buggy. Windshield wipers, run by a battery under their seat, swish-swished in front of them. The drumbeat of rain seemed to seal them together in the swaying black box.

It had been a grueling day for Kat. After the attack at the school picnic, the teachers and the three mothers had tended to the children's injuries as best they could. Fear was the worst damage, Kat thought, though several kids had swallowed paint or gotten it in their eyes. As if stung by giant bees, most of them, including Kat and Lee, had painful welts on their skin.

But Kat realized that three good things had come from the assault. She'd glimpsed a bumper sticker that was going to lead her to pursue an investigation into the Patriot Knights. Second, the Amish had decided that, even though it was nearly harvest time, fathers would take turns patrolling the school grounds. And the Amish community, which had once again refused to report the outrage and were praying for their attackers, was even more firmly behind her efforts, although that did not keep her and Luke from arguing.

"Whatever your painful past with Reuben Coblentz," she told him as the buggy rolled down the deserted rural roads in the misty darkness, "you should have told me."

"I told you what was necessary. He's being shunned, he drinks, he could be bitter, yes."

"And you sound bitter, too."

"Not against the Amish."

"But he's your father-in-law. Your children's grandfather, your deceased wife's—"

"That made his betrayal worse, not easier to deal with."

"But, Luke, with some people, alcoholism is a disease, not just a desire—a sin."

"I know that, but he didn't even want to change. He refused help and shunned our ways first, before—"

"All right," she said, and just then the turn onto Greengrove slid his shoulder and hip harder against hers. Luke's prickly reaction to her questions about Reuben reminded her of how cops fill out reports that could get them in trouble extra carefully. What could Luke be hiding in his relationship with his former father-in-law?

"Let me just ask one other thing, then," she said. "Do you think Coblentz has it in him to do any of these terrible things? Especially since the attacks have hurt Eli and Sarah?"

"He told me once, since I kept Eli and Sarah from him after Anna died, that I'd regret it and the children would, too. But that could have been just a general comment, or an angry man, or the liquor talking."

"Which could be the same anger and liquor behind these attacks. Do you know if he owns a black pickup?"

"Kat—Katie, lots of folks around here own a black

pickup. Yeah, he does, but it's an old one, and you said this one was newer.''

She wished again that she was savvy at spotting makes and years of vehicles from their silhouettes, back, front or side, but it just wasn't her thing. She'd always left that up to her partner, Mike Morelli, who could tell a Toyota from a Honda a block away. And certainly none of the other panicked eyewitnesses today would have a clue about the type or year of a truck.

"Does Coblentz own a motorbike?" she asked. "You realize, when it left your property, it probably turned toward his.''

"A motorbike, I don't know.''

"All right, let's change the subject,'' she said as the narrow road took them between walls of thick trees that seemed to lean toward them, shuddering in another sudden shower. "Tell me about the carpenter union problems at Amish Acres.''

"I've been meaning to. The guy who heads the union is in the list I'm giving you tomorrow. His name's Clay Bigler.''

"Clay Bigler. Tell me about him.''

"I don't know him personally, but he's the new head of the United Working Carpenters, the UWC. He's been trying to bring a lawsuit against our Amish carpenters for underbidding the union for jobs around here. The union used to live and let live, but not under his leadership. He's been taking photos of our men for things like not wearing safety harnesses and hard hats on the job.''

She knew the Amish didn't like to have their pictures taken. "Why not wear those on the job?" she asked. "It's just common sense.''

"Wearing those means you're not trusting God for

your safety. And the Amish never join unions—no groups but the church. It's like not having lightning rods on our barns or houses. We trust in God, not man's inventions. We don't carry insurance, so if disaster strikes, we just get together and rebuild.''

''But Eli told me you wear a harness working on windmill installations.''

''That's higher than a house roof,'' he explained. ''I never used to before Anna died, but if something happens to me, I won't leave those kids alone, though my brothers' or sister's families would take them in after my parents died. Since their mother passed away, both Eli and Sarah get panicked about me leaving them—dying. Despite having to convince the elders and the bishop, I wear the harness for them.''

The urge to argue went out of her. She'd been wondering why Sarah seemed to dislike her so, and was going to ask, but now was not the time. Kat had even overheard the little girl tell Luke this afternoon that Kat had shoved her down on the ground when the evildoers came with the paintballs—as if Kat were in cahoots with the shooters.

''But,'' Luke had told the girl, ''you are about the only scholar with not one mark on you. So Katie helped and protected you, didn't she?''

''Teacher Leah helped me,'' the stubborn child had insisted, and Kat had puzzled anew at the girl's dislike for her.

''There's the bridge,'' Luke said now, taking one hand off the reins to point ahead through the blur of plastic window. ''Looks like the sheriff's here already. There, parked off to the left in the fishing spot.''

Kat gasped. It was not a patrol car but a black pickup truck.

''See what I mean about lots of folks having

them?'' Luke said as he reined in, opened the flap and jumped down.

He held up his hand to help her, and she took it. He felt rock solid, while she was still jumpy from the attack today. Though she saw the sheriff emerge from the depths of the covered bridge, she took her time, going by his truck to look at the back fender. Its only bumper sticker said, Go Eagles Football! but it did sport an American flag with an eagle perched atop the flagpole. Surely that was not what she'd seen on the other truck's bumper.

"Let's step in here," Ray Martin said, gesturing to them. "This is the perfect place to meet when we got us this kind of weather, or in case any of us is followed. I'll park farther away next time and sneak in from that other direction." He kept fidgeting and seemed quite nervous. "No one would know," he went on in a rush, "if a courting couple, like you two supposedly are, didn't just see this as a real romantic spot for making out. Luckily, it's off the beaten path, since a lot of beautiful old bridges like this have been attacked by vandals lately."

Just like the Amish themselves, Kat thought as the three of them stood just inside the bridge before the deeper blackness began. Quickly, she filled the sheriff in on the attack at the school, yet omitted telling him about the bumper sticker. She hadn't told Luke either and was going to look into that herself.

She did outline some things she'd like the sheriff to do, though. "As I said, that motorbike was leaking oil, so if you get a chance to ask around at local gas stations or repair shops, you might latch on to something."

"Will do. I could try to check paintball supply stores, too, but I know for a fact equipment and supplies like the protective masks and goggles you described can all be ordered online pronto.''

''You've done paintballing yourself?'' Kat asked.

''No, but the church youth group did once, out in the woods, and I helped order supplies. Piece of cake.''

Kat saw again the lovely Welcome, Teacher Katie cake Lee's mother had sent from her Bread of Life bakery. The Amish women at the school had thanked Kat repeatedly for thinking to turn the table over to give the kids better shelter, but the entire cake had been smashed.

''One other thing about that, though,'' the sheriff was saying. ''I've heard the Patriot Knights have a paintball range, set up with targets for their kids to use.''

Bingo! Kat thought, though she merely nodded.

''Probably to get their interest up in shooting guns,'' Luke put in, with a shake of his head. ''Some of our boys learn to shoot, but only hunting rifles in deer season when we can use the meat.''

''Something else, too,'' Sheriff Martin said. ''I've been doing some research on anti-Amish hate crimes, which have been prosecuted some places in the Midwest as ethnic intimidation.''

''Is it widespread?'' Kat asked.

''Worse some places than others, of course, but unfortunately, growing in numbers. I kind of got a profile of the most common offenders. I thought it could help you keep your eyes open. But you just let me know if you zero in on any individuals for me to question or arrest.''

''What sort of profile?'' she asked, not promising him anything of the kind. She fully intended to keep him informed and let him do any enforcement, but she was starting to realize she'd make no progress if she had to clear everything with either Luke or the sheriff, not to mention Bishop Brand.

"The perps are almost always men, of course, mostly late teens on up to thirties or so. They may have a specific beef against their targets, but it usually boils down to the fact that they just plain hate someone who's different or they don't understand. They can't stomach folks who evidently aren't fearful of their attacks, of giving them 'proper respect' as one guy put it."

"In short," Kat said, "they're like any bullies picking on those they consider weak, because it makes them feel like big men and helps them hide their own insecurities and inadequacies."

"And all that makes you sound like a shrink," the sheriff said. "But yeah, I think you're right. And, Kat," he went on, laying a hand on her shoulder, "even though these attacks have been more malicious than violent so far, the government now prosecutes this as serious stuff."

Luke said, "These are terrorists, that's what I've been thinking."

"Exactly," the sheriff said. "A man in Wisconsin recently got twenty-five years in prison for burning a buggy. Yet these bastards around here are already way beyond something as tame as that."

"So," Kat said, "people are taking a big risk when they commit such acts. So much of a risk that they must have a motive beyond just harassment or bullying."

"And that's why," Luke put in, "you have to be very careful. Just observe, just gather evidence but don't really act."

"And don't get yourself caught," Sheriff Martin added.

"I'll be sure she's careful," Luke said.

Fortunately, it was dark, so he could not see her roll her eyes. Rain tattooed the wooden roof of the bridge, covering the frustrated *humph* she snorted. She didn't want a guardian angel, especially not a compelling, macho, Amish one. His mere presence made her lose concentration, and her reactions to him careened back and forth between fascination and frustration. She had to start making things happen, and she couldn't do that while focusing on Luke Brand.

Kat couldn't sleep that night. Every time she nearly nodded off, she kept seeing that black truck with the guns pointed out the dark windows, shooting bright blotches of blood. The Amish kids all shrank to one little boy who was afraid of his bullying father and needed her help. But the father's gun pointed at her too, shooting real bullets, not with paint but with pain and real blood....

She sat up, drenched with sweat, the sheet and quilt clutched around her. Shaking, she put her head in her hands. She had to act, had to do something right now to stop her nightmares and start solving the one the Amish were caught up in.

The clock on the bedside table read three-thirty. She got up and went to her window and pulled open the dark-blue drapes on their single rod. Tonight, unlike last night, moonlight flooded the yard and silvered the corn tassels. She wouldn't even need a flashlight to go outside, but she'd take it along. She'd used it as protection far more than she'd ever used the collapsible baton from her equipment belt. How much more natural it would seem to her, even now, to strap that belt on her hips instead of donning this Amish garb.

She wore the royal-blue dress and left the apron off. Not putting up her hair, she covered her head with her bonnet, and pulled her black shawl over her shoulders for camouflage more than warmth.

Kat opened her bedroom door stealthily, closed it behind her in the hall and tiptoed toward the back door of the *daadi haus*. It was locked—she'd heard that only lately had the Maplecreek Amish begun to secure their doors—but the key was in the keyhole. She turned it slowly, let herself out, then locked it behind her, and hid the key under the pot of geraniums Ida kept at the back door.

She strained to listen. The rain had long stopped and the wind had stilled. She heard no raccoon cries, no *click-click,* only crickets and a distant frog. She cut across the yard, then behind Luke's windmill shop and house. Glancing up at his dark windows, she wondered how well he slept without his wife at his side. Did he still long for her in bed and out?

The grass was wet and the corn, too, but she plunged between two rows. At least they were planted quite straight along the road, unlike on the hills behind the farmhouse, so she knew a row would take her where she wanted to go. She'd simply look around at the Coblentz place close up—she and Luke had passed it on the road in the rain tonight—and assess if it was worth coming back to in daylight.

Before she'd been injured, Kat used to run at least four miles a day, and she had been starting to get her stamina back, lately. The Amish sometimes walked long distances, but she'd have to get used to using the buggy instead of jogging. Tomorrow she'd find a way to take a look at Amish Acres to see if any of the union carpenters were around, and somehow, figure out how she was going to get onto the land where the Patriot Knights met, played and, perhaps, plotted. She had to learn more about possible suspects—fast.

Rain had made the going muddy; the rows of corn seemed endless. Kat was getting skittish from having heavy ears bump into her shoulders or hips as if someone from behind or beside tapped or grabbed at her. Suddenly, she emerged from the field and gasped. Just a few feet away lay a huge metal object on its side, like a giant, toppled erector set.

A windmill. Brought down by the wind...or by a man who hated Luke and the Amish?

Looking through the struts of the fallen tower, Kat saw she'd come out between Coblentz's farmhouse—smaller than Luke's—and the back buildings of a single squat silo and small barn with its doors ajar. Or was that barn more like a large storage shed or garage?

Even from here, Kat noted the house was in bad repair, with an eavestrough askew and paint peeling. The flower beds had run to riot, and the vegetable garden was nothing but weeds, no doubt both cardinal sins around here. The yard, which looked like it hadn't been cut in weeks, seemed to sprout tipsy-looking lawn chairs by the back door. Old-fashioned, horizontal venetian blinds, most of them bent or crooked, covered the upstairs windows while the downstairs ones seemed starkly naked.

Staying between the corn and the windmill and off the gravel driveway, Kat skirted the property until she was hidden from the house by the silo, then darted for the open doors of the storage building. Two vehicles sat within, a truck and a tractor, a modern one like the Amish would never use. Still wary of being seen from the house through the open double doors, she ran her hand along the truck. It was mud-splattered, she could tell that by mere touch. But the other truck had seemed newer, a more recent model. Or had her panic and rage kept her from remembering right?

Holding her breath, she stepped deeper into the darkness, then clicked on her flashlight. The truck was not completely caked with mud, though some of the dirt could have fallen off by now. The tractor, too, was dirty and looked as if it had been in a wreck—its front was dented and its single front tire was flat. She hurried behind the truck and shone her light on its back fender. The license plate was dirty, but she could read it. No bumperstickers, but it looked as if many had been there once and had been peeled or scraped off.

She played her light around the interior of the building, where piles of junk of various types ate up the space in the corners and along the walls. Cans of oil, but no motorbike. Clicking her flashlight off, she stepped outside, using the moon shadow of the building as a shelter from which to study the house.

She stepped back when a light downstairs flicked on, then two. They startled her not only for their suddenness but from the shock of their cold brightness compared to the softer glow of lanterns she was becoming used to. Had someone inside seen or heard her? Search warrants were a thing of the past; she was getting desperate.

Then she heard a car, saw its headlights swing across the house and gravel drive as it backed out and drove away. Could it be that Reuben Coblentz was just coming home? Could he have been out drinking this late and have arranged for someone else to drop him off?

"At least he has the brains to get a designated

driver,'' she muttered. ''And he's about to become a designated suspect.''

When the lights stayed on, Kat crept closer to the house, coming in from the back at an angle. Standing in the dark under an old apple tree in the side yard, she peeked out from behind the trunk.

A first she thought the man—no doubt Coblentz—was dancing, but she saw he was throwing something over and over. Pitching a baseball in his kitchen? She shifted her position slightly. No, he was throwing something—darts?—at a bull's-eye tacked up on the wall or the cupboards. Or was the crudely painted red-and-black target painted right on the woodwork?

Coblentz looked to be about five-five, maybe sixty. His salt-and-pepper hair was cut Amish, but he wore no beard. It looked like he was attired in worn, dark jeans and a navy-blue sweatshirt, though, she realized, his clothes could have been all black. She could hardly make out his features from here; it was his raw anger that defined him.

Kat stood transfixed for a few moments, wondering what he was thinking. How did he feel to have his dead daughter's family, who had shunned him, living right next door? A new thought hit her: could he blame Luke and the Amish for Anna's death? Ida said Anna had died in childbirth when she had Sarah. It had been in a hospital, but he could still hold Luke—maybe, in a warped way, even little Sarah—responsible.

Kat jumped as she heard something shatter in the house—a sharp, yet muffled sound. Had he broken a window with a dart? If so, looking out, would he see her?

But no, he was heaving drinking glasses at the bull's-eye, maybe plates too. Whatever demons possessed this man, she only prayed that they weren't ones that turned his anger on the Amish.

She hurried away, carefully climbing through the fallen windmill. Darting back into the cornfield, she headed toward home—toward Katie Kurtz's home, that is.

Despite having hardly slept, Kat was up early the next morning. She tiptoed into the kitchen with her shoes and stockings in her hand, but found Ida already preparing pancakes, hickory-smoked bacon and scrambled eggs, a definite improvement over the toast and instant coffee Kat usually called breakfast.

"I'm going out to talk to Luke to be sure he'll be taking the children to school," she told Ida, who stared at Kat's crimson toenails, which, unfortunately she'd forgotten to take care of. "And I'm taking Dilly and the courting buggy out today for the first time."

"You need my help with the harnessing, then?" Ida had asked as Kat hastily stuffed her stockinged feet in her shoes.

"If you'll let me trade you that for doing your grocery shopping after I run a few other errands," Kat said as she followed Ida's lead to pour honey on her pancakes. "Anything special you need in town?"

"That I do," Ida said, giving her a rare smile. "The elderberries out on the back forty are ripe, and I need some yeast and pectic enzyme."

"For pie or jelly?"

Ida looked at her strangely. "That and something else." Kat didn't know a thing about baking or canning—what the Amish called "putting up"—but she wondered if pectic enzyme could have something to do with the bishop's stomach ailments. No, she told herself, that would be peptic pills or something like that.

"Here, let me show you how nice the berries are this year," Ida said when they were finished eating.

"I'm sorry, I don't have time for a walk right now."

"No, here," Ida said, opening the freezer of her refrigerator. "It works best to freeze the fruit whole on their stems, then knock the berries off—see?" she said, plucking out a small branch and shaking it over the sink.

Kat had never so much as heard of elderberries before, let alone seen them. They were small, a beautiful purplish black against the white sink enamel. "I'm glad it's a good season for something," she told Ida as she took a short list of things she wanted from the grocery store in town.

With Ida's help, Kat got Dilly harnessed to Luke's little courting buggy, but she only drove as far as the hitching post of his shop. His workers' buggies were not here yet; the door stood ajar.

"Luke!" she called, knocking. "Luke?"

No one answered. Perhaps he had opened it, then had gone back into the house to get the children up. She could just leave him a note—and, while she was here, borrow some paint remover or turpentine to get this polish off her toenails.

She stepped inside. One end of the shop had an office set up with a desk and file cabinets, but, of course, no computer equipment. Yet Luke did have a plain black phone—one with a rotary dial, no less. Although the telephone line must be buried, she bet even getting that old phone had taken discussions with the powers that be here. All around the open room, on long metal worktables and shelves, lay pieces of windmills. She saw directional vanes, buckets of bolts and things she couldn't name, not to mention power tools linked to a generator.

In the end of the long, open shop, farthest from the office, stood the assembled metal towers for the seven-foot decorative windmills that Luke had said were becoming popular in the yards and gardens of the English and the Amish. On shelves behind that leaned the wheel of blades with their tips painted as red as her toenails. She laughed. He must have some brush cleaner in these cans and metal containers.

She found turpentine clearly marked, but it was in such a large tin container, she could hardly cart it back to the privacy of her room later. She decided to use it here, now. Hurrying, she took the turpentine and a rag and sat on the floor, which looked immaculately swept. She yanked off her shoes and stockings, then poured some of the acrid-smelling stuff on the rag. She rubbed hard at her left big toenail. Yes, the polish came right off, though it smeared the rag red. She'd have to take it with her, but at least he had a lot of rags and wouldn't miss it.

Kat concentrated on her task with one leg bent up at the knee almost to her chin so she could easily reach her foot. Her bare, extended leg got cold in the draft on the floor, but she kept going. Only two more nails on this last foot—

"Now, that's something I've never seen before," the deep voice beside and above her said.

"Oh! Luke, don't sneak up like that!" she protested, yanking her skirt down over both legs. "You weren't here so I just borrowed some of this."

"So I see." His voice was warm and heavy. He had one foot on a workbench and his arms nonchalantly crossed over his knee.

Her belly fluttered, and she looked away from him,

concentrating on finishing her task by bending way over her now-covered legs.

''That's fine—more than fine,'' he added.

She made the mistake of looking back up at him to assess if he was being sarcastic or teasing. He was neither, but looked transfixed. Though he didn't touch her, she felt as if he had, as if he'd run his big, hard hands, instead of his eyes, up her legs. How long had he been watching? But what rattled her even more was the burning intensity of his deep blue gaze. In a shop where electricity was *verboten,* she felt a jolt of sensual energy arc between them.

She knew she should just turn away and finish the damn job with her back to him, but she found herself saying, ''You've never seen nail polish on toes before?''

''Or bare English legs, to tell you the truth.''

''Or cops' legs, no doubt,'' she threw back at him, trying to play along as if she didn't feel flushed and shaky from the way he studied her, toes to the tip of her bonnet.

What the hell was wrong with her? She felt like some middle-school kid at her first party, or like one of the naive, virginal Amish *maidals,* when she was neither of the above.

''I meant,'' he said as he turned slowly, almost reluctantly, and started away, ''such brown and beautiful legs.''

Kat just gaped at him until she realized he must mean he was surprised she was tanned. Of course, the legs of Amish women would be all white, while she'd spent some of the summer in a bathing suit in the backyard. But she had no more time for such silly agonizing because just then Lee rushed into the workshop. At least by then, Luke was down by his desk, and Kat had her shoes and stockings back on.

"Komm schnell!" Lee cried to Luke. When she saw Kat, she startled, then added, "Oh, Katie, come quick, into town!"

"What?" Luke said, as he swung his jacket on and hurried toward them. "I have to take the kids to school."

"Windows broken in a lot of Amish shops, Mother's Bread of Life, too. She sent back word to us before I left for school. And the worst is that what broke them was those!" she cried, pointing past Kat.

Kat turned to see what she was looking at. Leaning against the wall, looking now more like miniature flying saucers or sharp metal Frisbees, were Luke's round windmill blades.

7

In five Amish-owned shops on the main street of Maplecreek, broken glass gritted underfoot and glittered in the glow of lanterns—and under the electric lights in two of Marnie Girkins's establishments, her Dutch Table Restaurant and Amish Treasures craft shop, which sat among those the Plain People owned. Luke and Kat saw the sheriff was in the craft shop, so they headed there.

Luke had not taken time to hitch his own buggy, but had asked Lee to take his children to school while he rode into town with Kat. "*Kristallnacht* all over again," he muttered as they crunched shards on the street.

"Crystal night? What's that?" Kat asked as she followed him up onto the sidewalk.

"When Hitler's bullies broke the windows of Jewish shops," he told her, his eyes wide as they surveyed the wanton destruction. "And that was even before the war started."

Kat stood doubly amazed: at this mess and at an Amish man quoting historical facts she knew nothing about, something that sounded as if it came from a college course.

They saw Sheriff Martin was already talking to Marnie Girkins, no doubt the only shop owner who would press charges—if they found the culprits.

"I'm just grateful none of my Amish staff was at

work yet next door at the restaurant,'' Marnie was saying. ''You know we open early for breakfast, Sheriff.''

''Got any idea when this happened, Marnie?'' he asked, writing on a small spiral notepad.

''I have no idea,'' she said, throwing her hands up. She looked as if she'd been rousted from bed; she wore no makeup and her hair was flattened in back. ''Well, at least before five-thirty,'' she went on. ''My manager, Martha, opens then. It figures, in this quiet town, no one was around to see it happen,'' she said, folding her arms across her chest.

''We're working on that.''

''And you might know it's Friday the thirteenth,'' Marnie muttered. ''Sheriff, could this have been done by the same jerks who've been after the Amish?''

''Don't know, but I'm gonna find out—promise you and the Amish that much. Now, nobody touches those windmill blades,'' he added, raising his voice, ''because I'm gonna have my deputy dust them for prints.''

Kat sucked in a sharp breath as the sheriff's gaze briefly snagged hers. If he thought she was worried Luke's prints would be on the metal, he was wrong. She was recalling that Reuben Coblentz had come home late last night and broken glassware, as if he were in a rage. That proved nothing *per se,* but it would be enough to prompt her to keep an even closer eye on him. She'd tell the sheriff if anything panned out.

''I thought word would get to you, Luke,'' Sheriff Martin said as Luke's big work boots crunched through glass.

''None of these bladed mills are missing from my

shop," Luke said as he hunkered down beside the two-feet-wide wheel.

"I heard where they came from already," the sheriff said, ignoring Kat as if he didn't know her. "All seven were taken from windmills you put in folks' yards. They been phoning in about them. Sometime after eleven last night, your windmills got beheaded, so to speak, and were used to bust out all these windows. Would it be hard to get these metal rotor wheels off their supports, Luke?"

"Not with a hacksaw, which these serrated edges suggest. It would make a little noise, but they could quickly be detached from their towers."

Kat was itching to ask if anyone who had called in had heard or seen them being sawed off, but she held her tongue. Surely the sheriff would pursue that. She did note that the time frame for this vandalism would fit Reuben Coblentz's return home. Of course, if the driver of his car was in on this destructive spree, they could both lie to act as an alibi for each other.

While Luke and the sheriff talked, Kat walked out onto the street. She scanned the area as she had watched the roads into town, looking for black pickup trucks, but she saw no vehicle that fit the description.

She strolled from shop to shop, looking in, as if she were just another curious bystander, but she wanted to see if the M.O. was the same in each establishment. In Bread of Life, the middle-aged, stout Amish woman sweeping up both window and display case glass looked so much like Lee that Kat was certain she must be her mother. Kat went in and stooped to hold the dustpan for the woman. "Do you know who I am?" she whispered, keeping her back to the people looking in through the jagged window pane.

"*Ja.*"

"There was no note, was there?" Kat asked, still keeping her voice low. "Did you see anything but this mill wheel and broken glass on the floor or outside?"

"Nothing but the hate that came with it," the woman whispered back.

"You're Mrs. Kurtz, Lee's mother, aren't you? I know it's not the time, but the cake you sent to the school was beautiful. I'm sorry I ruined it when I tipped the table."

"You ruined nothing," she told Kat as she kept sweeping and Kat kept dumping the contents of the dustpan in a plastic garbage can. "I heard you were only doing what you could to shelter the children. Bishop Brand, Luke and my Leah say you are here to help. When you catch the ones who hate us so, I will bake you another cake. You just call me Emma or Levi Em, like the others do."

The tacit support bolstered Kat and made her feel more determined to make headway before more attacks occurred. At least this one was not aimed directly at Amish children. But, as Luke had said, Crystal Night happened even before the real war got started.

"The question is," Kat said to Luke later as they huddled by the buggy, "did the jackasses who did this just take your metal mills to throw because they worked well for that? Or because they were Amish-built, and they wanted to ruin the windmills too, or—"

"Or what?" he cut in. She could tell he was seething beneath his forced calm demeanor. "No one, not Amish or English around here believes I would do this."

"I don't mean that. But could the vandals know

you're pushing to find and stop them, and, besides this being another attack on the Amish in general, could it be a warning to you?''

Luke rode home with a friend, while Kat drove the buggy to school to assure the students they were safe, though she couldn't help but wonder if she was telling them the truth. She informed them that, in addition to Amish men taking turns guarding the school grounds, the sheriff or his deputies would be driving by more often.

She left just after eleven-fifteen and drove the buggy out toward Amish Acres. She supposed that if Luke had already erected another little windmill at the charming entrance to this development, it too would have been decapitated and its metal rotors heaved through some window in town. Without insurance, the Amish would bear a heavy financial burden to replace the broken glass in their shops.

Kat was pleased with how she was getting along with Dilly and the buggy. About three miles northwest of town, she managed to make a perfect left turn into Pinwheel Quilt Road at the entrance to Amish Acres. She had to admit that whoever was building this place knew all about curb appeal. A picket fence surrounded the spot staked out for Luke's windmill, and clumps of russet mums bloomed around a small ersatz water- fall that poured frothing water from a carefully sculpted miniature rock cliff. The carved wooden sign that proudly announced Amish Acres had a back- ground that looked like a bright quilt pattern.

Kat had learned that the housing development was being built on what was formerly farmland. As such, it had no large trees, but new ones had been planted already. Two colonial-style model homes were completed with sod set in around them. She counted twelve other houses in various stages, though other sites stood empty. All the concrete streets looked poured. Pinwheel Quilt Road circled the area with various cul-de-sacs radiating from it.

At some building sites, large equipment, from bulldozers to dump trucks to small forklifts, was at work, making noise and whipping up dust. The roofs of the buildings under construction swarmed with both Amish and English workers, identifiable by their broad-brimmed straw hats or their molded, plastic hard hats. But, she noted, the worldly and Plain People did not work on the same buildings.

Trying to decide how to proceed, Amish Katie reined in, when cop Kat would have just approached several workers for questioning, then asked to see Clay Bigler himself. Her dilemma of how assertive to be seemed partly solved when a handsome, sandy-haired young man in a sharp navy-blue suit, which seemed out of place here, emerged from the large model home where she noted the sign Sales Office.

"Hi there!" he called, smiling. "Can I help you, ma'am? Are you here to deliver a lunch bucket to someone?"

"Oh, no," she told him, careful not to look directly into his eyes for long. Besides not wanting to seem English, that let her scan the area as well as watch the man from her peripheral vision. "I'm just new to Maplecreek, *ja,* and wanted to see what Amish Acres looks like, that's all."

"Hey, I'd be glad to show you around. My name's Grayson Gilmore, called Gil, Amish Acres sales rep at your service."

"Katie Kurtz, just moved here from Pennsylvania. No, not with all the men so busy, I won't take a tour."

"It's almost their lunchtime," he told her, putting one hand on the buggy and continuing to bathe her in his toothpaste-ad smile. Grayson Gilmore—Gil—had a lean face framed by an expensive-looking haircut. A square-cut emerald ring dominated his right hand, but he wore no wedding ring on his left. He was probably about five foot ten and one-hundred-eighty well-placed pounds.

"That's why I thought you were bringing food," he explained. "No one can cook like the Amish. I eat at the Dutch Table uptown a lot, but I'll bet that's only half as good as your home cooking."

"Did someone Amish own the land, so it got this name?" Kat asked, ignoring the way he kept assessing her. She was sure it was just because she was a young Amish woman, not because he could be onto her cover in any way. Or was he flirting?

"It's an amalgam of several big farms bought at auction," Gil said. "No, it wasn't Amish land."

"Bet they wanted it, though."

"Well, yeah, I suppose they did, but it's doubly valuable because they make such great builders and neighbors, though they—your people—are obviously not buying houses here. These have all the modern conveniences."

Kat wanted to argue that the perception that the Amish lived totally in the past was wrong, but she didn't want to get sidetracked. Besides, she realized, she should refer to the Amish as *we,* not *they.* "So who owns all this now, before the lots are bought?" she asked.

"A board of directors, no one local. Hey, I've never had the honor of speaking with an Amish lady before, not counting all the ones at shops or the waitresses in town. In case anyone asks, we're doing this development up right to keep the Amish ambience of the place, in homage to your culture and all. Oak floors laid by Amish carpenters, streets named after quilt patterns, the whole nine yards.''

Tempted to tell him what Bishop Brand and the Amish really thought of such homage, instead she nodded. "It's real nice that the Amish and English workers get along," she said.

Gil Gilmore narrowed his eyes at her, but perhaps it was because he stared up into the sun. "You *must* be new around here," he said with a nearly imperceptible shake of his head. His voice got a bit huffy. "Unfortunately, there's some strained feelings between the workers over wages and safety conditions. Just ask your menfolk, but remember that's not the whole story. The union guys need to make a living, too, and it's harder for them to cut corners, like the Amish can."

Kat sensed she'd overstepped, however safe she felt behind her facade. This cover was both a help and a hindrance. She could hardly ask this man to point out Clay Bigler so she could question him next. She would indeed have to ask some Amish menfolk about him. Was Bigler a man who would go to greater lengths than protests and a lawsuit?

"I'd best be going," she told him. "I shouldn't be driving in here, but the houses looked so pretty, these models here."

"As I said, even though you have no intention of buying, I'll show you around. Or since I know that's *verboten*," he added with a little grin and either a wink at her or a blink in the sun, "you just come on out with some other women, and I'll show you all around."

"*Danke*," she told him. "*Ja,* maybe I will do that." She snapped the reins and blew Dilly an exaggerated air kiss. Let the smooth-tongued salesman wonder if an Amish woman had dared to flirt back at him.

Kat drove the buggy along Roscoe Township Road, locally called Crookcreek Road, toward the area where the Patriot Knights owned a large parcel of land. Luke had told her where to turn off in a general way, no doubt supposing she wouldn't actually check out the area without him along. And that was all she was going to do, she assured herself, merely assess the scene. After all, if she was trespassing, anything she learned by surveillance would be inadmissible in court. She hoped, though, she'd come up with something that she could use against someone who could be prosecuted.

This was the first road she had driven on where traffic was heavy. She tried to keep over on the berm; Dilly seemed more steady than her driver as vehicles whooshed by. Kat soon came to understand something else about Amish life. As if she were an actor in a play, nearly all who passed her turned their head and gawked. Two teens in a truck—not a black one— honked as they went by, and Dilly pulled hard to the right. For one moment, Kat was tempted to shout at the morons, but again, she forced herself to be Amish and do nothing but grit her teeth. She pictured how Luke's square jaw had set when he heard about the paintball attack or saw his metal wheels had broken all those windows. She recalled Bishop Brand's tone of barely leashed contempt when he'd said the words *Amish Acres.* Yes, the Plain People were human, though their superhuman dignity and self-discipline awed her. But she, cop Kat, had a boiling point and, just as she had on patrol, she was going to have to keep her emotions from ruling her head.

She was surprised it was so easy to find the lane

that led back on to Patriot Knight land and amazed to see the metal gate stood open. About ten yards from the road, wire fences, maybe electric ones, set off the property itself. The Stars and Stripes flapped from a flagpole just inside the fence, and, under that stood a nearly four-foot-tall sculpture. Glinting in the sun, a metal eagle swooped down on what appeared to be the globe with its talons extended and its hooked beak open in a silent scream.

Her heartbeat quickened. The bumper sticker clue was flimsy, but any good detective work was always in the details. She also had the paintball connection. And surely these men would fit the sheriff's profile of hate criminals. But if they were behind the intimidation, were they picking on the Amish for real reasons, or were the Plain People just the best targets of general ethnic hatred such groups fed on? The Amish were pacifists, so that could be one bone of contention.

But her pulse pounded for another reason. If she drove right onto their land without an invitation—even under the pretense of being Amish—it was trespassing, possibly even entrapment. Since she was working for a government agent, albeit a rural county sheriff rather than a big-city police department, the rules she'd had pounded into her still held. Maybe she'd just ride in a little ways, she told herself as she circled back and turned in the lane. However much she didn't want to screw up, innocent kids being hurt and scared sucked, and she had to find out who was responsible.

Hoping that if she were stopped she could claim she'd just made a wrong turn, she drove in as far as the first copse of trees along the one-car-wide, rutted dirt lane. Luke had said several buildings were set back from the road; she saw them now. They reminded her of pictures of midwestern adobe ranches, but she realized these might be poured concrete. She could see a single van parked in front of the largest building.

Kat tied up the buggy behind some bushes where it was certain to be hidden. "Look, Dilly," she said, "I think these are elderberry bushes. We'll have to take some back to Ida." She snapped a heavily laden stem of berries off the bush and walked up a slight incline that overlooked the buildings.

She could see a gravel parking lot behind the main building with spaces for about twenty cars. Several wire fences, taller than the peripheral ones and topped by barbed wire, surrounded four of the six outbuildings. Two of them were the size of garages, and she wondered if they hid a black pickup truck.

Beyond them was a shooting range that looked a lot like the outdoor-indoor one at the Academy, with paper, man-size and man-shaped targets that could be pulled across wires. Kat supposed it could be a paintball range as well as a live ammo one. Could those smaller buildings, which looked like bunkers, be an arsenal? As if the breeze had chilled her, she shuddered. Kat shifted her position slightly, careful to stay behind trees or bushes and not silhouette herself on the top of the hill. The only thing she could see that softened the quasi-military scene was on the far side of the largest building. It looked as if there was a wooden-floored parade area under a canvas shelter edged with autumn decorations.

Kat shaded her eyes and squinted. Yes, piled bales of straw, sheaves of corn and several scarecrows were arranged there. Then she saw two men in khaki fatigues. They wore square, billed caps, but she could tell nothing else about them from this distance except that they seemed young.

One was setting up long, wooden tables and clusters

of small chairs under the large awning. The other was stringing lights on the edge of the canvas. It looked as if the Patriot Knights were going to have some sort of party, maybe a harvest dance. This was Friday; it was probably tonight or tomorrow. What she wouldn't give to be able to call in some police officer techies to plant a bug down there so she could eavesdrop.

But she had no permission, really, no authority. Still, she'd love to get a closer look. If only she could wangle some sort of invitation on to the grounds. Maybe Luke could tell them they'd won a free decorative windmill—if that would lead to evidence to show the Knights were suspects. She had no evidence that would get her or the sheriff a search warrant.

She realized she'd best clear out before others came in with supplies. But just before she turned away, she saw another reason for coming back tonight and possibly Saturday after dark to keep an eye on this place: a Patriot Knights banner that was larger and flew higher than the American flag. And on their banner was a perfect copy of the image on the bumper sticker on the black truck: the swooping, open-beaked eagle—

"Wanna come to the dance with me?" a sharp voice behind her said.

Kat turned and gasped. A man in fatigues stood not ten feet away with a semiautomatic rifle. He had his finger on the trigger but was not pointing it at her. Rather, he bounced the barrel in his other hand. His youth and jumpiness was both good and bad. She might outsmart him, but he'd want to prove himself.

Adrenaline poured through her with a force she hadn't experienced since John Seyjack's father had pulled that gun on her. She'd overstepped. She'd been caught again.

"You're trespassing on Patriot Knight land," he

said when she didn't answer. He was chewing gum—bubblegum, no less, she thought, as he popped it inside his mouth.

"Oh, I am? I was just looking to see if there were more elderberry bushes on this hill, see?" she said, holding out the single stem of berries toward him. He was almost six feet tall and stocky, with a clean-shaven face once ravaged by acne. His nose was long, his brown eyes close set.

Pointing down the hill, Kat went on. "Then I saw those real pretty decorations down there, *ja.* We're having a contest, see," she said, her words racing faster than her brain, before she realized the Amish wouldn't have a contest over anything. "Whoever brings back the most elderberries wins. I'm new in town, but my friends said try here—no one probably picks berries if there are any down this lane."

"Oh, yeah? Wins what? A ride in one of them old, flea-bit buggies? Say, you're kinda cute, not a plain old broad like some I seen uptown—plain, get it?" He snorted a laugh but his thin-lipped mouth didn't smile. "Want to win going to the dance with me tonight, honey?"

Kat faced him warily, but she almost smiled. That invitation to the dance could hold up in court if she got in trouble for being here. Anything, as they used to say, you could really justify and testify to honestly could work in your favor. But she realized she wasn't going to be able to just walk away from this jerk.

"Or better yet," he said, "how 'bout a nice roll in that hay down there with me?"

He laughed in a single sharp bark. Kat would have liked nothing more than to sucker punch and disarm him. But she kept telling herself, *think Amish, Amish.* She didn't want to blow her cover.

She tried to look both shocked and annoyed, but knew better than to play scared. If weasely men like this scented fear, it made them even bolder and more dangerous.

"I'll show you the berry bushes," she said, daring to start to walk away from him as if his threats and jokes had gone right over her bonneted head. This was a risk too, but she gambled that he wouldn't shoot her in the back, especially without permission from a higher-up, and it didn't look as if there was anything but lackeys around here right now.

"They make *ser gut* pies and jams," she said as she heard him striding to keep up with her, his sling strap for the weapon bouncing against it.

"I'd rather have a taste of you, Amish. You know, all kinds of bad things could happen to a little piece of pacifist tail comes on Knight property."

Pacifist! Then that was one reason the Knights could hate the Amish. People obsessed with playing militia who were ultrapatriotic could hate a group that didn't believe in violence or war.

Kat decided to continue to play dim bulb. That surely must be what the Knights thought of the Plain People anyway. "You upset I'm taking these berries?" she asked him, feigning confusion. "You want me to pick some for you to give your mother or sister?"

Hoping she could defuse his intent, she snapped off a few more stems. But as she nonchalantly began to untie Dilly's harness from the bush, the man assaulted her, spinning her around and pushing her back against the buggy with his hands and then his body. Stems snapped, berries smashed between them. Dilly jumped and snorted when the buggy bounced. Kat's assailant lifted a knee to spread her thighs and shove her skirt up.

Damn, she'd really miscalculated that she could deal with him calmly.

"Look, honey," he said, his breath hot on her neck as she smelled his sickeningly sweet bubblegum, "there's a penalty for little Amish babes coming on our land—and far as A.J.'s concerned, this is it."

Thank God A.J. held his rifle out to the side, but he pressed her harder against the buggy. He spit his gum out on the ground, then tried to kiss her. Instinctively, she lifted her knee to his groin hard, just once. He gasped and doubled up, going to his knees.

She grabbed the reins, then on second thought, not knowing how soon he'd recover, she picked up his rifle where it had dropped on the ground and put it under her feet in the buggy. As he retched under the elderberry bushes, she clucked to Dilly and snapped the reins.

Dilly headed back toward town at a good clip, but Kat turned off Crookcreek as soon as she could in case they came after her. She stopped only long enough to remove the rifle's magazine. Then she hid the rifle— a Colt AR-15 semiautomatic with rear peep-sight and flash suppressor—in a spot where she could send the sheriff to retrieve it. She kept the magazine under her foot—the one not stuck to A.J.'s discarded gum.

Kat was still shaking as she drove a roundabout way back to the Brand farm. But, when she glanced down at herself, she had to laugh. Since she'd been in peaceful Amish country, she'd had paint blotches all over one dress and now this one was speckled with purple berry stains. She'd have to get that idiot's gum off her shoe and the floor of the buggy. Kat didn't consider herself superstitious, but as Marnie had said, this *was* Friday the thirteenth.

Yet she had a plan now. Somehow, she was going to roll in the hay all right, only not the way that smug SOB had suggested. She was going to consider his lewd remarks an invitation—and legal excuse—to attend their little dance, even if undercover. She was going to hide amid the straw bales, corn sheaves and scarecrows, and go to school on everything those bigoted bastards said and did.

8

Eli was doing his chores in the barn when he saw how messed-up Katie's dress and apron looked. She drove the courting buggy in, got out and hurried to look closely at Dilly.

"What happened?" he asked and stopped forking hay for the three big Percherons in their stalls. She jumped because she hadn't seen him. "Did those bad men shoot more paintballs at you? Little ones this time?"

"It's smashed elderberries," she told him, looking kind of guilty. "Now Dilly's acting sick. Do you think if I ran her too fast it might make her vomit?"

"What does that last word mean?" he asked, frowning. He put the pitchfork down and went closer. Katie's hair was messy too. She had her *kapp* and bonnet on, but her hair was pulled out on her face like it was straw in a feed trough.

"You know," she said, "like she'll be sick to her stomach."

"Oh, not from running fast, even if they foam a little, like toothpaste caught in the corners of their mouth. But if she's been eating elderberries, all parts but the berries are poison."

"Poison!" she gasped and pressed both hands to her bonnet. "I didn't know. I've got to go tell your fath—"

"He went to put that little windmill in at Amish

Acres. He was looking for you to take with him. He was worried you weren't back."

"But poison? Does your grandmother know some antido—some cure?"

"Dilly won't die, so don't worry 'bout that, not 'less she ate a whole lot of them. Big as she is, she'll just mope around for a while. Raw berries can make people get the up-chucks, though. I'll just give her some water, but you better not drive her anymore today."

"Not tonight, either?"

Eli shook his head. He really liked the English woman and thought his father did, too. Sarah didn't, though, maybe because Katie wasn't too smart about important things and wasn't really Amish. Grandma Ida would probably make her wash her messed-up dress and apron until those stains came out.

"Eli," Katie said as he helped her unharness Dilly, "do you know anything about the kind of animal fences that have electricity in them? I know the Amish don't use that, but I just wondered."

"Oh, *ja,* I know a bunch," he said, grinning, "'cause we played a trick on someone once. See, those fences have a kind of off-on beat. If you listen real good, you can hear when it goes off. If you get over the fence real quick, between the beats, you'll be okay, but the next guy gets the surge. Then he jumps and squeals like a stuck pig, I guess."

He couldn't help laughing, remembering how the boys had done that to Amos Manz once. Katie was nodding, but not laughing, so she probably didn't like the idea of him talking about a stuck pig. But if she stayed around Amish country long enough for butchering time, she'd know what he meant.

"*Danke,* Eli," she told him and squeezed his shoulder before she took down the sack of groceries from the buggy. "You've been a big help to me, and it's great to know I can rely on you."

Eli watched her walk toward the *daadi haus.* His dad always seemed to be keeping an eye on Katie. Eli smiled. Maybe that would make his dad stay around here more.

It was nearly nine under a cloudy, pitch-black sky when Kat arrived at Lee's home. The lack of moonlight, at least, made Kat think her plan to eavesdrop on the Patriot Knights was meant to be.

Since the Amish community's teacher was unwed, she still lived with her parents on a farm two roads over from the Brands. Kat was out of breath and had worked up a sweat jogging over. While her other gowns were soaking, she'd borrowed a black dress of Ida's and belted it up with twine so her feet were free. A dark gown was much better for what she intended tonight, anyway.

Kat did exactly what Lee had said she should if she ever needed her at night but didn't want to wake her parents. Picking up several small pieces of gravel from the driveway, despite shuddering at the thought she could accidently break the glass, she threw them at the south back window that Lee had said was hers.

Courting couples did that all the time to meet on the sly, Lee had told her. Kat had wanted to ask what had happened to Lee's come-courting friend, if there had ever been one. Her single status only made Kat empathize with her more. After all, every time Kat had become romantically involved with a man, either she'd panicked about commitment or he had.

No light came on overhead, but the window sash scraped up and Lee's face appeared behind the screen.

Her hair was long and loose. Kat stepped back from the house to be seen clearly.

"Katie?"

"Yes, it's me. Can I borrow your buggy?"

"What happened to yours?"

"The horse got sick, and I don't want to ask Luke for his."

"Where you going?"

"I can't tell you—so you don't know."

"Oh. I'll be right down."

Carrying a lighted lantern, Lee came out the back door in her nightgown with a big black shawl wrapped around her. Stockingless, she wore someone else's too-large shoes.

"I appreciate your help," Kat told her.

"Help you don't want the Brands to know about, I guess."

Kat could only hope Luke assumed she was in her room, as did Ida and the bishop, who had gone to bed early. Marnie Girkins was driving the two of them into Columbus first thing tomorrow to visit with Brooke and Daniel and see how Melanie was doing in person. The girl was still comatose, though her parents were hopeful she was responding to more stimuli now. She opened her eyes occasionally, but stared unseeing.

"You should have asked Luke for his buggy and just said you couldn't tell him what it was for," Lee insisted as they hurried out to the barn.

"Are we talking about the same Luke?"

"But he's taken with you, that's sure."

"Lee, he isn't taken with me. It's just, he worries I'm going to ruin everything, because he doesn't think a woman can do the job."

"Oh, Amish men think we can do the job all right, but it has to be women's work. That is, unless a woman like Brooke or you comes along to shake things up. But Luke doesn't want anything bad to happen to you, so he'd skin me sure if he knew I was doing this. You going to Amish Acres? My friend Paul Yoder works there, and he says they got a guard on night watch.''

"Does Paul know Clay Bigler?"

"Sure does. Paul's in charge of the Amish work crews, so he's more or less Mr. Bigler's counterpart. Now, you watch out for that night guard, if that's where you're going," Lee warned.

Kat said nothing else, though she almost confided she'd bet a month's pay that an Amish Acres guard couldn't compare to the idiot on Patriot Knight property. She didn't want to alarm Lee more than she already had, though. When they had the buggy hitched, Kat pressed a note in a sealed envelope into the younger woman's hand.

"For Luke?" Lee asked.

"No, for Sheriff Martin, in case I don't have your buggy back in the barn by dawn. Otherwise, tear it up. You said you'd do anything to help, and I'm taking you up on that."

"I meant it, I really did," Lee said and hugged her.

Deeply touched, Kat hugged her back. "I owe you, Teacher Leah."

"You owe none of us anything but keeping yourself safe." After Kat climbed into the buggy, Lee reached up to grip her hand. "But I owe the kids," Kat told her, "your precious scholars and ones you don't even know. I owe them that they'll be safe."

She tugged her hand free and snapped the reins to move the carriage out from the dim depths of the barn into the vastness of the dark night.

* * *

Approaching Patriot Knights land this time, Kat pulled off on a small lane that skirted the property. Looking down the road at the regular entrance, she could see cars turning in, and, distantly, lights emanating from the main building and the area they had been preparing for the party.

This must be an old farmer's lane that provided access to crops when they had grown here. It took her longer than she wanted to find a place to hide Lee's buggy. Blessing the darkness, she tied the horse securely to a wooden fence that framed the fields abutting Patriot property, then walked up and down the road to be sure the buggy and horse could not be spotted. She also made certain she could find the buggy again quickly by tying her white *kapp* on a limb. Only when she had established a quick getaway plan did she turn toward the lights of the Patriots' party.

If she strained to listen, she could hear music drifting from across the field. She wondered if they had a live band, but it sounded like a recorded Beach Boys song. She might have known it would be something clean-cut, something from the past, she thought as she walked the outside of the fence she was certain was electric.

When a moment's silence settled between songs, she listened intently to the fence. Yes, little Eli was a genius! The fence did emit a slight pulsating, syncopated hum.

She walked it until she found a good place to go over, by stepping on a fallen tree to give her a leg up. Tucking even more of her skirt in the twine around her waist, she waited for the next lull. This song was that one by Lee Greenwood, "Proud To Be an Amer-

ican.'' She was pretty sure the party guests were singing—bellowing actually—along with it.

The music stopped; the pulsing hum of the fence
hesitated. With one hand for support on a post, Kat
cleared the fence. She had been in great shape before
being shot, and she was getting back some of that lost
strength and skill lately.

Banking on the hope no guards with guns would be
out in the fields tonight, she pulled the brim of her
black bonnet over her forehead and tied the strings
tight to cover her cheeks. Eli's description about the
men who'd ruined the quilts flashed through her mind.
Black ski masks. The paintball shooters had worn
high-tech goggles and masks. She just had an Amish
bonnet.

Keeping low, running a zigzag path, Kat headed for
the lighted canopy over the dance floor. Loud laughter
vied with the *clink* of glasses or bottles. Was this just
a harvest dance or was it a celebration of how well
the campaign to degrade and drive out the Amish was
going?

There were women here tonight, too, but it was the
inner circle meeting of men she hoped to overhear,
men who thought they could judge and control others
different from themselves, and, no doubt, bully them
into submission. When she'd worked the streets, she
had always been tempted to arrest such slime.

Individual voices began to stand out. Kat caught
separate words, even sentences. As she got closer, she
was nearly crawling. Damn, she'd probably ruin this
dress she'd borrowed from Ida, too.

Earlier today she'd seen that she could approach the
pile of straw bales from the back, where she hoped to
worm her way inside to overhear and watch the action.
She rolled against the rear of the straw bales and

quickly backed in to wedge herself between two that supported the pile. Today she'd noted such spaces in front, and she was relieved they were here, too, but she was forced to huddle in a very cramped gap.

The woody smell of grilled steaks or hamburgers floated to her. It smelled good, and her stomach rumbled. She had intentionally not eaten much tonight, knowing she was going for a run—not, as Ida had wondered, in an attempt to atone for letting the horse get sick. She almost sneezed, but she jammed her finger under her nose and held it in. Fortunately, another recording started, one that only the men sang along with. She recognized the melody of "To Dream the Impossible Dream" from the old musical *Man of La Mancha.*

Everything these people did seemed retro to her, but that made sense. They wanted to turn the clock back to the so-called good old days, though she'd hate to hear their definition of that. Then it struck her that *Man of La Mancha* was about Don Quixote, a hero who tilted at windmills. Surely there was no tie between the choice of this song and what they'd done to Luke's windmills. But the words to the song weren't right. Somehow they'd perverted the lyrics, written their own:

To dream the possible dream,
To strike boldly out at our foes,
To rid our homeland of cowards,
To soar where eagles dare go.

To save true patriots from harm,
To lift our flag starred and bright,
To fight and to die for our freedom,
To struggle for all that is right.

Kat was astounded and angry. Did they judge the Amish to be cowards because they were pacifists? Did they consider the Plain People their foes?

Huddled there, she got a cramp in her left calf muscle. Trying to massage it out, she strained to hear as the song ended and no other music played. Were they breaking up already?

But she heard the *clink* of glassware again, reminding her of the shattered window glass last night in town. Separate conversations occasionally drifted by her hiding place. Disembodied male voices talking about the coming World Series and whether the Cleveland Browns football team would do better this year. Two others were talking about what they called "Prize P.K. recruits." They talked about a few of them—they called one A.J....

When people shifted past her, their voices sometimes became muted or eerie. A gruff-sounding man told two women they'd better get in more food supplies, in case more terrorist attacks in the East cut import supply lines. Two, maybe three men came close. The bales of straw that surrounded her creaked and tightened. Were they sitting down just outside of or on her little lair?

The sharp smell of cigarette smoke drifted to her. She prayed they'd be careful with their matches, lighters and butts.

"...not only won't serve in the military, but most don't even vote. But then, with eighth grade educations, who'd want them to?"

"So we could more easily get Eagle One elected mayor and do some of this legally."

They were talking about the Amish! Alluding to doing something illegally.

"Such as?"

"Such as charge them road taxes—which they don't pay either—for repairs from those damn buggy wheels putting grooves in the asphalt, let alone the horse apples all over our roads."

"What a bunch of crap, right?"

That voice she knew. It was A.J., who thought he was funny when he wasn't. A.J., who thought nothing of trying to assault or even rape a lone Amish woman.

"Yeah," the older man said, not laughing. "And the way they tear the electric out of their homes just brings down property value in the whole area. No wonder somebody's giving the German-spouting morons a hard time, know what I mean?"

Snickers and laughter—because they were behind the attacks, or just appreciated whoever was?

"It's about as bad," a new male voice said, "as the Chicanos flooding in over our borders and the blacks jumping off beat-up boats from Haiti or wherever. The Amish breed like rabbits, too. Hell, coupla years, America won't be America at all, and we'll all be speaking in German, Spanish or black talk."

"I heard the Haitians speak French," A.J. put in.

"So? You standing up for them, boy? You want your kids—if you could find a decent woman who'd have you—speakin' that wimpy, up-your-nose French?"

The two older men laughed as they all moved on.

Kat lay there longer, tense, straining to hear, not daring to move a muscle. She listened to fragments of more conversations about commonplace things. Praying they wouldn't take their decorations apart tonight, she stayed until she heard people walk away, cars start and conversations cease.

When the lights went out, Kat counted to a hundred and inched out of her little den as straw snagged her skirts, bonnet and hair. She tried to dart into the dark field, but both legs had gone to sleep and she landed on the ground sprawled flat on her face.

Waiting until the prickly sensation of fresh blood in her legs made her feel them again, she lay in the weeds. Looking back at the scene—there were lights on only in the main building now—she wasn't sure what she could prove from all this. Still, it certainly gave her another theory to pursue. Even if the Patriot Knights had come right out and boasted that they were the ones harassing the Amish, it all would have been hearsay, which probably wouldn't be enough for a conviction. And, as ignorant as they sounded, she did believe in the right of free speech. But somehow she was going to get the hard evidence she needed.

Out of breath, she was clear across the field and over the fence to the buggy before she realized she'd lost her black bonnet somewhere.

Kat figured it was nearly midnight when she finally jogged back to the Brand farm. She'd taken time to unharness Lee's horse and rub it down. She could only hope that her bonnet had been lost in the vast, weedy field, not next to the straw bales or, worse yet, under them. If someone found the bonnet and showed it around, and A.J. put two and two together...

She shook her head and stopped to get her breath. At least she hadn't given A.J. her name. But she had told him she had just arrived from Pennsylvania, so she wouldn't be that hard to trace if he started asking around. She could only hope that he, as a new recruit, had been so embarrassed by how an Amish woman had kneed him and escaped with his rifle that he'd keep the incident to himself. Still, that didn't mean he wouldn't be looking for her, maybe gunning for her, on the sly.

Kat decided to check on Dilly before she went inside, hoping the horse was not still sick. She certainly hadn't meant to harm the poor animal. Mistreating a car engine from sheer ignorance was one thing, but she really did like Dilly. Why hadn't Ida told her that those leaves and twigs were poison? The horse had munched them while she was tied to the elderberry bushes, and then Kat had run her hard.

Kat entered the barn through the side entrance so she wouldn't have to open the big double doors. The small one creaked. It was pitch black inside, but her eyes were accustomed to the dark and Dilly's stall was close. Despite the cloud cover which had smothered the moon tonight, the door she'd left open threw a pale gray rectangle on the barn floor, so she could see to step inside. "Dilly? You okay, babe?" Kat said and reached to pat her flank. The horse whinnied gently and shuffled through her straw.

The door behind her creaked, then banged closed. Wind? Or had someone else come in? Kat pressed against the stall, undecided what to do. Could the Patriot Knights have found her already?

"The question is," the deep, angry voice said, "are you okay—babe?"

Luke.

"What are you doing out here so late?" she demanded, as he lit a lantern hanging on the wall by the door.

"I've been sitting in my bedroom window, agonizing about what could have happened to you. Eli said he saw you go out after dinner, and when I checked, you weren't in your room. And then a few minutes ago I saw a blur running up the lane, a white *kapp* bobbing along."

"I lost my bonnet."

"You lost your mind. Where have you been without a buggy, so long, so late?"

"Luke, you are not my keeper, nor do I have to report in to you!"

She stood facing him now, hands on hips. Fists clenched at his sides, he stepped closer, nearly pinning her against the stall.

"But I'm responsible for you!" he insisted, raising his voice, too. He came closer. The awkward angle of lantern light etched his face in sharp shadows. A frown furrowed his brow and darkened his eyes.

"You are not. You invited me here to do a job, so you'd better let me do it. I can take care of myself!"

"But do you really *want* to take care of yourself?" he demanded. "All of your life, do you really want to?"

"All of my life? We're talking about here and now. If you must know, I've been keeping an eye on the Patriot Knights."

He muttered something dire in German. "I can't think of anything more dangerous," he said.

"This is not some—some picnic, Luke. Whoever is doing this to your people, your children, is obviously playing hardball, and I intend to, too. If I'm out at night, if you don't know where I am, just go about your business. I can go to meet the sheriff alone, too. I know you're not used to a woman being in charge of things, but…" Her voice trailed off.

He was so close she could smell the pine-scented soap he used. Kat had faced down some furious men, but never one who awed her as this man did.

"Who took you there?" he asked. "Who went with you?"

"I borrowed a buggy because Dilly was sick."

"Lee's, I suppose. You could have borrowed mine."

"Oh, right. And have you worry to death, or have you argue about it—or, the way you're acting, have you try to tell me I couldn't go. Look at you. I rest my case."

He lifted his hands—heavy, hard hands—to her shoulders. She shivered involuntarily at his touch. Her hair had come loose, spilled from the *kapp,* and his fingers snagged in it. He tenderly brushed strands from her damp forehead and cheeks.

"I— My hair must look like a haystack," she said, amazed how breathy her voice sounded.

"More than you know," he whispered as a slight smile tilted his firm mouth, and he pulled a few pieces of straw from her hair. She expected questions about that, but he only looked at them quizzically, then glanced across the dim aisle at the pile of clean straw Eli had forked into a big pile. Was Luke thinking she'd been rolling in the hay with someone, or was that look stoked by his own dark desire?

Again, as if she'd run for miles, Kat felt out of breath. She was dizzy. Or perhaps her problem was that she had forgotten to breathe when he looked at her that way.

"I've got to remember this is all a sham," he said. "But I still will not see you hurt, however much I need—we need the help."

"And I won't see you and your people hurt again, and that takes risks, Luke."

"Risks," he repeated. "Yeah, it takes risks."

He lowered his head and brushed her lips with his.

Shocked but savoring his touch, Kat went absolutely still. Or at least she meant to. But when he kissed her again, she slanted her head to mold her mouth to his and lifted her hands to grasp his wrists which had returned to her shoulders.

The kiss started slowly but soon careened out of control. Luke leaned into her, and only the stall held her up as the barn spun and the world tilted sideways.

Kat propped her bottom against the wood and held on to him with her arms around his strong neck as his hands dropped to her waist to pin her to him. They moaned together, clinging, keeping the kiss going. Then, at the same time, they pushed each other back.

His breathing was as ragged as hers. She could taste him on her lips, feel his hands as if they were yet on her, as she wanted them to be again.

"I don't know how that happened," he said, sounding as dazed as he looked. "But I'm not sorry."

"That—makes two of us. It's just the tension, with all that's happened," she added as she tried to shove her loosed hair back under her *kapp*.

"Tension, that's for sure," he said and stepped farther away, gesturing for her to precede him out of the barn. "But our discussion isn't over yet, even if this is."

"We'll see," she said as she went on shaky legs out the door into the cool night. She had meant that only in reference to their argument, and she hoped he didn't take it to mean she wanted more of his gently rough kisses or his touch.

Truth was, she did.

9

The next morning, Kat couldn't find Ida in the kitchen so she fixed her own breakfast of cereal and coffee. It was the first meal since she'd been here that resembled something she used to think of as normal. Sitting by herself, she heard strange sounds in the basement, a crunching and clinking. She rose from the table and went down a few steps into the lantern-lit, small area. Holding to the banister and bending down, Kat looked below.

"Jacob Ida?" she said, using the name by which the Amish called Ida. So many Amish had the same first names that the women sometimes went by their husband's name as well as their own. The Plain People kept the men straight by saying Young Dan, Old Dan, Carpenter Dan, or other designations. She'd heard Luke was not Windmill Luke, as she'd expected, but, strangely, Speaker Luke, as if he, rather than his father or the church elders, were chosen to talk for them.

"You slept in late," the old woman called up to her, stepping in front of something as if to hide it.

But Kat had seen a large plastic jug of dark liquid as well as four plastic colanders full of what appeared to be elderberries on the worktable. Ida had evidently been crushing them through a sieve with the big wooden spoon she held in her hand.

"Making medicinal liquid," Ida told her. "Rich in vitamins A and C and good for what ails you, especially sore throats and flu. Only, I could use more berries.''

"It's getting so I can spot elderberries a mile away. If you want to tell me where they are out back, I'll pick you some more.''

"Would you take Sarah with you?'' she asked, not budging. "She usually spends Saturday mornings here while Luke works a half day in the shop, and I don't want her in this mess. Besides, she knows where the bushes are on the back forty.''

At first, Kat wished Ida hadn't included Sarah in the favor, but it would give her time to try to improve relations with the child. To convince herself, Kat said, "That will keep things quiet around here for Bishop Brand to sleep in, too.''

"Oh, he's feeling some better today,'' Ida told her with a nod. "Gone uptown on his regular Saturday routine with the elders to have some breakfast, talk a while. Wanted to see how the window repair is coming.''

From above, Kat heard Sarah sing out at the back door, *"Grossmutter Ida!"*

"We'll take some paper sacks and gather what we can,'' Kat promised. She could see Ida was anxious to go back to her work. Remembering that she had bought Ida yeast at the store, Kat wondered if that medicinal brew could be elderberry wine.

As she went upstairs, Kat smiled at that thought and at little Sarah as she let the child in the back door.

"You got your dress clean,'' the child said by way of greeting.

"Your grandmother was kind enough to dry it outside and iron it for me. Everyone's being so very nice to me here,'' she said, hoping the child would take the hint.

Sarah nodded without comment. But she didn't balk when Kat suggested they go out to pick elderberries together.

Although Luke did not have to return to Amish Acres to check on the small windmill he'd put in at the entrance yesterday, he went anyway. He intended to try to assess Clay Bigler's current mood before Kat attempted to. She seemed bold to the point of reckless, and what excuse could she possibly give to be talking to an English man—a union boss—as an Amish women, especially one who was unwed?

As Luke gave the windmill a perfunctory examination, he looked over the fence into the development. Yes, as he'd heard, Clay Bigler was here, like most Saturday mornings, to check up on how things were going. He'd parked his bright red SUV in front of the house-trailer office. Luke had heard the man's work was his life. It was well-known among the Plain People that Clay Bigler was divorced; Luke had once overheard some of the Amish carpenters joking that it was no wonder, since no one would want to live with him.

Luke decided to walk, leading Sandy and the buggy, so he could move more slowly through the work area. The men were working in good numbers today, and since they were paid time and a half on Saturdays, there was obviously a push to finish some houses. Luke had heard a big opening was already scheduled for the near future.

He nodded to the Amish men he knew. Because of seniority, Paul Yoder was more or less the Amish foreman, though their crews worked together with no one really in charge.

Luke tied Sandy's reins to a young maple, then

knocked on the door to the trailer. Someone looked out a window at him, then the door opened halfway.

"If you're looking for work, this job's full up of Am—" Clay Bigler said, then evidently realized who he was and opened the door the rest of the way. "Luke, the bishop's son, right? The windmill man?"

"Yours truly, so I'm not looking for a job here, whether you're full up with Amish or not."

"Didn't mean that like it sounded. Just trying to keep a lid on this labor dispute thing till I can get a ruling in court. And I don't give a damn that you people don't pay a bit of heed to what courts say."

"That's not true. We always render unto Caesar—"

"I don't want to argue here," Clay interrupted. "Anyhow, the windmill at the entrance looks good."

A sinewy man of around fifty, Bigler was built lean and lanky, like the rare joggers Luke had seen on the side roads around town. He was so tanned he looked carved from wood. Luke noted his prematurely silvered hair was cleverly cut to obscure his large ears and long face. His chiseled cheeks and prominent jaw dwarfed his narrow nose, and his sharp eyes were the deep brown of good field loam.

Bigler seemed dressed up with his crisp jeans and knit pale blue shirt. The initials on the shirt's pocket read *YSL,* so maybe it was borrowed. Bigler seemed to seethe with energy, as if the cigarette smoke that clung to him was his own steam. Luke had heard he was a chain smoker, and the stench of a cigarette in his hand matched the smell that also emanated from the small, enclosed space of the trailer. Inside was a young salesman, whose name Luke could not recall, who had been huddled with Bigler in some sort of private conversation.

"Frankly," Luke told Bigler, "I almost didn't sell the windmill to Amish Acres."

"That right?" Bigler said, his voice instantly challenging. "Your people want to boycott all this, that would be fine and dandy with me."

Luke tried to keep his temper in check. "It's just that I didn't want to appear to be putting my stamp of approval on a place that's probably going to grow and bring in more gas stations, supermarkets and mega-malls."

"Can't have it both ways, can you? You people like to sell your homemade stuff and food, don't you?"

"But there has to be an end to suburban sprawl somehow, especially in rural areas."

Luke noted the salesman's eyes had grown wide and his mouth had fallen open. Did he think the Amish had no backbone just because they didn't fight force with force? And even if the salesman was the type to live and let live, would Bigler strike back undercover as well as openly?

"You're just looking at one side—your side," Bigler argued, his voice rising as he gestured with his cigarette. "You're like your so-called Plain People carpenters who underbid my people all the time."

The young guy behind him stood, looking real uneasy. "Clay," he said, his voice smooth, "give it a rest. You know confrontation never does any good with—"

"Why'd you sell the little windmill to the place, then?" Bigler demanded, ignoring the other man. "Money talks and the Amish jump."

"I didn't come to argue, Mr. Bigler," Luke told him. "I simply wanted to get a sense of how you were feeling lately about men who ask what they feel are fair prices for their labor."

"Meaning my union boys are gouging?" A vein in his tanned temple began to throb.

"Meaning that there is obviously work for everyone."

"Not if I have my way, so don't come around here with your union-busting piety. You Amish sticking together, that's the ultimate union I've ever come up against, and I won't stand for it! You call the Amish brethren. Well, we have a union brotherhood!"

Luke had never imagined this could get so out of hand so fast. But as Clay Bigler cursed at him and slammed the door in his face, he was really glad he'd come instead of Kat.

"Can you tell me who lives on the nearby farms, Sarah?" Kat asked the girl as they snapped off stems of berries and put them in the paper sacks they'd brought with them. The back forty, as Ida called it, lay between the Brand and Coblentz farms. A tangle of various types of berry bushes grew near the ravine where Melanie and Eli had been hurt the night of the bonfire.

"*Ja.* I mean yes," Sarah said. "The closest one's Uncle Moses across the road, and his family what helps us farm, and that way, Mr. Coblentz."

Ordinarily Kat would have corrected the child's English, but she wanted her to talk with no negative feedback, as they seemed to be getting along today. Since Amish kids first learned conversational English at Sarah's age, she was doing well, although when the Amish had older siblings like she did, that seemed to help, too.

"I haven't met Moses and his wife yet," Kat said.

"He's called Mose and her Mose Susan. My *mamm's* name was Luke Anna, but she is died."

"I know. I'm sorry about that."

"Me too, *ja,* very. You can meet my aunt and uncle at church tomorrow, but *mamm's* in the ground on the hill. Her name on it, the stone has, real nice. Sometimes I talk to her but she don't talk back."

They were both silent a moment. Kat blinked away tears. She had once pretended to talk to her departed mother, until she finally figured out that, though her dad was dead, her mother had deserted them. Kat had also been a very fanciful child at Sarah's age, creating more than one imaginary friend, even before she lost Jay. After that, she'd been bitter, believing no one cared.

"Sarah, you do understand it's only pretend that I'm going to marry your dad? I won't take your mother's place."

"If you did, you'd sleep in *Daadi's* bed," she said, with a decisive nod. "But if you tried to take her place you might get died too."

A chill swept Kat. Was that a childish threat? Or did Sarah have some sort of premonition, not of any potential relationship Kat could have with Luke but of the possible dangers she faced here? "I haven't met Mr. Coblentz either yet," Kat said. She wanted to change the subject and hoped to find out if Sarah knew Reuben was her grandfather. "Can you tell me anything about him?"

"You could just ask him," she said, nodding toward his farm. "Right there, been watching like he does sometimes."

A vivid imagination, indeed, Kat thought, until she glanced toward the Coblentz farm. She gasped and dropped the sack.

A man—yes, Coblentz—was staring at them through binoculars from about forty yards away. She was not only shocked but angered she hadn't spotted him. A good cop should always be aware of her surroundings, but Sarah had sidetracked her.

"He won't hurt you," the child said, still snapping stems. "Never comes up and talks, but does this sometimes—what the word is, Teacher Katie?" she asked and flopped one hand up and down in an exaggerated wave. Or was Sarah making a beckoning sign, as if the man had been summoning her?

When Kat put down the sack and started to stride toward him, he disappeared into the foliage as if he hadn't been there at all.

Once Kat left Sarah with her grandmother, she stood under Luke's tall windmills and agonized. She was certain Luke didn't know Reuben had been following Sarah around, even if he evidently hadn't spoken to or approached the child. Had he done the same to Eli?

She realized that this was the perfect excuse for her, supposedly Luke's future wife and Sarah's future stepmother, to speak with Reuben. In a way, she had him at a disadvantage, and she wanted to move on this right now. If Luke were here, of course, she'd have asked his opinion or at least taken him with her to the Coblentz farm.

Besides, she'd been grappling with how the paintball attack at the schoolhouse was planned. What if someone with binoculars had hidden in the woods behind the school or in the wheat field to spy on the children, then climbed into the truck or summoned the men waiting in it? Since having the picnic outside was a last-minute decision, had their attackers originally planned to terrorize the students at their regular noon recess?

Quickly, Kat strode across the front yard of Luke's

house and plunged into the cornfield as she had two nights ago. The tall stalks didn't seem as daunting as they'd been in the dark. She wondered how soon these would be harvested. When the field lay bare, would Coblentz take his binoculars and watch Luke's yard and windows for the children?

She emerged near the downed windmill again and saw Reuben instantly. He was bent over a black pickup with its hood raised, his head so far in that, from this angle, it looked as if the open mouth of some monster was devouring him. He had driven the truck—she was quite sure it was not the one from which the paintballs had been shot—out from the garage she'd been in the other night.

Realizing he could be holding a wrench or some other impromptu weapon, she approached him carefully and stopped at a distance of about thirty feet, near the short, squat silo.

Reminding herself again that she was Amish and approaching an alcoholic who might be guilty of more than spying on his granddaughter, she called out, "Mr. Coblentz!"

He stopped and looked up. His face was smudged. His eyes were so bloodshot she could see that from where she stood.

"I take it you're Luke's intended?" he asked, and then went back to tinkering under the hood. His voice echoed. "Least it took him five years, even though folks tried to shove more than one willing woman his way."

"*Ja*, Luke's betrothed. Why did you run when I saw you today?"

"Just done looking, that's all. Anybody over there tell you Sarah's my dead daughter's girl—my grand-child?"

"I knew that, *ja*."

"Sarah know?"

"I don't think so."

"Better get on outta here," he said, standing, this time without the wrench. "This damn thing's leaking oil—blowed a hose—and I might just blow, too. Just like that windmill there the storm brought down— that's me. It may be good for salvage," he said, gesturing wildly, "but I'm not." When she stood her ground, he shouted, "Didn't they tell you I'm under the *meidung,* curse of all curses?" His voice was bitter, his face sharp with suppressed anger.

"*Ja.* That's a sad thing."

"Glad someone Amish thinks so," he muttered, still glowering at her, although that might just be his perpetual expression. "The Amish treat everyone real nice and fair 'less it's one a their own strayed a bit. You here to tell me to keep clear of the girl?"

"Have you been sneaking up on Eli, too?" she countered, still coming closer. She knew better than to accuse him outright of spying on the schoolkids before the paintball attack.

"Used to. Look, I don't need Luke telling me off or raising his hand to me again."

"Telling you off, I can see, but hitting you?"

"Aw, I hit him first. But see, he was the one who was not honoring his father-in-law—he was breaking the rules, too. After I was shunned, Luke used to look the other way when Ida sneaked me baked goods and stuff, but when he caught me and a friend following little Eli one day—whew! In short, *Fraulein* Katie, you'd better not tell him about today, if you don't want him beating up an old man again."

The fact he knew her Amish name shook Kat as much as his accusing Luke of violence. If Reuben wasn't in touch with the Amish anymore, who had he been talking to who knew her? Or had he merely heard town gossip?

"Forgive me for asking," she said, "but are you still angry with the Amish for the shunning? Or for keeping your grandkids away from you?"

"Now, why," he said, staring hard at her, "would I hold a grudge for being castigated and cast out, for having my only child's—my dead daughter's—children kept away from me because I might get drunk and do or say something dreadful?"

"You could change your ways, *ja.*"

"Have *they?*" he shouted, throwing both hands up.

"You haven't been spying on the other kids, have you?" she dared to ask. "At the schoolhouse the other day, since Eli and Sarah were there, when—"

"You 'cusing me of being some sort of pervert or something?" he thundered. He began to speak in German, maybe cursing, maybe questioning or accusing her. The man was not only deeply angry but volatile. Since she had no idea what he was saying and most certainly could not reply, Kat took a few steps backward, toward the cornfield, still keeping an eye on him.

By the silo, she nearly slipped in something sticky, but kept her feet under her. She hoped he thought that he had scared her off, not that she didn't understand one damn thing he was saying.

Just as she thought he was going to lift the wrench from the hood and throw it at her, he pulled out what looked like a whiskey bottle. He took a big swig from it, straight down, then hurled the empty bottle at the side of the silo, where it shattered. It missed her only because she'd started to move away.

As Kat hurried into the cornfield, she felt she wasn't

one step nearer to knowing if Reuben Coblentz was
guilty of more than breaking bottles, boozing and having a bad temper. Did he have the taste for revenge it
would take to attack the Amish who had kept his
grandchildren from him? Worse, could he become so
drunk or desperate that he would try to hurt those children in return?

The second Luke drove Sandy into the barn, Kat
told him all about Reuben's spying on Sarah and her
visit to him. He didn't like what he heard, but at least
she wasn't operating behind his back. "And don't tell
me I shouldn't have faced him alone," she added.

He'd managed to keep his mouth shut so far, but
she was reading him right in heading off that comment. "Besides," she added, hands on hips, "you
weren't here when I needed you, and I had to act."

"Nice to know you needed me for something," he
said. Luke fought to keep calm and concentrate on
unhitching the horse, when he wanted to jump right
back in it and take on his father-in-law. "I'll talk to
Sarah. She should have told me."

"Don't take it out on her, and please don't make
her mistrust me for telling you," Kat pleaded, as he
put Sandy in her stall. "I'm trying to build bridges
here, not tear them down."

"I hope that includes me," he muttered. He regretted that they'd fought last night and that he was
tempted to argue again. Yet he was still haunted by
the feel and scent and taste of her. "Which reminds
me," he added, hoping she wouldn't guess what he
was thinking, "do you want to walk or ride—or run—
to see the sheriff tonight?"

"I'd like you to show me the shortcut through the

fields to get there, in case it's not a good idea to go out on the roads.''

At least, he thought, she wasn't insisting on going alone to the meetings with the sheriff.

"You think Reuben's a suspect, then?'' he asked.

"I think he is. I think the Patriot Knights are prime candidates, too, but I'm not sure about Clay Bigler yet.''

"I talked to him when I checked on the windmill I put in at Amish Acres. I'd say he's in the mix.''

"Will you tell me everything he said?''

Luke explained how things had gone from bad to worse at Amish Acres. "I'm going to talk to Paul Yoder about what he thinks,'' Kat said. "Lee mentioned he'd be a good contact about Bigler.''

Luke only nodded as they walked out of the barn and headed toward the *daadi haus*. He wanted to protect her, but he knew better than to say so. This crazy idea of bringing in someone English—a female former cop, no less—was all his fault. And yet he was starting to believe there was a greater hand in all this than that of Luke Brand, Amish farmer and windmill maker.

"Look, Eli's waiting for you,'' Kat said, pointing.

The boy was watching from the kitchen window. Luke knew he'd have to talk to both kids about Reuben. It was time to question and warn them. But perhaps he could put off telling them the man was their grandfather, at least until he was sure Reuben was not the evildoer.

Luke had never been able to fathom why his father-in-law had not been able to stop the drinking and the destructive binges the booze sent him on. He could only pray that, when Kat or the sheriff finally trapped the person behind the attacks, it would not be the man

whom Anna on her deathbed had asked him to help—
and whom he felt he had betrayed.

Kat watched as Eli came running from the back
porch of the *daadi haus* and hurled himself into
Luke's arms as if he hadn't seen him in years instead
of hours. The boy still wore the patch over his eye,
but lately he had said the lacerations didn't hurt as
much as they had.

"I got all my chores done, Dad! Are we still going
fishing before you do farming with Uncle Mose?"

"You bet we are. We'll walk out the back way to
the pond."

As crazy as it was, Kat got tears in her eyes. She
couldn't help getting emotional around here, especially with the kids—and Luke. So often as a child,
she'd longed to have a dad to run to, a family to really
call her own. Surely that was the only thing setting
her off like this, when she was trying so hard to stay
objective. Too, she was tired and the strain of waiting
for something else to happen was wearing away at her.
Perhaps she should consider setting some sort of trap,
but how?

While Eli told Luke all about his morning, Kat sat
on the back porch step and took a deep breath. At least
Luke was not going to question Eli about Reuben right
now.

Looking down, Kat suddenly noted her shoes were
a mess. She had some sort of motor oil stain on the
white leather, If the oil had been on her soles, that had
worn off already. Which maybe meant she hadn't just
gotten it in the barn.

She didn't know whether to laugh or cry. Two
dresses dotted with stains, her bonnet lost, Ida's black

dress dirtied and snagged by her crawl through weeds and straw, and now this.

Then she remembered. She'd almost slipped near Reuben's silo, but that hadn't been the spot where he was fixing his car. Besides, he said the problem with the truck was a bad water hose. Worse, she'd seen the oily consistency of this stuff before.

"That motorbike," she muttered to herself while Luke laughed at something Eli had said. "Oil drippings, or something like it, near Reuben's silo."

She knew Luke didn't want her going back. But since there was such bad blood between him and Reuben, she didn't want him storming over there to accuse Reuben of having that motorbike. Her old police training also made her feel conflicted: when she was a cop, filling out forms and warrants had been necessary for a search such as she intended. Evidence obtained when she was trespassing might not hold up in court. Still, even if the attackers couldn't be prosecuted, exposing them would at least stop them. Working undercover, she had to play by different rules. If she could prove Reuben Coblentz was at fault, he might even confess and turn himself in, at least to his former fellow Amish.

So she was going back to Reuben's place one more time, to see if that oil had made a trail, and to where. Many machines or vehicles could leak oil, so she'd have to check this out. As soon as Luke and Eli went fishing, she'd just go fishing for more evidence against Grandpa Coblentz.

10

When Kat peered from the cornfield, Reuben was still fussing with his truck. She definitely didn't want him around when she searched his property in daylight, so she went back to the Brand barn, hitched Dilly to the courting buggy and rode into town. Most of the broken windows were boarded up, except for the shiny new ones in the Dutch Table Restaurant, which had a line of people waiting to eat lunch.

Kat rode around the block, heading for the hitching posts at the back of the restaurant. The boarded-up windows on the surrounding stores looked like crude bandages on the facade of the charming town. Where else, she thought, could you find a blacksmith shop next to a gas station and a buggy and harness shop near a video rental? The Maplecreek General Store still stood proudly in the middle of the block, but a new superstore outside town threatened its survival. If it weren't for tourists, would the cheese shop, gift stores and Levi Em's bakery last long?

Kat tied up her buggy next to several others and went in the rear entrance of the restaurant. Just inside the door, she stood for a moment so she could look the place over. Delicious aromas assailed her as Amish female servers in their crisp white *kapps* hurried by from the kitchen with trays heaped with homemade Amish food. Kat's stomach rumbled, but she hadn't thought to bring any money with her.

In addition to the authentic waitresses, the restaurant dripped Amish ambience. Wooden shelves on blue, country-patterned wallpaper displayed everything from old-fashioned kitchen utensils to faceless Amish dolls. Small, framed quilts hung around the large dining area. The two booths nearest the front door were set in buggy frames. Beautifully crafted oak tables and chairs, perhaps made by Luke's brother Dan, graced wooden-pegged floors. Polished brass gas lanterns hung from the ceiling, though they were electric.

"Katie, hi there!" a cheery voice behind her called out. It was Marnie Girkins, coming in the back entrance with sacks in her arms which the hostess came running to take. "Did Luke ask you to pick up the windmill wheel for him? Once the deputy took prints from it, he said it could go back to Luke to be reinstalled."

"Oh, sure, I can take it back. Truth is, I wanted to see if the windows were in yet. Luke and little Eli went fishing," she added, as if she should explain why she was here alone.

"I actually sent someone to Cleveland to get a piece of glass this big quickly," Marnie said, gesturing toward her front window. "I've arranged for glass the other shops need, too."

"I think you must be the Amish guardian angel."

Marnie just rolled her clear blue eyes at that. "Have you had lunch?" she asked. "I'm going to have a tray brought in my little cubbyhole back here. Why don't you join me?"

"Oh, that's so kind, but I can just take the wheel and get going." With no money the last thing she needed was to have this woman think she was trying to take advantage of her. That was hardly Amish behavior.

"No, my treat," Marnie insisted. "Just sit down in here." She opened the door to a small, crowded office, shooed Kat in and told her, "I'll be right back."

As Kat sat in the ladder-back chair across from the desk, she could hear Marnie talking to someone in the hall and caught the words *elderberry pie.* So Ida wasn't the only one rolling in those berries right now.

Kat quickly assessed the office. Much of Marnie's desk was buried under stacks of stuffed manila folders; her file cabinet was topped by tiered, wire in and out baskets, six of them. Behind her desk hung an Amish quilt, the one called Building Blocks. As the observer stared at it, the stacked, shadowed blocks seemed to shift perspective and direction. Yet, unlike most walls in Amish country, the ones in Marnie's office also held photographs, black-and-white ones of Amish buggies, farms and distant shots of the Plain People.

"Excuse the photos," Marnie said as she bustled back in and took off her black sweater. She wore a midi-length denim skirt and stark white blouse, and looked as if she could have stepped from one of her own photos. "I keep them in here, so as not to offend my workers."

"I see there are no close-ups of faces, so you know to avoid the graven images," Kat said, as Marnie began to clear and stack papers. Kat had read somewhere that the Amish refused to have their pictures taken in deference to the Fourth Commandment.

Marnie stopped stacking papers and smiled at Kat. "I always thought the Amish refused to have their photos taken because posing for photos implies personal pride and vanity. Mustn't have that in a man or woman, must we. So, Luke and Eli went fishing, did they?" she went on. "I'm hopeful the boy's eye will completely heal."

"He goes back to the doctor this week. We're hopeful, too."

"And that reminds me that your soon-to-be niece-in-law Melanie is still comatose, though they're praying round the clock that she'll come out of it. I was so glad the senior Brands let me drive them to the hospital to see Melly, as they call her. They said they'd been to see her once before, and an English friend of Luke's drove them. Someone, I suppose, he met installing windmills. I bought a lovely decorative one for my garden."

Kat smoothed her dress over her knees rather than giving Marnie a probing stare. Was she playing with her, setting her up somehow, or was she as kind and concerned as she seemed?

"How are Melanie's parents doing?" Kat asked.

"They're strong, those two, but then, they've had to be." Marnie slid her stacks of papers away to give herself more room. "It wasn't easy for Dan to leave the Amish to marry Brooke, and for them to remain in the community. Needless to say, the Plain People were not enamored of Dan's wedding a lawyer, and a female one at that."

Kat could imagine how they would regard a female former cop making out in the barn with the man they called Speaker Luke.

"As for Melly," Marnie went on, "she's *got* to get well. She's always seemed to me the living proof that the English and Amish worlds can blend and produce something beautiful. Well, so how are you settling in?"

"Very well—*ser gut.*"

"If you ever need a job, you just let me know, though I believe Luke makes quite a good living, and you'll no doubt be busy with his children, as well as having a brood of your own.''

"I— Only time and God can tell, but that's kind of you about the job."

"Besides the waitresses and hostesses working here, other Amish women cook in the kitchens and bake the pies and the breads we serve, provide the honey, even make the cornmeal mush. To help Emma's bakeshop get going next door, I now buy the pies through her."

"You must love the Amish. It's so good to know that, when some folks around here obviously don't, *ja*. Do you live near here or drive in?"

"I live in the back part of the downstairs at my bed-and-breakfast, the Valley View Inn, here in town, but I'm building a house in Amish Acres. And, yes, I love the Amish and understand them better than most, since I was born to Amish parents."

Kat missed a beat on that. Why hadn't Luke told her, or didn't he know? "And, like some of the young people here, you left for the world?" Kat asked.

"My parents did, when I was very young. It happens, you know. This was over in Bird-in-Hand, Pennsylvania, near Lancaster, not far from where your people in Intercourse live—but then, you know what's what there. Sometime we'll have to compare notes. Ah, Mary, we appreciate the special service," Marnie said as a young Amish woman Kat did not recognize came in with a tray laden with food.

"We could clear a table out there for you, Mrs. Girkins," Mary said with a smile and nod at Kat.

"No, just put my things here on the desk, and Katie can eat off the tray, if she doesn't mind. The Amish sure love their *katsche und schmatze,* don't they, Katie?"

Kat had no idea what that meant. "*Ja,*" Mary said

with a quick wink at Kat over Marnie's head. "We love our talking and our eating, all right."

Kat blessed the clever but careful way the Amish had of bailing her out of trouble. All she needed was to get quizzed about Pennsylvania or her supposed people there. So during the delicious meal of broasted chicken with noodles and slaw followed by elderberry pie, she tried to question Marnie.

Kat soon learned that her hostess—whose real name was Margaret—had been widowed young and had reared her two daughters alone. The girls were in separate Ohio colleges. Most amazing to Kat was the fact that Marnie's father had been lured from the Amish fold by his passion for photography, and these were his photos in the room.

"It's lovely that you can help your cousin Leah with the school," Marnie said in one of her obvious attempts to circle back to focus on Kat. "She works very hard and has been the teacher longer than most young women labor at that task, but then, she was greatly let down by her come-courting friend. But of course, she's told you all about that."

"Oh, *ja,* but she doesn't like to talk about it, and I understand that," Kat said, silently cursing the Amish for being so tight-lipped about things. Again, she wondered what had happened to keep Lee single when she was so attractive and endearing.

"Amish old maids are few and far between," Marnie said, "but they do exist, and Leah's quite independent. I'm trying to recall if there have been others in this community, though I knew several in Pennsylvania and suppose you did, too."

Kat knew she needed to get out of here before she really put her foot in her mouth. She'd thought she'd be safe with an English woman. When the phone on

Marnie's desk rang, Kat quickly thanked her for the meal and told her she'd get the windmill wheel on the way out. She asked the manager, Martha, where it was, and the two of them carried it together toward the back door.

"Here, let me help with that," a voice said. Gil Gilmore suddenly appeared, holding open the door for them. "Man, I heard what happened," he said, staring at the wheel. "Is this one of the weapons? I'm sure you ladies never saw that old James Bond movie where the villain threw metal wheels like this at the good guys."

Kat and Martha exchanged guarded looks. "No, that's for sure," Kat told him, though she remembered the movie well where the villain had spun metal disks to decapitate statues and people.

Why was this man coming in the back door from the buggy area? Kat wondered. Or was he waiting to see Marnie? She had said she was buying a house in Amish Acres. As much as the Brands liked Marnie, that wouldn't sit well with them.

Gil hefted the windmill wheel up into the buggy for Kat as Martha hurried back inside.

"So you're the mail-order bride I've heard about," he said, his tone hovering between pleasant and amused. He smiled broadly at her again.

"Not exactly by mail," she told him.

"Is it more like a matchmaker got you two together, you and Luke Brand?" he pressed, clapping from his hands the residue left on the wheel from lifting fingerprints.

"Look," he continued, "I don't mean to be nosy or insulting, but I think it's fascinating—your people. I just asked around about who you were after you visited yesterday."

"Mrs. Girkins told me she's building a house there."

"Yeah, custom-built, complete with darkroom in the basement and small greenhouse on the back. I don't know where she gets the time, but she's a lady with a lot of hobbies."

"Thanks for the help," she told him, and intentionally went around the other side of the buggy because she was certain he was keeping close so he could help her up, and she didn't want him to. She didn't like something about him beneath the smooth, salesman facade, though she couldn't figure out what—yet.

"I wonder if there's going to be weird weather every night we go to meet with the sheriff," Kat teased Luke as they trudged past the back forty and cut through adjacent fields, heading toward the covered bridge. Low-lying clouds and a strange mist hovered in the air—not quite rain, not quite fog.

"This isn't my idea of a Saturday-night date with my betrothed," he said, and they both laughed nervously. Their voices seemed to bounce back to them in the silver miasma they plunged through. Luckily, Luke knew the way by heart.

"When are you planning to talk to Reuben?" she asked.

"I wanted to rush over, but I needed time to calm down. I'm going over on Sunday evening. Maybe he won't be drunk for once, since the bars he hangs out in are closed that day."

Kat thought she might be able to take a look in Reuben's silo while Luke spoke to him in his house. Yes, that might work.

"When I was talking to Marnie today," she said,

"I almost got trapped by several things she said. I had no idea she used to be Amish."

"Not since she was eight years old, I think. It's interesting that she shared that with you, because she doesn't like to dwell on it."

"Really? One thing she almost got me on," Kat continued, not wanting to get off track, "was Lee's sad loss of her betrothed."

"Lee hasn't told you about that?"

"No. It must be a touchy subject. Did he leave Amish life for the world, or die? I'm not asking for gossip's sake, Luke. Marnie tried to nail me on it, and I am supposedly Lee's cousin."

"She and Joseph Yoder, the man she loved, even had the *banns* read in church, which some think is as good as being wed. They were both very young. Anyway, to everyone's amazement, he evidently took off for the world."

"Evidently?"

"He left a note but told no one. Many of our youth leave for a while during their *rumspringa* or running-around time. They're even encouraged to spread their wings to be sure they really want to commit to the demands of Amish life. But Joseph just plain never came back. Some say he moved west, others that he must have met with some fatal accident and no one knew who he was."

"What does Lee think?"

"I've never asked her. She put it behind her and never looked back. I think other guys got the idea she was too bright for them, maybe too dedicated to teaching and the kids she's loved as her own. She has friends, but was never courted again."

"At least she isn't bitter."

"It's a testimony to her that her betrothed's parents,

Paul and Mary Yoder, still look upon her almost as a daughter.''

"One more thing," Kat said as the hulking silhouette of the covered bridge emerged from the mist. "Is that Paul Yoder the same one Lee mentioned is a friend, the guy who works at Amish Acres and knows Clay Bigler?''

"Right. He's a church elder, too.''

"And a witness to Clay Bigler's actions, who I want to interview as soon as possible.''

Sheriff Ray Martin was waiting by the bridge for them again.

"Least there's not much worry someone's gonna tail us out here in this soupy mess," he said by way of greeting, shaking both their hands.

"Did you get any decent fingerprints from those windmill wheels?" Kat asked.

"I'm gonna have to print Luke and the owners to eliminate their prints," he explained. "I'm thinking weather should have worn off all but the most recent ones. It'll take some time, but I'm on it. You got anything new?''

"I've paid two visits to the Patriot Knights," she told him. "The first time, in daylight, I pretended to be there to pick elderberries but got stopped by a recruit named A.J.''

"Clay Bigler's kid," the sheriff muttered.

"What?" Kat exploded, smacking her hands on her skirt. "There's the link, then! A.J. and Clay could work together. A.J. could have been on the motorbike, and both of them could have hit the Amish quilts with manure spray and the schoolkids with paintballs! Can you check out their alibis for those time frames? I'm sure A.J. is trigger-happy. Is Clay in the Knights, too?''

''Just calm down,'' the sheriff said, putting a hand on her shoulder. ''Not only is Clay *not* in the Knights, but he's estranged from A.J. for throwing his lot in with them when he was fresh out of high school. I hear A.J. moved out of his dad's house to live on Knight property, and they hardly speak.''

''Still,'' Luke said, ''that could be a front or ruse. If they are in this together, it unites two apparently separate but powerful groups who seem to hate the Amish.''

''Something else, Sheriff,'' Kat said, feeling deflated after jumping to conclusions. ''The second time I went back on Knight land it was dark, and I was able to get in a position to overhear some of their conversations.''

She and Luke exchanged pointed stares, his angry, hers defensive. She'd finally told him where she'd been Friday night, and he hadn't liked it. Ray Martin looked from one to the other.

''And?'' he prompted.

''They alluded to the fact that if they could get someone named Eagle One elected as mayor of Maplecreek, it might allow them to do some anti-Amish things legally.''

''Which means,'' Luke muttered, ''they are doing things illegally otherwise.''

''So,'' Kat said, ''since you knew right away who A.J. was, Sheriff, any idea who this Eagle One might be? The Patriots' head honcho, I assume.''

''Right,'' he said as he shifted sideways to look off into the distance instead of maintaining his usual intent gaze at her and Luke. ''Their leader—their commander, they call him—is Tyler Winslow, my wife's brother.''

Kat saw Luke startle, but he kept quiet.

''Your wife's brother—your brother-in-law—is head of the Patriot Knights?'' she demanded, her voice rising.

''I'm not proud of it, don't agree with it—with him,'' the sheriff said. ''Only thing we do see eye to eye on is the need for law and order, though we come at it from two diametrically opposed positions. He's all for vigilantism, if need be, standing up for one's rights, no matter what the state says. I'll look into things with him, real careful like, so's not to blow your cover.''

She nodded, but realized the sheriff had not looked back at her since she'd asked about Eagle One's identity. Why hadn't he questioned Tyler Winslow before? Was there something he wasn't saying or was he just ashamed to admit the family connection?

''Anything else?'' he asked, clearing his throat.

''Only that I've drawn a sketch here,'' she told him, giving him a folded piece of paper she'd carried in her damp palm. ''It shows where you can confiscate a Patriot Knight semiautomatic Colt rifle. I took it away from A.J. when he wasn't looking, so to speak. And here's its ammo clip,'' she added, pulling it out from inside her sleeve.

The sheriff seemed surprised, but Luke looked really riled again. In her telling him about Kat's Excellent Adventure in Patriot Knight Land, she'd intentionally left out that she was assaulted and had to assault in return. And that she'd taken a gun.

''I'll keep it locked up,'' Ray Martin said, frowning at the clip before he clenched it in his fist. ''We don't want them knowing you have any ties to me. I'll talk to Tyler about things. The guy's just a law-and-order freak, that's all. Hell, he just got voted onto City Council here. I swear to you, knowing Tyler, I can't believe his people would be behind any of this.''

''After what I overheard,'' Kat said, despite realizing she should stop pushing so hard about Tyler Winslow, ''I'm not so sure.''

''Anyway, the gun is probably legal,'' Luke put in, his voice sharp. ''I don't think they'd make that mistake, do you, Sheriff?''

''No, I've asked him before if the guns are legal. Damn, but you'd think this little town wouldn't have one bit of trouble compared to the big cities!''

Kat was grateful Luke did not explode at her as they walked back toward the farm. But of all the disturbing things she'd learned tonight—the A.J.-Clay Bigler connection, the Sheriff Martin-Eagle One tie—something else troubled her more.

She'd begun to love Maplecreek and, like the sheriff, had made the mistake of thinking its problems must be smaller than big-city ones. But the real difference here was that the enemy hid not in the anonymity of a large population but was probably in plain sight. Her cop mentality that said the enemy was ''them'' had to be changed to accept the fact the enemy might be some form of ''us.'' And, considering that the sheriff hadn't told her about Eagle One's identity from the beginning, that now seemed much more menacing than she'd ever imagined.

The next morning was still strangely foggy as Kat rode with Luke, Eli, Sarah, Ida and Jacob in the large family surrey to church, held in Paul Yoder's home. The Amish usually had services in a member's house or an immaculately swept-out barn every other Sunday, but lately, in the light of the attacks on them, they'd been meeting every week. Moving the services around and never erecting a stationary church was a tradition from the days when the Amish in Europe were hunted down, tortured and martyred for their beliefs. Now, she'd overheard the bishop tell Luke, moving around might just keep them from being attacked even as they worshiped.

After the lengthy service, partly preached by Bishop Brand and all in German, Kat had the opportunity to meet the entire church community of fourteen families, about one hundred and twenty-five people. The Amish churches, like their schools, needed to stay small and within a short buggy ride of the farms.

At the lunch provided after the service, Kat thanked everyone for their support. She knew not to single out individuals like Lee, her mother Emma, or Mary, who worked at the restaurant, for special praise, though she did thank Bishop Brand and Jacob Ida for housing her. The social time after church also gave her an opportunity to question Paul Yoder about Clay Bigler.

"Don't like to speak ill of anyone, as the Lord is the only true judge of character," the red-bearded man had told her. "But, God as my judge, *ja,* I think Mr. Bigler would step over the line to scare us out of Amish Acres—and Maplecreek, for that matter—*ja,* I really do."

Mid-afternoon when things broke up, Luke dropped off Eli and Sarah across the road at the farm of his brother Mose and his wife Susan. Kat could tell that Eli was torn between wanting to play with his six cousins and not wanting to let Luke out of his sight.

When Jacob and Ida went to take a nap, Luke told Kat he was going to walk over to Reuben's to speak with him alone.

"Are you going to cut through the cornfield?" she asked.

"I'm going to walk the road. Is that how you've been going over, cutting through the corn? You'd better be careful sneaking up on someone like that, because it can work two ways."

Pondering his warning, she watched him head for the road. Sometimes it seemed that whatever way she turned here, someone said or did something upsetting. Not that she didn't trust Luke, Lee and the sheriff, but, as with walking through the tall, thick corn—well, Luke was right: it was scary when you couldn't quite see what was coming next.

But that wasn't going to stop her from going through the adjoining cornfield right now. Something near or in Reuben's silo had dropped oil. There was no motorbike in his garage—but why would he be stupid enough to store it where it could be found? With Luke keeping Reuben's attention, she could peek into the silo and in a few seconds be gone.

Kat darted into the *daadi haus* to get her flashlight, then cut across the field so she'd come out near the silo. She blessed this lingering ground mist; it was as if the clouds had come down to cling to the earth. But as she moved through the field this time, she heard someone behind and slightly to the side of her, coming through the corn.

Nonsense, she thought. Luke had spooked her, that was all. But did she smell smoke? Was someone burning leaves?

As she hurried on, she became convinced she heard rustling on this still day, a body aside from her own bumping into the ripe ears of corn. She looked back, stopped and held her breath to listen. It might be a deer moving through the field; she'd seen them nibbling nearby. She sucked in a breath. The smoky smell was gone, or else she had imagined it. But she still heard something or someone in the field. And the sound was coming closer.

She pushed faster through the corn, shoving heavy ears out of the way. But she realized the noise could tip someone off to her location.

Though she longed to flee, she stopped dead still again. For one moment she heard only the breeze swishing the corn tassels and rustling dry leaves. A crow cawed somewhere overhead, but she did not look up. Instead, bending her knees in case she had to run or spring, she held her breath, straining to listen.

Something or someone moved again. Close. Maybe two or three rows over. Surely Luke had not changed his mind and decided to come through the corn. She'd give away her presence and position if she called out. And no way could she sneak around to get to whoever it was without making her movements known. She could lunge toward the sounds, but what if it was A.J. with a gun? It was better not to startle her pursuer, but to lure him into view.

She moved again, toward the Coblentz farm, intentionally making a lot of noise. She bumped corn shocks with her elbows and faked a cough. Then, swiftly, she spun about and headed back in the next row, hoping she could glimpse someone through the screen of corn and mist, then decide whether to fight or flee.

The cool breeze and patchy fog made the sweat on her face cold. Her heart beat in rhythm to her strides. Her breathing quickened, so she wasn't certain if she heard the sounds again or not. Surely it had not been just strange echoes of her own noise that made her panic. Wouldn't corn, even on a foggy day, absorb sound, rather than bounce it back?

She froze again. Nothing unusual now. Rather than play a game of cat and cornfield-mouse, she plunged away toward Coblentz's farm, praying someone was not lurking in the field just to watch. Since she'd earlier been fooled by a raccoon, maybe it could have been a deer.

Kat got to Reuben's just in time to see Luke walk up from the road and onto the front porch. She suspected, since Reuben was still shunned, Luke might not even go into the house but talk to him outside.

Seemingly disembodied voices floated to her, so Luke and Reuben must be talking. The mist sat on the roof of the house and swallowed the top of the small, squat silo, which was about three times her height. At least this daytime-twilight was good cover for her.

Kat ran to the silo before she saw a big, green metal wagon attached to some sort of tractor with a tall metal arm that sat between the silo and the barn. A mountain of corn kernels filled the wagon.

She gasped, but saw no one around, not even in the cab of the vehicle. This certainly hadn't been here Thursday or Saturday. As a matter of fact, it was parked right where Kat had slipped. Luke had said Reuben no longer put in crops, but perhaps he'd rented his silo to some English farmer. Maybe this vehicle or machine had dropped the oil, if it had been here before.

Kat hoped there was no corn in the silo already, because she was going to open the single, small door to look inside and she didn't want any to spill out and show she'd been trespassing again. The door was elevated about two feet off the ground.

She unlatched the outside hook on the door and

opened it carefully, then peered around it. Nothing spilled out; there was no corn inside. Nor was the interior pitch black. A gray circle of light shone in the middle of the floor from an opening on the roof. And in that gray circle, as if in a dim spotlight sat a black motorbike. Even in the door light, it gleamed as if it were on the showroom floor instead of in a silo.

Bingo! she thought, exultant. Closing the door behind her and snapping on her big flashlight, she tiptoed toward the bike. So it had been Reuben who had tossed the fireworks in the bonfire. Skulking around the back forty with binoculars, he'd known exactly when and where to strike and had easily escaped to hide the bike in this small silo. Now if only his fingerprints could be found not only on this bike but on the windmill wheels that had shattered the glass in town. She'd have to get the sheriff to try to fingerprint Reuben at once.

Then she realized that Luke was now probably accusing Reuben of stalking Eli and Sarah. Who knew what Reuben would do if he were cornered? Perhaps she'd best go around the front of the house to see that Luke was safe. Then they could phone the sheriff and let him question Reuben.

But her flashlight illumined drops of water on the bike. A wet sponge and a rag still stiff with what looked like paste wax lay on the ground behind the back tire. Her hopes plummeted. Had Reuben just washed and waxed the bike? Because it was a sort of trophy, a testament to what he'd done with it—or to remove any remnants of fingerprints?

Kat jumped at a sound nearby, a rumble that became a roar. Someone must have turned on the motor to the machine next to the silo; the metal skin of the structure vibrated hard enough to rattle her teeth and bones.

She ran to the door she'd come in, but it was stuck—no, it must be latched from outside. The shudder increased. She tried to shine her light up through the hole, but a big funnel covered that opening in the roof, blocking out the wan light and flow of air.

And from the funnel a cascade of corn kernels began to fall, pinging off the metal motorbike and hitting her.

11

Kat pounded on the metal interior and shouted, "Stop it. Someone's in here! Let me out!"

Her voice echoed; the stream of corn increased. Panicked, she searched for a second door, then banged her flashlight against the thin gray outline of the door she'd come in. She turned back to get the motorbike to roll against the door like a battering ram, but it was already smothered by the onslaught of corn, now nearly up to her knees. Slogging through it like mud, she could barely move. Soon she'd be swimming for her life in the kernels. And Luke was so close and didn't know...wouldn't know, until they found her weeks later when someone came to get the corn....

"Help me—ee-ee!"

She pounded flashlight and fist against the silo, but the roar of the machine only increased. Swirling chaff choked and blinded her. She was shocked at the weight of the kernels, piling up, pressing in.

Buried alive. By accident, or by intent because she'd stumbled on the person behind all this and he knew it? Murdered? Instead of keeping the peace on city streets, she was at war with someone in Amish country. As Kat gagged in the thickening dust, she could not accept that she was going to be crushed to death by tiny, golden kernels of corn.

Dizzy, light-headed, she reached out to comfort her brother, but he slipped away in the heavy flow of memory and little John Seyjack stumbled at her, wide-eyed, beaten, afraid. John started to follow her brother upward, climbing, then motioned to her. She couldn't see him, but she thought his mouth moved to say, *Come on up! The circle of safety is here...come on up...*

Kat tried to follow, but the weight of the paintballs and berries and bullets was too strong against her...against her chest and in her eyes and ears and mouth, so she couldn't hear or see or cry anymore.

Luke was shocked to see Tyler Winslow, the man Sheriff Martin had said was the Patriot Knights' leader, come around the corner of Reuben's porch and put one foot up on the step. Luke and Reuben had been talking on the porch when someone had started up some machinery in back to fill a silo Reuben said he'd rented out. Since then, the two of them had been shouting at each other to be heard—not, thank the Lord, because either of them had lost control yet. The old man had admitted he sometimes spied on Sarah simply because he longed to see her.

"Hey," Tyler interrupted, raising his voice, too. "Didn't think you two were on speaking terms any-more."

Luke was surprised the man knew that and could keep the Amish straight, for many of the English could not. Luke only recognized him because his political posters for town councilman had been along the roads at election time last year. Tyler Winslow was a mid-dle-aged blond man with short, stand-up hair who was one of the most successful English local farmers, mostly because he owned so much land. Though Win-slow had no children, he had been long married to a local woman named Louise, who, Luke had heard, hardly ever left their farm. At any rate, Winslow was evidently the man who had rented Reuben's old silo for his corn overflow. He was harvesting early, but then, he usually put in popcorn, which peaked before other varieties.

"You got a problem back there?" Reuben shouted to Winslow over the din.

"Just wanted to tell you I saw an Amish woman dart out of the cornfield earlier. She must have gone in your garage, Coblentz. You got a little something going here on the side?" Winslow shouted a laugh and turned away. "We'll be done in a couple of secs." His voice floated back to them. "My man's almost got that little thing filled."

Luke jolted alert. An Amish woman came out of the cornfield? Kat could have followed him over. But she'd already searched the garage, she'd said. Surely she wouldn't look in the silo, and if she had, the noise of the machinery or falling grain would have scared her out. But it was so like Kat to just plunge into things.

For some reason a dark foreboding clamped his chest. It would also be just like her to look around, once he had Reuben occupied. Or what if she'd seen Winslow coming and thought she'd just duck inside the silo? It was a long shot, but he had to check this out.

Luke left his surprised father-in-law standing on his front porch and ran around the side of the house. A huge John Deere combine spewed grain from its chute into the top of the silo. If Kat was in the garage, she was as good as trapped if Winslow decided to follow her in there. If she was in the silo...

Although the man stopped at the door to the garage

and just peered in, Luke stepped past him to shout, "Katie? Ka—tie!"

"Hey, that pretty little thing following you instead of Reuben the Rube?" Winslow goaded with a sly grin. "Is that the bride-to-be you've imported? You and her—now that's more like it," he added, rubbing his hands together.

Luke ignored the implication. "Katie!" he shouted, this time outside the garage. He cupped his hands to his mouth and turned toward the cornfield between the Coblentz property and his. "Katie!" Over the noise of the machinery, he told himself, she might not hear him, even if she was heading for home.

Yet he ran to the silo and pressed his ear to it. Unless the combine had something wrong with it and was echoing funny, some sort of metallic clanking was coming from inside the silo's shell. "Turn that off!" Luke roared, pointing at the combine. He lunged toward the latch of the silo door.

"Hey, no way!" Winslow shouted and tried to yank him away.

"She may be in here!" Luke shouted.

He shoved Winslow off and opened the door. He jumped back as grain poured at him, slamming the door against the side of silo.

And saw Kat—at least her feet, legs and the bottom of a ladder.

"Get help!" Luke shouted to Reuben. "Call 911!"

"No." The raspy voice came from the silo. She started choking but she managed to say, "I fought my way up—until I found this little—ladder stuck on the side. If I can just get out—I'll be all right."

Though Tyler Winslow still wanted to call the emergency squad on his cell phone, Kat kept shaking her head. After Reuben and Luke pulled her out of the silo through a small trap door in the roof that she and Luke hadn't known existed, she sucked in great, wheezing gasps of air. Gratefully, she drank water Reuben brought her and pretended her throat was too sore to answer the questions he and Winslow peppered her with. She wanted to question them but wasn't quite sure how to take advantage of this opportunity, especially since she'd made a fool of herself, not to mention she could have been killed.

But *had* this been a freak accident or not? Had Tyler Winslow been tipped off by the sheriff's questions— or warning—or had she been identified by A.J. Bigler? Or was Reuben in league with Winslow? No, she told herself. Impossible. No one could have known she wanted to look in the silo.

"I just...came over, following Luke to be sure he didn't argue with Reuben," she finally said, when she'd considered all her options for proceeding. The four men—the operator of the machine was Jake, who worked for Winslow—leaned closer to hear. She felt they were blocking out her light and air again.

"*Ja,* I admired the big machine," she went on. "I just looked in the door of the silo to see if any corn was in there yet. I saw a motorbike and—"

"A motorbike?" Reuben interrupted. "There's no motorbike in there. I don't own a motorbike. You been hallucinating, hit by all that corn."

Kat knew that was true. She *had* hallucinated, but only after the corn started to deprive her of air. Now she tried to watch both Winslow's and Reuben's reaction to the mention of the bike. Maybe it wasn't Reuben who had planned for it to be buried under that load of grain, though Tyler Winslow hadn't reacted, either.

As for uncovering the bike to discover fingerprints or its ownership, it had taken all four men to close the silo door, and they'd hardly be willing to empty it all right now. If the prints hadn't been washed and waxed away, they could have been scoured off by the corn and chaff. She felt deflated as well as beaten up: unless the sheriff had traced the bike's owner through its oil leak or its purchase, its presence might not be the solid evidence she had hoped for.

"So, what's with carrying a flashlight?" Winslow asked nonchalantly, sticking his hands under his armpits and rocking slightly back on his heels.

He'd evidently decided to not be so intense, she thought.

"If you just kind of wandered in and got trapped," he went on, "why are you carrying it around in broad daylight?"

"All right, I'd best tell true," she said, and felt Luke's hand clasping her shoulder tighten. "Luke's mother said she was short on canning jars—you know, for putting up things for the winter, storing things like all the berries coming on." Kat wasn't sure why, but his fingers tightened even more.

"*Ja,* I was hoping, Mr. Coblentz," she plunged on, concentrating on sounding Amish, "there'd be some old ones in your outbuildings that should rightly go to your daughter Anna's girl, Sarah. Soon she will be my stepdaughter, and I wanted her to have her mother's family's things to inherit, just so nice that way. I would have asked you for them, though, not just taken them, that's sure."

If Reuben believed that flimsy line, Kat thought, it was because he desperately wanted to. He had tears in his eyes. Winslow looked bored, and she regretted she was in such a defensive position that it didn't allow her to go on the offensive with him—as if an Amish woman would or could.

"Forgive me, all of you," Kat said, hoping she sounded contrite, "for getting caught like that— caught not admitting right out about the canning jars too. And for spilling some of your corn, Mr. Winslow," she added, looking down at the ground when she'd rather be skewering him with a hard stare and harder questions.

"Hey, don't worry about it," Tyler Winslow told her. "Thanks to Luke Brand, another catastrophe was avoided, so we were all pretty lucky. This combine can suck up spilled grain as well as shoot it out, so Jake can clean up this mess. I'm used to the Amish getting in the way," he said with a chuckle. "On the roads in buggies, I mean."

Kat studied him in a glance. A dark undercurrent clung to everything he said, as if he were secretly sniggering at a dirty joke only he was in on. It reminded her of A.J.'s sense of humor, only more shrewd. She didn't believe Winslow's nice-guy approach, especially not after seeing—or hearing—the Patriot Knights up close. And this was Eagle One, their commander, and an in-law to the sheriff. But could he be the sort of outlaw who would either attack the Amish, or at least order an attack? *Thanks to Luke Brand, another catastrophe was avoided,* Winslow had said. Was that a backhanded compliment or a subtle dig?

"I'm taking her home," Luke said, and, before Kat could decide what to say next, he lifted her easily in his arms. Bouncing her once to get a good hold, he started out, not plunging through his cornfield but skirting it closely, following Reuben's lane and then the road. She could not tell if he was relieved—she'd seen tears in his eyes when he'd first pulled her out of the silo—or furious.

"You could have been killed," he said through gritted teeth.

"But I found that motorbike. And you just interrupted the only interview time we might get with Tyler Winslow. I wonder if the sheriff's talked to him yet, and if he was able to shake anything out of him."

"But if the bike was in the silo, Reuben's behind everything."

"With Eagle One showing up to fill the silo, who knows?"

"If the motorbike was in Winslow's possession, he could have ditched it a million places on his big farm or Knights' land."

"What if he wanted to set Reuben up?"

"I think that grain knocked you silly. You're seeing sin and guilt everywhere you look."

Cop Kat wanted to swear a blue streak and order Luke to put her down. Amish Katie wanted to tell him how good it felt to be carried so masterfully. Her breast bounced against his hard chest, her hip against his flat belly. She had to fight herself to keep from simply clinging to him. She had to think—to stop this roaring rush of emotion and hold on to reason, instead of this man.

"Luke, I think I was followed through the cornfield today, or someone was watching you from it."

"See what I mean about seeing suspects everywhere? At least you won't tell me you don't need my help anymore. You had very little air left in that silo. People have been crushed to death or suffocated by grain storage."

"You think I don't know that? And that you're angry with me?"

"Angry because you were almost killed. And that your headstrong nature is making you take risks I can't allow."

"How did you know to look for me in the silo?"

"I had to risk checking. If you had darted back into the cornfield, that wouldn't kill you. Suffocation in the silo would."

"A risk, see. You take risks, too."

"One that saved your life, not endangered it."

She tried to squirm from his grasp. "I can walk, Luke. Put me down."

To her chagrin, he shouldered his way into the cornfield, snagging her feet and bumping her head on the laden stalks. He went two rows in and sat, cross-legged, with her sprawled across his lap.

"This isn't working," he said, as she wriggled free to sit, exhausted, wedged in the row tight beside him. "I thought you'd just gather information."

"You'd rather have your children threatened and hurt? I've only been here a little more than five days, and we're making progress."

At that, his head snapped toward her. His blue eyes seemed to darken; despite the magnetism he radiated, she forced herself to look away, down at her hands in her lap.

He cleared his throat. "Then that progress," he said, "means we have a list of suspects we can turn over to Sheriff Martin."

"No way. I don't have enough on anyone yet." *And we don't know if we can trust the sheriff,* she wanted to add. "Besides, my ability to pass as Amish is too good to let go." She shifted around to get to her knees. He mirrored her movements as if they would stand at the same time. "Luke, listen, if Ray Martin and his deputies start going after people we name, everyone will go to ground.''

"About your ability to pass for Amish," he said. "I'm only grateful none of those men back there seemed to know that no one cans berries. And you claimed you were looking for jars in a garage in daylight with a flashlight?" he added with a little snort that infuriated her. He was as bad as that mocking Tyler Winslow. She shook off his hand when he touched her shoulder.

"Katie—Kat, you are really going to get in over your head—I didn't mean to say it like that," he amended and reached out to brush several kernels from the edge of her rumpled, dusty bonnet.

This time she didn't flinch but let him touch her, *wanted* him to touch her. He was driving her nuts with this mix of toughness and tenderness that evoked wild, confused feelings in her.

"Okay," she said, "so I may not be able to can or cook up a storm, but I do know a good lead when I see one, and I'm not letting up on this. I won't have another window broken or windmill beheaded—or worse. I won't have any more kids like Melanie and Eli hurt, or so much as another Amish quilt ruined or kid paintballed…"

She tried to keep her words rolling as a barrier between them, as some link to sanity, because she knew what was going to happen, and it scared her.

Both still kneeling, they came together in a crushing, mutual embrace. She held tight, grateful for the solidity of his body, his strength. His arms clamped her against him, tight around her waist.

They didn't kiss this time, just held on, breasts to chest, soft hips to hard, thighs pressed together.

Minutes rushed by and stood still until they heard a familiar roar coming closer on the road.

"Winslow's combine leaving Reuben's," Luke said, and they got reluctantly to their feet. Moving over one row, they peered through to the road as the big green monster rolled by. Winslow and Jake sat up in the lofty cab as if they were kings of all they surveyed. As the ground under their feet seemed to shake, Luke told her, "Our old-fashioned machines make a lot more noise than that."

Kat almost laughed at that bravado from an Amish man. She recalled the humorous sign one of her friends had that claimed the difference between men and boys was the price of their toys. That was only part of the difference between Amish men and worldly men, she thought. Horses versus horsepower might be no contest for the outside world, but the impact Luke Brand had on her was way off the charts compared to any other man she'd ever known.

When they emerged from the field and started up the drive toward Luke's house, a black pickup truck pulled across the bottom of the lane and honked. They both turned back and gasped. Its motor had sounded like a muted machine gun, and Kat's first instinct was to dive for cover.

"Wait!" she cried, grabbing Luke's arm as he tried to pull her back into the field. "It's Reuben. And what he's holding out the window isn't a gun."

Again she recalled the paintball guns leveled at her and the kids, but this glinted like glass. Was he going to throw glassware again? And on Luke's land?

"Canning jars, I think," Luke said. "Stay back."

But Kat walked to the truck with Luke. Reuben was reaching out, she thought, in more ways than one, as he extended two glass Mason jars to her, then handed out to Luke a cardboard box that clinked and rattled—more jars.

"For little Sarah," Reuben said with a sharp sniff. "And if you tell her they were ones her *mamm* sent over to me—filled with food, so her hands actually touched them all—I'd count it a real favor. And, Luke, Anna told me you didn't say a word to stop her, though you knew she was doing it, so guess I'm beholden to you for that much. Actually, your mother sometimes done the same."

"We'll give them to Sarah," Luke managed to say. His voice was rough, too.

Reuben nodded, and the truck chugged away. Kat wondered if this could make a real difference: if Reuben had been behind any of the attacks, would this end them?

"I'd guess you and Reuben got along all right today," Kat said, "before you came looking for me."

"I didn't even give him my ultimatum to keep away from Sarah, though he said he doesn't follow Eli anymore, because Eli got too adept at ditching him." Luke grinned, then sobered. "I've tried to keep peace with my neighbor and father-in-law, but it's been hard. When Anna was dying, I telephoned him from the hospital in Cleveland that he could come to see her, despite his being under the *meidung*."

"And did he?"

"He started out—probably in that same ramshackle truck—but was so drunk he drove into the water ditch on the other side of that very road, got stuck, and never made it to the hospital in time. I guess I was furious with him for that, too. But no, we haven't patched things up. When he drinks, he's a maniac, another man, so he's got to stay on our list of suspects."

"But he should be allowed to see those kids sometimes, under supervision, I mean," she whispered, touching Luke's arm. "We've got to make sure he's not the guilty one first, but if he isn't, *meidung* or not, we could meet him with the children halfway, when this field is cut, at least to say hi."

"We? After this is all over, it would be *ser gut* if there was a 'we.' And I think I owe you an apology," he added as he fell into step with her along the lane, "for saying that Reuben wouldn't believe your excuse for snooping. He evidently did, and I just hope Tyler Winslow did, too. The thing is," he added, "I'm used to strong women, but not ones who always tell me I'm wrong."

"You're not always wrong. The Lord knows, I've been wrong more than I'd like to admit."

"You believe in the Lord, Katie?"

"Of course I do. Not many cops don't. They say there are no atheists in foxholes, and cops, sooner or later, are deep in those."

"But not ones filling fast with crushing corn," he said, turning toward her so abruptly the glass jars clinked. "Just be careful."

"I will," she promised, as they stopped walking and stared at each other for several moments. He nodded and smiled tautly, and they started to walk again. "Look," she cried, pointing with one jar, "here comes Eli."

"He didn't stay long at his uncle's," Luke murmured, as they watched the boy sprint down the lane toward them.

"Of course," she told him, "because you weren't there."

"*Daad!* Katie!" Eli shouted before he was even near them. "Grandfather took sudden sick again! He ate a lot of Grandmother's pie, so can we call the doctor·on the office phone?''

''Probably just another ulcer attack, but...'' Luke said.

Kat took the carton from him, and he ran with the boy for the windmill shop. Despite suddenly feeling exhausted and beaten, Kat hurried up the lane.

Kat went quietly in the back door of the house and took the Mason jars into Ida's pantry. On the kitchen table sat the pie in question, no doubt, for only a single piece was left, and Kat had seen it was whole before she'd gone across the field. She said a quick prayer for Bishop Brand's recovery.

As the day wore on, in the hush of the house, Luke and Ida sat with the ill man in his bedroom, waiting for the doctor. Eli and Sarah rocked together on the back porch swing; its creak was driving Kat to distraction. Because there was only one bathroom in the small *daadi haus* and she thought the ill man might need it, Kat, who longed for a bath, just washed off and changed clothes. Not knowing how to help except to keep an eye on the kids, she stood in the kitchen and glanced in the door of the pantry where she'd put the jars.

Indeed, no canned berries sat among this rainbow array of jars. Some sweet cherries were the only thing that vaguely reminded her of berries. Green beans, crimson beets, applesauce, peach halves, tomato juice, jars of multihued, pickled vegetables including what looked like salsa. Even chicken broth for soup—imagine, she thought, making homemade soup like Marnie had brought, when it could just come from a store-bought can.

Kat let the doctor in when he arrived. Dr. William

Barker was an elderly, white-haired man from Pleasant. It seemed so old-fashioned to see a medical man make a house call, carrying a small black bag.

He stayed with his patient for an hour as daylight grayed to dusk. Kat shuffled things around in the refrigerator, noting there were various leftovers in plastic containers, but she finally made scrambled eggs and toast for Sarah and Eli. She told them everything would be all right—and again wondered if she was lying. Why was all this taking so long? If Bishop Brand was quite ill, she would volunteer to move out of her bedroom next to theirs to give them more privacy.

As she sat at the kitchen table with the children, helping with their homework, she wondered if she should take them to Luke's house to get ready for bed. At one point, the doctor and Ida stepped out into the hall, and she heard Dr. Barker raise his voice. Ida's gentle tones carried too, although in snippets.

"No hospital, Doctor, he won't go…"

"Mrs. Brand, without some sort of specialized care, he won't…time is of the essence…I can't be responsible…"

"My husband says the Lord's responsible…"

After they went back in and closed the door, Kat began to shake. They had to take the bishop to a hospital. Jay's foster family had not taken him, and he'd died, though this was a grown man, a religious, strong man, making his own decisions.

Kat continued to sit with the children, waiting for news. Luke's brother Mose came to the back door and spoke to Kat on his way in to see his father. Suddenly, she remembered how she'd thought she'd seen her own brother in the silo today. Jay had been slipping away, but John Seyjack had been there, telling her to come up, come up.

Goose bumps gilded her flesh. Surely she'd imagined all that, and yet it had seemed so real.

She sensed Luke's presence behind her and turned. He leaned in the doorway, looking drawn and exhausted.

"How is he?" Kat asked, at the very moment that Eli said the same thing in German.

"Gone—" Luke's voice broke.

"Gone where? To the hospital like *mamm,*" Sarah piped up and scrambled from her chair to throw herself at Luke.

Luke picked her up in one arm and, when the boy rushed to him, put his other hand on Eli's head.

"His last words," Luke said, sounding dazed, looking at Kat rather than his children, "were that he trusted us to stop the evil. Then he whispered, 'Come up, come up,' and that was all."

Kat tried to stand, but her legs were shaking too hard. She gripped the edge of the table with both hands. Luke's haunted stare held hers. But he could not possibly know how stunned she was, not only by the bishop's death, but by her sudden certainty that her life had been spared today so she could risk that same life to help these people.

12

Kat was astounded at how quickly the Amish community took over for the bereaved family of their dead bishop. As far as she could recall, only a handful of people had attended her father's funeral, and even fewer her brother's.

The body had been sent to the funeral home in Pleasant to be embalmed, but the plain oak coffin was soon returned with the bishop clothed in white trousers, shirt and vest. Amish coffins were handmade of oak with both ends tapered, and the top hinged from shoulder height up so the face could be displayed until burial. Two days before the funeral, relatives and church friends gathered at a round-the-clock wake.

With outsiders arriving, at first Kat felt uneasy. She didn't want to intrude, but even the Brand relatives from western Ohio treated her as if she belonged, so someone must have explained the situation. Most of the conversations swirling around her were in German, though Lee translated for her when she could, and Eli helped, too. Kat hardly saw Luke in the purposeful hubbub as he comforted his mother and welcomed guests, most of whom were housed in Mose Brand's home across the road or with other church members.

"Katie, you will come up to my room with me?" Sarah asked, tugging at Kat's hand as they stood in the front room of the *daadi haus,* staring out the side window at the rows of parked buggies and the boys tending them. Eli was helping, although most of the boys handling the horses were bigger than he was; he wanted to be a part of it. Kat had put drops in his lacerated eye this morning. The doctor still didn't know whether the boy's blurred and double vision would improve. So many things were in limbo—Eli's eye, Melanie's coma, and solving the anti-Amish crimes.

"I want to show you something," Sarah said.

The child's invitation was a great gift, considering how badly they'd started out. But Kat had only briefly ventured into Luke's house where the lying-in was being held, and she hesitated to go upstairs without his permission.

"Will you?" Sarah pleaded.

"Of course. I'd like to go with you."

Sarah pulled her by the hand across the yard and past the barn, which men were sweeping out and filling with plank benches. So many mourners were going to attend the funeral that services would be held in the downstairs of Luke's house with the overflow in the barn.

Kat and Sarah went in the back door to the kitchen. Women in black bustled about to lay out a lunch for the family, visitors and workers. All the food had been brought in. In German, Kat briefly greeted those who spoke to her and wondered what they really thought of the impostor in their midst.

The farmhouse kitchen was spacious and lovely with its gleaming oak cupboards, matching table and chairs, and pegged floor. Down the hall was the large dining room; two living rooms took up the front of the house. In the more formal one, called the parlor, the coffin was laid out on sawhorses. Close relatives, including Jacob and Ida's sons Luke and Mose, with

Mahlon and Gideon from western Ohio, took turns sitting near the coffin as others came to pay their respects. Though Dan was no longer Amish, he was going to leave Melanie's side at the hospital to attend the funeral, and Kat had heard that Brooke was coming briefly today.

Kat followed Sarah upstairs and down the hall onto which four big bedrooms opened. Each one Kat glimpsed had white walls, bright blue drapes and a double bed adorned with a colorful quilt. She lingered to look into Luke's bedroom. It was masculine, without a bit of the clutter that was always strewn around her inner sanctums. His double bed had a beautifully grained wooden headboard and a massive chest of drawers. A graceful rocker sat between two windows. Even from the hall, she glimpsed the stunning view of fields and trees. A crisp breeze through the partly open windows made the curtains dance.

"In here," Sarah said, sounding impatient. "Since I keep your secret, you keep mine, *ja?*"

Kat nodded as the child sprawled on her stomach to reach under her bed and pull out a battered cardboard box. "Mrs. Marnie gave me something and said not tell— This is my real mother."

Again Kat felt uneasy that Sarah worried she would take her mother's place. Perhaps a young, practical Amish child couldn't grasp what *pretend* really meant. The truth was, when Kat got caught up in everything here, she sometimes started to believe she belonged too, especially when Luke looked at her with such intensity and they touched....

Sitting on the floor, Sarah untied the string around the box and lifted the lid. In it lay a single photograph of a young Amish woman, her face partly hidden in the shadow of her black bonnet. Barefoot, a baby in her arms, she walked across a road to a mailbox, evidently with no notion or concern that her photo was being taken.

"So that's your *mamm,* Sarah," Kat said, sitting on the edge of the bed and leaning down to look. It was obvious the child had no intention of handing the photo over for closer inspection. In the slant of window light, Kat could see fingerprint smudges all over it—maybe a mouth-print of a kiss, too.

"Oh, *ja,* but the baby's Eli, not me."

"And Mrs. Marnie gave you that picture?"

"She said she shot it." Sarah looked up frowning. "But she didn't mean with a gun."

"I know that. She took it with a camera."

"*Ja.* And told me not show *daad,* 'cause it would make him mad."

"You mean sad."

"No, mad."

"How long ago did Mrs. Marnie give you that?"

"I don't know. A goodbye gift, she said."

"Because your mother went away?"

Sarah shrugged, stroked the photo, replaced it and slid the box back under the bed. "Good at secrets, I know you are," Sarah said. "No one else really Amish can see it."

So Marnie Girkins had inherited her father's passion for photographing the Amish, Kat thought. Gil Gilmore had told her that Marnie wanted a darkroom in her new house. It made sense that she wouldn't want the Amish to know about this hobby. Since Marnie had evidently taken this photo without Anna Brand knowing it, did she take others secretly?

"Where were you when Mrs. Marnie gave you that picture?" Kat asked, as Sarah got up to look out the window.

"With Grandmother Ida at Mrs. Marnie's house, taking back Toppedware."

"Tupperware," Kat corrected automatically. "At Mrs. Marnie's Valley View Inn in town?"

Sarah nodded. "Talking, they were. So I went out back and saw her mushy garden. She said to get away from it, kind of mean, but gave me that shot and said not tell. You think Mrs. Marnie will give me a shot of Grandfather, since him gone too?"

Kat's eyes prickled with unshed tears. "I tell you what. I'll ask her for you. Is that all right?"

"Oh, *ja*," she said, and her face suddenly lit to see whoever had stepped into the room behind them. As Kat spun around she had two thoughts. She had forgotten her training to always be able to surveil the scene, especially who came in the door—and...it might be Luke.

"Aunt Brooke!" Sarah cried and ran to hug Brooke Brand. "Did you hear Grandfather went to see my mother, but I can't go, too?"

After Brooke paid her respects to her father-in-law and the immediate family in the parlor, the Amish ate lunch in shifts. Brooke was going to see her niece, Jennifer, then drive back to Columbus, but before she left, she and Kat walked out to the pond on the very edge of the farm.

"Luke says you've made some headway here," Brooke said as she leaned against a gnarled tree by the water. "I wish I could say the same for Melly. She's not worse, but not much improved."

"I'm so sorry. But I'm sure she'll recover. A coma is the brain's way of healing itself, even if it takes time."

Brooke only nodded as she stooped to pick up a flat

stone and skip it across the pond. In this light, Kat noticed strands of silver etching her honey-hued hair. Could her desperation over her daughter's condition be turning her gray almost overnight?

Brooke went on. "Luke says he believes there's real danger involved for you here, maybe more so than for the Amish."

"And he asked you to ask me to be careful?"

"No, but I could tell he was concerned for you. Kat—Katie, how are you doing here, acting Amish?" she said, turning to her with an anxious expression. "I've been hoping things were going well for you. I think we have a lot in common."

"Two English women adrift among the Amish?"

"Not only that. I've done a little homework. Right now I have a lot of time on my hands, and the tendency to look into crimes and their causes dies hard, though I haven't done criminal law for over ten years. In short, I read a few old *Dispatch* articles about what happened to you in Columbus."

"I see," Kat said. She picked up a stone and skipped it much harder and farther than Brooke had.

"Since you don't know much about my past," Brooke said, "I'll just say that I was responsible for getting a murderer off, and he abducted another victim. They were both killed. I couldn't face up to that, not to mention that someone was stalking me, so I fled to Amish country. I blamed myself for someone's death, actually two deaths, and I...just thought you might, too."

"Not for that damn child abuser's death!" Kat exploded, before she got hold of herself. She continued more softly. "Yeah, for the boy's, I do. It wasn't my bullet that hit him, but I blame—"

"Don't! It will eat you up. You need to let the past

go. Just concentrate on the present, on not letting *this* criminal get away with anything else. He—or they— hurt Melly and are evidently determined to force the Amish away or punish them for something.''

"You know, cops are trained to look into the what and how, not the why," Kat admitted. "But I've got to keep digging for the motive, too. The thing is, I'm getting obsessed with all this."

"There was something else I wanted to mention," Brooke said, throwing one more stone that sank almost immediately. "Another thing I think we might have in common is the Brand brothers."

Kat's stomach cartwheeled. "But—in what way?"

"Dan and I couldn't hide how we felt about each other, and we tried most to hide it from each other. Luke cares for you, and he implied you return his feelings. Kat, just let me warn you," she plunged on, speaking faster and faster, "my Dan was what the Amish call a fence-jumper, a rebel who'd lived away from this life, so it was possible for him to leave the faith. But Luke's been the backbone of this community, especially lately, the solid rock for the Amish and yet a bridge between the two worlds."

"It seems you, Dan and Melly have been, too."

"Not like Luke, because he's still one of them," she insisted. "If Luke were married—bishops have to be married, unless they become widowers in office— I think the selection of the new bishop would have to go his way."

A new bishop. Kat hadn't thought of that. She re- called that Bishop Brand had explained the process of nomination and selection to her.

"Our situation demands we work closely together, but Luke and I aren't involved like that," Kat said, trying to convince Brooke—and herself.

"Enough said," Brooke murmured as she gave Kat a quick hug. "Thanks for not telling me to butt out. You know, it's so quiet here—" she changed the subject as she gazed at the pond "—but I can still hear in my head those machines and monitors in Melly's room, the little sounds she makes when she stirs or snores. Can you believe it, even deep in a possibly deadly coma, she snores—?"

Brooke burst into tears. She covered her face with her hands, but, as Kat stepped forward to clasp her shoulders, she got hold of herself. "I really loved Jacob Brand," Brooke said, swiping at her tears. "I screwed up his son's life, as far as he was concerned, but he and Ida were always good and fair to me, and they loved Melly just as much as one of their all-Amish grandkids."

Kat put her arm around Brooke's shaking shoulders. "He treated me well, too. And Luke said that the bishop, even as he died, was worried about the evil, as he called it. Brooke, somehow I'm going to root out that evil. I just wish he'd be here to see it happen."

Kat soon saw she was wrong about this time of mourning being lost days for her investigation. Sitting in Luke's parlor the next day, she was shocked to overhear Paul Yoder say to Lee in German—which she was starting to grasp more each day—"Well, look at that. Parked his red truck, Clay Bigler coming this way with flowers. Since Luke's inside, best I go meet him halfway."

"Can Lee and I come with you?" Kat asked quickly in English. "I've been wanting to meet him. I'll stay in the background, but if you could just talk to him a bit while I listen…"

"*Ja,* okay," Paul said. He walked down the front

porch steps and headed across the yard with her and Lee behind. "If he's here to mend fences," Paul threw back over his shoulder, "he's welcome."

That eternal Amish forgiveness, Kat thought as she followed the burly, red-haired man. The quotation "The meek shall inherit the earth" must refer to the future, because she was afraid meekness wasn't helping them around Maplecreek now. Someone had to fight for the Amish, and she was coming to feel so protective of them all.

Kat immediately noted that Clay Bigler was not the muscle-bound, cigar-chomping union boss she'd stupidly envisioned. He was slim and nattily attired in gray slacks, knit shirt and a sports coat that matched his silver hair. He carried a graceful arrangement of yellow gladioli. But hadn't this man figured out by now that Amish funeral practices would be as plain as the people?

"Yoder," the man said to Paul and extended his hand.

Bigler was either squinting into the sun or bore a look of distrust and dislike. Even from here, she could tell he smelled of cigarette smoke.

Paul shook his hand and said, "You are welcome here."

The two men stepped apart, with Bigler still holding the flowers. "Sorry to hear about the bishop," he said. "I know he was pretty old, but what happened?"

"He's had stomach problems for some time. Mr. Bigler, this is Leah Kurtz and Katie Kurtz—cousins."

"Ladies," he said with a dip of his head. "Here, guess you can take care of these," he added, and passed the bouquet to Kat. She sniffed at the flowers, but they reeked of cigarette smoke, too. "Consider it from all the union boys. Disagreements aside, you people are all a big part of the community. Well, it surely wasn't something like food poisoning,'' Bigler said, ''not with the great way you all cook.''

''Much appreciated, your kindly thoughts,'' Paul said. ''Would you like to come to the house?''

''Uh, no, that's okay. So, any idea who will take the bishop's place—his office?'' Bigler asked, jamming his hands in his pants pockets.

''Not decided yet. The Lord will decide.''

''Oh, sure. Well, I gotta run.''

He almost did, as he turned and headed for his van, bloodred among all the black buggies.

''So,'' Paul said as the three of them headed back to the house, ''what do you think, Katie?''

''I think,'' she said as she set the flowers on the front porch, ''he's hoping the next bishop can be bought off or cowed, now that Jacob Brand is gone.'' She didn't share her second thought: Clay Bigler's comment about food poisoning was really strange.

''Sheriff, it's kind of you to drop by,'' Luke called to Ray Martin about an hour later as the sheriff drove up in a car that was neither his sheriff's vehicle nor his black pickup.

Kat hurried to join Luke in the farmhouse lane. She was disappointed that the sheriff had two other men with him—deputies?—because she'd like to talk to him alone. But the two who climbed out behind him were Tyler Winslow and a young man she'd seen in a photo in the sheriff's office, his high-school-age son. Despite driving the civilian car, the sheriff was in full dress uniform.

''Luke, ma'am,'' the sheriff greeted them, looking strangely guilty. Was he uncomfortable to be seen in the presence of the commander of the Patriot Knights,

even though Winston was his brother-in-law? Or had
he not expected Kat to come out with Luke?

"This here's my son Mark, and I guess you two
know Tyler Winslow," he said, taking his hat off and
turning it repeatedly in his hands. "Luke and *Fraulein*
Kurtz—"

"You can call me Katie," Kat put in.

"Okay, Katie. Tyler's been telling me what happened with the near disaster at the Coblentz silo and
all."

"I hope there's no hard feelings over that freak accident," Winslow said. "We're here to pay our respects to a community leader. I'm representing the
Maplecreek City Council."

Kat was both dumbfounded and annoyed. If Sheriff
Martin had not told her that this man was the Patriot
Knights' leader, she would probably vote for Tyler
Winslow for reelection or even for mayor of Maplecreek. Was it possible that a few of the Knights, raw
recruits like A.J. Bigler and the idiot she'd overheard
raving about minority groups, were way out of line,
and Winslow and his Knights weren't really that de-
viant or dangerous at all? The man looked dignified
and charming. But then, she warned herself, she had
to remember he was a politician, albeit on a small
scale.

She let Luke do the talking and turned her attention
to study the sheriff and his son, Mark. The boy, though
much younger and thinner, was basically a clone of
his father in height, features and coloring. She wondered if Mark had liked shooting a paintball gun so
much with his church youth group that he'd kept it
up. Or had his uncle ever taken him out to the Knights'
range to shoot paintball guns or worse?

And then she realized Mark Martin, under his new-

looking jeans, wore scuffed western boots with
pointed toes. Luke had said the motorbike rider had
worn boots that were not square-toed. But she could
not get Luke off to the side right now to ask him if
Mark's physique and boots matched his memory of
the motorbiker with the fireworks. Fireworks that
Sheriff Martin had claimed had not come from the
stash used at the homecoming game, where Mark was
the star quarterback.

Kat recalled that Brooke's niece, Jennifer, was a
cheerleader at Mark's school. She was staying with a
family friend of Brooke and Dan's so she could go to
classes while Melly was in hospital. Maybe Jennifer
would know something about Mark, and, for that matter, about A.J. Bigler, who'd graduated last year.

After the sheriff came out of the house where he
and Winslow had expressed their condolences to Ida
and the family, Kat managed to press a note covertly
in the sheriff's hand. Mark had waited outside, talking
to some of the Amish boys handling the horses. Kat
would have loved to grill him, but she didn't dare.
Besides, she was crazy to think that the sheriff could
have anything to do with the Amish attacks. She'd
thought A.J. and his father Clay could be a connection,
and the sheriff had set her straight on that. Surely, he
and his small-town, all-American son could not be in
cahoots for anything darker than something like a par-
ent's note to let the kid skip school to sleep in before
a big football game.

Her note to the sheriff read, *Let's not meet until
after the funeral. Too much going on here.* The truth
was, she needed time—to think, to sort things out and,
she hoped, to talk to Jennifer.

"The sheriff," Luke said as the two of them
watched him drive off, "wanted to lead the funeral

procession of buggies in his cruiser. But I told him my father never would have allowed it. Even if word gets around and people come to stare, we've faced that before and don't need the sheriff for that.''

Ordinarily, Kat might have argued that a little police protection might be a good idea, but she was getting paranoid about the sheriff and his family.

"Mark Martin—the boy," Kat said. "You haven't seen him before, have you, Luke?"

"I've seen him around. He used to court Dan and Brooke's niece, Jennifer."

Kat just gaped at him. Was it getting so she could predict things around here? She'd been especially shaken by the fact she'd dreamed that little John Seyjack had whispered, "Come up, come up," when she was being deluged with the corn, and then Luke had said those were his father's last words. Now she'd suspected that Jennifer might know something about Mark and then...

"Kat," Luke said, "are you all right? You look pale."

"I'm okay," she told him. "I'm just grieving, too."

On the morning of the funeral, the lane and yard were filled with black buggies and a few cars waiting to leave for the cemetery. In both the house and barn, the ministers preached funeral services. As a soon-to-be family member, Kat was seated in the house with the women. Lee sat at her elbow and translated from time to time.

"He's preaching on Jesus being a carpenter, a builder," she told Kat. "Like Bishop Brand was a builder, helping his people with their lives. Besides, when he was younger, he used to work with wood."

"Maybe he's implying that the Amish carpenters

should be proud of their calling, too,'' Kat whispered. ''To stand up to Clay Bigler and the union.''

''No,'' Lee whispered back. ''What an Amish preacher says is what he means, no more, no less. But some of the visiting Amish have been stressing a different message. Jesus told his disciples, if you are not welcome one place, shake the dust off your feet and move on.''

''The Maplecreek Amish can't be thinking of leaving? Of giving in to this evil and moving on?''

''It's our way, if we have no choice, because we can't fight evil with evil. If our children are at stake, we can only take so much.''

Kat saw Luke level a stern look at them from across the room where the pallbearers sat. No one else seemed to be bothered by their whispering, but he had evidently noticed. Or were those around them simply being kind and tolerant?

Kat only knew that if the Amish would not fight back, she was going to do it for them. They could not leave this beautiful area and all they had built here. Her dedication and passion for her challenge became stronger, fiercer.

As everyone got into buggies or cars and the casket was carried out to be placed on the back of the one-seat, open-back spring wagon that served as a hearse, Marnie approached. Kat had seen her pop in and out, bringing food during the last few days. She'd evidently been in the service in the barn. She patted Kat's shoulder and said, ''I closed the shop all day and the restaurant for the morning, but I've got to run back to get things geared up to open at noon.''

''It was nice of you to do that so the workers could attend,'' Kat told her, but Marnie only patted her again and hurried away.

Just then Dr. Barker walked up. "A great loss," he said, shaking his white head. "You're Luke's fiancée, right? I know you let me in at the house that night, but things were so rushed."

"*Ja,* that was me."

"I know everyone's headed for the cemetery, so I won't keep you. I just wanted to tell you, as I have the others, how sorry I am. I wish I could have done more—if the bishop had just been willing to go to the hospital. Usually the Amish are, of course, but I believe he was so sick that he saw the handwriting on the wall and wanted to die in his own bed. I guess we should all be so lucky—blessed, as Mrs. Brand puts it."

"Did you determine the actual cause of death?" Kat asked before she realized that hardly sounded Amish.

He looked surprised. "It could have been several things," he admitted as his brow furrowed. "Without an autopsy, which of course is out of the question with your people, I can't say. A great loss..."

Kat wanted to ask him if it could have been food poisoning, but she didn't want Ida's pie to be suspected. Besides, people ate elderberry pie all the time, including herself and Marnie just four days ago. And Eli had said you had to eat the leaves and twigs to get sick from it.

Kat climbed in the back seat of the big Brand surrey, which sat directly behind the hearse. She wanted to beg off riding with the immediate family, but she knew, even here among the Amish, she must keep up appearances. And Luke had said that gawkers with video cameras might be along the road. He sat in front to drive, with his mother on the seat beside him. Eli and Sarah sat on the middle seat. Kat noted the kids were subdued. For Eli, this no doubt brought back memories of burying his mother. For Sarah, who knew what went on in that little mind?

As the procession began, Kat looked between Luke's broad shoulders and Ida's stiff, sloped ones to keep an eye on their surroundings. People in cars parked along the road watched them pass. Some bowed their heads or removed their hats. Kat noted a few cameras, and despite what Marnie had said about leaving, she looked for her. As they left the farm road behind, spectators dwindled.

Craning her neck to gaze through the plastic window behind her, Kat could see Mose, Susan and their brood in the next buggy. Beyond them, the long black line snaked from the lane and out onto Ridge Road toward Hillfarm Road. Soon they would turn onto the narrow single lane that led up to the Shekinah Amish Cemetery. The simple, identical tombstones were laid out atop the hill with a fine view of the gentle valley. Kat had only seen the cemetery as she had driven past, but it seemed a pretty and pleasant place. She was sure Bishop Brand would have agreed.

They heard a buzzing, not from behind them or before them. Kat's head jerked around; Luke looked from side to side. Not an airplane swooping low? Where was it?

"What's that?" Eli asked.

For one moment Kat thought Reuben might have come uninvited in his old truck, but this was a much smoother sound. The noise was loud, but could not compare with Tyler Winslow's combine. An image of a police motorcycle patrol at a fallen officer's funeral flashed through her mind.

But Sheriff Brand had been asked not to bring an escort. It must be someone—something—else.

"Luke," Kat said, "that doesn't sound like the motorbike, does it?"

"No."

"It's not like that one that threw the fireworks," Eli said.

Before Kat could grab for him, the boy jumped up and leaned out of the buggy, looking up and down the road. "Don't see a thing," he said, just as a large motorcycle burst from behind the thicket between the two cornfields they were passing.

Kat thought it was two vehicles at first, but it was one with a sidecar attached. Two men rode the motorcycle, one on the bike, one in the sidecar. Dressed in black, they wore knitted ski masks and goggles, the sort sported by the paintball attackers. Kat saw no weapons, but that didn't mean they weren't carrying.

She yanked Eli into the back seat with her and put her arm around Sarah to drag her back and shove her under the seat. "Stay there!" she ordered the girl, and pushed Eli down in the space between the second and third seat so he blocked Sarah in.

Without a word, Luke took Ida's hand and helped her climb toward Kat, who helped her sit on the protected back seat. Like a mother hen, Ida spread her skirts to hide the children. Kat squeezed Ida's arm, then clambered up in front with Luke.

All that had taken mere seconds, but it had felt like an eternity. Damn but she wished that she was armed. Why had she ever let the sheriff talk her out of at least a cell phone?

The hearse had gone on but the motorcycle, a big Harley, forced the horses off the road. It tipped one wheel into a ditch, slanting the wagon. The coffin slid backward but did not fall out.

"What do you want?" Luke shouted and stood in the surrey. "Leave our people to their mourning!"

Kat grabbed his arm. "They might have a weapon," she whispered, but it was soon sickeningly clear that it wasn't Luke or any of the living these ghouls wanted to harm here. The men jumped into the hearse and opened the hinged lid of the coffin, which would not be screwed down until the final moment before burial.

"No! *Nein!*" Kat cried when she realized the outrage they intended.

Luke jumped down and, as Mose appeared at his side, strode to stop the man who had pulled the bishop's body out of the coffin and then handed it down into the sidecar of the motorcycle. Kat heard Ida gasp, and then another woman—Mose Susan?—shrieking. The hearse driver, shaken and pale, came around the corner of the tipped vehicle, wiping blood from his forehead.

Kat was certain Luke was going to attack the attackers. After all, he had struck Reuben once. His fists clenched at his sides, a vein standing out on his neck above his white collar, he advanced on them. Sounding as if he spoke through gritted teeth, Luke said, "What is it you really want? What's the message? Just give it like a human being, not a ravening wolf."

The men turned to Luke, then jumped back on the motorcycle, one man sharing the sidecar with the corpse. When the Amish just stood, shocked, it hit Kat hard that they would not commit violence even to halt this violation of human decency. If Bishop Brand were alive, he'd no doubt approve of their response.

"The message—you're cowards!" the bike driver called in a low, rough voice that Kat did not recognize. But she was thrilled he had spoken. Surely someone could identify who in the community owned that big Harley and its sidecar.

Kat heard Sarah whimpering from the surrey; fury racked her again. Despite knowing she should act Amish and not call attention to herself, she stood in the surrey and, fighting to keep her voice calm, said, "*You* are the cowards, *ja,* picking on women, children and the dead."

While the intruders stared at her, Luke stepped forward to lift the body from the sidecar, but the motorcycle driver slammed him in the side of the head with a back blow of his arm. In his hand, he held a pistol.

Kat almost screamed, *Gun! Gun!* but she stopped herself from giving her cover away. At the school picnic, she'd shouted that, but over the truck noise and kids' screams the attackers apparently hadn't heard her.

Luke staggered but did not fall.

"That's the message," the driver shouted. "Get away! *Go* away—or else!" He revved the engine and pulled away, nearly running Luke over.

Kat jumped down and ran to him. Leaning on her, he stumbled to the edge of the lane. They watched the motorcycle pass about half of the Amish, who were stopped in their vehicles, before veering off the lane onto a dirt road. And all the way, one of the perverted bastards lifted and moved Bishop Brand's arm as if he were waving goodbye.

13
___

Luke and Mose walked back along the line of buggies to tell their families what had happened. Then all five Brand brothers made their way to the rear of the procession, explaining to everyone. Kat could see buggies begin to turn around and head toward the farm. Meanwhile, Mose Susan comforted Ida, while Kat tried to answer Eli and Sarah's questions.

Kat managed to keep calm until Sarah clung to her skirts. Tears in her eyes, Kat bent to pick the child up in her arms.

"Is that where my *mamm* went, how she left?" Sarah asked, glaring at the open coffin still in the hearse.

"No, Sarah, no! Your mother's buried under that pretty stone with her name on it you told me about," Kat said, rocking her side to side as if she were a much younger child. "You saw her buried, didn't you, Eli?" Kat prompted.

"*Ja,* Sarah, I was there," Eli said. Dry-eyed but frowning, he patted Sarah's back and the arm that Kat had tight around his sister. "She wasn't stole like this by the evildoers."

"But I didn't want them to take Grandfather!" Sarah wailed.

"Listen to me, both of you," Kat said. "I know how you feel because my father died when I was young, and I was very sad. But the thing is, once someone dies, if they loved the Lord the way your *mamm* and *grossvater* did, they leave their bodies behind and go to live with Him. It's like a butterfly leaves behind its cocoon. Even if the cocoon gets taken, it doesn't hurt the butterfly. It's all right, Sarah and Eli, because we can always remember how strong and kind Jacob Brand was to all of us...."

As Kat looked up, she saw Luke was back, standing, listening. Tears tracked down his face. He stepped forward and embraced her, Sarah and Eli in one big, silent hug. Kat felt stunned. Harsh times or happy, was this how it felt to have a family?

The Brand brothers helped to right the hearse and, together with their surrey, it brought up the rear of the line of buggies straggling back to the farm. Some of the older women accompanied Ida inside the *daadi haus,* so Kat gave them their privacy. Lee took Sarah and Eli off with the other children. As Kat watched Luke conferring with the church ministers under his windmills, Dan strode toward her with Brooke's seventeen-year-old niece, Jennifer. Not perfect timing to question the girl, Kat thought, but an opportunity she couldn't pass up.

"I'm so sorry for your loss," she told them, rising from Ida's rocking chair on the front porch of the *daadi haus.* That was the standard opening cop line for interviewing bereaved witnesses, but Kat had never meant it more.

"No, sit," Dan said, indicating Jennifer should take the other rocker while he lowered himself wearily onto the top step. Both Dan and Jennifer were dressed English but in dark clothes. "I wish I wouldn't have been so far back in the pack, so to speak," Dan went on, after introducing Jennifer to Kat. "I would have knocked the SOBs' teeth down their throats. But if I had, no one would have forgiven me but Jen.''

"And me," Kat said. "Frankly, that's about what I hope to do. But I saw a gun, Dan, so we're blessed they didn't use it.''

"That's for sure. We've got to hit them back somehow. Which reminds me, Brooke said you should call her at the hospital or the Ronald McDonald House in Columbus if she can help in any way—contacts, research, whatever.''

"If I could get a cell phone or laptop in here, I could contact her. The sheriff told me he thought it wouldn't be a good idea since I was going in undercover. Where would I recharge my batteries on Amish property anyway with no electricity? I guess I could just carry around new batteries all the time.''

"Let me give you a key to our place in town," Dan volunteered, digging in his suit-coat pocket. "You could stop by there to recharge. It wouldn't look strange if you dropped in—pretend to water plants or whatever, collect our mail, even though Jen's doing all that for us.''

"If you want," the girl said, "you can hide your buggy in our barn, too. My horse is usually the only resident, but he's staying at Mose's farm across the road until Dan and Aunt Brooke and Melly get back from Columbus.''

"Do you know where our place is?" Dan asked. "It used to be the Melrose Manor Bed-and-Breakfast, kind of catercorner from Marnie Girkins's Valley View Inn on the edge of town. But since Melly arrived,'' his voice snagged ''we haven't been taking in guests, so stop in whenever you want.''

"I really appreciate that. I'll get my laptop, too, and

leave it there. It's no problem to buggy into Pleasant to get my things.''

"I know all about what you're trying to do, Katie,'' Jen said, "and we're really grateful.''

"Everything depends on people keeping my secret,'' Kat told her.

"For sure,'' the attractive blonde said, nodding vigorously. Perhaps in deference to her Amish family, Jen's hair was pulled into a French braid she'd pulled to the back of her head. She wore no makeup and had not worn earrings in her pierced ears.

Dan opened his key ring and slipped a key off. "Be sure to get the sheriff's phone number and e-mail address,'' he told her. "Here, I'll write Brooke's e-mail down for you. Sorry we're in Columbus with all this going on. I'm heading back right after I drop Jen off at Verna Spriggs's. She's staying there, at The Sewing Circle Quilt Shop.''

"If you have a second, I'd like to ask Jen a few questions,'' Kat said as she took the key and slip of paper from Dan. She stood and walked toward their car with them. "It's a long shot, but...''

"Sure, ask away,'' Jen said. "I'd personally like to brain the morons that hurt Melly and Eli and now— now everybody,'' she said with a sniff as she glanced back at the Amish, still milling about and talking on Luke's lawn.

The women had sat the children in a group on the grass and stood around them as if they'd circled the wagons. Kat noted even the teenaged *younge leit* were in that group, being given drinks and sandwiches, while the men made a second outer circle of protection. Kat shuddered. She recalled teaching the kids in Columbus about circles of safety. But from here, it looked as if the Amish had made a huge bull's-eye, the perfect target for brutal bullies.

"If what's happening to the Amish turns into gossip at school," Kat said, facing Jen as the three of them stopped next to Dan's van, "please don't mention any of this even to a best friend."

"Is someone I know involved in something?" she asked.

"She doesn't mean that, honey," Dan said.

"I hope I don't, at least. Jen, Mark Martin came out here with his dad yesterday to express his condolences. It was a nice thing, but I'd just like to know more about him."

"Mark or his dad?"

"Especially Mark, but both of them."

"He's not against the Amish—Mark—if that's what you mean. I guess you heard I used to date him."

Kat nodded.

"Mark feels just the opposite," Jen rushed on, sounding defensive. "I mean, some of the kids think the Amish are weird and all, but he doesn't. He just thinks they're interesting. He even wrote a paper on them once, about how they used to get picked on really bad in Europe and that's why they came here. I mean arrests, torture, really sick stuff. I told you about that paper, Dan."

"Yeah, I remember. The Martins are a real nice family, Kat. It was a mutual decision that Jen and Mark stop seeing each other."

Kat was beginning to wish she'd gotten the girl alone for this interview.

Jen went on. "It was just that Mark really ran with the wrong kids sometimes. I mean, not like I'm Miss Perfect, or anything. But some of his buds were into skinhead, neo-Nazi stuff, so completely weird. Mark thinks his Uncle Tyler's really awesome, but I thought he was, like, kind of two-faced. You know, like one foot in local government and one in that militia boot camp he runs out there that supposedly distrusts our national government.''

"Was A.J. Bigler one of Mark's buds?" Kat asked, studying the varied expressions that flitted across Jen's face.

"Oh, yeah, big time. And A.J.'s, like, such a chauvinist, I mean, a real pig about women. People think the Amish are anti-woman, but they're not.''

"Kat," Dan said as he threw a protective arm around Jen's shoulders, "you're not implying something's strange about Mark or his dad, are you?''

"I'm just trying to learn as much about everyone as I can. So, how well do you know the sheriff, Dan?''

"Not well. He's fairly new, but he's a huge improvement over the Neanderthal who reigned supreme here for years. Why?''

"I'm thinking about Sheriff Martin's family ties to Tyler Winslow. I'm sure a part of the sheriff wants to protect his wife's brother—Mark's uncle.''

"I suppose," Dan said, "you saw that Harrison Ford movie about the Amish, *Witness.*''

"Yeah, years ago. What about it?''

"Harrison Ford almost found out too late that his boss in the police department was the villain, remember?''

"I'd forgotten," Kat admitted. "Yeah, that's right. It's a good thing for me this is the real American Midwest, instead of Hollywood, right?" She tried to lighten up as Dan extended his hand and she shook it, then Jen's. "You two take care of yourselves," Kat said. "You know we're all praying for Melanie.''

"Luke's going to call me from his office phone if

he hears anything about—about what happened to Dad," Dan said as he slid into the driver's side. "And they're going to elect a new bishop this afternoon to replace Dad's leadership. That's the tradition when a bishop dies. Luke said if they don't get Dad's body returned in the next couple of hours, they'll have to go to the sheriff with this, even if it turns everything into a media and tourist circus."

"And ruins what I've been trying to do here," Kat said.

"Take care!" Dan called to her as he started the van. He honked twice as his taillights, like big, blood-shot eyes, stared at her, until they disappeared down the corn-lined lane.

Kat just stood where she was, agonizing. She couldn't believe these dreadful deeds could all come down to a bunch of boys like Mark Martin, A.J. Bigler and his ilk. That deep voice she'd heard from beneath the mask and goggles today was surely not that of a young man, was it? She'd heard both A.J. and Mark speak, and the voice hadn't sounded like either of them, though most men could lower their voices for a few words. Kat wished she could read Mark's paper on tormenting the Amish; had he and A.J. found it so grossly fascinating that they thought they'd try it? But as blatant and brutal as the attacks were, some level of perverted adult sophistication seemed to underlie them.

Kat tried again to picture the sizes and shapes of the men who'd stolen Bishop Brand's body. Usually she was good at assessing height and weight stats. But they'd worn black leather jackets, black jeans and gloves, just as the motorbiker had.

The theft of the bishop's body had happened so fast, so horribly, that she kept seeing those hoods and goggles in the dark blur of their movements. If only she weren't so emotionally involved. It was the kiss of death for cops on the streets to let feelings dictate actions, and that was happening to her here.

On trembling legs, Kat made her way back to sit on the *daadi haus* porch when Eli came running, out of breath.

"With this eye patch, I know I'm not s'posed to run," he blurted as if to head off a scolding. "But Dad said to ask you to come to his windmill shop right now. With the church leaders, he's meeting, and wants to ask you something, I guess."

Kat headed right over, but she was starting to feel even shakier. What if they wanted her to leave, to give up? What if they wanted her to agree they should bring the sheriff in on everything? Or could a call have come into Luke's office—a ransom note for the body or a threat? Maybe the media had already caught wind of this outrage against the gentle folk in the land.

Eli delivered her directly to the workshop door, then disappeared into the crowd of kids on the lawn.

"Katie, come in, will you?" Luke called to her, though she was already inside when he spotted her. She was the only woman in the room with a dozen men, including both ministers, the church deacon, Paul Yoder, and all the Brand brothers, but for Dan.

Everyone was standing around Luke's desk, so Kat joined them. They had been speaking in quick German, but now, went silent.

"We've decided to bring in Sheriff Martin if we have no word by sundown," Luke told her, glancing at the phone on his desk.

"There hasn't been some sort of ransom call?"

"Nothing. I figure our enemies are already kicking themselves for talking back to us, letting us hear a voice. I've told everyone here exactly what happened on the road, since no one else but you, me, the driver of the hearse and Mose saw it close up. We're going inside to choose a new bishop, but we wanted to speak to you, since you have a criminal background—finding them, I mean.''

"I'm trying," she said, "but whoever is the mastermind behind all this keeps coming up with such outrageous surprise attacks, I can't predict anything.''

"I know. But you're doing what you can, and you've made progress," he said, an intimate tone replacing his official one. She wondered if he realized it—if the others noted it, too.

"I haven't made enough progress," she said, feeling frustrated and angry with herself again. Unlike when she was on the force, now it felt good to confess her doubts to these men without feeling she sounded weak or scared. "I hope, though," she added, "you don't want me to leave.''

A few heads shook; she heard Paul Yoder whisper, "*Nein*, no.''

"We only want to know," Luke said, "if you can think of anything we should do besides bring in the sheriff—and if you have any objections to that.''

He gave her a knowing look that surely no one else could interpret. Could Luke too be having doubts about Sheriff Martin? She was going to have to ask the sheriff for help to learn who owned a motorcycle with a sidecar. She was afraid to trust him, but she was going to have to risk it. He'd wonder, though, why she hadn't come to him sooner about the motorbike buried in Reuben's silo, despite her theory it must have been wiped clean of prints. He might be suspicious of her terse note, putting him off when she had information she should have entrusted to him.

"I think you have no choice but to call him in at

some point," she admitted. "The drawback is that dragging in law enforcement and, as a result, the media, might mean the culprits will stay in their holes and dispose of the body so they don't get caught with it."

A general shuffling of feet followed, then more shaking of heads and some talk in German.

Kat plunged on. "But I would suggest that as soon as you select a bishop, you also pick several men to visit the grave site to be sure nothing is amiss there. And I'd like to go along, not in full view like today, but out the back. We can walk the way the local scholars go to school, maybe even after dark. In short, hold off calling the sheriff at sundown, at least until we check out the burial site."

Glances passed among the men. Paul Yoder and Luke both nodded. "Four of us, then," Paul said, as he smoothly took over the meeting Luke seemed to have commanded so far. "Luke, Mose, me and Katie."

"I'll get us some flashlights," she told them. "I realize you won't fight violence with violence, but I think we can use a bit of secrecy, *ja?*"

Almost to a man, they nodded. "Like Joshua sneaking in to spy out the promised land," Paul Yoder said, as she headed for the door. "And, remember, it was a woman helped them, too."

Brooke thought Melly looked like an angel sleeping, but she was so very pale against the white sheets. The lights from the medical monitors in the semidarkened room cast a wan glow over her flaccid features.

Brooke startled at the sound of quick footsteps, then silently hugged Dan as he entered the room. They kissed before she steered him away from the bed to pepper him with questions, whispered ones so they wouldn't disturb Melly.

"How's everyone taking it? I can't believe what you told me on the phone. It's horrible, an outrage. They stole his body?''

Dan nodded. "Luke said he'd call if they found it—him. And Kat questioned Jen about Mark Martin and A.J. Bigler. Jen told her about that paper Mark was so into. Kat didn't ask, but maybe you could look into it some.''

"Sure. I'd forgotten about that. Anything but sitting here staring at Melly, just waiting for her to—''

They both froze as their daughter moaned. They rushed to the bed, bent over her.

Should I get the nurse? Dan mouthed.

"Wait a sec,'' she whispered back. "Melly, sweetheart. Mom and Dad are here. We're right here, and we love you.''

It seemed to Brooke that she smiled, but she moaned again and started to thrash, muttering something. Brooke leaned close to try to catch any words that might make sense. Melly had been agitated before, had murmured, too, but this seemed like more, and it gave Brooke such hope.

"Co—mmm-in,'' she thought Melly said.

"Coming?'' Brooke said. "Or come in? Are you coming back to us, sweetheart? We'd like to come in where you are.''

The child began to flail about.

"Her IV's—'' Brooke cried and tried to hold her daughter's arms still as Dan rushed out to get a nurse.

"They're—coming.'' Brooke would have sworn her daughter said that, seeming to growl her words, but mere murmurings followed.

Dan's first words when he ran back in were those very ones: "They're coming."

And then all was lost in the bustle of two nurses and a doctor taking over.

It turned out that the new bishop went along as they set out at twilight, for Paul Yoder had been chosen by lot. It was sad, she thought, that his first act of office wasn't something happy, like presiding over a wedding or a harvest dinner.

Darkness descended like a pall; the wind picked up instead of dying as it often did when the sun sank. Part of their path was familiar to Kat. They soon emerged from the forest near the school and cut across the road toward the hill where the cemetery was. She wished they could do this by daylight, but she did not want them to be spotted. She'd been hoping their eyes would adjust to the dark so they could kill their flashlight beams, but they needed the light. Clouds had blocked out the moon and stars, and, since they weren't walking on the road, the terrain was uneven as they began their climb.

The iron gate creaked as Paul opened it, and the four of them went into the Amish cemetery they had never reached earlier today.

The regular rows of tombstones stretched out in both directions like ghostly heads rising from the dark earth. Kat wondered where Sarah's mother was buried, but this was no time to ask. Luke led them directly to a grave in the western corner that the Brand brothers had dug yesterday; it was covered by poles laid across its width.

"Nothing around here I can see," Luke said as their lights crisscrossed the immediate area. "They wouldn't dare come here."

"But they're unpredictable and brazen," Kat insisted. "Sometimes murderers even return to the crime scene or show up at funerals or grave sites."

"They feel guilty?" Mose asked.

"Or just like to revel in what they've done," Kat said.

She moved closer to the poles and played her light down through them. Her beam picked up something below—something light colored.

"Look," she said, seizing Luke's wrist and pointing with her light.

"That's the box to lower the coffin into," Mose said. "New, light wood, that's all." Paul—Bishop Yoder—stepped close and peered down, too.

"No," Kat insisted, stooping to point her flashlight between two poles. "It's more."

Luke leaned down to shift the poles apart. Four wide leather straps by which the coffin was to have been lowered into the ground were instantly visible, dangling into the deep of the grave. And on them, six feet down, lay the body of an old man, clean-shaved with cropped hair, dressed in a bright red, cheap Halloween devil's costume.

For one moment Kat thought it might be someone else in the grave, but Luke whispered, "Father!" and made a move forward.

"Luke, all of you—don't disturb anything until we can really look around," Kat insisted, gripping Luke's arm even harder.

"But such a contemptible, vile—" Luke said through gritted teeth.

"It doesn't matter what one wears," Kat argued. "You have all taught me that. It's what's within the person, and we know the bishop would want us to take our time with this, if it will give us a clue, a way to find out who's attacking his people—your people now, Bishop Yoder.''

"All right," Bishop Yoder said. "Luke and Mose?"

"All right," Luke echoed, and Mose nodded, but the men's gazes were riveted on the corpse.

"I know you all want to get him attired in worthy clothes and properly buried," Kat said. "But I'd like your permission to be lowered into the grave to look around before you bring him up."

They looked at her now. A moment's utter silence followed, stretching out into the vast, windy night.

"*Ja*, all right," Bishop Yoder said, as if answering for all.

Luke said, "We can gently pull up the strap on the end, then lower you on it."

Three of the men trained their lights into the hole while Luke let her down slowly, then dropped her flashlight to her. She was careful to stand at the corpse's feet to avoid disturbing the way it had been laid—or dropped, probably, since the limbs seemed to have flopped askew.

The grave smelled slightly, a mixture of dank earth and the new pine wood from the Amish's answer to a waterproof vault. She'd smelled death before and that was not the odor, not in this crisp weather and in this cold earth. It was a slightly smoky smell.

Kat trained her flashlight all around the body. "He's wearing his burial clothing under this suit," she called up to them.

"Thank God," she heard Mose mutter, and she too was grateful that the corpse had not been more abused. *Abuse of a corpse, stolen property.* Exactly what charges could the sheriff bring for this horrendous hate crime if they called him in? she wondered.

But she saw nothing that could serve as a clue to who had dumped Jacob Brand here, except of course the devil's outfit. Every time Kat turned to look another way, her own multiple shadows shot at her, as the men above shifted their beams of light.

"If we bring in the sheriff," she called up to them, "he could order a forensic examination of the scene." She'd known better than to mention an autopsy, but she thought they might go for this.

"But we've found him," Bishop Yoder said sternly. "No sheriff, no outsiders."

Kat straightened and looked up, blinking into the glare of their lights before they moved them away. "Bishop Yoder, we are desperate for any clues," she said. "And it's obvious that events are escalating."

"Trusting in God, that's what we're doing," he said. "God and the one He's sent us—you."

By midnight, so much had happened. Luke and Kat had hiked back to the Brand farm, leaving Mose and Bishop Yoder to guard the body they'd lifted from the grave and divested of its insulting costume. The Amish men had examined the corpse, still in its original white burial clothes; though the garments were soiled, they were intact. Kat had asked them to be careful with the Halloween outfit, so she could search it for clues, and they had allowed that, at least.

At the farm, after getting Ida and the coffin, Luke, Gid and Mahlon had returned with the hearse to bury Jacob while Kat stayed behind. She'd helped Luke hitch the horses and had lit the lanterns that hung on the back. She'd found herself waving goodbye as they pulled out on their somber task, though no one looked back. Her first instinct then was to check on Eli and Sarah, but Luke's house was full of guests tonight.

So she gathered and lit every lantern in the *daadi haus* and sat in the kitchen where she'd talked with Bishop Brand barely a week ago. Carefully, she laid the devil's outfit on the table in the bright light and started to examine it top to bottom.

The tags in it said only "Size Large" and "Made in China." The costume was thin, cheap material, the sort that looked like it would bleed red dye if it got wet. It smelled mildewy, as if it had been stored away for quite a while in someone's basement—or was that from the grave? It may have once had a cape or hood attached to it, for something had been ripped off behind the neckline.

Kat sucked in a breath. It had a pocket! What if they'd left a note, or at least something that would give her a clue as to who originally owned this tawdry thing.

She opened the pocket and peered in. Nothing. Sighing, she turned the costume over and noted a small, brown burn mark near the hem on the left hip. It looked like a cigarette burn. She sniffed at the faintest odor of smoke. Was it mildew and cigarette smoke that clung to the costume that she'd smelled in the grave?

The yellow funeral flowers Clay Bigler had brought flashed through her thoughts. They had smelled of smoke, and he did, too. If the burn mark here was on the left side—and if this costume had been worn by one of the evildoers first—did that mean a left-handed smoker? Was Clay Bigler a leftie?

Kat heard a horse snort and the jingle of harnesses as the surrey and hearse returned from the cemetery. She glanced out the window to see two of the men take Ida into Luke's house and the others take the vehicles into the barn. Gutting out three of her four lanterns, Kat carefully folded the devil costume and put it under her bed. Like the motorbike in the silo, this too was evidence she should hand over to Sheriff Martin. She was going to have to go see him, to determine once and for all if she could trust him.

When Ida did not come to sleep in her own home nor Luke to tell her how things went, Kat paced the house, thinking, planning.

She had to learn more about Clay Bigler, keep an eye on him somehow. She wanted to talk to Marnie about whether she still took photos of the Amish. Who knew what she might have seen or accidentally recorded? Without telling the sheriff, Kat decided, she was going to drive her buggy to her apartment in Pleasant and get her cell phone and laptop.

It struck her that she was alone in the house while many of the Amish clustered together at Luke's home and Mose's across the road. She'd never been afraid to be alone, not even at night, but now she surprised herself by wishing she was among the Amish.

She knelt in her back bedroom window and lifted the sash as she'd done on her first night here. The wind was still restless. Clouds raced overhead. Sleep was what she needed, but she was too tightly wound. With her cheek on her crossed arms on the sill, she half dozed. Being in that grave tonight, even though it was lit...being trapped in the dark silo filling with grain...being here among the Amish, and so close to Luke and yet so far... Every time she tried to close her eyes, she kept seeing black figures of death...taking the bishop's body, taking her father, whom she had both detested and loved, then taking Jay from her, and they had a gun, and she couldn't shoot one anymore, but she could hear the trigger click-clicking...

She jerked alert, the way her muscles sometimes did in bed when she was falling asleep.

A sound. Again that clicking sound, somewhere in the night.

The shutter of a camera?

She closed the window and yanked her curtains shut. The sound had definitely been coming from behind the solid-cornstalk wall in the field. And she was going to find out once and for all what it was.

14

Kat put on the black dress she'd borrowed from Ida, turned out the last lantern, took the screen out of a side window and climbed out into the blowing night. If the house was being watched, the focus would be on the doors. Keeping low, gripping her flashlight in one hand and a butcher knife from the kitchen in the other, she bolted for the cornfield that ran along the side of the house.

She went a short distance up the first row, then stopped to listen.

Yes, amid the rustling of the corn, the sporadic *click, click* carried to her on the breeze. It seemed a sound she should be able to place. But Reuben's tinkering with his old truck or breaking more glass could not carry clear over here. Nor did it sound like that. Could it be a camera, a computer keyboard? Or a gun being loaded?

She advanced slowly and carefully until she was sure she was behind the *daadi haus*. The clicking was no longer ahead but directly to her right. Did a faint light emanate from the place of the sound?

Kat moved slowly, holding her unlit flashlight like a club in her left hand and the butcher knife in the other. She hoped those months of isometric wrist exercises had helped; her right hand shook so hard she sliced a corn leaf with the knife. Ahead, at the end of the row, she could see the light growing, brightening.

Click, click. Pause. *Click, click.*

Someone crossed the end of the row! A blur in black—could the person be wearing a dark hood? She should go for help, get Luke, but she had to know, to see. "Situational awareness," one of her instructors had called it: assess the scene to know what you're up against.

Two stalks into the row, she leaned forward to peer out. Someone seized her and shoved her facedown on the ground.

Kat managed to land one blow with her flashlight. The man gave a surprised grunt. She tried to stab him, but the knife went skittering away across the smooth-cut grass.

Smooth-cut grass? Trimmed turf in the middle of a field? She was staring down into a small, neat hole with a white plastic cup containing three golf balls. And beyond lay a big-brimmed Amish man's hat next to a golf club.

"Kat?"

"Luke!"

He rolled her faceup and took his weight off her. Propped up on one elbow, breathing hard, his other hand on her stomach, he stared down at her, astounded.

"What's with the weapons?"

"What's with the putting green?"

"Thank God I didn't hit you with the club."

"Luke, what is all this?"

He sighed and shrugged. "You've found out my secret—my guilty pleasure, at least one of them." He still held her down, though gently now. As he said those last few words, his frown softened to a smile.

She reached up to punch his shoulder. "In other words, you're a closet—a cornfield—golfer? I've heard that ball clicking in that hole more than once, and it was driving me nuts. Do—did—your parents know?''

''They're both just hard of hearing enough that they never asked, and I don't come out here unless I know someone's with Eli and Sarah, day or night. In other words, not as often as I'd like.''

''Since I freaked out at a raccoon screech once, I thought I'd just figure this out myself, so I wouldn't look like a coward or an idiot.''

''A coward or an idiot, not you. But that's Kat Lindley, just charging in on her own, despite the fact it could be something dangerous. Still, she's getting to be more like Katie Kurtz lately.''

''Meaning?''

''Meaning those two women used to be very distinct people, but they're merging now. You really thought it might have something to do with our harassers, I'll bet. You should have asked me. You used to work with a partner, didn't you?'' He reached out to pick up the butcher knife, then heaved it away so it stuck in the sod by the single lantern.

''But a highly trained partner who was willing to use force if need be, more so than just pulling someone down on the ground and leaning on them. Listen, Luke, there is no real Katie Kurtz, even if I have to keep telling myself that. She exists only for one reason—though she's not doing too well with stopping these damn demons hurting your people.''

''But why do you have to fight reaching out and trusting others? I didn't mean to keep you from sleeping,'' he said, changing the subject with a sigh and flopping down beside her on his back. ''If you're like me, you've been doing little of that lately.''

She saw how drained he was; she too felt so strung-out that she was afraid she was going to cry. *"Ja,"* was all she managed to get out and then instantly wished she'd said it in English. But German—this life—was beginning to feel normal, despite her denial about Katie's existence.

"So, let me come clean about Luke Brand, then," he told her. "I clear a circle in this back field each year, then build a putting green when the corn's tall enough to hide behind. I bring in sod, but the green only exists for about a month before harvest, then it's chopped up by the big, antique combine we pull behind the five-horse hitch. And with Sarah and Eli so well cared for tonight at the house, I came out for a while. I do my best thinking here," he admitted, reaching to turn off his lantern and plunge them into darkness.

"As for guilty pleasures," Kat said, "your mother makes elderberry wine—and not just for medicine, right? Everyone has a secret, as well as his or her individual Amish personality."

"Their 'Amishalities,' you mean? Yeah. My sister Emma's husband Levi would give years of his life for a ride in an airplane. He stops plowing and looks up any time one flies over. We're human, Kat, that's all."

His voice drifted off again as if in utter exhaustion. She felt it too, creeping into her bones, yet she was so excited to be alone with him that her mind was on overdrive. Lying shoulder-to-shoulder on the grass, they stared up at the sky.

It seemed as if a massive hand had swept the clouds away. She'd never seen such stunning stars, certainly not around city lights. She felt awestruck at sharing such splendid solitude with him. Yet she was afraid he would turn those deep blue eyes on her again and see her scared and alone and wanting so much to belong. Not to be Amish, of course, nor to belong to him—except in a forbidden, physical sense—but just to belong somewhere, to someone special.

"I should go back," she whispered.

"No—don't."

"So much to do tomorrow—really, it's tomorrow already."

"Do you have secrets, Kat?"

She swallowed hard. "Some, I guess. That I blame my mother for deserting me and my little brother, and blame myself for not being there when he died from a burst appendix."

"Shouldn't you blame your mother for that, too, then? But it's best to forgive, or it poisons you."

She blinked back tears. One crept from the corner of her eye and slid into her hairline, but she didn't brush it away, hoping he wouldn't notice.

"Luke, it won't help to analyze my feelings. I'm here to do a job, and that's that. Katie Kurtz exists for a short time, for a season, and then disappears like this magical little lawn of yours."

When she made the slightest move to rise, he reached for her hand; hers closed around his bigger one so perfectly. They shifted their touch so their fingers linked and held tight.

"It's all right," he whispered. "We don't have to talk about it or philosophize or fight. I know all about trying to deal with losses and about wanting and needing someone special in your life."

She wanted to argue that, but she could only nod. How had he known exactly what she'd been thinking, dreaming? His voice mesmerized her, and she began to really relax. They were like a married couple, she thought, lying in bed together. The sweetest silence fell as they stared upward into the vastness. Luke evoked a deep peace in her and yet a restless passion.

They stayed that way for so long, she thought perhaps they both had slept. Dew began to settle on them, and she sneezed.

"When I was an outsider," she said, "I used to think you Amish were almost saints."

He laughed. "At least you're implying you're not an outsider anymore, Kat-Katie. I'm never a saint, not me," he added, squeezing her hand, then rolling to his side on one elbow to stare down at her as he had earlier. His face was in deep shadow, but she could feel his eyes on her, feel his breath. He smelled like new-cut grass and fresh wind and dark, sweet night. Slowly, he lifted his free hand to clasp her waist.

"I did notice you tackled me pretty hard," she said, trying to remind herself to breathe. Again, as with each time she thought her stoic facade would crumble, she was suddenly desperate to build a wall of words between them. "Are you longing to be a worldly football player as well as the first Amish Jack Nicklaus?" she teased.

"Right now I'm not longing to do anything but this."

They had both been sucked into an emotional whirlpool today. They were grieving. For the hundredth time, Kat told herself she had to stay objective, keep her head. To think, not feel. She knew a kiss was coming and that it was not a good idea.

But they met in the middle of their need, in the middle of what must surely be the only Amish putting green in the universe of galaxies overhead. They kissed, caressed and clung.

It was not the right time, place, person, or even the right planet for this.

But it had happened.

She thought—and feared—she was falling in love with Luke Brand.

The next morning, Kat decided she'd been bewitched by some fairy circle of a putting green last night. From now on, she would concentrate only on catching the culprits. The idea of loving Luke was not only impossible but insane.

Since Ida was still over at Luke's house, Kat ate breakfast and left early to help Lee ready the schoolhouse for the scholars. When the kids arrived, she spent an hour speaking English with the younger grades, then buggied into Pleasant to get her cell phone and laptop.

Sneaking into her own place dressed like an Amish woman made her feel silly at first. She was grateful her landlady wasn't home. She glanced around her small apartment. The place felt wrong now, too cluttered and lonely. It surprised her that she was not tempted to turn on the TV to check *Headline News,* or take non-Amish clothes with her, or even look in the mirror. She had no desire to phone anyone, check her e-mail or pile of snail mail. Not even staying long enough to charge up the batteries, soon she was on her way back toward Maplecreek, her brain going as fast as Dilly's hooves.

Kat knew where Dan and Brooke's place was, but what especially interested her was that Marnie's Valley View Inn was close by, and she wanted to talk to her. The whirling dervish entrepreneur was no doubt at the Dutch Table or her shop, so that would be the next stop after plugging in the laptop and charging the cell phone at Dan and Brooke's.

The next car she heard behind her on the road into

town did not pass; the driver tapped the horn. Kat looked back over her shoulder to see the sheriff's car.

"Do I need to hit the light bar and siren to get you to stop a sec?" he yelled out the window.

Feeling guilty, Kat turned into the next farmer's lane. Ray Martin pulled his cruiser straight across it, hemming her in. He got out and slammed the door. Kat quickly wrapped the reins but didn't climb down.

"What if someone sees us together?" she asked.

"Let them think I pulled you over for speeding." His voice was clipped; he didn't smile. "Why in the Sam Hill have you been playing hard to get lately?"

"I told you in the note. So much was happening."

She wondered if he knew Bishop Brand's body had been snatched. She hadn't told him, and if he'd learned that, he could cancel this assignment, even fire her. She had to decide whether to trust him or not. Or could she tell him just enough to hide her suspicions about him, his son and his brother-in-law?

"Yeah, well, even if you don't have anything for me, I've got things to tell you." He put a hand on the buggy so hard he rocked it on its springs. "First off, that Colt semiautomatic rifle you took from A.J. Bigler was registered to his dad."

"No kidding? You said A.J.'s supposed to be on the outs with Clay. I would have thought that was a Patriot Knights weapon."

"I talked to Clay. He claims the kid took it without asking. But just the fact that Clay owns that sort of assault rifle says something, even if he did buy it legally. He said it was just for his own protection since he's been in a volatile position lately."

"Oh, right. As if the Amish would come gunning for him. Where does Clay live?"

"Used to live in a real nice place he custom-built,

not far from the high school. Since his divorce a couple years ago, he's moved into a rented farmhouse about twenty miles north of here. Said he wants to move back here, though. Really likes the area.''

"Where do his ex-wife and A.J. live?"

"Ex moved somewhere out west after their divorce.''

"Do you know the grounds for their breakup?''

"Not really. I heard it was pretty bitter. Gossip said he was married to his job and that he dumped her for someone else. I think the guy's a loner, but for his dedication to the union. A.J. lives with a couple of young Knight recruits on Patriot Knight property, bounces around between menial jobs and refuses to follow in his dad's footsteps as a carpenter. Most of his time he's playing militia, as you know.''

"I suppose your questioning Clay tipped him off that I'm the link to the gun,'' Kat said with a sigh. "Anyway, A.J. could have told him.''

"Clay still claims they're on the outs and he hasn't seen him for a while. The boy blames him for the divorce. Yeah, I had to tell Clay how I got the gun, though, in case he checked with the kid.''

So, Kat thought, if A.J. and Clay were by chance talking, they could be onto her. Or A.J. might have tipped off Tyler Winslow about her. And who knows what Sheriff Martin might have told his brother-in-law. She would have to start watching her back even more.

"Plus,'' the sheriff continued, "we found no identifiable fingerprints on the blades of Luke's windmills that got tossed through the shop windows in town. Either the weather or the vandals wiped them clean, or the perps wore gloves.''

"I'll bet they wore gloves. The man who rode the

motorbike wore gloves. And, Sheriff, so did the three guys who took Bishop Brand's body from the funeral procession for a few hours.''

When he gaped at her long and hard, she held to the hope he had not known. He had not exploded with rage, as she'd expected, either at the insult to the Amish or at the fact she hadn't come directly to him when it happened. If Ray Martin was being straight with her, she'd been right to inform him. If he was crooked, and she didn't tell, he might figure she was suspicious of him.

"Get down from that buggy and let's walk up the lane a ways," he said, taking off his hat and raking his fingers through his short hair. "I think you and I got a lot to get caught up on, and you're right—we don't need folks spotting us talking."

Decision time again. Should she go off alone with him? But other cars had gone by already. Some people had even rubbernecked to see who the sheriff had pulled over in a buggy. If Ray Martin was involved with the Amish abusers, he was clever. He'd be an idiot to harm her when they'd been seen together. Still, the sheriff was the last person many would believe could be involved with something illegal and immoral, which meant he could act with impunity.

"It's so horrible, I hate to even recount it," Kat told him as she jumped down, then leaned against the back of the buggy instead of following him down the lane. She tensed as he stopped and came back, but she'd always been good at self-defense. "It's just that I need time to sift it all out, to get a complete list of possibles together for you."

"The bastards stole the old man's body?" he said, as if he couldn't get beyond that. "Just for a while?"

"It was recovered in the grave, no less. His family

has buried him now.'' She described what had happened, both on the road and later in the cemetery. ''I asked the family if they'd allow a forensic examination of the grave and corpse, but they said no. By the way, the body snatchers drove a black Harley with a sidecar, and waved a gun around—a 9-mm semiautomatic pistol, I think it might have been.''

''Another semiautomatic,'' he murmured, as if to himself. ''Man, I can't believe that horror didn't leak out. But I've seen from the get-go that the Amish can be tight-lipped. That's one reason I thought your masquerade would work. Hell, Kat, why didn't you let me know?''

''It's not easy without a cell phone or my laptop,'' she said, wondering what he would say if he knew both were hidden about four feet away under the buggy seat.

''Now, where would you plug those in, even if you had them? Besides, Luke's got a phone in that workshop of his.''

She stared at him for a moment, then realized anyone could know that. ''I think you realize,'' she said, ''that I'm caught between two worlds. The Amish made a mistake by not letting you give them the funeral security you'd offered. They also didn't want outsiders to know about the abuse of the bishop's corpse. They expect certain things of me and you do too. But I have to tread a fine line with them, Sheriff, even more than I do with you.''

''Yeah, yeah, I see that,'' he admitted, removing his hat again and running his fingers through his hair. Though the breeze was chilly, Kat could see he was sweating profusely. ''We're up against some real sickos. Yeah, Kat, I know you're being pulled both ways, but you're gonna have to keep me better and faster informed. Meanwhile, I can try to trace that Harley—and a sidecar?''

She nodded. ''You've never seen anything like that in the area?''

He shook his head. ''We've had bikers ride through, but they weren't locals and moved on. And with a sidecar?'' he added, scratching his head. ''I'll ask around, just like I am about that motorbike buried in corn at Reuben Coblentz's place. Don't go looking in any silos to see if a Harley's sitting there, ready to be hidden during the harvest next week—though I might just do some of that.''

She didn't dare ask if that would include searching silos his brother-in-law might own or rent. All this reminded her that she wanted to see Tyler Winslow's farm. Clay's ex might be out of reach for now, but Kat hoped to find a way to interview Winslow's wife. Paul and Mary Yoder's farm was one of several that abutted the big Winslow spread, and Paul had said that Louise Winslow was almost a recluse. In this small community where most people knew each other well, almost no one knew Louise. The obvious thing would be to ask the sheriff about his in-laws, but she still felt she shouldn't risk it.

''So,'' he said in the awkward silence, ''who's on your list of possible perps, so I can shake a few cages?''

''I think if you do, they'll go underground. Give me a little more time, please. And if you ask around, do it carefully.''

He narrowed his eyes and took a step closer as he jammed his hat back on his head. ''Sounds like you're the one giving orders now,'' he said, hooking his thumbs in his gun belt. ''Sounds like you know more than you're telling. Ask around about who?''

"The very people you put me on to in the beginning. I'm keeping an eye on Coblentz, who has some English drinking buddies and some real bitter feelings about being shunned. Clay Bigler and his union buddies, not to mention his son, A.J."

"And maybe some of the other Knights. I'm sticking closer to Tyler than usual, I'll tell you that."

Kat almost fell over. "Because you suspect him of something?"

"Hell, no. Because he's sitting on a bunch of time bombs out there with some of the guys that belong to the Knights, that's all. I've told him right out, if he overhears anything funny, he'd better tell me. You're not thinking he'd be in with Coblentz on this, are you, because it was Tyler's grain that hid the bike and almost hid you?"

"I don't know what to think yet."

"Then you better get your act together...quick," he said, starting for his car. "Stealing dead bodies is bad enough, but what if next time they take live ones—or *make* a corpse?" he threw back over his shoulder. He opened his car door, then turned back to point at her. "See you and Luke at the bridge tomorrow night, ten sharp."

As he drove away, his words echoed in Kat's brain. *You'd better get your act together...quick...* It may have been just his usual gruff advice, but it had sounded like a warning, or a threat.

15

After her unsettling interview with the sheriff, Kat drove into Maplecreek and used Dan's key to go in the back door of his and Brooke's large home. The sign out front said, Melrose Manor, Amish Furniture & Attorney-at-Law.

She plugged in her laptop in their den, where it looked as if Brooke had kept hers, and began to charge her cell phone. The house looked lovely, but felt empty. As could be expected from an Amish craftsman, the furniture was big and bold, and the woodwork superb. Kat realized that Dan also must have custom-made most of the pieces in Luke's big farmhouse. She pictured the farm now, its large, high-ceilinged rooms, which could either bustle with activity or breathe out serenity. Luke seemed to fill any room he entered, and Eli and Sarah lit each corner.

Kat shook her head to clear it and spent most of her time staring out the parlor windows at Marnie's large home and lot. She was surprised to see Marnie drive by, but perhaps she was coming home for a late lunch. As Kat locked the door to Brooke and Dan's house and headed out to unhitch Dilly, she decided to walk over to talk to Marnie. It was a short way across a vacant lot to her B & B. Both places had carriage houses and deep backyards that almost abutted in one corner. Kat was halfway across the weedy lot between the corners of the two properties when she saw another vehicle turn into Marnie's driveway. She could have picked it out anywhere. Clay Bigler's red SUV.

Fighting her instinct to hit the ground, Kat froze where she was in the open. Sudden movements sometimes called more attention than trying to blend in. She watched, riveted as Clay, who had been smoking a cigarette held in his left hand, tossed it down and ground the butt out under his foot in the gravel driveway. In the other hand, he carried a manila folder. She was afraid he'd see her, but he went up onto the deep back porch, expelling smoke from his mouth and nose in a rush. He knocked once on the door and was instantly admitted.

Kat hustled to get behind some tall hollyhock bushes just off Marnie's property line. It was obvious where Marnie's land began, because it was beautifully tended, every inch of it, back to the treeline. Apple trees, roses, shaped bushes Kat couldn't even name were clustered between paths and shady walkways. An evidently Amish-built gazebo was the crowning touch. When Kat darted forward to crouch behind some clumps of tall ornamental grass, she saw one of Luke's decorative windmills spinning madly in the breeze by the back porch.

Kat agonized over what Clay and Marnie's connection could be. Perhaps they had some business association tied to Amish Acres. Since Marnie was buying a place there, Clay's union guys could be working on it. Also, Paul Yoder had told her that Clay took photos of the Amish workers for the union's lawsuit to prove that they weren't wearing hard hats and safety belts. Maybe, if Marnie was still taking pictures of Amish life, that common interest could be a link. Surely they weren't intimately involved? Both were single, though, and it looked as if Clay had been expected. A clue might be in that manila envelope. Kat was tempted to go closer to the house and peer in a window, but that would be too risky.

She racked her brain for evidence against Clay. When he'd paid his condolences call at the farm, he'd been curious to find out who the next bishop would be. His comment about food poisoning had seemed off-the-wall.

Though she wanted to stay behind the tall grass until Clay left, Kat forced herself to head back to get her horse and buggy. She was undecided about whether to drive over to Marnie's, with the hope of overhearing or seeing something, or to just wait until Clay left. But as she hesitated, he came out and gave a long look back at Marnie, standing in her back doorway. He didn't appear furtive or mussed, so it must have been a business call. As Kat watched, he lit a cigarette, got in his vehicle and drove away. Kat longed for a plain car, to be able to tail him.

"Come on, Dilly-Dally," Kat said to the horse and patted her flank, "we're still hot on the trail of someone or other."

As if she were just arriving, Kat drove over to Marnie's. She wrapped the reins around the hitching post in the front yard next to several parking spots for guests. The post reminded Kat of Marnie's Amish heritage. It was thoughtful of her to treat the Amish and English as equals. But, since the parking spots were here in front, why did Clay drive around to the back? Didn't he want his vehicle to be seen from the street? To go in the back door seemed a familiar act.

The moment Kat walked up on the front porch, she heard Marnie's voice. Perhaps in casual conversation inside her own home, she would say something about Clay's visit. All this made Kat decide she would take

Gil Gilmore up on his offer to show her around Amish Acres. It was a good place to learn more about Clay and the union and to check out Marnie's new house.

Kat was up on the wide front porch before she realized Marnie must be on the phone. Her hand raised to knock, Kat stood like a statue, straining to hear.

"...can't believe I miss you so much already," Marnie was saying. "Yes, my darling, every minute we're apart." Pause. "It's not enough. I need you more and more..."

Kat flushed hot. This was eavesdropping at its worst and best. Were Marnie and Clay having an affair? But he'd left less than five minutes ago, so it seemed more likely she was talking to someone else.

"I know—I know you have a lot to do," Marnie was saying. "I just don't want her to find out about us. Until later, my love."

Who didn't they want to find out? Could they be onto her, or was there some other woman in the mix? Kat darted down the steps and strode away, praying Marnie didn't glance out her window to see that maneuver. Then, from halfway up the lawn, she called out, "Marnie, are you home?"

Marnie opened the front door. "Why, Katie, what a nice surprise. You've tracked me down," she said, evidently assuming Kat had gone to the restaurant first. "Come in! Is anything wrong? Ida's doing all right, isn't she? I meant to stop by, but I know how everyone will tend her without my help."

"*Ja,* she's doing as well as can be expected," Kat said as she stepped inside.

Unlike in Marnie's cluttered office, here in this eclectic living room nothing seemed amiss. A fine oak staircase led upstairs, and Kat could smell either lemon furniture polish or a scented candle. And, on the wall going up the staircase, she could see from here, were framed black-and-white photos, probably others Marnie's father had taken—or ones Marnie herself had shot.

"I'm really here for little Sarah, in a way," Kat said, taking a few steps in but not sitting as Marnie indicated she should. She'd felt trapped in Marnie's office when the woman started quizzing her, and today, she intended to ask the questions.

"For Sarah?" she said frowning. "I hardly know the child."

"Now, don't blame her for showing it to me, but I saw the photo you took of her mother."

"Ah, I see. I'm afraid I risked giving it to her in a weak moment."

"She treasures it. It was kind of you."

Marnie seemed to relax a bit. Kat went on. "I think you, like your father, have a gift for taking pictures. Sarah wondered if you had any of Bishop Brand for her to keep, and I told her I'd ask you."

"I see," she said again.

Only an hour ago, Kat might have asked Marnie if she'd taken any photos that might show someone watching the Amish, lurking in the background. Now she worried Marnie herself might have been lurking to take the photo of Sarah's mother. But why? Just her fascination with the Amish? The love of photography she didn't want to admit to? Some sort of tie to her father? Kat had often longed for photos of her parents, however bitter the memories.

"Obviously," Marnie said, one hand on her cocked hip, "that shot was taken years ago."

"But it's such a talent, if the photos are anything like your *Daad's*. Are those his on the staircase?"

"Some are, some might be mine," she said with a

slight shrug. "You know," she added, leveling a long look at Kat, "you're the first Amish person I've met who would praise a photograph."

Again Kat cursed her Amish cover. Frustrated, she longed to just flash a badge and grill this woman. But she got hold of herself again.

"Well, I'll be going. I just promised Sarah I'd ask. She told me your gardens were pretty, too, and she's sure right about that."

"You've been around behind the house?"

"Just saw a little from afar, when I drove up."

"What did Sarah say about my gardens?" Marnie asked as she opened the door. "I'm sorry I don't have the time to show you around right now. But I suppose, despite the Amish blood in me, I'm rather proud of them."

Kat knew exactly what Sarah had said, though it didn't all make sense. But she had the sudden instinct not to keep the child at the center of this conversation. Damn, she wished she could trust the sheriff, because she'd have him do a phony follow-up interview, say, about Marnie's windows being broken—anything to get her talking and steer her around to discussing her photography again. And maybe discussing her love life, whether it was with Clay Bigler or some other secret sweetheart.

As Kat drove Dilly back toward the Amish school-house, she admitted to herself she felt trapped. With a shudder she recalled being in Reuben's grain silo and later Bishop Brand's grave. Other than the Amish, she wasn't sure whom she could trust. She needed Sheriff Martin, but was afraid to tell him too much. She wasn't even sure that the local champion and guardian angel of the Amish, Marnie Girkins, was lily white.

Clay Bigler and Tyler Winslow and their Amish-hating minions were on her watch list, but it wasn't easy to get near enough to keep an eye on them. And kids like Mark, A.J. and their friends couldn't be discounted.

She decided to call Brooke.

Kat tied Dilly to the school hitching post, waved to the Amish guard who was walking the property and walked out into the trees beyond the playground. The scholars would be out soon; she'd promised Luke she'd get Eli and Sarah home safely.

She leaned against a tree and punched in the number Dan had given her. "Brooke? It's Kat. Anything new with Melly?"

"Oh, Kat. Dan said you might call. She's showing a lot more movement, so they had to restrain her."

"But that's good, right, the movement?"

"I guess, but I hate seeing her tied down. She's been talking, too. It's mostly nonsense, but, yes, I think it's good. Dan's gone to get some sleep. We were really relieved to hear Father Brand was found and buried. He said they had you to thank for that."

"I don't feel I'm owed thanks for anything. I just wanted to tell you that I've been in your house charging up my cell phone batteries, and I left my laptop there."

"That's fine. Which reminds me, Dan suggested I look up some info on hate crimes against the Amish. They didn't just happen in Europe years ago, unfortunately, but in the good, old U.S. of A.—currently too, especially in a neighboring state. Got time to hear it now?"

"Definitely. Shoot."

"It can't really be tied to what's going on in Maplecreek, I think, but here goes. This is in northern

Indiana. The Amish there have been targets of hate crimes for years. Their 'martyr mentality,' as a local newspaper put it, keeps them from going to the authorities, although it's become so bad, the police are in on it lately. So it's a real blessing our Amish have gone to the sheriff and have you on their side.''

''Is it young boys committing the crimes?''

''Right, and in groups, not as individuals.''

''Pack mentality.''

''Exactly. It's kind of a local heritage thing. The perps' uncles and fathers have done it as young men and it gets passed on.''

Their uncles and fathers... The words clung in Kat's mind as she pictured Sheriff Martin, Tyler Winslow and Mark coming to the farm to pay their respects to Bishop Brand.

''It's called *claping,*'' Brooke continued, ''which evidently comes from the fact the Indiana harassers call the Amish 'clay apes'—in other words, farmers.''

''That's so screwed up. And this is in the heartland of America in the new millennium, a kinder, gentler America? Doesn't this country have enough foreign terrorists threatening us that we don't need any within?''

''I know. It's tragic.''

''And local law enforcement is stretched to the limit right now,'' Kat said, ''which is partly why I'm here.''

''Which reminds me, months ago I had a conversation with Maplecreek's new sheriff about his son's paper on the Amish. When Jen was going with Mark, Dan and I both read it. The sheriff wanted to get it printed in the *Maplecreek Weekly,* but then he said he didn't want to give local kids any ideas. He'd have to lock every last one of them up, if they so much as threw rotten eggs at a buggy.''

Didn't that mean, Kat thought, that the sheriff could not possibly, not conceivably, be involved in any of this or be covering up for someone who was? Or did it mean he had just been diverting suspicion from himself?

Trying to concentrate, Kat squeezed the bridge of her nose between her thumb and finger. Talk about a martyr mentality. Her own cop mentality was imprisoning her again: she feared everyone was suspect, everyone was hiding something. But here in Amish country, maybe she had to change that thinking. Perhaps she had to risk trusting her police boss. She'd done that on the streets of Columbus. Even when times were tough, her sergeants had been stand-up guys.

"So Ray Martin's relationship with his son is pretty good?" Kat asked.

"I think so. I heard the two of them did have one knock-down-drag-out fight, though, over Mark's fascination with all kinds of guns. I suppose the sheriff saw enough of the damage they can do when he was a sharpshooter in the Marines, and didn't want his kid to get involved with guns."

Kat had known Ray Martin had served in the military, but not as a sharpshooter. And Mark was fascinated with all kinds of guns? Her stomach cramped.

Brooke went on. "And here, Mark's uncle is head of the Patriot Knights militia, and you know they've got guns galore out there on their shooting range. Well, as long as they don't hurt anyone, this is America, land of the free and of free speech."

"Brooke, could you do one more favor for me?"

"If I can do it from Melly's hospital room."

"I hate asking this since I have my laptop available now, but I've got to go back to being Amish. Could you background some top-of-my-list locals online?"

"I can Google with the best of them. I'm guessing you want Sheriff Martin included? I'd tell you you're crazy, but it pays to check every angle. I had a big run-in with his predecessor once, where I suspected his motives, and he turned out to be okay. I learned that you can't always tell a book by its cover, and this could be the opposite situation. Ray Martin might just look clean. Who else? Tyler Winslow?"

"Damn, you're good. And Clay Bigler, head of the UWC Union."

"Speaking of 'clay apes,' huh? Dan says he's got a really bad temper. Okay, you got it."

Kat knew not to bother with Reuben Coblentz, not because she'd deleted him from her list but because surely he wouldn't show up online. Unfortunately, research on him would have to continue to be the up-close and personal kind.

"And one more," Kat said. "Marnie Girkins."

"No way!"

"Just covering all my bases. Do you know if she dates anyone?"

"I don't think so. I always thought she was married to her many business interests and hobbies."

"Do those hobbies include photography?"

"Not that I know of. More like all kinds of gardening, *A* to *Z*—azaleas to zinnias."

"Brooke, I can't thank you enough. Listen, the school bell's about to ring and I've got to get Sarah and Eli back to the farm."

"Call me soon—it won't do to have your phone going off under that apron or bonnet."

Despite everything, they shared a laugh. Brooke, Kat thought as she gave her cell-phone number and punched off, was a blessing, a gift from God in all this. As she hid the phone up her sleeve, she shook her head. Just a few weeks ago, she never would have thought of anything as a blessing. Like it or not, she was being Amishized.

After dinner that evening, as dusk bled to darkness outside, Kat washed the dishes and Ida insisted on wiping them dry in Luke's kitchen. Kat had assembled a meal for the family from casserole dishes Amish neighbors had brought over today. A few weeks ago, that would have felt like a major accomplishment, but now it seemed like nothing.

"You know, Ida, I think I'm getting the bug to learn how to fix a few of the dishes I especially like."

"Next week's the corn harvest, with lots of food. You just ask the Amish sisters for recipes to take with you when you go."

Sisters, Kat thought. Even the word sounded wonderful to a woman who'd had but one brother and had managed to let him slip away. And, Kat mused, Ida's double-edged comments no longer bothered her. That was just Ida, kind and supportive but painfully honest. But still, Kat knew she should hope she would be leaving the Amish soon, because that would mean she'd found their tormentors.

Though Ida soon collapsed onto a kitchen chair, Kat saw her inner strength, especially in the way she reached out to others despite the loss of her husband. And Ida did not blame herself for Jacob eating her pie and falling fatally ill. Had Kat's guilt about her brother's death led her to make reckless choices as an adult? Perhaps it wasn't really her fault Jay died, even if running away with him had caused them to be placed in separate foster homes.

How far those foster homes seemed from this kitchen, this house, these people. What was the magic, the allure? Luke, sat in the front room reading a book on European history, but leaned back in his rocker now and then to glance down the hall at her. The kids were with him, doing homework, but they called out questions to her as often as they asked their father.

It was a simple but strangely sweet and peaceful scene, especially since next week the rush to get the ripe corn harvested would begin. But even then, order would prevail: Luke had said the church families shared a big old combine, now stored in Paul Yoder's barn. The Amish worked as a team, the women covering chores and fixing food, the men working in one field after the other until everyone's harvest was home.

"I'm going to sleep in my own bed tonight," Ida suddenly announced, jolting Kat from her musings.

After Ida said good-night to Luke and the children, Kat walked her toward the *daadi haus* while Luke oversaw preparations for Eli's and Sarah's baths. Eli, who wouldn't let anyone but Kat put the drops in his eye lately, came running out after them.

"Katie, Katie, are you coming back to put my eye stuff in?"

"I'll be back after you take that bath," she told him and bent to brush his bangs from his forehead. The boy needed a haircut as well as a bath. Luke usually trimmed it, so she'd have to remind him, because Eli certainly wouldn't.

As Kat turned toward Ida, she saw a dark form move against the barn. She gasped and pulled Eli behind her, then stepped in front of Ida so that the child was sandwiched between them.

Her heart thudded in her throat. Just when she was tempted to throw all three of them to the ground, she thought she recognized the slouched silhouette. "Reuben, is that you?" she called.

"*Ja,*" he said, stepping from the shadows.

For the first time, Kat feared the target might be Eli. The boy was the common factor in the three early attacks: he was with the sprayed quilts, at the bonfire, and at the school. He'd been in the surrey behind the hearse. If so, did that mean Reuben was out for revenge? But her female instincts, as well as her cop training, told her he meant no harm, at least right now.

"I want to hire Luke," Reuben said, coming closer, "to put my windmill back up—a business deal. I'll pay good, not a favor this time. Jacob Ida," he said in way of acknowledgement, taking another step forward. He must know he was close to Eli. Surely he hadn't been spying on them. Kat's heart still beat hard.

"Reuben," Ida said, her voice sharp, "have you been hiding in our barn?"

"No, though I wished I coulda come to Jacob's funeral, even if I'd had to stand outside for it, to pay my respects. Ida, I'm sorry he's gone, even if to a better place. I haven't been here but a few minutes. Walked over to leave this note, see?" he added and came closer, holding out a folded piece of paper. "And I haven't been drinking tonight."

Despite the growing dark, Kat had been scanning him for a weapon. He had none, unless it was stuck in his back waistband or a jacket pocket. He wore jeans and a dark leather jacket. Damn, were those jeans navy or black? And had Luke been sure the motorbike rider was in black jeans as well as a black leather jacket? Kat had asked Luke if the boots Mark Martin had on the other day looked like the motorbiker's, and he'd said he wasn't sure. What would he say about this outfit? The guy who threw the fireworks still could have been Reuben, however sympathetic he'd seemed lately.

"I'll give Luke the note," Kat said when Ida didn't reach for it. The two women still had Eli wedged between them, but the boy sidestepped, pulling free from Ida's hands on his shoulders.

"I can do it, 'cause I gotta go get my bath," he said.

Reuben handed him the paper but didn't let go of it right away. For one moment they both clung to it as if they held hands.

"Real sorry about your eye, Eli," Reuben said. As the man bent down to Eli's height, Kat wondered if he was apologizing or comforting his grandson.

"He got whipped in the eye with a tree branch," Ida piped up. "But you'd best get the beam out of your own eye, Reuben Coblentz. Then you could return to your people again. Maybe you could be a help, *ja,* since Eli just lost his grandfather and a boy needs at least one."

Reuben gave a loud sniffle and took off down the driveway at a quick jog, before, she surmised, anyone could see he was crying.

"Got something for you," Sheriff Martin said when Kat and Luke met him on the covered bridge at ten the next night.

She wondered if he was going to give her a cell phone and felt a twinge of guilt that she hadn't told him she had one, as well as access to her laptop. But he held something dark out toward her; she couldn't tell what it was at first. Then she saw it was a dirty black Amish bonnet, one with straw still clinging to it.

"Where did you get that?" she blurted.

"My brother-in-law's guards, as they call them, found it on Knight property. Tyler was nice enough to suggest I get it back to the Amish, so I thought maybe you could get it to the woman who carelessly left it behind.''

Kat's mind raced. She hadn't told the sheriff or even Luke about how close she'd gotten to the Knights during their party.

''Where did your brother-in-law's guards find it?'' Luke asked.

''Strangely enough, under some bales of straw that were right in the middle of a private party. And, frankly, like Tyler, I can't quite figure how it could have gotten there, 'cause you never told me a thing about going undercover to that foolhardy and dangerous an extent, Kat. And after you nearly got shot the first time, with that rifle? At least you told me about that.''

The sheriff, she saw, wasn't letting up on her. He was onto the fact she'd been holding things back, but did he suspect why? If he, or Tyler Winslow, for that matter, had anything to do with hate crimes against the Amish, why would they return this bonnet? Even if the worst-case scenario were true and the sheriff had told Winslow who she really was, why would they try to warn her off like this? Wouldn't they just try to stop her one way or the other?

''I know how that probably got there,'' Luke said, before Kat could decide which way to go with this.

''*You* do?'' the sheriff said.

''The roads and fields adjoining Patriot Knight land are the best place to see the Fourth of July fireworks the Knights shoot off every year. You know that, Sheriff. Some of the Amish buggy out to see them. An Amish woman lying on a blanket must have left her bonnet behind, and it got raked up or stuck somehow on the bottom of the bales. That would be my first guess—though, I suppose the bales could have been sold by the Amish originally and a woman helping to harvest or bale the straw just lost it.''

The sheriff looked annoyed; Kat was relieved that Luke had ridden to her rescue.

''Or,'' the sheriff said, ''it could be from some woman who lost her head as well as her bonnet. You got anything to add to that, Katie Kurtz?''

''Luke knows the Amish so much better than I do, Sheriff.''

''Well, I've got something to add,'' he said, flinging the limp bonnet at her so hard that a few pieces of straw flew off. ''Anything important happens—or you decide to go in to spy on the Knights or the carpenters' union up close, or whatever—you let me know first. Got that?''

''If it's possible, under the circumstances,'' she said.

''You don't and you're off this case, fired. And I'd hate to lose you, Kat. I'd *hate* to lose you.''

Luke managed to hold in his anger until he and Kat were in his buggy. He gripped the reins so hard that Sandy came to a dead stop before he eased up. He knew he was going to explode.

''You went onto Knight land during a party?'' he demanded as they headed back toward the farm. ''Up close when they were all there? You trespassed not once but twice?''

''Luke, do you think I can make any progress just playing proper Amish around the school or the farm? Yes, I went twice, and I wish I had some way to get in there again!''

''I covered for you, but I'm starting to agree with the sheriff. You can't keep this up.''

"Amish children—including your son and niece—have been abused and harmed, your father's body has been defiled, and you want me to back off or quit?"

"No, but I don't think your cover is working well enough. What if Tyler Winslow has guessed you're not really Amish?"

"What if the sheriff told him, you mean?"

"You're suddenly afraid to trust the sheriff. Do you know something dirty about him?"

"Only that he has personal ties I don't like—ones he didn't tell me about at first, when I should have been forewarned."

"Like I didn't tell you all about Reuben at first? So do you suspect me, too? Trust is a big problem with you and it's getting in the way."

He hadn't meant to be so confrontational with her. This woman was making his head and heart spin faster than a windmill in a gale. The other day he'd accused her of becoming more Amish, but she made him feel more English—as least less his stoic, steady self. Around her, he wanted to shout and worse—put his hands all over her.

"Don't be ridiculous," she argued. "Look, it's a mistake that you feel responsible for me. Our...your feelings are what's getting in the way. I want to do this job not only because I'm a cop at heart, but because I care deeply for your people. So you're going to have to stand back and let me do it—trust me to do it."

"Not if you can be hurt in the process. I can't allow that."

"Luke, you are my host and my friend, but you are not my boss, not my betrothed, not my husband. If you ask me to leave, I will, but I'm hoping you'll let me stay among the Amish."

I'm hoping you'll let me stay among the Amish. He clung to those words, wishing she'd said them at another time and meant another thing.

She continued. ''Both your father and now Bishop Yoder have said they believe it's God's will that I'm here to help.''

''Do you believe it's God's will?'' he asked as he turned out onto Ridge Road and saw the distant lights of the farmhouse.

''I'm starting to, I really am.''

''Then that's enough for me,'' he told her with a single nod.

But the more he saw her stubborn strength and lonely courage, the more he couldn't bear to leave her on her own. Next week he'd be busy with harvesting and he'd promised Paul Yoder he'd repair his broken windmill so his family would get water from their well again. He also wanted to get Reuben's windmill put back up soon as a statement of good faith, for his mother had said she sensed the old man yearned to return to the Amish fold.

How Luke wished he could protect Kat during those hours he'd be away from her. How he longed to keep her safe, locked in his heart and loved forever.

16

Kat flinched each time the *ba-bang* of nail guns sounded. Roofers were fastening shingles on two houses as Gil Gilmore showed her and Lee around Amish Acres on Saturday afternoon. The sharp cracks were so much like gunfire that Kat kept having reflex reactions.

Gil only laughed. "You get used to it," he said. "Just pretend it's a buggy backfiring—or the horse."

He chuckled, but Lee and Kat didn't laugh. They were both tense, and Kat was trying to take everything in without appearing to be nosy. She wished she could wipe the smirk off Gil's face by telling him she'd once seen a fourteen-year-old gangbanger with a framer's 16-penny stud nail driven to the hilt into his forehead by a nail gun. When the squad car that Kat had called to the scene was in an accident en route, she and Mike had driven the kid to the ER. Those nail guns were damn dangerous; the doctor who had treated the boy said they packed the same wallop as a .22-calibre pistol.

Today, except for the roofers, other workers had quit for the day, so Kat was doubly glad she'd brought Lee. So far, Gil had been on his best behavior, though his level of humor was starting to remind her of A.J. Bigler's.

"You don't realize," Kat said, "how big these houses are until you look in the basements." Gazing down into the cleanly cut-out rectangle, she couldn't help but think of Bishop Brand's grave.

"*Ja,* a lot could be stored down there," Lee said, nodding in agreement. "I hope no one falls in when it's dark."

"No one's around except the night watchman, in case someone tries to steal building supplies," Gil said, pointing at his sales office. Kat assumed—hoped—that was where the watchman hung out. "Even in small-town Amish America," Gil added, shaking his head, "weirder things have happened."

Kat was tempted to say, *Tell me about it,* but she kept quiet. "They'll be pouring concrete for this house on Monday," Gil informed them. "This way, then. I'll show you Mrs. Girkins's house, since you asked."

Kat jerked again as a nail gun sounded. They turned down Pinwheel Quilt Road, then continued to the back of the development. They had told Gil they'd walk instead of being driven in his car, but she hadn't imagined it would be this far.

Marnie's mansion—Kat could not call it anything else—sat at the back of a cul-de-sac at the very edge of the development. It was still in its skeletal form, beams and two-by-fours defining the rooms on three visible levels: downstairs, upstairs, and spacious attic above the poured basement. The bare bones of staircases were in place and window openings were framed. The ribs of a multi-gabled, massive roof hovered overhead. Like Marnie's present place, the house was backed by a large yard and small woodlot, one of the few in sight, since this area had formerly been farmers' fields.

"A great space and setting for her gardens, that's for sure," Kat observed as they stood in the dirt driveway.

"Oh, yeah. I guess I told you she's going to have an attached greenhouse, too. And some of the most fabulous custom-built woodworking you've ever seen."

"Amish-built?" Kat asked.

"Maybe Amish-finished," Gil said, thrusting his hands in his pants pockets and rocking slightly back on his heels.

He had a nervous habit of jingling coins in his pockets—something she hadn't noticed before. Perhaps he was especially on edge for some reason today.

"She's paying extra for union carpentry work," he added. "I've seen the drawings and specs for it. Mrs. Girkins likes special touches."

So that, Kat thought, might explain the manila folder Clay Bigler had carried into Marnie's house. Or did *special touches* mean more than Gil was letting on? He was good at double entendres.

"I guess Mr. Bigler's doing a lot of work here," Kat said.

"Oh, yeah. Even moved his office over there," Gil told them, pointing to a tan metal trailer pulled up close to Marnie's lot and situated back by the trees. "It used to be over by the sales office, but the union guys are working on these houses—though your carpenters are, too. Look, ladies, you should tell your menfolk there's no hard feelings on my part about the union-Amish disagreement. I think the Amish do great work and all. And obviously, you two are fine examples of that."

Kat leveled a look at him, then forced herself to glance away rather than stare him down. She had never quite been able to discern if the man was flirting. He was a much more clever guy, she suspected, than she'd given him credit for. She should have known better than to dismiss him as just another glib salesman.

From afar, Kat studied the exterior of Clay's trailer, where he probably kept that manila folder he'd carried into Marnie's house. Beyond the regular keyhole of the trailer, she saw no extra lock on Clay's office door. In her tough teenage years, she'd learned a thing or two about picking locks. Night guard or not, as soon as she could, Kat and her flashlight were coming back here. She knew she'd be crossing a line, committing a B and E, but she didn't know if she could trust the sheriff and she'd never felt more desperate. From now on, if she was going to protect Luke and his people, she really was on her own.

From Amish Acres, Kat and Lee buggied to Yoders' farm to watch Luke try to repair the jammed vane on the windmill. It sat behind a long, low storage shed so that only its upper two-thirds could be seen from the house or road. As much as Kat was intrigued to see Luke scale the tall tower, she especially wanted to talk to Paul and Mary Yoder about their neighbors, the Winslows.

When Lee and Kat arrived, Ida, Mose Susan, her kids, three Yoder grandchildren, and Eli and Sarah already made up an audience, sitting at a distance on the ground behind the shed and watching Luke high up and Paul halfway up the windmill. The spectators were all sitting, except Eli, who insisted on standing, as if that little extra height put him closer to his dad.

Eli's belly felt like that time he'd eaten too many green apples. His *daad* was doing the thing that worried Eli most, hanging high in the sky like he was in the clouds. Every time he did that, it made Eli think of *Mamm* in heaven up there. And it scared him that *Daad* could slip, even with that safety belt on. He could fall and die and join her and *Grossvater* Jacob in the clouds with God. And if *Daad* did that, Sarah and Eli would have to be without him, too.

That's why Eli was glad that Katie was coming now with Teacher Leah. Katie made him feel safer. His eye still on his *daad,* Eli ran to meet them.

"He's being real careful," Eli assured them. "He's got on his safety belt, but Bishop Yoder's only got himself tied on with ripped pieces of sheets."

Katie ruffled his hair like she did sometimes. He liked that a lot. He wished the story about her wanting to wed *Daad* could be true, but he knew better. She was still English under those Amish clothes.

"Don't you worry," she told him, shading her eyes to look up, even if the sky was kind of dark today. "Your father is very good at what he does."

"I'm going to help with our corn harvest!" he told her, hoping that didn't sound prideful. "Taking water out to the men in the fields, *ja,* watering the horses, too. The corn combine has a real wide cutting blade that goes back and forth. But I'm old enough now to stay away from it and know when they need water at the ends of rows."

"I can't wait to see all that," Katie said as she waved at Sarah and the child waved back.

At least, Eli thought, his little sister didn't hate Katie like she used to. Sarah might even cry some when Katie found the evildoers and went back to really being English. When Katie could drive a car again, Eli would call her on the phone from *Daad's* office and ask her to drive him to the hospital in Columbus to see how Melly was doing. Sometimes he kind of blamed himself for Melly getting hurt more than he did. The blurry vision in his eye was going away some, but Melly was still sick.

"Be careful, *Daad!*" he called up because he just couldn't help himself, even though he knew God up there in those clouds should take care of everything. But sometimes the way God saw things wasn't the way Eli did.

"You be careful, too, Katie," Eli added quietly, grabbing her wrist when she touched his head again. "I heard *Daad* saying to Bishop Yoder that you got to be careful."

"I will, Eli," she promised. "I will."

Kat estimated that Luke was at least forty feet in the air on the windmill platform, mounted where the legs of the tower joined, just under the rotors. Something had jammed the vane so the mill itself would not turn to catch the shifting winds. Paul was on one of the metal supports halfway up, watching more than he was helping, but occasionally he hoisted Luke tools on a rope pulley they'd rigged.

Mary came out with a big tray of cider and doughnuts to greet them. "Luke's refusing to take anything for the repair work," she told Kat. "He said he's never seen a vane get jammed like that before. Looks like it's been used for target practice, too. He says there's bullet holes in the vane."

Kat cupped her hands around her mouth and yelled up to Luke, "Shots from the direction of the road?"

"Can't tell, since the vane was probably still rotating then," he called down. "No, here's where one dinged the tower. Looks like from the east."

Kat gazed in the direction of the field of pumpkins that lay between Yoders' farm and Winslows' spread. But anyone could have stood in that field to take potshots at the new bishop's windmill. The shooter might have known Luke had installed the windmill or would come to fix it, if it were broken. Kat's adrenaline level ratcheted up; she began to sweat. She scanned the field and the Yoder property on the far side of it. If Luke's windmills had been targeted again, was it some sort of second warning to him?

"As Eli said, please be careful up there!" she shouted to him. "And enjoy the view!"

"I hear you. I'm looking around, but we're not going to live lives filled with fear."

"That's right," Paul agreed, leaning out from his makeshift ties to look down. "We fear only what the Lord can do, not men. We will not give in to their terrorism."

"Don't you fret about any of that right now," Mary told Kat, gently bumping her arm with the food tray. "You just sit on down with us. No, here—take one of the pillow-shaped ones, Katie," she insisted when Kat reached for a glazed doughnut-hole. "I got the big ones filled with custard, *ser gut!*"

Kat helped Mary serve the others and made sure she sat by her when they all settled down on blankets to watch again. But Kat stood from time to time, pretending to stretch, so she could assure herself no one was in the east field. Her ears were attuned to any vehicle that slowed down on the road, even though she had to walk out from behind the shed to see it.

"So your farm abuts Winslow land," Kat said to Mary, a plump, smiling woman who, Kat had heard, loved to read.

"Oh, *ja*. Tried to be neighborly more than once, we did," Mary told her as they both kept their gazes on the men aloft. "But Tyler is never at the house, and she's so—so different."

"Different how?" Kat asked, as she licked the last bit of custard from her fingers. "I heard she was reclusive, but why?"

"I don't think she's sick in the head, but she's strange. Dresses old-fashioned—well, I can see you're going to laugh at me for that—but not Amish. Louise Winslow dresses...just different. The only place I seen her this year was at the library bookmobile, which stops over there special. I'd missed it so I ran over, and there she was checking out a stack of books in a sort of angel dress."

"An angel dress? White and flowing?"

"*Ja.* Down to her feet. Had on lots of makeup, too, pinkish rouge, she did."

"Do you know any reason she might be eccentric?" Kat asked.

"Never had children and wanted to bad, I heard. Had visits about adoption but wasn't permitted or something. I hear Tyler said he'd have none of that fancy new medical test-tube baby stuff. Like I said, she stays home, and he's always gone."

It wasn't much to go on, Kat thought. And no cornfield stood between the two farms to hide her so she could sneak over to get a look at or least try to talk to the elusive Louise Winslow. Again, Kat eyed Yoder's pumpkin patch with its big, bulbous gourds. From here, their tangled vines made the field look like a plate of green spaghetti with orange meatballs.

"I'm not sure the Winslows even live together anymore," Mary whispered when Kat thought the subject was closed. "She has a little house out back I've seen her kind of float in and out of."

Speak of the devil, Kat thought, as Tyler Winslow's noisy combine approached on the road, with him in the driver's seat. Before she even saw it, Kat recognized the sound and went to look around the corner of the shed. No one accompanied him this time as he halted on the road at the end of Yoders' short driveway.

Kat almost panicked, since Luke was a sitting duck up there, but she saw no gun—only Tyler's face pressed against the window of his lofty driver's seat as he looked up at Luke and Paul. Kat thought he might turn in to inquire what the men were doing, but he ground the gears and drove on.

So, Kat thought, the coast was clear for her to visit Louise Winslow. She'd decided on her cover story: she wanted the Winslows to know that the accident at Reuben Coblentz's silo had not harmed her and she didn't hold them responsible in any way. That certainly sounded Amish.

But would a woman as strange as Louise Winslow even answer the door? It was worth the old CPD try. A glimpse inside or a few words with the woman would surely throw more light on the amazing Tyler Winslow. Just as Marnie Girkins was a sort of Renaissance woman, Tyler seemed a man of many talents. Successful farmer, Patriot Knight commander, city council member, possible mayoral candidate. Was all that to keep himself busy and away from home because his wife was "weird"?

When Luke came down for a break, Kat told him, "I'm going to walk over to Winslows' and see if I can meet his wife."

"At least he's not home. That was him in the combine, right?"

Kat nodded.

"But if she tells him, it might put him onto you."

"I'll say I just wanted him to know I'm fine and don't hold any grudges—forgive him."

"He could come back."

"You think I wouldn't hear him coming in that machine? I'll never forget the sound. Luke, from that vantage point on the windmill, you can practically keep an eye on me, can't you?"

"Don't stay long," he said, squeezing her hands in both of his. "The weather forecast is for thunderstorms—"

"I don't care if I get wet, and I— Oh, you mean the storm could be a danger to you."

He nodded. "The windmill's mostly metal, and I won't want to get down until I see you walking back."

She laughed and squeezed his hands in return. At least it was getting easier to convince him she could handle this investigation alone. "I promised Eli I'll be careful, and the visit won't take long."

Kat felt both curious and confident as she walked the edge of the pumpkin patch toward Winslows'. Their place boasted a big, handsome house that reminded her of prewar Tara in *Gone With The Wind*. They had two red barns and a white silo so large it looked like a rocket on a launching pad. So why, Kat wondered, had Tyler bothered to rent Reuben's little silo? A payoff, of sorts? An agreement to bury that motorbike? Or did he actually need extra storage space?

The twisted pumpkin vines snagged her foot, even on the edge of the field, when she looked back to see if Luke was up the windmill again. He was, silhouetted against dark clouds clumped on the western horizon. She almost tripped again when she stared ahead at the Winslow buildings. No one was in sight. She could only hope that Louise would come to the door when she knocked.

From this angle, Kat could see the little house Mary had mentioned. It sat behind the barns and was not so small after all, maybe a one-bedroom place. It seemed an enchanted cottage from a fairy tale, Kat mused, with elaborate gingerbread woodworking along the eaves, a fence spilling late red roses, and ruffled white curtains beckoning at open windows.

Pulling her attention away from the allure of the little place, Kat rang the doorbell next to the front double doors to the big house. She heard it ring inside, but no one answered. Shading her eyes to keep her image from staring back at her, Kat looked in a front window. Masculine furniture, leather and wood. Dark-paneled walls and Persian area rugs. Elegant old-English hunting prints next to laden bookshelves and a big-screen TV. And, over the hearth, in an impressive wooden frame, the too-familiar flag of the screeching eagle landing on the globe.

She descended the porch steps and made her way around toward the small house. Both barns and the big silo were shut. She resisted the temptation to look in, not because the sheriff had warned her to steer clear of such, but because she didn't want a farm hand like Winslow's Jake keeping her from the cottage.

As she neared the building she noted that, unlike most picket fences which had spaces between the white-painted boards, this one was solid with thorny roses past their prime clinging to it. Should she call out or just go up on the front porch and knock?

Kat walked close enough to be able to look over the fence—

She halted and gasped. Still as a statue and completely naked, a woman with closed eyes lay faceup on a white sheet spread on the grass. Splotches of stark white and brutal red scarred her skin; she looked severely burned or beaten.

17

Brooke couldn't believe what she read. After Google-ing "Tyler Winslow" online, she had opened the Patriot Knights Web site. Perched on the single chair by Melly's hospital bed, she hunched farther forward, her eyes wide and her mouth agape at the site's jingoistic, vitriolic language.

Not that it would prove anything directly, but she'd have to judge Winslow and his pseudo-militia a lot more dangerous than she'd imagined. At least whoever wrote this garbage was an equal-prejudice employer: "Our fatherland," one article on the visually dynamic site began, "is going to the dogs, namely, foreigners breeding like bitches, including Mexicans, Africans, Haitians and the German Amish."

"The German Amish!" Brooke whispered. "Wait until Kat sees this."

As she glanced up, she almost dropped the laptop off her knees. For the first time since the accident, Melly's eyes were not only open but were staying that way. She seemed to be staring straight ahead at the wall, as if looking into some vast space where Brooke could not go.

Putting the laptop on her chair, Brooke stood slowly, not wanting to startle her daughter.

"Melly? It's Mom," she whispered. Then, when the child didn't blink, turn her eyes or move, Brooke said louder, "Melly, it's Mom."

Dear God, she was breathing, wasn't she? Brooke glanced at the monitors. Nothing beeped or changed. Yes, her chest rose and fell. Brooke bent down to take her hand, though her wrists were still restrained. "Melly, can you see me?"

"I know who it is," she said distinctly.

Melly knew her! She recognized her. She was coming out of the coma. She would get better.

Brooke's heart slammed against her chest. Tears of joy blurred her vision. She had to get a doctor in here to be sure Melly didn't slip back. Though Brooke's hands were trembling, she grabbed the call button at the head of the bed and pressed it. Dan had gone to get carryout from a restaurant because they were sick of hospital cafeteria food. She wanted him back *now*.

"Do you know who Dad is, too?" Brooke asked. "And Jen? Do you remember what happened to you?"

"I know who it is," she repeated. "Who did it."

Brooke's hopes plummeted. Had Melly recognized her or not? Or was she just reciting something from her imprisoned memory? The last time she spoke it was about someone "coming," and now this.

The nurse was the first to respond. "What is it, Mrs. Brand?" she asked as she rushed to the bed. "Oh, good," she said when she saw Melly. "New signs of perceptivity."

"I— She spoke, and I thought she knew me." Brooke's voice shook as hard as her body. "But, if it wasn't that," she added, almost to herself as the nurse scanned the monitors and the doctor on the floor hurried in and bent over the bed, too, "could she know who did it?"

"Did what?" the doctor asked as he held Melly's

now heavy-looking lids open to shine a light into both her pupils.

Brooke went on, trying to keep her voice steady. "The neurologist told me that she'd probably never be able to recall the trauma—what caused this."

Busy with Melly, he nodded.

"Then she couldn't have meant that," Brooke murmured into her hands pressed over her mouth. "Just couldn't."

"What do you mean by this—this invasion of my privacy!" the naked woman cried and yanked the sheet over herself like a shroud. She had short, stark black hair that framed her head like a dark halo.

"I'm sorry," Kat said, turning her back. "I had no idea someone would be there. I just wanted to stop to tell the Winslows I'm all right, *ja,* that's all. I thought Mr. Winslow might be worried after my accident."

"Oh," the woman said. Kat could tell from the sound of her voice that she was standing now.

"I thought you might be selling produce or baked goods. I'm Mrs. Winslow."

Kat dared a look back. Wrapped in and hooded by the sheet, Louise Winslow was pulling on elbow-length white gloves. She stared at Kat through sunglasses so huge and dark they looked like goggles. And then, to Kat's amazement, she bent to retrieve a cigarette and lighter from the grass. She lit it and inhaled deeply. She was smoking left-handed. *Left-*handed!

"You startled me, that's all, and I suppose I startled you," Louise Winslow said, her voice now warm and calm.

She was a tall, sturdy woman with what once must have been a very striking face. It was striking now only because of its bizarre patchwork of deep pink and white coloring. Was she an albino burned by the sun?

"I don't mean to stare," Kat explained, "but, *ja,* you startled me."

"Did my husband hit your buggy? What accident?"

So Tyler hadn't told his wife. Perhaps they were estranged. Kat could not picture the handsome, self-confident man with this poor creature. If he had been at that Patriot Knights harvest party, she'd bet Louise wasn't with him.

"I was in a silo when he latched the door," Kat explained, "and then Jake in the combine started to fill it with grain."

"Dreadful! Almost buried alive—I can sympathize with that."

Kat realized she was dealing with a bright if odd person. For some inexplicable reason that went deeper than pity, she liked Louise Winslow. Perhaps her left-handedness was pure coincidence.

"I have psoriasis, if you're wondering," Louise said, exhaling perfect rings of smoke that the breeze immediately ripped to shreds. "Not many know. It comes and goes, but I don't come and go, not looking like this anyway. If you saw how I go out, you'd never recognize me." She muttered a strange little laugh. "It helps to sunbathe, you see, even though it's a bit late in the year. I'm in a very bad stage with it now. Lately my doctor is claiming it's stress-related, but then, isn't everything they can't really cure stress-related in this day and age?"

Kat racked her brain for what she knew about psoriasis and came up with nothing. "What is the treatment, Mrs. Winslow?"

She shrugged, then said, "I soak myself in the Dead

Sea salts I buy online. I do all my shopping and living online, it seems.''

Kat could not believe the woman was so talkative. Perhaps she was lonely, or thought an Amish woman was harmless or didn't count. She hadn't asked Kat's name, and Kat hadn't given it. "Life must be very difficult," Kat said.

"Sometimes I'm not sure who I am anymore," she admitted, holding out both gloved hands as if in supplication. "I get so scaly I don't even have fingerprints."

Kat nodded, as her mind raced for ways to keep her talking. How could she get her back on the subject of her husband? "Why do you have this cottage, when you have such a lovely house?"

"Because this is *mine*. I watched over every bit of its construction, even helped put the roof on. It's my escape, my refuge and haven, my Petite Trianon."

"Petite what?"

"I forgot you speak German. You see, Queen Marie Antoinette of France hated the grandeur and demands of living at the Palace of Versailles with the king. She disliked his friends, too. So she spent her time at a lovely place called the Petite Trianon."

Kat simply nodded again. She was starting to see that she was better off interviewing this woman by keeping her mouth shut.

"King Louis loved to hunt, he loved his clock collection, his workshops, his friends, everything but her, though she was faithful to him. As a matter of fact, she did things to help him on the sly. Do you know what she said, even when they took her away and imprisoned her, before they carted her out to the guillotine?"

Astounded at everything about Louise, Kat shook her head.

"'Courage!'" Louise said, gesturing grandly. "'I have shown it for years; think you I shall lose it at the moment when my sufferings are ended?'"

"Did the queen secretly resent her husband? She seemed to be harmless, living at the Trianon," Kat dared, wondering how much Louise was talking about her own life, "but would she do something to make him look bad or to bring him down?"

"She never did—but she should have," Louise declared with a decisive nod that pulled her head free of her hood. "As I said, the silly woman was so honorable that she helped him, even though he didn't deserve it one bit."

Louise's hair was wild and free; Kat imagined she yearned for her life to be wild and free, too.

"I'm glad," Louise continued, "that you weren't hurt by my husband's voracious nature to control everything—to rule, just like the French king, until, that is, he was ruined by a revolution he didn't see coming."

Kat thought she gave that low laugh again, but it was the rumble of distant thunder. She turned to see if Luke was still up the windmill across the field. He was. And a line of dark sky was splitting from the lighter part. She had to go back.

"I'm sorry I invaded your lovely space," she told Louise before she realized that she'd stopped trying to sound Amish. She had let her guard down with this woman and that wasn't wise. "But I'm not sorry I got to meet you, *ja*."

"Come back sometime, only don't come so close without calling out. What was your name again?" Louise asked.

"Katie Kurtz, come from Pennsylvania to marry Luke Brand," Kat said as she started away. Another roll of thunder echoed. She felt somehow worse about lying to Louise than she had about putting on an elaborate charade with so many others.

It was ludicrous to think the woman had anything to do with throwing windmill blades through windows or riding a motorbike, Kat scolded herself. Louise was a loner and a recluse, so how would she get a motorbike or fireworks, let alone a canister to spray chicken manure or paintballs? If she'd ordered any or all of that online, wouldn't Tyler find out, or did she have her own money? Surely a deserted wife wouldn't be working with her husband on any of that.

And then a thread of thought Kat had ignored occurred to her. Mary had said something about Louise that she had passed right over. Kat turned back and came closer again.

"Mrs. Winslow, do you have any children?"

The easy stance disappeared and her demeanor stiffened. She took another drag on her cigarette. "No, and to tell the truth, I think your people have far too many. Just too many for one family to rear well. If you're wedding Luke Brand, you'll have an instant family, won't you, as I believe he's a widower with a boy and a girl. And then you'll no doubt have a brood of your own on top of that."

Gooseflesh prickled Kat's arms. The woman's voice had gone taunting, almost goading. Louise knew specifics about Luke, about his children.

"Yes," Kat said. "The—we Amish love our children. Did Queen Marie have any?"

"Finally, when her husband began to cohabit with her—the ignorant, foolish man."

Kat saw distant lightning lurch from the clouds.

From her vantage point, it seemed a fiery finger pointed at Louise's head.

"I have to go," Kat called and, lifting her hem to her knees, broke into a jog toward the pumpkin field. Luckily, Luke and Paul were off the windmill. "Good to meet you!" she called over her shoulder.

Was that poor woman a saint in exile or a demon in disguise? Surely she was not so embittered that she helped her husband hurt children like the ones she could never have. Perhaps, if she acted without Tyler, she was intent on setting him up as the one behind it all. But, if so, who in heaven's name could Louise be working with?

Kat glanced back one more time. Louise Winslow stood before her little house, her shroud of a sheet whipped by the rising wind.

Luke had come down the windmill so fast he almost rappelled. The storm had come up quickly. He was grateful to see Kat had started back toward Yoders'. A moment later and he would have gone to get her.

"My new buggy horse is really skittish in storms," Paul told him as they gathered Luke's tools and put them in the storage shed. "You just go on in the house. I'll pull your and Katie's buggies in the barn too."

As Luke went into Yoders', he saw that Eli and Sarah were playing with Paul's grandkids while Lee oversaw everything and Mary chatted with Mose Susan and his mother. He went out onto the porch again as Kat, now dripping wet, emerged from the pumpkin field.

Luke thought she looked beautiful, not bedraggled. Her garments clung to her slim body and her skin shone. And best of all, her eyes lit like lanterns to see him waiting for her.

"Is everyone all right?" she called to him as she hurried up onto the porch. "Wait until I tell you about Louise Winslow."

He nodded and threw a protective arm around her. "Tell me inside!" he said, raising his voice to be heard. They stood for a moment looking at each other before they gazed out at the increasing strength of the storm. The wind slanted sheets of gray rain sideways, and the shrinking vista seemed to close them in together. Yet the power of all that did not awe him as much as his growing need for this woman.

"Is everyone inside?" she asked as they backed up toward the house.

"Paul's checking on the horses in the barn." He raised his voice to be heard above the thud of thunder. "He probably got caught out there."

"Did you get the windmill fixed before this hit?"

"Just. A bullet lodged in the cogs of the rotor. I saved it for you in my toolbox so the sheriff can identify it. It could have been shot by some random prankster, or by the ones we're after. I'm betting it's from some gun Tyler Winslow owns."

"I don't know what I'd do without you," she shouted, lightly hitting his upper arm with her fist. "You're my partner on this case, much more than Sheriff Martin could ever be."

Despite the rain encroaching on the porch, Luke wanted to lift and spin her around. Maybe she was coming not only to trust him, but to rely on him.

"But I've got a farming question for you," she said. "I see Paul's got a lot of corn, too. Can this storm hurt the crop just before it's harvested?"

"Not unless it makes the fields too muddy for the

horses pulling the combine. Corn's sturdier than wheat, which can be beaten down and ruined—at least with this much wind and rain. Now if it was an out-and-out hurricane or tornado…''

The center of the storm drowned his words and thoughts. He wasn't sure what he had just said. Kat made him feel swept away in a way he had never felt with another woman. She had begun to shake, no doubt from the cold, though his own trembling was of another kind. He was being selfish to keep her out here, yet he savored the feeling of being sealed away with her. Reluctantly, he led her toward the door on the Yoders' long porch.

But between the two windows, she turned and leaned into him, and they pressed together. A jagged bolt of lightning struck nearby. Its reverberating thunder didn't jolt them apart, but a boy's voice did.

''*Daad?*'' Eli called out the back door. ''Oh, Katie, too. I heard you yelling like a fight. I see you are all right, kissing like that, for sure!''

Luke chuckled as he escorted Kat inside, and Mary hurried her off to get some dry clothes. The storm was letting up; it was going to depart as quickly as it came. Luke looked down at the Monopoly game Lee was playing with the kids on the living room floor.

''Hi, *Daadi*,'' Sarah said, grinning up at him and waggling her fingers in a wave. She'd had her hands clamped over her ears to mute the thunder. ''These are not hotels but barns, see,'' she said, holding up a red plastic piece.

''Sarah, it's going to be your turn next,'' Lee said, then went back to talking to the circle of children. Paper money lay in neat piles on the floor while Lee tried to explain how it bought things on the playing board.

"But this pretend money, just like real money, can't buy happiness or safety or forgiveness or goodness or anything really worthwhile," Lee told them. Her gaze snagged Luke's; he nodded. "If it did," she blurted, "I'd just buy a husband and children of my own, but I still love all of you."

For a moment he thought she'd cry. Her face showed mingled sorrow and shame. He was surprised she'd said that, for no one seemed more dedicated to duty than Leah. She must be holding so much inside. He wished he'd thought of her plight more, maybe tried to match her up with someone. But others had attempted that and failed, and she was caught in an age gap between men too immature for her and the rare widowers, who, like himself, already had broods of their own.

As the rush of rain in the drainpipes became mere dripping from the eaves, Kat came out in dry clothes. Damp ringlets of blond hair peeked from the starched white *kapp* Mary must have loaned her. With a nod and shift of her sky-blue eyes, Kat indicated he should step out in back again, no doubt so she could tell him about Louise Winslow.

"Luke," Mary said before they could move, "maybe Paul had real trouble with that mare. With all that noise she's like to kick him or something. I'll go out and—"

"No, I'll go," he told her. "He took two buggies in with him so he's tending a lot of skittish horses, that's all. I'll be right back," he said, looking at Kat, who nodded again.

He went out into the damp, heading toward the barn. Leaves lay littered underfoot where the wet wind had spun and stuck them. As he went in the barn door, which had been left ajar, presumably to give Paul light in there, he saw the buggies his friend had pulled inside. The new horse Paul was worried about banged around a bit in her stall, the white of her eyes showing as she snorted and neighed nervously.

Luke's stomach clenched. Surely the horse hadn't kicked Paul as Mary had feared. He walked closer and sighed in relief. Paul was not on the bed of straw in the stall, nor anywhere in the barn, as far as he could tell.

"Paul, you in the loft?" he called out, looking up, thinking he might have gone to check the old roof for leaks.

A big drop plopped in the middle of his forehead. After this corn harvest, Paul would have money to patch the roof, even before the pumpkins were ready. In that respect, it was going to be a good year.

"Paul!"

He went out toward the storage shed to see if he'd gone there, perhaps to lug Luke's tools to his buggy or the house for him. No, things were just where they'd left them in the dark building. Had Paul gone outside after it let up, to be sure his newly repaired windmill had withstood the storm?

Luke walked around the corner of the shed and stared. Paul lay crumpled at the foot of the windmill, the back of his shirt charred from what must have been a blast of lightning.

"Paul!"

Luke ran to him and fell to his knees to feel for the pulse at the side of his throat. Nothing.

Luke tilted his face to the pearly sky. "Kat!" he shouted before he realized he'd used her wrong name. "Katie!"

Kat and the other women laughed when Sarah asked if the Monopoly card she drew, *Take a ride on the*

Reading, had anything to do with reading books in a buggy.

"What's so funny?" the girl demanded.

"The Reading is a railroad, not a buggy," Lee said, pointing to the place on the board.

"But I'm not allowed to go near the tracks, so I can't take a ride on it!" she protested.

Kat looked up and saw Luke standing in the doorway to the back porch. No, he wasn't standing, but was propping himself up, arms stiff on both sides of the threshold.

Kat stood in one quick movement and went to him. As the kids quieted, Mary Yoder followed her.

"Lee," Luke said, looking past Kat and Mary, "run down the road to Smiths' to use their phone and call 911. Paul's been hurt out back. Mary and Katie, come with me."

"Hurt?" Mary cried, twisting her apron in both hands. "That mare kicked him, didn't she. Did it break a bone?"

"Running to Winslows' will be quicker than Smiths'," Lee said, grabbing her shawl.

"No," Luke said. "Go to Smiths'."

A hand on each of their upper arms, he steered Mary and Kat outside. On the back porch, he released Kat and said, "He's by the windmill."

Kat ran even as she heard Luke tell Mary, in the German she was coming to grasp all too well, "He got struck by lightning, Mary. I think he's gone."

Kat tried to block out Mary's cry as she tore around the corner of the storage shed. Although she'd never seen an electrocution, she knew instantly what had happened.

"Oh, no. Dear God, no!" she cried as she dropped

to her knees beside Paul. She rolled him onto his back. His clothes were soaked. Something—Paul—smelled burned.

He must have been touching the metal legs of the windmill, but why? He knew better than to do something so stupid. Had he forgotten something out here, or had come outside, thinking the storm was over, to be sure the windmill was working?

Kat opened one of his eyelids. Pupils fixed and dilated. She put her ear over his mouth. Not breathing. She checked his airway and adjusted his head. As Luke and Mary joined her, she began CPR.

"Is he yet alive?" Mary asked, her voice tremulous.

"I thought he was gone," Luke said. "Kat, what can we do to help?"

Kat was sure he was gone, but she didn't answer. She just went on and on, trying to bring him back, counting compressions and breaths until she thought her arms would break and she would pass out. But Paul was going cold already. How long had he been like this? Or had the chill rain just made his skin feel clammy?

Then she felt furious at herself. She had a cell phone in her buggy that she hadn't told Luke about yet. She was becoming so Amish, she hadn't even thought of it until now. Cold comfort that a quicker call for medical help wouldn't have made one bit of difference for Paul. But she tried to make up for it now, for all her failures. She went on and on, until Mary said something to Luke, and he tried to lift her away.

Finally, Kat sat back on her heels, her arms limp at her sides. Her back felt it was breaking, but her heart hurt worse. Mary held Paul's hand. Luke's face was running tears like rain.

The three of them sat silent until they heard the

distant whine of a siren. Then Mary broke into sobs while Luke prayed in German over the man who had long been husband and friend and, so briefly, bishop.

As the EMS vehicle came closer, Kat staggered to her feet and scanned the scene. Her legs were numb; she nearly stumbled. She saw a short strip of white sheet, probably what Paul had used to tie himself to the windmill before the storm. But this shred was twisted, sopped and caught in the farthest leg of the windmill, which was not the side Paul had climbed.

Even as Lee brought the medics to them, Kat quickly studied Paul's body. His shoes—one *side* of each shoe was mud-coated. Maybe he'd writhed on the ground in a death spasm. Or had he been dragged to this spot through the mud in the rain? And was then tied to the windmill in the worst of the storm?

At she looked closer at the sides of Paul's shoes, Kat saw bits of straw and even a corn kernel stuck in the mud there. As far as she could see, no straw or corn was strewn on the ground where he'd died—if he'd died where he lay.

When Mary loosed her husband's limp hand, Kat caught a glimpse of some sort of ligature marks on Paul's wrists that suggested he'd been tied tightly or that he'd struggled.

Kat overheard the older medic whisper to his partner, "Maybe this trauma on the top of his head is the entry wound, and it exited at the back." Kat shifted her position. Yes, she saw a head wound, but one that evidently had not bled into his hair, unless the rain had washed the blood into the ground here. Some head wounds bled badly, some didn't.

Or, Kat surmised, Paul could have been attacked in the barn, hit, dragged and tied to a metal windmill in a violent electrical storm. After the lightning hit him, he'd been untied. But that was the weak link in her theory. Would his attacker have risked standing near him in the storm, between a metal windmill and a metal shed, *hoping* lightning would strike Paul alone? Someone could have come out looking for Paul earlier and spotted his attacker. Or, if lightning had not struck him, couldn't he have identified his assailant?

"Luke," she whispered, touching his sleeve as he, with his mother and Mose Susan, comforted Mary. "I'm going into the barn to call the sheriff on my cell phone."

Dazed, Luke looked at her. She thought he might be angry that she hadn't mentioned the phone before, but he only nodded.

Though she wanted to cry with the rest of them, she was not going to accept this tragedy as they would. She was certain the hate crimes against the Amish had escalated to the clever killing of the new bishop. This might look like an accident, but she was convinced she had a murder on her hands. With Bishop Brand's death earlier this week, maybe two.

18

"I'm already on my way," Sheriff Martin told Kat on the phone. "But if you're at Yoders', where're you calling from?" His patrol car's siren muted his voice.

"I decided I was going to have to get a cell phone to keep you better informed," she told him, shoving the barn door open farther to give herself more light. "I'm in the barn. How long before you'll be here?"

"Five to ten. Gotta call the coroner to come out too. Hell, two bishops in the same week. *There's* a message of some sort. Sit tight."

Kat indeed saw a message in these deaths of the two leaders of the Maplecreek Amish: a terrorist who had amused himself with aggravated assault and abuse of a corpse had morphed into a serial killer.

Punching off, she hid the phone back under the buggy seat. She was glad she'd called the sheriff. As she'd expected, his dispatcher had picked up the 911 call and relayed it to him. At least he would know she wasn't trying to stonewall him on Paul's death to give herself time to investigate on her own—which was exactly what she intended to do. That, and try to finally figure out whose side the sheriff was really on.

If she tried to convince him that Paul had been murdered, would he cancel her assignment? She couldn't bear not to see this through, to not nail whoever was behind all this. Maybe, considering the odds of lightning hitting the windmill while Paul was under it—

and possibly tied to it—it had not even been a lightning strike that killed him. The Amish might argue again, but she was going to get the sheriff to insist on an autopsy.

Head down, she began to walk the concrete floor of the barn, just the way she'd seen the forensic team do after they'd gridded a crime scene. She noted spilled straw and corn but no deep mud that could have ended up caked on the sides of Paul's shoes. She peeked carefully in the stall of the nervous horse Paul had come out to comfort. Yes, both straw and some corn were spilled here and there was a bit of mud made from the horse's water, or a roof leak.

"What did you see?" she asked the mare—as if she'd answer. "*Who* did you see in here, besides your owner?"

As Kat searched for signs of a struggle, she could not erase the picture, as if it reran on a TV set in her brain, of Tyler Winslow looking through the window of his combine at Luke and Paul. He'd gone on, but had he then come back and—?

"Kat, are you all right?" Luke's voice interrupted her thoughts. His shadow stretched across the barn floor in the late afternoon light, as he walked toward her. "What are you looking for?"

"For proof that Paul was hit on the head, dragged out of here and tied to that windmill in the storm."

His eyes widened and his fists clenched. "Murder? Tyler Winslow, then?"

"He's gone to the top of the list. This practically happened in his backyard, too."

"He would have had to hide that noisy combine and sneak in, though Yoders' cornfields would make that possible. But how could Tyler or anyone else have known lightning would strike the windmill and kill

Paul? If it didn't, they ran the risk that Paul could identify his attacker, unless he was struck from behind.''

''I know. Did you see anyone in the fields besides me when you were on the windmill?''

''No. Kat, I just wanted to tell you, I can't deal with all this right now. I assume the sheriff will. If it's murder, you need to turn it over to him.''

''I know you have a lot to do, telling everyone about the tragedy. There will be another big funeral, right?''

He nodded solemnly. ''One we'll ask the sheriff for security on.''

''Luke, one quick thing—no, actually, two. The sheriff's called the coroner to come. You know that he can order an autopsy for any suspicious death...''

''I pray it doesn't come to that. Mary would be appalled, and it's not our way. Try to understand that, Kat.''

He'd called her Kat, and he seemed different now. Stunned, yes, as they all were, but it went deeper than that. He looked somber, almost austere. Dear God, she prayed, don't let Luke be the next leader of his people. If Paul hadn't been out here in the storm, and Luke had come out to pull their buggies into the barn instead, he could have been the one targeted, just as his windmills had been.

''What else?'' he asked as he raised his big hands to her shoulders. She longed to throw herself into his arms and hold tight, but she stood stiffly. Since he'd asked her to turn this over to the sheriff, was he saying she should leave the Amish? His touch and tone made her feel this was some sort of farewell blessing he was bestowing.

''Just be careful,'' she choked out, gripping his

wrists in her hands. "For yourself, Eli and Sarah—and me."

His lower lip went taut and his eyes narrowed. "The same to you, Amish cop," he whispered, and darted a quick kiss on her lips before he turned away.

"Coroner says it's electrocution for sure," Sheriff Martin told Kat as she handed him the bullet from the windmill. "All the facts lead to a lightning hit."

He held the bullet between his right thumb and index finger and squinted at it. He'd been at the scene for a half hour. With Luke's permission, Kat had taken the bullet out of his toolbox and given it to the sheriff, but she wasn't just going to hand over the investigation of Paul's death.

Martin went on. "He says he's seen several other similar cases in the county over the years, with similar exit and entry wounds and burns. He thinks the voltage might've leaped from the windmill through Paul—who never should have been out here—into this metal shed."

Kat looked up at the roof's interior while he continued to study the bullet. "But wouldn't there be some sign," she said, "that it passed through here and was grounded?"

"Kat, the man's dead from a lightning strike—that's what's going on the death certificate. Neither the coroner nor I want to upset Yoder's people by insisting on an autopsy."

"But I saw you look the scene over carefully," she challenged. "And the body."

"Why do I think you're gonna give me chapter and verse that I did something wrong?"

"You saw the mud on Paul's shoes?"

"Yeah, on two sides only, opposite sides, one inner,

one outer. Either he slipped before the jolt hit him or
he kicked a bit when it did. The coroner said people
are often blown back a ways, too. I saw no sign of
footprints on the ground under the windmill, but the
rain could have washed them away.''

"It's mostly grass under the windmill," she countered.

"There's some soil the rain churned to mud.''

She almost blurted out that the mud there had no
straw and corn as she'd seen inside the barn, but instinct told her to quit arguing with him. At least, she
thought, he had not just glossed over what he'd seen
but had tried to reason it out.

"I hate to say it, but I think you or the coroner
should insist on an autopsy.''

"You're the one who's been preaching to me about
having to walk the Amish line to get along with them.
You think county officials like me and the coroner
don't need to, too?''

"Did you see the torn strip of sheet on the windmill
and the ligature marks on his wrists?'' she said, unwilling to give up.

"'Course I did. But both Luke and Paul's wife told
me he tied himself to the windmill with strips of sheets
earlier and ran rope over his wrists more than once to
hoist himself up and down. Where were you during
all that?''

Kat wondered if someone had told him she'd spent
some of that time over at his in-laws', talking to Louise. She was starting to distrust Ray Martin more, not
less. Still, while she might not tell him that Tyler had
taken a good look at Luke and Paul on the windmill,
she had to come clean on this much.

"I walked over to the Winslow farm to let them
know there were no hard feelings about the silo ac-

cident, in this county of *so many* accidents,'' she said, realizing too late it sounded as if she were baiting him.

''You talked to Tyler?'' he asked, finally pocketing the bullet.

''Actually, to Louise. I found her fascinating.''

''Oh, she's something, all right. But if she fed you some sort of bull about Tyler, take it with a grain of salt. She hasn't been a wife to him for years. She's lucky he doesn't boot her out of her back-lot hideout and out of his life.''

Though Kat tried not to react to that, her thoughts raced. She was on the trail of someone so clever, with such a bizarre sense of humor, that, after getting bored with shooting manure, fireworks and paintballs, he'd gone to the next step. He was now creating what appeared to be accidents: Kat's near suffocation—which could have been attempted murder; maybe Bishop Brand's death; now Paul's. Tyler Winslow had been at or near the scene of at least two out of the three apparent mishaps. And, unless she was just over the edge of desperation again, Sheriff Martin was still trying to protect him.

Kat wanted badly to prove that Ray Martin had underestimated her. Maybe he thought it was safe to bring in a former cop—a mere woman—who'd screwed up on the job and gotten shot—one who was going to hide behind a dispatcher's desk from now on, one who could no longer shoot a gun or maybe even think straight. One who'd be overwhelmed by trying to fit in with the pacifist, forgiving Amish.

But he was wrong, very wrong. Aside from her sense of justice spurring her on, she'd fallen in love with the Amish—yes, with Luke, too. Though he was unwed, which meant he could not become their next bishop, Luke had always seemed their *de facto* leader, and that could make him the next target. And the cop in Kat—Amish cop, as Luke had called her—could not let that happen.

Kat and the sheriff watched from the door of the shed as the coroner signed Paul's death certificate and the EMS guys zipped him into a body bag. The gurney rattled as it rolled past, bumping through the wet grass and mud. Heads bowed, Mary and Luke followed close behind with the others, including the children, bringing up the rear in a solemn, silent procession. Kat amazed herself by wanting to fall in with them, to be there when decisions were made and the Amish began to comfort one another in this new loss.

"I'm gonna turn this over to the crime lab, even though it's bent all out of shape," the sheriff said. He patted his shirt pocket where he'd put the bullet.

"Good. Sheriff, one last thing, and then I'll just go back to preparing for another Amish funeral. I hear you'll be there, too, this time."

"You bet I will. No one's gonna bother anyone at the mourning or burial for Paul Yoder, not if I can help it. The Amish are learning they need me sometimes, at least that much good's coming out of this string of tragedies."

"Is there any way," she asked, pressing her palms together, "that Paul could have been electrocuted, if lightning didn't strike the windmill?"

"Kat, give it up. Both Luke and Mary Yoder said they heard a big bolt hit nearby. You telling me you didn't hear that, too?"

"I heard it. But is there some other possible source of electricity that could have killed him?"

"Pardon the pun," he told her, "but I'd be shocked if there was. You're on an Amish farm with no electricity, got it?"

"Yeah, got it," she whispered to herself as he strode toward his cruiser. But she wasn't giving up on this.

It was barely dark that evening when the food began to arrive with the mourners at Yoders'. When Mose Susan and her children had finally left, Kat had volunteered to buggy Ida and Luke's kids home, but he had wanted them to stay until he could go with them. Once again, Lee was overseeing the children, who were well-behaved, so Kat busied herself helping the Amish sisters lay out or store food.

"Will the funeral delay the corn harvest?" Kat asked Lee's mother, Levi Em, as she took potato loaf and corn fritters from her.

"By a day, maybe. When the crop is ready, it's ready, for sure. Bishop Yoder would not have approved of a delay. The harvest is the future, that's an old *Deutsche* saying, *ja*. We must have a *gute Ernte,* a good harvest."

"And," another woman put in, "Luke said it will go on—that no tragedies shall overcome our strength and resolve."

Kat's insides went into free fall. Luke was stepping to the fore, guiding the people, the church. She could only pray that word of that did not get out to their enemy.

"Here," another woman said, coming in the door and switching to English when she saw Kat, "*schnitz* pies I had already baked."

Kat recalled that elderberry pie that Bishop Brand had enjoyed just before he died. Ida would have been careful that none of the toxic leaves or twigs got in it, but could anyone have tampered with the elderberry bushes themselves? Maybe sprayed them with some sort of poison, just the way those quilts had been sprayed and ruined?

"Reuben!" she said as she carried the pies into Mary's pantry to put with the others. She'd seen him sneaking around, spying on Sarah, but he could have had another motive. Perhaps he'd known Ida would pick those berries and bake them up for her husband, the man who had overseen his shunning.

She pictured Reuben lurking around the Brand barn the night before last, carrying a note saying he wanted Luke to resurrect his fallen windmill. If Reuben feared they were onto him, could he be just trying to look contrite? She couldn't afford to overlook any suspect, especially since she feared that Eli was the common link in the attacks. And Eli had been here again today.

But as more of the Amish arrived with food and comfort for Mary and her family, Kat recalled someone who had directly mentioned food poisoning. Clay Bigler. He had greeted Paul in the Brand front yard that day. He'd asked what they thought was the cause of death. *It sure wasn't something like food poisoning,* she remembered Clay had said, *not with the great way you all cook.* But how in heaven's name would Clay have managed to poison the old man's food? No, none of that made sense. She was getting paranoid.

Kat started to rake her fingers through her hair, but she snagged her *kapp* and remembered who she was. And why she was here. She went out of the pantry and, in German, told the women she had to leave. From the laundry room clothesline where shawls and bonnets hunched like black crows, she grabbed her still-damp things and went looking for Luke in the front room.

To her dismay, Luke was speaking to the growing assembly of the brethren. No way could she bother him now—but then he looked up and saw her dressed to leave. Frowning, he excused himself and joined her in the narrow hall.

"I don't want you going out alone," he said, clasping her wrist. His hand felt like a wide, warm bracelet. "I'm starting to get a siege mentality."

Rather than go through that argument again with him, she said, "The suspect's probably off lying in wait for our—your—next move before striking again. But I just wanted to ask you if you know of absolutely any way Paul could have been electrocuted, if lightning didn't hit the windmill or that metal shed. I've examined both but found only a shred of sheet tied to the side he didn't climb and no sign of electrical burns on that cloth or the shed."

He looked as if she'd sucker punched him. His eyes widened, then narrowed. "I thought there were holes in your first theory, but yes..."

"Yes, what?"

"Possibly a backup generator."

"A portable one?"

"I own one."

"Tell me about it."

"It's back in my shop. I think it weighs about twenty pounds. Since there's no electricity that comes onto Amish property, if we need power tools..."

"Oh, right—I've seen that generator. But it's big. Nobody could cart that around."

"No, you've seen the one I never take from the shop. There are newer ones, smaller ones. I buggy mine around with me for setups. I think Reuben has one. He used it before he got electricity put back in his place after he left the church."

"A small one?"

"I don't know, because someone only told me

about it, and I can't recall who. But it's not only the Amish who use them.''

"Small, portable generators would be used for power tools, on construction sites, right?''

"Sure. If you're thinking Amish Acres, it could be. But, stay here until we're all ready to head home,'' he said. He touched her cheek with his curled fingers and hurried back among the men.

How enticing that invitation sounded. *Stay here until we're ready to head home.* How she wanted to stay, to belong. But not now. She had things to do, and however risky, she prayed she could do them before Luke was the next one hurt or killed.

No moon or stars lit the night as Kat buggied into town. For a city girl, she was becoming used to the dark depths of a rural night. She let herself into Brooke and Dan's house with their key, which she kept on a string around her neck. Rushing to her laptop, she got online and searched for Web sites selling backup generators.

Ideal for camping, fishing or using power tools outdoors, one site read. "And for electrocuting someone,'' Kat whispered. *Ten pounds for a small unit, up to 80 pounds for a large, but the 20-pound ones can pack a real punch. The charger is so tiny you can plug it into a wall outlet or a car cigarette lighter. Charge it while you drive.* "While you drive your big, noisy combine,'' she muttered.

She gasped as she read the next selling point. *Or it can even be charged by small windmills.*

Could the same diabolical mind that cut off the tops of small windmills, heaved Luke's rotors through shop windows, and shot at the Yoders' windmill, have charged up volts to kill the Amish bishop? Or had Luke been the target and Paul just happened to tend that skittish mare, and so had been jumped instead?

Kat wished she could convince the sheriff to try to get search warrants for Reuben's place, Tyler's combine and Clay Bigler's truck and office, for anything to link them to a portable generator with traces of mud or blood. But there was hardly enough evidence for that yet. Besides, if the sheriff was clean, that would tip off the suspects. If he was dirty, she and Luke could be in more danger than they already were.

She decided to e-mail Brooke about what had happened, and where she was going and why. Though they had spent little time together, she felt close to Brooke. If anything dire happened, someone could carry on to nail the bastards behind all this.

Kat also wrote Brooke that she was going to borrow some jeans and a dark sweatshirt and scarf from her. No more leaving bonnets behind; she needed pants to move quickly through the construction site, her first stop tonight. She took a little knife and a walnut pick from Brooke's kitchen. Mike Morelli had always said hairpins worked best but that no one had those anymore. Kat smiled grimly. Mike would be surprised to know her hair was partly held up by them.

She pulled her shawl around herself and put her bonnet on, hoping to disguise her worldly clothes while she was in the buggy. As she drove by Marnie's house, she noted the place was all dark. Perhaps Marnie was still at her restaurant or shop. To avoid passing directly by either building where she could be spotted, Kat took a side street and headed northwest, out of town.

19

A noisy, old black pick-up truck whizzed by Kat on the road. At first she almost panicked, but it surely wasn't the newer one that had carried the paintball gunners. Actually, this one resembled—and sounded like—Reuben's old rattletrap, but, as Luke had said, many around here had similar vehicles.

Yet her heart pounded even harder as she assessed what Morelli had always called the best-case-worst-case scenarios. At best, the driver was some idiot wanting to shove an Amish buggy in the ditch for the hell of it. At worst, could Reuben be driving drunk and following her with evil intent? Whoever it was, the back of the truck was filled with dried corn shocks, for pieces kept whipping loose and hitting her.

When the truck appeared a second time, she got way over and tried to read the license plate, but it was a blur. She craned around, even leaned out of the buggy to be sure its taillights disappeared back toward town. She shuddered and shook her head. Since the day she thought she'd been followed through the cornfield en route to Reuben's silo, she was sometimes sure she was being watched.

Finally, the only sounds were the *clop-clop* of Dilly's hooves and the occasional *creak* of a cricket soon doomed to die by autumn frost. The only light at Amish Acres emanated coldly from Gil Gilmore's sales office windows as Kat approached the entrance to the development. A single car was parked nearby, one she didn't recognize, no doubt the night watchman's. Kat hoped he was the sort she'd often seen during graveyard shifts in the city, the guy who got paid time-and-a-half but mostly slept while gangs looted supplies or hot-wired cars.

She drove Dilly past the entrance, where Luke's windmill spun in the chill night breeze, and turned down the rain-rutted side lane the construction trucks used during the day. She hoped Dilly could see better in this thick dark than she could. If there had been moonlight or starlight, she would not have felt half as safe.

But she did feel sure of what she was doing. It was time for bigger risks. She and Luke had been talking about a list of suspects since she'd arrived in Amish country. Starting tonight, she was going down that list to pin mayhem and two murders on more than one: Clay and A.J., or Tyler and Mark—perhaps with the sheriff abetting them—or Reuben and his drinking buddies. If those possibilities didn't pan out, she'd try to bluff or shake information out of Marnie and Louise, even Gil Gilmore.

She hid Dilly at the very back of the cul-de-sac, in the trees behind Marnie's mansion. Dressed in Brooke's jeans and sweatshirt, her lock-picking gear in one hand and her unlit flashlight in her other, her cell phone stuck in a back pocket, Kat emerged from the clump of trees and looked around.

Clay's trailer office lay silent and dark as a coffin. She tiptoed toward it, hunched over as if ready to spring or run away. The ground was muddy from the rain, so she'd have to be careful she didn't leave tracks inside. She hoped she could get in, and if so, that the watchman would not see her flashlight as she looked around.

Working by feel, as she'd learned to do years ago, she tried the tiny tip of the knife in the lock on the only door. The blade was too wide to go down far enough to move the tumbler. She switched to the nut pick. No luck. Hairpin time.

Kat pulled one from her hair, then turned it in the lock. She began to sweat. Before she turned her teen-age life around, she'd done more than graffiti walls. Thank God no one had ever caught her at it, even though it was petty, neighborhood stuff done just for the heck of it after Jay died. Yet she could have landed in juvie detention or had a record that could have kept her from becoming a cop. She'd always hoped that helping people, especially kids who were hurting, partly paid back for how screwed-up she'd once been.

Kat bent the first hairpin out of whack, so she pulled a second one out. The knot of her hair loosened and a thick tress swung free over her face. She half wished she was still dressed Amish so she could try one of the straight pins from the front of her dress.

Kat gasped as the lock clicked. Glancing behind her, she turned the handle and the door creaked open. Light was still visible from the sales office near the road, where a pair of wide-beamed headlights went by, then shrank to red taillights and disappeared. Taking a deep breath of fresh air and scraping her feet on the mat, Kat shoved the door open and stepped inside.

She could just imagine the headlines in the *Maple-creek Weekly* or even the *Columbus Dispatch*: Former Cop Caught Breaking and Entering. Amish Admit They Harbored Her, Say They Regret It. Sheriff Insists on Letter-of-the-Law Justice...

The trailer was neat and spare, but it reeked of cig-

arette smoke, and soon she would too. Being careful
not to make a mess and to remember where she took
things from, Kat began to search. Among the pile of
purchase orders, she prayed she'd find a receipt for a
motorcycle or paint guns, anything to put her on track.
In a plastic organizer on the desk, too many folders
looked like the one Clay had carried into Marnie's.

She found something, though it wasn't much. Clay
had paid five-hundred dollars for fireworks last week
for the official opening of Amish Acres on Saturday,
September twenty-eighth, just one week away. It was
stapled to bills for booths and food, both to be provided by Marnie Girkins at the Dutch Table Restaurant
of Maplecreek, Ohio.

"Damn! Maybe that's why he went to see her."

But she memorized the phone number of the Fire
the Works Company anyway. She'd phone them to see
if Clay had ordered fireworks previously. She found
one more piece of paper stapled to those—an invitation list for the grand opening. At the top were the
names of members of the board of directors of the
Amish Acres Corporation, which consisted of three
divisions: Rural Residences, Country Club and Golf
Course.

"What country club and golf course?"

The names of board members she read didn't narrow her search one bit, but this could be a momentous
find. Because among the names of people she didn't
know were ones she did: Tyler Winslow, Marnie Girkins, Clay Bigler and Ray Martin.

"The sheriff. Oh, no!"

She jerked so hard, the contents of the folder scattered on the floor.

Gilmore had lied to her; he'd said none of the board
was local. But would anyone want to drive the Amish

off land that could be simply purchased, as this land had been? At least for ambience, didn't they want the Amish living near a place called Amish Acres? Maybe the Plain People were too much trouble or their numbers multiplied too fast.

Tucking her flashlight under one arm, she knelt to get the spilled papers back in place. She had just opened the desk drawer when she heard a muted sound outside, maybe a car door slamming. She'd been so intent, she wasn't sure if the sound had been close or far.

She could get caught in here if she didn't get out now.

Not even taking time to look out the window, Kat cut her light, cracked the door and peeked out. Through the skeleton of Marnie's mansion, she could see a second car had arrived between here and the sales office, at the end of the cul-de-sac. Its interior dome light was on, one of those that eventually went out on its own. She saw no form in the car or silhouetted by the distant lights. The person had no doubt gotten out, but where had the driver gone? She'd make a dash for the copse, then wait to be sure the coast was clear again.

She saw the dome light in the car go out.

Kat quickly, quietly, closed the door behind her, before she realized it wasn't locked. Though she heard only night sounds, the hair prickled on the nape of her neck. She sensed someone close, a predator after prey.

Bending low, she started away, but something pinged off the metal trailer, inches from her head.

Gun! she screamed to herself. But something strange echoed in its retort. Nail gun? Yes, nail gun!

She hit the ground as the *ba-bang* sounded again. Her flashlight rolled away on the ground. Where was the shooter? Should she cry out, so they would know it was her?

No, someone already knew—and wanted to kill her next.

She didn't dare make a dash for it, for she'd be exposed. How far did those damn things shoot? She rolled to a crouch, then darted for Marnie's house. It would provide partial protection until she could run for the trees or jump her attacker.

Had the guard shot at her? More likely it was whoever had just arrived in that car. Someone who would use a nail gun. Clay? That wasn't his van. One of his roofers? Any moron could pick up a nail gun left here from the shingling and shoot it in the dark.

Kat couldn't decide whether to go up or down in the house, so she crawled into the protection of the fireplace, the only solid wall standing so far. At least her back was covered. Still, it meant she was trapped. Her breathing was ragged, her heart thudding. Shuddering at the memory of that kid with the nail in his forehead, she held her breath and squinted to try to pierce the darkness. Silence. She could identify no form or human sound. Was the person waiting for her to show herself? Though she'd love to ID the shooter, all she really wanted was to get out of here in one piece. From her Academy days, she heard her sergeant's voice, *Don't take a knife to a gunfight.* Hell, she didn't even have a knife.

Uncertain how much time had passed, she decided to risk coming out. It was black as the inside of a box, even though she could pick out the beams and boards of the framing.

Moving slowly, she lay down on the plank floor and gut-crawled toward the back of what Gil had said would become a huge kitchen with an attached greenhouse. She'd just slide through the two-by-fours and tear like hell for the trees where Dilly waited.

Ba-bang!

She heard the nails whistle by, felt them, just like live ammo. They careened off the chimney bricks. Kat rolled away, then glimpsed someone standing at the back of the house.

Thwack, thwack. The nails hit the wood near her.

He wore all black. A hood. Goggles!

He ran at her; instinctively, she kicked at his legs. Her mind threw at her the terrible scene where she'd rolled at Seyjack's feet in that death house in Columbus. She'd ripped his glasses from his face, thrown herself at his legs while he'd pointed his 9-mm at her. That gun shrieked through her terror. She remembered the pain and her own cry for help over her radio, but there was no one to call now.

But she had her cell phone. And the number on redial would be the sheriff's mobile number!

Kicking again at the person who stood over her, Kat fumbled for her phone. All sounds seemed to mute to nothing but her own inner screams. The world went into slow-motion as the person above her lifted his arms stiffly toward her. A nail gun? A real gun?

Kat wanted to scream *Who are you?*, but her voice snagged. She expected no mercy, only another murder.

She kicked again and skewed his aim. The nail gun banged and another nail struck near her hip. She forced him off balance and rolled the other way, but suddenly there was nothing to hold her.

Kat broke her fall partway down the basement stairs. Grunting, hitting, rolling, she fought to get to her knees on the hard concrete. She scrambled away, but she was trapped down here. In the far corner of the basement, by feel, she punched the redial button of her phone.

The moment she heard someone pick up, she screamed, "Sheriff, Marnie's house at Amish Acres! 10-3, 10-3!"

Her attacker came partway down the basement steps, squatted, shot twice more—though wide of where she huddled, covering her head with her phone and both hands—then thudded up the stairs. She heard him run across the plank flooring above. Then there was silence.

Where in hell was that night guard, Kat thought. Or had that been him? She'd hurt her hip on the tumble down the stairs. At least it was the other hip from the one that had taken John Seyjack's bullet. It felt more like the hip-pointer she'd suffered learning self-defense.

She touched her hip: her hand came away wet and hot.

Shot! Worse, she'd called for the sheriff, so he'd know what she'd been up to. But maybe not, if she could get to the trailer to lock Clay's office door first, and then get out of here. Of course, if he was the person who'd answered her panicked phone call, she'd have to think of some explanation.

In pain, she went up the stairs she'd fallen down, pulling herself up step by step with her arms and one good leg. Pressing one hand to her hip hard so she wouldn't leave a trail of blood, she used her clean hand to lock Clay's office.

Still dragging one leg, she shuffled toward the trees until her foot hit her flashlight. She'd forgotten about that. She'd have to bend to pick it up.

"Aarw!" she cried aloud as she retrieved it and went on toward the trees. Just before she reached them, she saw the sheriff's car—or possibly his deputy's. No siren, but the barlight was blinking, throwing strobe flashes even to the trees. Should she go back out and ask for help, come clean on all that had happened? But she didn't want the sheriff to know she'd been shot. Not only because he could pull her off the case for her own safety, but because he could be the shooter.

She only wanted to go home, home to the Brand farm, even if Luke had a fit when he learned she'd done this. He'd said once that Dilly would take her home if she gave the horse her head. If she could just get up in the buggy...

Kat heard footsteps nearby, someone panting for breath as she reached the trees. She froze as a large beam swept across her, then shone full in her face.

"What in the Sam Hill are you doing here, dressed like that?" Sheriff Martin. She thrust a hand up to block the light from her eyes.

"I just—needed to look around," she said, trying to stand straight and not flinch. "I fell down the stairs onto a nail, so I called you on your cell."

"Come on, girl. Enough lies and stonewalling out of you. Either you don't trust me worth a damn, hope to impress Luke and the Amish, or want to wrap this up all by yourself because you screwed up in Columbus. But as far as I'm concerned, you're screwing up now, too."

"That's not tr—"

"Hey, guys," he bellowed, turning away, "I got it under control. You can quit looking!" He lowered his voice again. "I was in the office playing cards with the night guard, my deputy, and Gilmore. Deputy took my squad car and went out to get us some pizza. Said he got a crazy call from you on my phone. Kat, I'm gonna have to pull you from this case before you get really hurt—or worse.''

"But who had that second car, the one parked partway back?'' she demanded.

He glanced in the direction she stared, then shook his head. "The only second car is mine. The deputy just drove it, I said. Gil's is in the shop getting repaired and that one by the office is the guard's.''

So there were three cars, she thought, and she hadn't heard one leave because she was still in the basement. It had been a medium-size sedan, but she couldn't ID it beyond that. At least the sheriff evidently didn't know she'd been shot. Or was he now stonewalling *her?*

"More than once,'' he went on, "you crossed the line, ex-Officer Lindley. You've been insubordinate, so that's it.''

"You gave me a job to do, and I've been trying to do it. But Katie Kurtz can only go so far before she needs Kat Lindley. Or did you know that assigning me to this case in Amish guise would hamstring me—''

"Hell, I can't even see holding that office dispatcher's desk job for you. You just tell the Amish you're off the case and clear on out of Maplecreek.''

As he started away, he focused his light at the ground to guide his steps. Getting fired hurt more than her throbbing hip. At least he hadn't realized she was shot, and she wasn't going to give him the satisfaction of telling him. She couldn't see trying to work with this man anymore, either—especially since she might have to get someone else to come in here and arrest him.

For as he turned away, she had seen that someone had kicked a mud footprint on his pants leg. The lighter, drying mud outline showed up well because he was wearing, not his uniform, but black jeans and a leather jacket.

How she made it up into the buggy she wasn't sure. Just in case the nail wound was bleeding bad, she made a tourniquet from Brooke's bandanna and tied it around her upper thigh, right over her jeans. As Luke had said, after she got the buggy through the last intersection—she saw no one on the roads, thank heavens—she loosed the reins and let Dilly head home.

Home? Not anymore. Not if the Amish asked her to leave, for she would not keep back from Luke what had happened. Here, amidst all their upheaval about Paul, she was going to be their burden too.

She began to feel faint, and she put her head between her knees. Wait until Luke and Ida saw her in English pants, bloody English pants...

She jerked and sat up again. Had she fallen asleep or passed out? What if the sheriff or whoever seemed to follow her around at times came after her through the dark, through the corn? Coming through the rye...if a body shoots a body, need a body cry? Was someone coming through the corn to lock her in the silo or throw her down the steps into a basement or a grave...

The buggy ride lulled her. Luke was bringing her to Amish country to meet his parents and his kids, to be one of them. A family, and Eli so much like Jay and Sarah the child she'd never had and all those sisters with all that food...

She jolted awake again, sprawled across the buggy seat. Was she home? Yes, heading toward the barn, past Luke's house.

Kat saw the barn doors gaped wide. The barn was

blacker than the night. She should have taken Dilly's reins at the end to go to Luke's house, under his back window...

"Kat? Kat!"

Luke, climbing up into the buggy.

"When you didn't come back, I was going out to look! Kat?"

"I went to check out Clay Bigler's office at Amish Acres," she told him. "Someone shot at me with a nail gun and hit me in the hip. And I phoned the sheriff and called him in—unfortunately—and he fired me."

He muttered something dark and angry in German. She was sure the Amish didn't curse, but that's exactly what it sounded like.

"Please don't give me a bad time," she said. "Please don't send me away, because the sheriff may be working with everyone else."

"Everyone else?" he said as he got down and pulled her gently toward him, to the edge of the driver's seat, before he lifted her down into his arms. "I'm taking you into the house to see how that wound looks and maybe call Dr. Barker."

Kat laid her head on his broad shoulder. Being jostled and held hurt like hell, but she never wanted him to let her go. She started to tell him the names she'd seen on the board of directors list and that Gil had lied to her and that she worried Marnie might be involved and that she was terrified Luke was in grave danger, but she felt so weak and dizzy that she wasn't really sure what she said.

Pain shot Kat awake again. Her eyes flew open. Soft lantern light illumined a large room. She was in a big, soft bed. Her gaze darted around. Luke's bed, in Luke's bedroom.

She turned her head as he came in with a basin and towels.

"I know I should have taken you to the *daadi haus*," he said as he put the things down on the bedside table, "but I didn't want to wake my mother, and I didn't want the kids to see you like this on the couch downstairs tomorrow morning. You can sleep here, and I'll go in with Eli. But I think we'd better take a look at your wound first, so we know whether I should call Dr. Barker."

"I got hit with a nail from a nail gun, but I've had my tetanus shots. I think it's more blood than wound."

"I'll take a look at it, and we can decide. I can't believe the sheriff fired you."

"I just hope he didn't fire *at* me. Like I said, he may be behind all this. Or be working with Tyler."

"Is that what you meant by everyone else could be in on it?"

He sat on the edge of the bed, rolling her slightly toward him. He'd pulled the quilt away, but she was afraid she'd bleed on his sheets. She was still fully dressed and couldn't bear to think of the pain it would cost to get out of her jeans—Brooke's jeans. Maybe they could just cut them away, as she'd seen done when the ER guys rushed to get to bullet wounds. Her pain had now subsided to a dull throbbing.

"Kat?" he said, making her realize she'd been silent for a while. "What did you mean, everyone who could be in on it?"

"I saw the list of the board of directors for Amish Acres. They have bigger plans than that, including a country club and a golf course."

His eyes widened; his mouth set hard. "And the Amish are in the way? And they figure we'll just move on if it gets bad enough? They're right, you know."

"No! No, you can't do that."

"But who is 'they'?" he asked again as he slid a piece of plastic under her hip and produced a huge pair of scissors.

"Besides Ray Martin," she told him, "Tyler Winslow, Clay Bigler *and* Marnie Girkins."

He whispered another epithet in German. "You don't believe in conspiracy theories, do you?" he said. Without asking her permission, he began to cut up the leg of her jeans from ankle toward knee along the outside seam. The denim was stiff with blood.

"I'm starting to," she said, wondering how far up her pant leg he would have to—dare to—cut.

"But they would have too many people in the know to keep things secret. Attacks on children, maybe eliminating Paul. Too many cooks spoil the broth, they say...."

"And two people can keep a secret if one of them is dead. But maybe I can't find the person behind it because there isn't one, but several."

He kept cutting away at the thick material. The scissor blade felt cold against her skin but each place Luke's knuckles brushed her felt so...hot. She fought to keep her thoughts on their conversation. She had to tell him what she'd been agonizing over since earlier today.

"Luke, if Paul was killed, could it mean your father was too?"

He stopped cutting, then went on, carefully edging around the blotch of blood on her lower hip. At least she hadn't been hit higher up, for Luke finally stopped cutting.

"I think this might be encrusted," he told her. "I'll try to soak the cloth away, not just pull. Sarah screams when we even say we have to take a bandage off her."

"Did you hear me?" she demanded, seizing his free wrist with as good a grip as she could manage. "You don't think I'm way off, do you? I know you said before that I'm seeing sin everywhere, but—"

"You should see it everywhere. It's rampant in this world."

"But about your father—"

"How? He was sick for weeks. Doctors looked at him and said it was ulcers or acid reflux."

"Did they think to look for poison? Food poisoning?"

"You don't mean pie my mother made for him that last day."

"No—I don't know. Luke, please let me look into this. The sheriff expects me to leave the Amish, but just give me a little more time here with you. I'll concentrate strictly on how your father could have been killed, because if I can prove that—who did it—it will help prove everything else. The sheriff will either have to arrest someone, or we'll call in the feds. I know you have to be at Paul's funeral and will be busy with the harvest for several days, so just give me that long."

"And I'm re-erecting Reuben's windmill," he said as she released his hand, and he gently held the wet towel against the scrap of blood-soaked denim on her hip. His strong features clenched in a frown and he didn't look at her now. "He came over tonight and wants to rejoin the church. He wants to be a grandfather to the children and help Mose and me farm. Paul's funeral is Monday morning, so I told him I'd put his windmill back up first thing Tuesday, just before the harvesters arrive here to cut our fields."

"Was Eli here when Reuben came over tonight?"

"In bed, just like now."

"But you ran out to the barn when I came in. Were they here in the house alone then?"

When she tried to sit up, Luke pushed her back. He leaned close again, holding the cloth to her hip. "Kat, they're fine. I looked in on them while I ran this water. You've got to calm down."

She shocked herself more than him when she threw her arms around his neck and held tight. The sudden movement pained her hip, but she didn't care.

"I can't calm down," she whispered in his ear as he braced himself on his elbows on either side of her. "I can't bear to see anyone hurt, Sarah, Eli—you!"

"Or you," he said, lifting his head just enough to position his mouth over hers. "Yes, you can stay through the three-day harvest. I'd like it to be longer. But if you don't turn up anything, we'll have to call Katie Kurtz an experiment of mine that didn't work. The Plain People will have to go back to trusting the Lord to work this out another way."

He lowered his lips and took hers. Despite her mingled fear and pain, pure pleasure flooded her. His free hand cradled her head to hold her mouth to his. Though he held himself away from her wounded hip, his chest pressed her breasts as his weight anchored her to the mattress.

Despite the whirl of emotions, Kat knew one thing. Whether she was Amish Katie or Cop Kat, she wanted to be in Luke's home, in his bed, in his arms.

"Just these few days, then," she said when they finally took separate breaths. Tears blurred her view of him, so strong and yet so vulnerable. She was terrified that Luke would be the next one attacked, maybe killed. She was going to keep that from happening, even if she was the one who went down instead.

20

Despite the fact Kat mourned with the Amish for their second fallen leader, she also savored the Sunday at Yoders' farm. She tried to treasure each friendly comment, each word of encouragement within the atmosphere of solidarity that emanated from the Amish. When Eli and Sarah were at her side, she watched their faces and cherished their words. She pitched in to help, and was grateful the sisters expected it from her now, as if she belonged. Above all, Kat mourned her waning days here and that she had so little time to solve two murders before a third one could occur.

When Sheriff Martin arrived to discuss security for the funeral tomorrow, Kat saw that he walked straight for Luke amid the press of people, including church deacons, elders, and Paul's son Sam, who, with his wife Barbara, was helping the new widow.

The sheriff, and no doubt anyone who knew the Amish, regarded Luke as the community's new leader, at least until another bishop was chosen. And that, Kat feared, meant Luke had a bull's-eye on his back. As if in sympathy with her tense emotions, the wound that he had tended so well last night began to throb again.

Halfway toward Luke, hat in hand, the sheriff noticed Kat. He frowned at her, looked away, and kept on going. Defiantly, she went to join Luke in the Yoders' front room, where family was waiting for Paul's body to be returned from the funeral home.

"I see she's still dressed like Katie Kurtz," the sheriff said to Luke.

"She's our guest through harvesttime," Luke told him. "She wanted to see how it was all done, and we're beholden to her. I know you'll be willing to keep her secret at least that long."

The sheriff's jaw clenched. He cleared his throat. "The point is, you're all in my jurisdiction, and I need to know anything that's turned up. The whole undercover thing was a bad idea on both our parts, Luke. I expected she would just find information and hand it over, not keep jumping in with both feet—"

"Hey," Kat cut in, glaring at Luke and ignoring the sheriff as he had her, "would you stop discussing me as if I'm not here? The sheriff knows I don't work well with him. He also knows how this case of harassment has turned into hate crimes of the worst order, terrorism in the heartland of America. I'm not worried that the sheriff will let on he set up my presence here. It would make him look very bad and get in the way of his solving these crimes."

"Throwing down the gauntlet?" the sheriff goaded, turning toward her, hands hooked in his gun belt. "I blame something on you, and it comes back to bite me, is that it?"

"I haven't thrown down a gauntlet since I've been here," she said, facing him squarely. "Now I'll just let you gentlemen discuss security for the funeral tomorrow, because I'm officially off this case. However, as Luke said, I expect you to continue to keep Katie Kurtz's secret, Sheriff Martin. No one needs to know that it was your idea that bombed, now do they?"

"And after harvest, my little undercover agent will

just fade away?'' the sheriff challenged. ''Luke's Amish fiancée just didn't work out, so she goes back to Pennsylvania and gets out of my way so I can solve this?''

''Let's just say,'' Kat said, ''in three days it will all be over.''

He looked both puzzled and alarmed at that, but she decided not to push him further. Trying not to limp, she made her way toward the women, who had moved to the front windows of the house. She soon saw why. The same wagon from which Bishop Brand's body had been stolen was coming up the driveway with Paul's coffin.

When her cell phone vibrated, Kat quickly made her way out of the crowd. She'd hung it on a piece of twine around her waist under her dress and apron, so she'd have to hike up her skirts to use it. Without even taking time to grab her shawl, she hurried outside toward the storage shed to take the call in private.

''Kat here.''

''It's Brooke.''

''How's Melly?''

''She keeps opening her eyes and talking, but not really focusing. I guess it's progress, but we still don't know what's going to happen. I wanted to tell you that the Patriot Knights have a vile Web site that rants about the German Amish, among other ethnic groups, breeding like dogs, et cetera. And Tyler is openly linked to it. He probably wrote the crap.''

''He's a Dr. Jekyll and Mr. Hyde, so it doesn't surprise me. Thanks, Brooke. I'll check it out.''

''Luke called Dan late last night and brought him up to speed. I'm sorry your cover's blown.''

''Hopefully just with the sheriff, who set it up anyway, but I'm going to have to be really careful now. If he's at all culpable in all this, I can't trust who he's told.''

"In other words, you're not giving up during these last few days? You intend to do more than just watch the harvest?"

"I'm going to do whatever I can to stop anything else those guilty have planned."

"Please, just don't go near the Knights again or even Tyler's house, not Clay's office, either."

"I hear you—and Luke's message through you and Dan. Did Luke tell him I think Paul Yoder could have been intentionally electrocuted and their father poisoned? Bishop Brand's ailments might have made him susceptible, but I'm going to focus on finding out if something deadly could have gotten into his already weakened system."

"Yeah, Dan told me your theory."

"And you think I'm crazy."

"Not for looking into Paul's death as a possible murder, no. After all, Melly and Eli could both have ended up dead in that fireworks attack. But Father Brand was old and ill. And I just have the funniest feeling you're still looking into a long shot, so—"

"You mean Marnie. Why do you say that?"

"Please, just let me get this out. She's been a friend of mine for years, not a close one, but a generous one. We've gone to the same church and once had the only two B & B's in Maplecreek."

"I understand all that. But Ida certainly didn't harm her husband, elderberry pie binge or not. And the bishop did eat at the Dutch Table on a regular basis, including the day before he died."

"But he always ate there with other brethren, sometimes with Luke and Dan, too. I've seen them at their favorite table in the front window. And they often ate family-style—you know, shared the dishes at the table.''

"So you think Marnie's a dead end—sorry, I didn't mean it that way.''

"I can't get past how much she's done for the local Amish, and how much she benefits from their goodwill and trust. For heaven's sake, she used to *be* Amish. Tyler, Clay, maybe even poor Reuben Coblentz have viable motives, but not her. In my years as a defense attorney, I've seen a lot of weird cases, but I don't think it's her. I know I'm looking at all this from a distance, but it gives me a certain objectivity.''

"Which you don't think I have?'' Kat asked, though she silently questioned Brooke's objectivity about Marnie.

"I didn't mean that. I only know when I was falling in love with Dan and was so swept up in learning about his people, I became so passionate, so overwhelmed at times— Kat, I'm not criticizing.''

"I know. I value your input and support.''

"I'm sorry you'll be leaving Maplecreek. If you come back to Columbus after harvest, come see us, okay? There's no reason why you can't visit Luke and his kids sometimes, maybe come stay with Dan and me at our old bed-and-breakfast when we get Melly home. Dan's coming to Maplecreek today for the funeral, so you just tell him if we can help in any way right now. And if I learn anything else online about the powers that be in Maplecreek, I'll get back to you, pronto.''

"Including Marnie?''

"Of course.''

"I can't thank you enough, Brooke. As for after I leave, I haven't even thought about that. My dream was to start a country antiques business when I first came. About visiting—I think it would be painful to be so close and yet so far from Luke and his kids. It's been almost like play-acting having a family to love— to love me...."

Kat surprised herself by sucking in a huge sob. When she blinked, tears matted her lashes and speckled her cheeks. She managed to say a hoarse "'Bye, Brooke" and punched off.

When Kat got hold of herself, she phoned long distance to the Kentucky company from which Clay Bigler had ordered fireworks for the grand opening of Amish Acres. Pretending to be a ditsy secretary tracking a lost purchase order, she learned that was the first time he had ordered from the Fire the Works Company.

"But," the bright, elderly office manager told Kat, "that name of Maplecreek does ring a bell."

"Oh, maybe someone else around here ordered them, too," Kat said. "I'd sure like to know, because if some locals here can recommend the fireworks, I'd urge our town council to buy them for the Fourth of July next year."

"Why, I think that's it," the woman said, and Kat heard her shuffling papers. "I've had to learn to use these computers, but I've been here for years and I have my own system. Yes, two orders. My dear, Maplecreek must already be using our fireworks for the Fourth. A goodly order was placed online by someone named Winslow."

Kat's heart almost beat out of her chest. "Is there a first name or initial? I mean, there's more than one Winslow around here."

"Hmm—Tyler Winslow. Nice name, isn't it, kind

of aristocratic? And, oh yes, an order from Maplecreek Consolidated High School, a small order for a halftime show at a homecoming football game just this month. Why, no wonder Maplecreek sounded familiar.''

"And who were those ordered by?''

"Hmm, paid for by a personal check. Now I file that different, but I'm sure you could find out at the high school. My dear, it sounds as if you have a cold. You're awfully stopped up and sniffly.''

Though Kat had stopped crying, she did sound stuffed up. "Thanks, but I'm all right.''

"Now, you just get a cup of hot water, squeeze some lemon in, add some apple cider vinegar and a bit of honey, stir it up and drink it straight down. It's good for what ails you. Did you want to order now?''

"I'll call back. And thanks for all the help.''

Kat washed her face at the laundry sink and went back to the dining room table where she'd been sitting with the sisters. The Amish were eating in shifts, and she wanted to be in the first one. She'd heard that Marnie was coming out to pay her respects this afternoon. Kat was also expecting Tyler, as town council member and neighbor of the deceased, and Clay, as union head. After all, Paul was his Amish counterpart at the construction site.

But this time, she wouldn't be here when they arrived, hanging on their every word. She was going to buggy into town and sneak in the back door of the Dutch Table to look around Marnie's office. The place was closed on Sunday since the Amish refused to work in or patronize a business on the Sabbath. That meant Marnie was giving up big profits from weekend tourists. Surely that spoke well for her intentions and character. Brooke was probably right about Marnie being completely innocent of hurting the Amish.

Kat hoped she could pick the lock on the back door of the restaurant to get in. She was not certain what she was looking for in Marnie's office or at her house, but she had the strangest feeling something she was missing could be right under her nose.

Kat stared down at the bowl of vegetable soup a sister had set in front of her. Marnie and vegetable soup...that first day she was in Amish country...the Tupperware bowl with "that herbal chicken noodle soup with extra vegetables the bishop likes from the Dutch Table," as Ida had explained it.

"Stop eating! *Halt!*" Kat cried, mixing German and English in her alarm. She rose at her seat. *"Wer hat diese Suppe gemacht?"*

The sisters stared at her, spoons halfway to open mouths. "I made this soup," Lee's mother, Emma, answered as Ida gave Kat a sharp look.

"Ah, it's very good. Ida, could I speak to you for a moment?"

Ignoring the sisters' glances and whispers, Kat and Ida went into the laundry room. "Ida, how often did Marnie Girkins bring Bishop Brand that special soup he liked?"

"Oh, that. Off and on," she said, tapping a gnarled index finger on her lips. "He loved the angel hair pasta and the extra vegetables. I think it's all gone, though— What? Katie, what?"

"Did he eat any before he got ill that last time—or the earlier times?"

"He could have, *ja,* probably did, but didn't take ill right away. So it was not canned right—or are you saying more? But Marnie brought it either fresh or frozen, not canned, no."

"I wish there was another jar of it."

"Eli might have brought one here. This funeral's happening so fast because the Yoders don't have many ties outside this area. And because of harvest. So folks brought in what they had at hand, sure did. Eli could have brought that last one, because when I looked in the freezer it wasn't there, so—"

Kat rushed out. The kids had been fed first, both at the kitchen table and in the dining room, and were now upstairs with Lee. She might be too late, to help—to save Sarah and Eli!

Yanking her skirts up above her knees, ignoring how her wound screamed at her, Kat took the steps two at a time. She tore though the open bedroom door through which she heard Lee's voice.

"Eli!" she cried. He looked normal, healthy, sitting with other boys on the floor as Lee led them in some sort of recitation. Sarah was with several girls on the bed with Lee. Kat sagged against the door frame. She almost burst into tears again. Her emotions were out of control. Her sergeant would have pulled her off the street—just the way Sheriff Martin had.

"What's the matter, Katie?" Eli asked, jumping to his feet.

"Did you bring any soup from home, Eli?"

"*Ja,* but grandmother told me I could."

"Where is it? Did you have any?"

"It was grandfather's favorite," he said, shaking his head, "but I think I left it in the surrey. Did the lid come off and it made a mess? I got it out of the freezer, not the pantry, but she said I could."

"It's all right. Sorry to interrupt, Teacher Leah," Kat said as the scholars stared at her. Lee kept mouthing, *What? What?* But Kat rushed downstairs, grabbed her shawl and headed out by the barn where the older boys had unhitched the horses to let them graze in a corral. The rows of vehicles were neatly aligned in what looked like the Amish version of a used-car lot.

Kat went from surrey to surrey, the eight identical ones that sat among the other, smaller buggies. Finally, she recognized the Brands' by Ida's lap blanket left on a seat. Though her hip hurt again, she hauled herself up in it and got down on her hands and knees.

Bingo! A still-sealed Tupperware bowl had rolled under the back seat. Kat lifted it and stared through the opaque plastic at the half-defrosted swirl of pasta and vegetables including mushrooms, potatoes, celery and carrots.

Asking the surprised teenage boy watching the horses to tell Teacher Leah she was borrowing her buggy, Kat had it half hitched before he could even help her. Keeping the container of soup between her feet, she took the back route toward town at a quick pace. No way did she want any of her suspects who might be heading for Yoders' to pass and recognize her.

On her way into town, Kat recalled one time that she and Morelli had been called to a 10-17—what they thought was a domestic dispute. It was a dispute, all right. The lady of the house had a boyfriend on the side and had been trying to poison her husband with arsenic, slowly, over a long period of time.

Could Marnie have slipped arsenic in Bishop Brand's soup? But why? One thing Kat intended to check out was whether Reuben's soup from Marnie had been all right: had he eaten it and did it match what she had here sloshing around between her feet? But Brooke was right that Marnie had no motive—no apparent one, at least. And Kat couldn't even imagine her electrocuting Bishop Yoder.

It was only then that she realized she hadn't told Luke where she was going. She'd been so excited and incensed at this poison-soup lead that she'd just run out. Kat fished up under her skirts, grabbed her cell phone from the twine around her waist and punched in Brooke's number again.

"Brooke, it's Kat," she said when her friend answered. "You said Dan's coming to the funeral today?"

"Right. He's going to meet Jen at our house and go out to Yoders'. I should come, but I just can't bear to leave Melly right now, with how she—she looks and sounds. She's so agitated."

"Can you reach Dan by phone?"

"Sure."

"Please have him tell Luke I'm checking on some things at Marnie's restaurant, then her house. Tell him I'm being very careful."

"Sure, okay. No, hey, the Dutch Table's closed on Sundays."

"I know. Brooke, just cut me some slack on this, okay?"

"Be careful. And since you're still that hot on her trail, even though a lawyer couldn't talk you out of it, I'll get busy right now researching her for you. She's the one I skipped before because I thought you had to be wrong. Is there anyone else?"

"One other woman, but I'm going to have to eventually look into her, I'm afraid. Louise Winslow is supposedly a recluse and dresses like an angel, but she smokes left-handed, which could link her to the devil's costume Bishop Brand's body was dressed in."

"But how?"

"Assuming the costume wasn't just bought for the bishop, it looks—and smells—like the person who first wore it smoked. There's what appears to be a cigarette burn on the left side, which may mean nothing—or everything. Louise Winslow admitted she likes to wear costumes, even disguises. She's bright and could be trying to set up her estranged husband, but I'd still rather have you look into Marnie first. Female cop intuition, I guess. It's like…she's almost too good to be true."

"You got it, although partly because I'm sure anything I find will clear Marnie. As I said, I'll call Dan, too."

Kat felt instantly better, braver. Dan would be in town, and Luke would soon know where she was. No more night forays alone into Patriot Knight territory or Amish Acres. From now on Kat was going to do her investigations, and if need be, make her accusations in broad daylight.

To safeguard the sample of soup, she'd stop at Dan and Brooke's to put it in their freezer, labeled with a note and skull-and-crossbones sketch. Hopefully, Dan could take it back to Columbus for her. One phone call to Mike Morelli, and she was sure he could get that CPD crime lab buddy of his to test it for arsenic.

She fixed her eyes on the two-lane road ahead and blew a kiss to Lee's horse, speeding her up even as her brain raced with new possibilities. Everyone knew the Amish loved to fix and eat food. Perhaps the same diabolical, perverted mind that reveled in using chicken manure, paintballs, electricity and nails for ammo thought it was a great joke to use killer food.

As Kat turned onto the narrow lane toward town, she saw a black pickup truck barreling at her. It looked like the same one that had buzzed her the other night en route to Amish Acres. Yes, for again a plume of dried corn shocks arched into the bright autumn air in its wake.

No mystery this time who was in it. Reuben Coblentz slowed, then slanted the ramshackle vehicle across the road, hemming her in against a water-filled ditch that kept the road from having berms or pull-offs. He climbed out so fast she didn't even have time to reach under her skirt for her cell phone.

From the cab of his truck, Reuben dragged out a long, curved machete and brandished it as if he were an attacking barbarian.

If Reuben had been behind everything, was he going to try to eliminate her with that brutal-looking blade? She could leap out and try to vault the ditch. The field here was planted in early winter wheat, short and pale green, no tall-corn refuge. No, perhaps her best defense was a good offense.

She stood in the buggy and pointed stiff-armed at him as he came closer. Her flight rush kicked in.

"Reuben, keep away from the horse and me with that thing! Have you been watching me, following me?"

"I knew you'd catch on sooner or later," he said, holding the massive, thick sickle in both hands before him. Either squinting or frowning, he looked up at her. "And I have something for you and Luke, see?"

The bright noon sun flashed off the blade as he lunged and swung it in a wide arc toward her.

21

Kat hurled her shawl at Reuben and slid to the other side of the buggy seat. She leaped off, despite the wrench to her hip wound. At least she had a barrier between them.

"Now see," he cried, "I accidently sliced your shawl. I just want you to give this corn knife to Luke, 'cause it was Bishop Brand's once. I'm just swinging it like what they do in those fancy Japanese ninja movies. Ain't it a beauty?"

Kat grabbed the buggy wheel to keep from falling into the ditch. "That thing's for Luke?" she demanded.

"This here's an antique, the kind the Amish used to cut the crops by hand in the old days, then make shocks. *Stooks*, they're called, to stand in the field for later shucking. I been using it to cut my small stand of corn by hand," he went on as he came around the horse, holding the scimitar-looking thing down at his side. "I bind the shocks, make decorations for the English. I been selling them here'bouts. I haven't been spending the money on booze either—you can just tell Ida that."

The pace of Kat's pulse began to slow, her thoughts settling. Though Reuben stood at the front of the buggy, she came around the rear to give him a wide berth.

"Don't ever come at someone again with that thing.

Just put it in the buggy, and I'll get it to Luke. Why didn't you give it to him yourself?''

He did as she said; the corn knife thudded onto the buggy floor. Without it, he looked sad and sorry, a scarecrow blown by winter wind. "Because,'' he said, his hand on the buggy wheel, "I know he's busy with Paul Yoder's death, on top of everything else, and I just happened to see you.''

"You recognized me from that far away—one Amish woman among the hundred others who could be in a small buggy? You've been following me sometimes, haven't you?''

He shrugged. "Anyone been Amish can spot a certain horse.''

Since it was Lee's horse, Kat assumed he was lying. Yet Lee's mare resembled Dilly. She pictured Reuben lurking in the bushes behind the farm with his binoculars trained on her and Eli. The hair prickled along the nape of her neck again, and she edged closer to the buggy, hoping he'd back away.

Kat realized he could have seen the plastic container of soup under the seat. She had planned to question him about Marnie's bringing him the same soup she gave Bishop Brand. But if Reuben were somehow involved—maybe as a cover for Marnie—Kat didn't want him to know she was going to check on the woman.

"Please move your truck,'' she said as she climbed up into the buggy and took the reins.

"Sure, no problem. Did you hear Luke's putting my windmill back up for me right after Paul Yoder's funeral? He's doing it in good faith, won't take a fee. I wanted him to have his dad's old knife—wanted to clear the books with him.''

"I'll see he gets it and hears what you said.''

He nodded and finally went to the driver's door of his truck. "I think you're a healing power in his life, maybe mine, too," he blurted, his words coming faster. "I haven't really been following you, only watching at times to be sure you stay safe. Luke's been aching for a wife, needing one, a mother for my Anna's Sarah and Eli. I don't hold no resentment 'gainst you for taking her place—just wanted you to know."

As Kat watched him get in, start the truck and pull away, her fear faded but the ache of looming loss blossomed again. Reuben actually thought she was Amish and had come to wed Luke and mother his grandchildren. But soon—in three days—she'd have no part in their lives. She'd lived among them for only two weeks, but she could not bear to leave. It would be worse than losing her parents and Jay. As she snapped the reins, she felt as if the horrid knife under her feet had sliced her in two.

Kat went to Melrose Manor to put the soup, carefully labeled with a Do Not Touch sign, in Brooke's freezer. Dan apparently hadn't arrived yet. After locking up their house, she drove to the back of the hardware store across the street from the Dutch Table. After tying the horse to a hitching post, she crossed the main street and strode toward the back entry to the restaurant.

Though Kat hadn't expected it, Marnie's car was parked down the alley by the back door.

Kat stepped behind a Dumpster a half a block away and waited. After about ten minutes, Marnie came out, dressed in black. Kat was relieved to see she wasn't taking food to Yoders'. She recalled how Marnie had sent suckers for the kids at school right before the paintball attack. Had she made suckers of them all?

Kat watched her get in her car, but she just sat there, primping in the rearview mirror, brushing her hair, applying lipstick. Gil Gilmore drove up with Tyler Winslow, and they got in Marnie's car and drove off together.

Were they all just friends, or could Tyler be cheating on poor Louise with Marnie? They could be in cahoots for the terrorism against the Amish, as well as each having an interest in Amish Acres. Later she'd have to ask Luke if the three of them had showed up at Yoders' together.

Kat walked to the back entrance of the restaurant and, looking both ways in the alley, jiggled the doorknob. To her surprise, the door was unlocked. She opened it quietly. Thank heavens she wouldn't have to pick the lock. But the open door might mean someone else was inside. If so, she was determined to look as if she belonged.

Glancing down the back hall into the deserted restaurant itself, Kat saw the clock read nearly two in the afternoon. Without knocking, she tried the door to Marnie's office. This knob too turned easily in her hand.

The room was lighted but deserted. The comfortable clutter was gone. No photos on the walls, no folders on the desk or piled on the filing cabinets. All that remained on the stripped walls was the Building Blocks quilt. Kat didn't realize anyone else was in the room until she heard the sound of ripping masking tape come from behind the desk.

"Oh!" Kat and the girl on her knees by a big carton cried in unison. The girl was an Amish teen, though not one of the church members she knew. Perhaps she was from the church on the other side of town.

"Sorry, I didn't see you," Kat said in English before she realized she should have used German. "I was hoping Mrs. Girkins was in. Is she moving her office?"

"Just storing some things for moving later to her new place at Amish Acres. I'm going to be one of her housemaids there. Already I work at the bed-and-breakfast."

Kat stared at the neatly closed carton which probably held the folders and photos she had hoped to glance through. She weighed questioning this girl about whether Marnie made her special soup at home or here, but it wouldn't take much for her to figure out she was suspicious of Marnie—and wasn't Amish at all.

"I can tell her you were here, *ja?*" the girl said.

"Oh, that's okay. I'll just catch her later."

"You are the one come to wed Luke Brand?"

"*Ja. Auf Wiedersehen,*" Kat said and beat a hasty retreat. Maybe this was a sign—a second sign, she told herself—that she shouldn't risk rifling through suspects' offices like she was some sort of special ops instead of a street cop. She would go where she should have gone first, to Marnie's house. Somehow she had to look around her kitchen, check her pantry, maybe even look in her cellar, even though she never wanted to risk getting trapped in another basement as long as she lived.

Kat left Lee's horse and buggy in Dan's barn and approached Marnie's property from the back this time, coming through her woodlot. A charming white trellis with clematis and climbing roses arched over a flagstone path that twisted through the trees. Birdhouses and birdbaths enhanced sheltered spots along the shady walkway. Just before Kat emerged in the back of the yard proper, she found herself in an area where Marnie kept her woodpile.

It wasn't really a woodpile but large logs leaning against a wire fence from which torn strips of sheets fluttered. The strips reminded her of the piece she'd seen caught in Yoders' windmill. Were these tied here to keep birds off the wire fence?

She approached the logs—six of them, hardly a woodpile. Each one had holes drilled in it at regular intervals and straw packed in the openings. Glancing around to be sure she could not be seen from the house, Kat leaned closer. Some of the holes were sealed with what appeared to be wax. From others sprouted clumps of mushrooms. She had to step carefully, for all around her feet, fungus had popped from piles of sawdust and the grass.

The clusters of colored caps ranged from white to tan to pink to mottled brown. Some were stubby and fat, others up to six inches tall. One type looked like tiny parasols in a fairy circle, nodding to each other in a dance. One pure white variety resembled oyster shells, and she was sure she recognized the ones called shiitake.

"A mushroom garden," Kat whispered. "Marnie grows her own mushrooms."

Another memory darted at her: when Sarah had shown Kat the photo Marnie had given her, the child had said she'd seen Marnie's "mushy" garden. Kat had assumed it was some sort of baby talk and hadn't questioned her on it. Marnie told her to get away from the mushy garden and was "kind of mean." Perhaps she had either wanted Sarah to stay out of here or was angry the girl had found the place. Had she given Sarah the picture as a bribe to keep her from telling about the mushrooms?

"The hell with my arsenic theory. These mushrooms—some, at least—could be poison."

Again Kat studied the area, from the backyard to the fringe of the woods. She saw no one, however much she felt she was being watched again. Darting another look back at the house, she assured herself that she could not be seen from its windows.

Kat stepped behind a big tree and reached up under her skirts for her cell phone. From memory, she punched in Mike Morelli's number. He answered almost immediately, his voice so familiar yet so foreign that she blinked back tears.

"Morelli here."

"Lindley here."

"You gotta be kiddin' me!"

"Nope. I know who to call when I need some help."

"Kiddo, if you haven't needed help since you left the big city, you're not my old partner but some damn impostor. What gives in Amish land?"

"I'll explain everything later, because I may be moving back soon. But I need you to get me some intel from your old tox lab pal."

"Jimmy Lowe?"

"Affirmative."

"Wait—okay, got a pencil, shoot."

"I need to describe some mushrooms to you to see if they could be poison."

"You got a vic?"

"I'm afraid so."

"The local law in on it?"

"That's sensitive—part of my problem."

Kat waited a second for further reaction, but there was none. She'd almost forgotten that Mike had seen about everything by now, and that his nickname was Whatever Works Morelli.

She started describing the five distinct kinds of mushrooms she saw here—size, color, shape.

"Affirmative. Anything else?" he said, and she silently blessed him for being so willing to help. They'd been through a lot together. In a way, he'd almost been the father she'd lost too early.

"The only other thing is there's a compost pile nearby," she said, "at least, that's what I think it is. It seems a strange mix of sawdust, maybe ground corncobs, and manure—chicken manure's my best guess."

"Getting really countrified, huh?"

If he only knew, she thought. Wait until he heard she'd gone undercover Amish—and didn't want to leave.

"You still on your old cell number?" he asked. "I'm gonna try to have Jimmy call you, especially if this info's not enough for him."

"Great. Also, tell him I'll send a sample of mushroom soon. Say hi to Peg and the kids. I miss being dragged to the Morelli reunions. Is the department hiring any dispatchers lately?"

"You want the job, kiddo, I'll whack one of the regulars for you."

Ordinarily, she would have laughed, but that hardly seemed funny now. "Thanks, partner. Thanks for everything," she said and punched off.

Kat hid the phone, then carefully gathered a bouquet of fungi, two of each kind. She peered at the house from behind the tree. Had she found what she came for? Poisonous mushrooms? Chicken manure that could be used to spray on Amish quilts? The corn cobs could have come from Tyler Winslow—or any of a hundred other places around here. Clay Bigler could have brought Marnie the sawdust—or not. This was all circumstantial so far, but she felt, finally, that she was getting somewhere. But was it where she needed to go to save Luke and his people before it was too late?

The next day, despite the sheriff and one of his deputy's escorting the procession, Kat was continually on edge. In fact, the funeral and burial passed without incident. But then she worried that the meal back at Yoders' farm could have been tampered with, even though she trusted the cooks and the farm had been watched by four teenage boys during the trip to the cemetery. Kat asked more than one Amish woman if Marnie Girkins had brought any food when she'd paid a condolence call on Saturday, but they'd all said no. For once, Marnie—or the other English visitors—had not come bearing gifts.

Kat filled in both Luke and Dan on what she'd discovered in Marnie's backyard, and Dan had taken the soup and one each of the mushrooms to Columbus. He'd promised he'd get everything to Mike Morelli or Jim Lowe as soon as he could.

Kat had been in a quandary about where to hide the rest of the mushroom samples she'd picked at Marnie's. She'd finally packed them in straw and secreted them in a box under her bed in the *daadi haus*—the same place she kept the devil's costume.

Kat's thoughts remained in turmoil: Mary Yoder had said Louise Winslow dressed like an angel, and Louise herself had said that when she went out, no one would recognize her because of how she dressed.

What if Kat was wrong about Marnie? What if Louise was either working with Tyler and lying about their estranged relationship or working hard to set him up to take the fall?

Kat shoved everything back under the bed. "I'm not spending my last few days in here," she muttered as she closed the door and went outside. She could do nothing else until she heard from Morelli or Jim Lowe, but she could do something to make more memories with these dear people she would soon have to leave.

Since the funeral meal had been in late morning, Kat knew Luke and the kids would be hungry. She marched into his kitchen. Ida was reading to Sarah, and Eli was with Luke in his shop, preparing to resurrect Reuben's mill tomorrow morning. It would be a busy day, for the harvest team was coming at about two to cut first Luke's, then Mose's cornfields. And during all those busy hours and the following days when Luke helped others cut corn, she knew she'd be hard-pressed to get him to herself again.

Though her idea of a home-cooked meal used to be reheating Szechuan carryout, Kat went to work. By four-thirty, when she rang the dinner bell outside the back door, she had set the table for five. She'd made a pile of cranberry pancakes, which she kept warm, along with fried country sausage patties, in the big oven, while she melted orange marmalade for a topping. She poured iced milk for everyone, made coffee, and, at the last minute, put together a Waldorf salad from apples, celery, walnuts and raisins she found in the fridge.

When Luke came in and saw the spread, his jaw dropped.

"Yes," she said, "I did this, and it's all edible, though cooking's never been my thing."

"Until now," Luke said and hurried to wash his hands in the sink.

"Wow," Eli, two steps behind Luke as usual, cried as he came in with Sarah and Ida close behind. "It smells good in here! I mean, *Daad* does pretty good fixing food, but *Grossmutter* Ida's kitchen's the one that smells good—usually, that is."

"Sit then, all of you," Kat said.

To her amazement, despite the fact she'd expected Ida to have the place opposite Luke at the foot of the table, everyone left it for her. After the silent prayer— during which Kat prayed fervently that she could keep everyone here safe and have loved ones of her own like this someday—they ate family-style, each taking what they wanted from passing platters.

"*Ser gut,* Katie," Ida said. "The orange glaze, now that's a fine idea, goes good with the pancakes, for sure."

"So what's this salad called?" Eli asked, spearing apples and celery with his fork as if they needed killing.

"Waldorf salad, named for a hotel in New York City, I think," she said.

"Waldorf sounds *Deutsche,*" Eli said, nodding approvingly.

"Mmm" was the most Sarah said.

And then Kat's gaze met Luke's down the span of busy table. His eyes glowed with warmth and happiness and even, perhaps, forbidden Amish pride. And his expression made him look as if he'd like to devour her along with the food.

Her fork halfway to her mouth, Kat stared back. He smiled the way that moved the right corner of his mouth in a slight slant before his lips parted and the single, deep dimple showed in his cheek.

Kat felt dizzy. The entire room seemed to tilt toward him. For one blinding moment, she saw nothing but Luke Brand.

"I'm starving," he said, a dark flicker in each eye as he winked at her. "Everything looks great," he added, as his eyes both assessed and caressed her. *"Wunderbar."*

How Kat managed to eat, she didn't know. Her stomach felt filled with butterflies. When Luke excused the kids to their nightly chores and Ida, exhausted from the day, went back to her house, Kat made a move to clean the table.

"No, wait," he said. "Let's just sit like this a minute."

She nodded. Sinking back into her chair, she put her hands in her lap. She gripped her apron and felt the cell phone against her thigh. *This isn't real, this can't be,* she told herself. She was English, he was Amish, and the world was out there, not only waiting but threatening.

"Kat—my Katie—things are going to be really busy the next few days, but I just want you to know how much it's meant to me to have you here. And not only for the help to find whoever's behind all the harm and hurt."

"It's been great for me, too, a revelation."

"What was revealed?"

"How I need and want a family—the possibilities of that."

"How you need and want a man to share that dream?"

"Luke, I—" She bit her lip and said no more.

"I'm forcing myself to sit down here so I don't do something insane, like pick you up and carry you upstairs to my bed. And never, ever let you leave."

Tears blurred her view of him—two tables, two Lukes. Stunned, longing for all he intimated, she nodded.

"Katherine Lindley, it's in your reach," he said, his intense gaze burning into her as he slid one hand down the long table as if they could touch. "It's in yours but not in mine. I can't leave the Amish and my children, however much I want a life with you. But if you could leave the English world, we could consider so many things…"

The kitchen door opened and Eli poked his head in. "Mr. Coblentz is out here to see you, *Daad.* About tomorrow morning."

"Tell him I'll be right there, son."

When Eli left, Kat jumped to her feet and looked out the window over the sink. The boy strode back to Reuben and stood chattering away to him. From here, she could see the smile on the old man's face.

"You still don't trust him," Luke said, coming to stand behind her. He put a hand on each side of the sink close to her waist and leaned his chin on her shoulder to look out too. His pelvis touched her bottom as if she sat in his lap. He slid his hands up to clasp her upper arms.

"I can't help worrying about Reuben," she said, "even if he gave you that corn knife peace offering." She glanced above the back door where Luke had mounted the curved blade. "And I'm going to be a nervous wreck every second you're hoisting that windmill of his tomorrow and then climbing up there to get it working again."

"In other words, I can take the English cop out of the city, but I can't put the Amish in her without a lot more work," Luke said, leaning back against a tall chair and pulling her toward him in a gentle embrace.

"I wish you'd give me more time to try to make it work. Don't be afraid, Kat. Katie wouldn't be afraid. 'For God has not given us a spirit of fear, but of power and of love.'"

For a man who seemed so calm and controlled, he kissed her with hunger, slanting his mouth against hers, opening her lips and crushing her to him. Then he set her back hard, roughly, as if forcing himself to do so, and strode for the door.

Deeply shaken, Kat alternated between cleaning up the table and glancing out at the two men and the boy outside. Surely Luke's instincts were right about Reuben. The old man just wanted to be Amish, to have a part in the lives of his long-lost family.

"Damn it!" she cried. "That's fine for him, but it's absolutely impossible for me!"

She nearly dropped a stack of dishes when her cell phone vibrated against her. Hurrying into the dining room, Kat pulled her phone from under her skirt and punched it on.

"Kat Lindley here."

"Officer Lindley, Jim Lowe, CPD crime lab."

Officer Lindley, he'd called her. Didn't he know she wasn't with the force anymore? "Thanks for calling back. And thank Mike Morelli for me, too."

"He owes me for so many favors already, this is a mere blip on the radar screen," he said with a chuckle. The man spoke fast; she had to really focus on each word.

"Besides, this was a fun assignment," he said. "I haven't heard of anyone either accidently or intentionally cultivating *chlorophyllum molybdites* for years, though I'm only hazarding a guess so far, going on your descriptions of one of the fungi varieties you gave Morelli."

Her stomach knotted. "So that variety is harmful?"

"To say the least. Its nickname is Green Gill or Green-spored Parasol, but they might as well call it the Kiss of Death. And the crazy thing is, it's beautiful and prolific, sprouting in lots of American lawns in late summer or fall. It has a big fruiting body, but for what you see above ground, there's a lot more mycelia hidden beneath."

"What specifically happens if a person ingests it?"

"Depends on the dose, size of the person, age, health. Symptoms would usually occur within a couple of hours but then could hang on. Possible combinations of nausea, vomiting, weakness. There could be some brief period of improvement. Sometimes it mimics influenza, virus or stomach problems."

"Like an ulcer? Or acid reflux?"

"Sure, it could. It's hard to diagnose. Continual, even sporadic ingestion would cause liver and kidney damage and eventual death. Yeah, old Green Gill's bad, bad news. Got any actual samples I could check out?"

"I've sent what must be Green Gill mushrooms to you in a chicken broth soup mix, and one in the flesh, so to speak. A friend, Daniel Brand, will be dropping them off today at the medical examiner's office for you, and I have extra samples here."

"Keep your fingers out of your mouth if you've been handling them. The spores on those babies are as dangerous as that mottled flesh, however beautiful they are."

Horrible, not beautiful, Kat thought. The only thing beautiful about them was that they all pointed their poison caps right at Marnie.

22

"Brooke," Dan said, jumping up from his chair in Melanie's hospital room, "I'm going to go drop the cooler of soup at the ME's office for Kat. I'll be right back."

"You know where it is?" she asked, keeping her eyes fixed on Melly. "On King Avenue, in the same building as the coroner's office."

"Right. That's what you said."

She lifted her eyes to Dan's worried frown. "Oh, I guess I did. I just get so distracted, so—"

"You can't keep this up, Brooke, staring at her for hours on end," Dan said, keeping his voice low. "You have to take a break now and then. Sweetheart, *you're* starting to look comatose."

"I know. I'm sorry." She slumped back in her chair and folded her arms over her chest. "I just keep thinking I can will her to wake up, to come back to us, so we can go home, stay home."

He knelt by her chair and hugged her. "I know, I know, but—"

"I know, I know," Melly said distinctly.

Still in a half embrace, they stared at their daughter. Brooke was expecting the cryptic phrase to be followed by the usual disappointment where Melanie's eyes stayed open for a while before she faded back into fitful sleep. But this seemed different. Brooke held her breath.

"I know who I am," Melly whispered. "Have I been sick?"

This time, Brooke didn't call for a nurse. She tried not to get her hopes up, but Melly seemed so clear, so aware. She had turned her head, and her eyes seemed focused on them. Brooke was terrified that if she spoke or moved, she'd shatter this new hope.

Both Brooke and Dan stood slowly and, gripping each other's hands, approached their daughter's bed.

"Yes, you've been sick for over two weeks," Dan said as he stroked Melly's cheek and Brooke held her hand. "You hit your head," he went on when Brooke couldn't find her voice. "But—you do know who you are?"

"I'm Melanie, Dad," she said, her raspy voice sounding slightly annoyed. "Where's Jen?"

Brooke could feel her pulse pound. When she first heard the ringing, she'd thought it was in her ears or her heart.

"Brooke, your phone," Dan said.

"Let it ring."

Dan moved away to take it from her purse and answer it. "Kat, hi. What? I was just going to take it over, but Melly's conscious. Yeah, tell everyone! The doctor hasn't seen her yet but..."

"Who's Kat?" Melly asked.

That snapped Brooke back to total reality. Her daughter had come to life, but her father-in-law and Bishop Yoder might have been murdered. "Let me talk to her a sec," she said, still holding Melly's hand as Dan gave her the cell phone.

"Kat, listen, I can't talk right now. But I just wanted you to know I did find a single lead about Marnie online. Nothing came up under her married name, Girkins, but I remembered she'd once said her maiden name was Byler. Margaret Byler—B-Y-L-E-R. There was some link to a Lancaster, Pennsylvania newspaper that was cross-referenced to a new book about the abuse of children by priests in the Catholic Church. That's as far as I got until Dan came, and now Melly's back. Kat—tell everyone Melly's back with us!''

When Kat told Luke and the kids, the house erupted in a wild melee of hugs, cheers and shouted prayers. Eli ran to the *daadi haus* to tell Ida. Luke put Sarah on his shoulders and was heading out the door to let Mose, Susan and their brood know the news.

"Wait, wait just a second!'' Kat called, grabbing his arm. "I have to buggy in to Dan and Brooke's house to get my laptop computer. Brooke has turned up something I have to check out. Ten minutes into town, five minutes there, ten minutes back—I'll be here in about a half hour, before it's dark.''

"I should go with you.''

"I'll be fine. You go tell your brother's family the good news. If my batteries for the laptop run down, I'll just plug it into your small generator in the shop, okay?''

"Sure. But, Kat, come back to Mose's instead of here,'' he called after her. "With all the bad things that have been going on, we need some family time to rejoice.''

Family time, Kat thought as she hurried out to the barn. Time to rejoice. Luke had included her in family time. But her time here was slipping away....

Luke sent Eli out to the barn to hitch Dilly for her. Though she didn't need the boy's help, she took it. "I can go in town with you,'' he told her as they both climbed into the little buggy.

"I'll just drop you at Mose's driveway,'' she said

as she blew a kiss to Dilly to get her going. "You run straight up to your uncle's house, you hear me?"

"I hear you," he said, half polite and half pouty. "But I'm not a baby who needs watching, you know. I can keep an eye on *Daad,* and you, too."

"And we both appreciate it," she told him. Before he jumped down, she ruffled his hair, and he hugged her.

In Brooke and Dan's house, Kat started to unhook her laptop, then glanced out the window over the desk. Across the vacant lot between the two old homes, Marnie was putting a box in the trunk of her car, which was parked at the side of the house in her driveway. First her office disappeared into a cardboard box, and now this? Why would Marnie be preparing to move her things when her house at Amish Acres was still a skeleton? Could she know she was a suspect? If so, she could be disposing of evidence or planning to flee.

Kat plugged the laptop back in and sat before it in the darkening room. Glancing out the window to watch Marnie, she turned the laptop on, went online and searched for Margaret Byler. She had no idea what Brooke had meant by there being some link to abused Catholic children.

She found nothing relevant; Marnie put another box in her car.

Kat tried Margaret Byler + Child Abuse. Nothing.

Amish + Margaret Byler + Lancaster, Pennsylvania. "Yes!"

She traced more links until, of all things, Amazon.com popped up on the screen, offering a book called *Gifts From God: The Amish Love for Their Children,* by

Charles Jensen. Also listed was a much newer book on the abuse of children by Catholic priests.

She backed up again and tried the site of the Lancaster, Pennsylvania newspaper, the *Intelligencer Journal,* where she searched the archives. She was relieved to see that historic articles on the Amish community were included in the archives, whereas the records didn't go back very many years on other subjects.

But this was all taking too long and turning into too many dead ends. If Marnie closed her car trunk, Kat decided, she would rush over to talk to her about where she was going. Even if the mushrooms were poisonous, even if Marnie had murdered Bishop Brand, a big piece of the puzzle was still missing. As Brooke had said, Marnie had no motive, unless she was doing it for someone else who had some sort of control over her.

"Bingo!" Kat cried as the screen slowly loaded an article from June 30, 1958, with the headline "Abusive Amish Bishop Jailed." She skimmed it wide-eyed, trying to remember to watch for Marnie across the empty lot. Although Marnie's car trunk was still open, she hadn't reappeared from her house for a few minutes.

Bishop John Byler, age 30, was arraigned at the Lancaster County Court House on Monday for physical and psychological abuse of both his wife, Naomi, age 29, and their daughter, Margaret (Marnie), age 8. Although the Amish usually judge and control their own, even church members, who wished to remain anonymous, admitted that both the woman and the child were often bruised and the child has had bones broken.

"The saddest thing is," said non-Amish Milt

Miller, owner of the Bird-in-Hand Nest Restaurant, age 45, who tipped off authorities to the alleged abuse, "the child [Marnie] also told me she'd been locked in a closet and made to fast for being bad."

Fasting is a voluntary going without food, though this starvation, said Lancaster County Judge Clark T. Wilson, "was for punishment, as was the minor's being beaten and locked for hours, if not days, in a dark place."

According to Professor Charles Jensen, author of *Gifts from God: The Amish Love for Their Children,* it is highly unusual for the Amish to mistreat their children, for they are greatly loved and valued within the community.

Bishop Byler faces not only a jail sentence but shunning by his own people. When asked for a statement, John Byler told this paper, "It's all lies from the pit of hell. The Plain People know I like to take photos, and they're blackballing me for that."

Naomi Byler has been indicted for child endangering and six counts of permitting child abuse. The child in question has been taken in by the Amish community until her parents' trials.

Kat sat stunned. She turned on the printer and hit print. Through the window she saw Marnie come outside again, this time with a small box and her purse over her shoulder. She slammed the trunk so hard Kat could hear it even here. Kat now had a motive for Marnie's possible guilt: she could hate the Amish, especially bishops. And she could definitely be warped by that abusive, traumatic childhood. She watched Marnie walk around the car. Kat only had a few more days here, and it was possible someone—surely not Brooke?—had tipped Marnie off and she was going to flee.

Leaving the printer still chugging out the document, Kat dashed out the front door, hiked her skirt hem and tore across the lot toward Marnie. When Marnie opened her car door and the dome light popped on, Kat realized that this car could have been at Amish Acres Saturday night. She'd been so certain, though, that the person shooting the nail gun was a man.

Marnie tossed her purse in the front seat and got behind the wheel. She wasn't looking Kat's way and evidently didn't see her until Kat crossed the driveway behind her. Though Marnie hadn't started the motor, Kat was terrified she would lock the door. Kat yanked the driver's door open.

"Oh, Katie! You scared me to death! What in the world's the matter? Don't tell me something else terrible has happened."

"Yes, yes, it has. Do you have a minute before you leave?"

Marnie pulled her key—it was on a big, jingly ring—out of the ignition and got out. She had evidently not caught on that she was a suspect or she would hardly have been so cooperative.

"What's the problem, then?" she asked, looking puzzled.

"The problem," Kat said, out of breath, "is that the person who's been harming the Amish is someone they love and trust."

Marnie's face went blank for one moment, though whether in shock or self-denial, Kat was not certain. Then she squinted; growing dusk etched lines in her face and hid her eyes. Her face suddenly looked older and sharper. "Someone's been c-caught?" she stammered.

"That's right."

"I certainly hope whoever it is pays dearly not only for scaring those poor children but for breaking the windows in town, including mine."

"That was a clever move, too, wasn't it? What a perverse sense of humor's behind all this."

"What are you talking about?"

"Arranging for your own windows to be broken with the Amish ones. I think it's time to come clean, Margaret Byler Girkins."

Her features seemed to shift again, clenching in a frown. "I suspected almost from the first you weren't Amish," Marnie said, her voice cold and outraged. "And that the local Plain People—certainly the Brands—had to know that you were a phony."

"Perhaps it takes one to know one, but this isn't about me. Nor is it about windmill rotors breaking windows, or even about scaring kids. It's about poisonous mushrooms, Marnie. And, I guess, trying to get back at your father somehow."

Despite the growing darkness, Kat could see Marnie's face drain of color. She seemed frozen in a pose, a black-and-white photo like those she'd taken of Luke's wife and of other local Amish in her morbid fascination with them. Kat was almost sure Marnie would admit her guilt. She'd seen that moment in others, when they knew they were cornered on the very edge of the roof with no way down but flinging themselves into thin air.

"You're demented," Marnie accused, "and I won't listen to any more snide, insane accusations. What are you, some sort of spy? If you're a cop, this is entrapment."

"Hardly. And I'm not a cop, though I can let you make these accusations to the sheriff," Kat bluffed, still not certain she could fully trust him. "Or I could just chat with some homicide detectives I know in Columbus to see what they'd advise."

"You're a Columbus cop or detective, that's it! I knew it was something like that! Your German is pitiful, and Luke Brand's not the type to marry someone he hardly knows."

"I said this isn't about me. It's really about you hating the Amish—your father, maybe your mother too—for what they did to you. Fascinated by the Amish, wanting to belong, yet resenting and hating them."

"You don't know the first thing about being abused and deserted! You—"

"Hating the bishops, wanting Amish kids who are loved, as you weren't, to suffer, so that—"

"Do you know he got off?" Marnie screamed. "Because he was Amish and a bishop, he got off, and my mother, too? The Amish family that took me in had to give me back to them. They left the Amish, but nothing much changed, and I ran away when I could and met my husband when I was working in a restaurant. If he hadn't found me, then left me with some money when he died, I never could have started here. I've made a success of myself, so no one will ever believe anything bad of me, either," she insisted, crossing her arms over her chest and tossing her head.

"Let's just test that theory. You and I are going to the sheriff's office so that—"

With her keys protruding from her fist like sharp brass knuckles, Marnie took a swing at Kat. When Kat ducked, Marnie, thrown off balance, lunged for the open car door. Kat came at her waist-high, butting her shoulder into the woman's belly. Marnie gave a grunt as Kat slammed her into the back door of the car.

They grappled against it until Kat managed to get a "come along" hold on Marnie's hand, which she twisted up behind her back. Kat might not be able to shoot a gun, but she hadn't forgotten this, and she found the strength she needed in her once-shattered right hand.

Marnie went to her knees beside the driveway; Kat knelt behind her, holding on.

"I'm sorry, Marnie, really sorry about what your parents did to you, but it doesn't excuse what you've done. Yes, I do know what it is to be betrayed by parents, to be desperate and hurt and deserted, but it doesn't have to come to this."

"To what, damn you! You can't—can't prove—"

"I'll bet I can prove that some of the delicious veggies in the soup you fed Bishop Brand will match those poisonous Green Gill mushrooms you're growing out back!"

She gasped. "He was old—ill."

"So that makes it all right to slowly poison him? But who helped you with your other acts of terrorism? Tyler? Clay? Gil? The sheriff? Tell me!"

"I'm telling you I want a lawyer."

Kat knew she should let go, *had* to let go. But Melanie lying in that hospital bed for weeks, Eli's eye, the smell of Paul Yoder's burned flesh, and Bishop Brand's body in that damn, cheap devil's costume flashed through her mind.

"All right, all right!" Marnie cried. "I hired two guys from Cleveland so they couldn't be traced. I— You're breaking my arm..."

"The Amish trusted you, even loved you, and you threw it all away. Such a precious people, and you did more than betray them. You not only killed Bishop Brand, but I'm going to prove you and your hired thugs murdered Paul Yoder, too, and could have killed those kids—Melanie, Eli and the rest, for all you cared.''

Gasping for breath, Kat let up her pressure. Her heart beat so hard it shook her whole body. Though Marnie had started to sob, Kat hauled her to her feet.

Kat hadn't meant to lose control. She'd forgotten the rules of arrest. But what shook her more was that she'd forgotten what it was like to make an arrest. That high-five, exultant feeling she'd experienced so often on the force when she'd followed leads or taken someone off the streets was muted now. When she saw Marnie looking so broken, she felt for her, almost understood her—and that reaction was so Amish it scared Kat stiff.

When Marnie begged to be arraigned in some other jurisdiction and not to be handed over to Sheriff Martin's custody, Kat realized two things. First, that part of Marnie's punishment should be facing those she'd tried to harm. Second, that Ray Martin was evidently a man to be trusted.

She dialed the sheriff's cell phone number just as Luke drove at breakneck speed into Brooke and Dan's driveway. "Luke, over here!" Kat shouted. He vaulted from his buggy and raced over on foot.

"Even with everyone together and so happy about Melly," he began as he came closer, "I worried about you...."

He came to a dead stop as he rounded the car. "Marnie?" he said, when he saw Kat had tied her hands behind her back with bonnet and apron strings. "It was Marnie?"

Kat nodded as Ray Martin answered his phone. "Katie Kurtz here," she told him, holding up one finger to Luke, "but I think I can admit to being Kat Lindley now."

"You're either leaving or you got something for me," he said.

"Someone," she corrected. "Caught, confessed and almost delivered."

"Where are you? You okay?"

"I'm in the driveway of Marnie Girkins's bed-and-breakfast. Luke's here, too."

"You mean it's her? You sure as hell better have proof."

"It was Marnie?" Luke repeated as the woman just hung her head.

"Yes," Kat told the sheriff while nodding to Luke. "Marnie Byler Girkins has admitted to poisoning Bishop Brand and to hiring hit men from out of town for the rest, but you'll have to take it from there, Sheriff—Melanie Brand came out of her coma tonight, and I'm missing a big celebration over that."

Kat smiled at Luke. Though he looked stunned and shaken, he reached out to grip her free hand. "A celebration, but a time of mourning and remembrance," he said. "For our gains but losses, too."

They stood like that over the sobbing woman until Sheriff Martin pulled up with his light-bar flashing in their eyes.

23

"It's going to be a great day, *Daad!*" Eli told Luke as Kat and Ida put a big breakfast on the table in Luke's kitchen on Tuesday morning. "'Specially 'cause we got some days off from school, so I can help you with Mr. Coblentz's windmill and water the horses when everyone cuts our corn!"

Luke grinned and, to Kat's surprise, high-fived his son. They were all excited, not only over the resurrection of Reuben's windmill and of his Amish ties, but over the lifting of the dark cloud of threat and fear in the community. Sheriff Martin had called Kat on her cell phone early this morning to tell her that Marnie had given up the names and addresses of the two Cleveland men she'd hired to harass the Amish while she slowly got rid of their leader.

"Did she admit to anything about Paul Yoder's electrocution?" Kat had asked.

"She claims she merely mentioned to her cronies it would be good if Yoder was out of the way, too, and they may have acted on their own."

"Who are these guys? Were they hanging around, or did they just drive in for the hits she set up for them?"

"They evidently drove in. She says they have a motorcycle shop outside Cleveland."

"That fits. But does everything else?"

"Like what? You did a fine job, Kat, and I want to

apologize for overreacting to your style. I know Luke couldn't bear to have you hurt, and I couldn't, either, but I guess your ends justified the means. Listen, I'm on my way to Cleveland to help the cops collar Marnie's hired hands. Gotta go, but I'll get you back in the loop when I can. You're staying for the harvest, right?''

''Ja, ja.''

''You always did look Amish. Hey, you want that dispatch job, it's yours.''

''Thanks, but I don't think I could stay around now. I'd feel like I had one foot in the English world and one in the Amish—and I'd be doing the splits.''

''Yeah, but you seemed to handle a split personality pretty well. Enjoy your last coupla days there. You got a payday coming with me.''

''Katie.'' Eli's voice interrupted her thoughts. ''How come you don't look happy? You can watch *Daad* lift the windmill with me and Sarah and *Grossmutter* Ida, then watch the harvest. It's real loud with the combine.''

''Why is it loud with the horses pulling it?'' she asked. ''It doesn't run itself, does it?''

''Daad,'' Eli said, rolling his eyes as if she were the most ignorant thing in the world, ''tell her how it works.''

Kat was thrilled that Eli's eye was better. The vision was still slightly blurred, but he never would have rolled his eyes if the pain weren't gone. That ointment and time would heal Eli, the doctor had theorized. How she wished she had some magic medicine and the promise that time would heal her heart when she left here.

''Why don't you tell her how harvesting works?'' Luke suggested as he forked up more eggs.

"See, Katie," Eli said, sitting up straighter, "the horses come first, pulling the combine. They have to stay way out in front of it, 'cause it has a real long blade—how long, *Daad?*"

"Almost four feet."

"Right, and real sharp on two sides. It goes back-forth, back-forth to cut through about four rows of corn at once. Is that right, *Daad?*"

"Right."

"Then the stalks fall back and kind of get caught in these teeth things that grab them up into the wagon part. That makes all the noise, like *bump-chug, bump-chug,* the gasoline generator engine working the blade and the teeth."

"Oh, I see," Kat said. "And then the machine takes the ears and husks them?"

"No," Eli said, sounding exasperated. "That's how the worldly machines work, like the one Mr. Winslow drives around, big as a monster. The Amish 'round here have a man up on the machine—not the driver, but the binder man. They take turns, don't they, *Daad?*"

"They sure do, because it's hard work. After the machine lifts the bundles and binds them with twine into shocks, the binder man throws them off behind the combine. The others walking behind pick up the shocks and stand them up so they can dry and the corn can be shucked by hand later."

"*Ja,* that's it," Eli told her with a proud grin, as if he'd explained all that himself. "We do that in the fall and winter when we're not so busy, when there's lots more family time."

"I see," Kat said. She did see. She could imagine it all—the crisp, deep autumn nights to come, the snowy winter mornings with the family staying in together. The peaceful, rural views out over the snow-blanketed fields from this warm, bright kitchen or from Luke's bedroom window upstairs.

Sarah spoke up. "Katie, you're still sad. Everyone's going to have fun today. The evildoer is gone and it was Mrs. Marnie—but, *Daadi,* what will happen to her houses and shop and restaurant if she has to go away now?"

"I don't know, Sarah," he said, shoving his chair back from the table. "Just remember, thanks to Katie—and the Lord—we don't have to be afraid anymore."

"Amen," Ida put in as she lingered over a piece of toast spread with what looked to Kat like elderberry jam. "And some of us don't have to fret that we might have done something to hurt those we loved, for sure. We lost my Jacob too early, but the Lord seems to be giving us poor Reuben back. But your father has something to tell you children about Mr. Coblentz, too, don't you, son?"

Luke sat back down. "I was going to do it later, but yes."

"I'll just step out—" Kat said.

"*Nein,* Katie," Ida said. "It's partly you that brought Reuben back to the fold. And since you know how that's done, maybe you will want to do it again."

With whom else? Kat almost blurted before she realized Ida meant Kat herself. She blinked back tears as Luke began, "Eli and Sarah, you are both old enough to understand that sometimes the Amish brothers and sisters don't get along—"

"Eli and me haven't been arguing," Sarah said.

"Shh! Just listen, *meine liebe,*" Ida scolded.

Luke sighed and his shoulders heaved. Kat knew he blamed himself for some of what he had to say. "Mr.

Coblentz—Reuben—is not just a neighbor to us—he's really a member of our family. Years ago, Reuben didn't want to act Amish, so he left the Plain People for a while, and we had nothing to do with him. But now Reuben wants to be taken back. We are happy and grateful to have him with us again.''

Ida held her half-eaten toast, and Kat gripped her coffee cup.

"You see," Luke said, looking from Eli to Sarah and back again, "Reuben is really your mother's father—a grandfather to you, just like *Grossvater* Jacob was."

"I knew it was something like that!" Eli blurted, grinning. "I knew he liked me a lot!"

Everyone looked at Sarah to see how much she had taken in. "Then, if he's our grandfather, too," she said with a wise nod, "we better make sure he doesn't get kilt and stolen like Grandfather Jacob did. Eli and me—we don't want to get stolen neither."

By 9 a.m. that morning, while the Amish were cutting corn on other farms, Luke and his windmill installation crew of three used his portable generator to hoist Reuben's old tower. It looked a bit worse for wear, Luke thought, but it was good to have it—and its owner—back in place.

"Make sure the legs are down far enough in the old holes, then let's get the new cement filler in!" he called to his crew. "I'm going up to give the mill a last check."

As he put on his safety harness and climbed aloft, Luke glanced down at Kat, sitting with his people. He knew it was insane after just a few weeks to convince her to stay, but he desperately wanted to try. He thought of all the ploys he could use, because he couldn't offer a worldly woman a betrothal without being shunned, just as Reuben had been.

Brooke would need help with Melly when they got her home from Columbus. The doctors had warned them that she would not easily return to normal, especially her motor skills such as walking, even feeding herself. Because Kat had been through a lengthy period of physical rehabilitation, he knew both Melly and she could profit from the time together.

He was frustrated that Kat had turned down that dispatcher job this morning. If she still wanted to open a country antiques shop, he knew the Amish would help her, even donate pieces to get her going. But he knew not to push her.

He had noted that Kat still wore Amish garb, although she didn't need to. He was both surprised and touched that she seemed reluctant to get back to English clothes. As he reached the top of the windmill and pulled a screwdriver from his leather work belt, he tried to picture Kat looking like a worldly cop, wearing a gun belt, pants, a badge, and a cap over those golden flyaway curls.

He was really glad he was up here where no one else could see him close, because tears ran down his cheeks.

Just as they had watched Luke put up Paul's windmill, Kat sat with Ida and the kids on a blanket, this time on Reuben's lawn as Luke hung aloft. Reuben darted everywhere, smiling, bringing out drinks and store-bought cookies for everyone. Mose's kids were here, too, and Lee had appeared through the rows of corn after she dropped some pies off at the farmhouse to feed the harvesters later.

"I feel like a double weight's been lifted from our

shoulders,'' she told Kat. ''Melly's on the road to recovery, and we're rid of poor Marnie. I never would
have imagined her—almost one of our own.''

''Why is she *poor* Marnie?'' Sarah asked. ''She has
lots of money.''

''Because we feel sorry for her,'' Lee said, ''not
just because she will go to prison. Also because she
is a sick lady.''

''Sick in the head and the heart,'' Eli put in before
he popped up again. Kat understood that Eli would
always be marked by losing his mother young, but she
hoped he'd win the struggle to stop fearing for his dad.
Marnie had been horribly damaged by her sad childhood. And Kat could finally admit, in her own way,
that she had, too. But now she knew—really knew—
it wasn't her fault that her brother died, or John Seyjack, either.

''I hope we can stay friends, even if from afar,''
Kat said when she saw Lee staring at her.

''Does it have to be from afar? You know I don't
get to Columbus, if that's where you're going.''

''*Ja*, it is. I can't stay here if I can't *really* stay
here.''

Frowning, Lee would have said more, but Kat got
to her feet and stretched, looking up at Luke as he
checked the gears and cogs. It was wonderful not to
fear for his safety, Kat thought, but somehow, she just
couldn't sit here, watching him, wanting him.

''Guess what I see?'' he called down to everyone
as he pointed back toward his own farm. ''The harvesters are bringing the combine already!''

Eli had been right about the *bump-chug* sound of
the old McCormick corn combine, Kat thought. It was

so loud as it began on the side field that the women preparing the noon meal in Luke's kitchen had to shout when it passed close to the house. The whinny of the big Percherons that pulled the thing and the shouts of men, pierced by the higher pitched voices of the water boys, made a raucous music Kat would never forget.

And how strange it seemed when the cornstalks were cut, for it widened the vistas from the farm. Kat could see to Mose's place across the road and almost to the bell tower of the schoolhouse. But she already missed the tall walls of swaying corn. It would have been so much fun to watch them sprout and grow next year.

"It's sure been good to have you lend us a hand these last weeks," Levi Em told Kat. The Amish were not big on emotional thank-you's, but Kat knew that each one, indirect or not, was from the heart.

"*Ja, gute, ser gute,*" another sister said. "We're going to miss you bad," she went on in German, for they knew Kat was picking up much more of what they said, even though her own vocabulary needed a lot of work. But why try anymore?

Kat sniffed hard and bent over to pop a casserole of macaroni and cheese in the oven. Taking off her padded mitts, she went back to the counter next to the sink where she'd been cutting celery for Levi Em to stuff with peanut butter. As Kat glanced out the window, she saw Eli sprinting toward the door from the back field that the harvesters were just beginning to cut.

The look on his face scared her. Without getting her shawl or bonnet or dropping the knife, she hurried out to meet him.

                    *   *   *

"I can't wait to go home!" Melly told her parents as they sat on opposite edges of her hospital bed. "They said they might release me soon!"

"Maybe even tomorrow," Brooke said, "depending on how all the tests come back."

Brooke felt as if she were the one coming out of a long coma, one of fear and agony. But now that Melly was talking so animatedly, despite her pale skin and the loss of weight, she seemed almost normal again.

"The therapist said I actually talked when I was in the coma," Melly added.

Brooke and Dan exchanged wary glances. They'd decided not to quiz Melly about that now, in case it would upset her.

"Yeah, you did, more than once," Dan admitted.

"Like—crazy stuff?"

"Once," Brooke told her, holding her hand tightly, "you said, 'They're coming,' as if you were reliving the accident again. And once you said you knew who it was—and I thought you meant you recognized me."

"Yeah," Melanie said, drawling out the word and looking past them, as if into the distance. For one moment, Brooke feared she was going to drift off again, but Melly said, "I think I did have dreams—nightmares—about it all. Not about falling, because I don't remember that, but of running with Eli. And I—I thought, despite the sort of disguise on the biker, I did know him, who it was."

"Don't think about it anymore," Dan urged. "You couldn't have known the biker, because he's someone from out of town who was more or less hired to do it. And he's being arrested today."

"No—I..." She paused and her voice faltered before becoming stronger again. She tugged her hands back from them and crossed her arms as if to hug herself. "Dad, Mom, I *did* recognize who it was. Whatever people have been told, he's not from out of town. He's from Maplecreek."

"I can't find *Daad!*" Eli shouted to Kat.

"He said he was going to be the binder man when they started on the back field."

"But he's not where he should be."

"Eli, you've been water boy, right, assigned to the end of a row? Don't worry. You're not going to see him in all that corn until it's cut. When he takes his turn up on the combine, you'll see him again. This isn't like being up on a windmill—"

"No," the child cried. "He's not where he's supposed to be!"

Kat groaned as he ran around the corner of the field, heading toward his post. Her first instinct was to run after him. Her second was to find Luke, but she didn't want to get in the way of the harvesting. And, despite all that had happened for good, she couldn't shake the feeling something could go wrong. What if Eli tried to dart down a row to find his dad and got in the way of those massive horses' hooves or the thrust of the huge blade?

The noise of the machine cutting wide swaths grew louder, then softer, as Kat ran in the direction Eli had gone. From outside the field, gazing down its length to what Ida called the back forty, Kat could see the men waiting their turns; the water boys stood ready with their buckets for the horses and plastic jugs for the men.

But she did not see Eli or Luke. Had that boy run into the field when it was being cut? Since the machine cut multiple rows at once, it would be easy to misjudge how close it was. Besides, with all the noise, no one would hear a child cry for help.

Kat darted back to the front of the field and tore along the edge of it to the other side. The combine seemed to be stopped or idling, its roar somewhat muted. Down this side of the field, she saw more men and boys, this time watering the horses and the harvesters as they paused, about halfway back in the field.

Then Kat realized where Luke could be. Before it was his turn to be a binder man, he might have gone to say a quick farewell to his little golf green. But that didn't tell her where Eli could have gone, unless he knew of the hidden spot and had gone to find his dad there.

Since the combine was stopped and she knew right where it was, she'd just check the golf green.

Kat started into the field. From this direction, she had to step through the rows instead of running down them. Shouldering past heavy ears, sturdy stalks and thick leaves, she realized she still had the paring knife in her hand. Wishing she could use it like an antique corn knife to cut her way in, she pushed through more rows.

"Eli? Luke?"

The green was not far in. This would not take long. If she heard the combine rev up again, she'd get out before the next few passes brought it through this section.

"Eli! Luke! *E-e-e-l-i-i!*"

She pushed free, into the small area of trimmed grass where she'd spent such precious hours with Luke the night they'd buried Bishop Brand.

Luke was there. But he was facedown on the ground, hatless, unmoving, with a bloody head. Wearing ski masks and goggles, two men in black jeans and jackets stood over him.

As the combine roared to life again, they bent their

knees and pivoted, extending their arms stiffly as if in slow motion. It reminded her of the hours she'd spent on the CPD shooting range, because both men held semiautomatic handguns in a perfect, two-hand stance.

And these were pointed right at her.

24

As Kat was targeted, it wasn't her life that flashed through her brain, but two split-second scenes. Seyjack shooting her in Columbus. The man with the nail gun at Amish Acres.

She was too far into the clearing to run. She threw herself flat on the ground. Neither man fired, but they rushed her and stepped on her, pinning her down with their feet, then hands before she could roll away.

The two men working for Marnie! She must have contacted them somehow.

"What have you done to him?" Kat shouted over the roar of the combine. She was suddenly so dizzy, she couldn't tell where the machine was, how close... Was Luke wounded or worse? She was so angry that if they hadn't held her down, she could have ripped both of these bastards apart, guns or not.

"Marnie's given you up!" she shouted at them, though her mouth was shoved into the turf. "The sheriff's onto both of you!"

One laughed. She knew that laugh, didn't she? The last thing the sheriff had said to her was that she had a payday coming. Surely, he didn't mean this!

"You've been interfering since the first, but you're a big help now!" the heavier man shouted, his voice mocking. "We were going to get rid of you later, but this will do just fine. Yeah, Marnie got to make two calls, one to a lawyer—and one to me."

The one with the younger voice snickered. "Two lovers together in the field will make more coleslaw, chop-chop, than just the new Amish leader here."

He sounded like A.J. She'd only had one run-in with him, but his voice and stupid sense of humor ID'd him. She wasn't sure whether to let on that she knew him or not. Thank God the bigger, older man wasn't the sheriff. But was it Tyler or Clay?

"Luke is not the bishop and won't be," she cried. "He's not married. You're picking on the wrong guy this time. Just leave us alone! No one knows who you are! Clear out of here—"

They dragged her by her hair and dress toward Luke. Her skirt ripped, her cap snagged and came off, her hair pulled free.

"Not very Amish-looking to me!" A.J. said, yanking a handful of hair so hard her entire scalp burned.

They turned Luke on his side and pressed her against him. Fresh blood bloomed under his nose. They hadn't been here long. Had they broken his nose? She couldn't tell if he was breathing. Had he fought them? Was he unconscious or dead?

Only when they started to tie her to Luke, feet and hands, did she realized he was tied, too. If he was dead, they wouldn't tie him. They didn't use rope but strips of sheets.

This close to him, she could feel him breathing. He was alive!

"I'd really like to put a bullet in you, city cop," the older man said and leaned down to press the cold muzzle of his pistol against the nape of her neck. Her entire body went ice cold, then numb; she could feel only the hard circle of the muzzle. She waited, holding her breath, trying to concentrate on something lovely and coming up only with the memory of Luke's smile.

"But even in all the mess you two are gonna make," he went on, "I'm not going to risk them finding a bullet to trace. Let's go," he added to A.J.—and then the press of the muzzle was gone from her skin.

It *was* Clay, she thought. She smelled the stench of cigarette smoke, even in the open. She forced her thoughts to the fact she had to get loose before the horses trampled them and the combine blade hacked them to bits. Lying here, tied tightly to Luke in their special place, was like a dream turned frenzied nightmare. She'd had that paring knife with her, as if God had given her the means to cut them loose and escape, but now she had no idea where it had gone.

"Luke. Luke, wake up! Wake up!" she shouted, trying to shake him alert.

Then Eli ran into the clearing.

"Eli!" she screamed. "Untie us!"

Falling to his knees, leaning over them, the boy picked at the knots. "A man was chasing me, a b-bad man with a black mask," he cried, his voice and hands quaking. "And he had goggle eyes like when they shot p-p-paintballs at us! Is *Daad* all right?"

"Yes, he just got hit on the head."

"Not like Melly! That was my fault, but—"

"It wasn't your fault, and don't ever forget that. Just untie us!"

This wasn't working. The boy could not manage the taut knots or break the stretched strips of linen. Kat knew she had to get him away to save himself. She couldn't tell where the combine was, but it was closer, so close. The crunching *thwack-thwack* of the big blade as well as the roar of the old engine grew louder. But she knew, unless she outfoxed the boy, he'd never leave his father.

"I'm going to roll your dad and me away!" she

shrieked. "Get way back! Go out where the corn's already cut, and we'll be right there!"

But she couldn't pull Luke up and over her. Besides, Eli hadn't budged except to stand up. The ground seemed to shudder as she saw the horses' ears and the top of the combine with its busy binder man bent to his task go by, several rows over. On the next pass, they'd be here for sure.

"Eli, I dropped a little knife here somewhere! Can you see my knife?"

"No, but I'm l-looking!" he screamed, crisscrossing the small space. "I've got to go tell the harvesters to stop. I'll stop them."

"Only on the end of a row or else they'll never see you!" she yelled.

But as she watched Eli turn to run, she knew she'd never see him again. He'd be too late. She and Luke would be gone, leaving him and sweet, spunky Sarah to be reared by Ida or Mose and his family. How she'd wanted to be Luke's children's new mother. Impossible! As impossible as salvation was now.

She gasped as the two men in black darted onto the putting green again. "I told you he came this way!" Clay shouted. She was so tempted to tell him she knew who he was, but time was too precious.

To her horror, A.J. scooped up the squirming, shrieking child, threw him over his shoulder and shoved into the corn again behind Clay.

Like a trapped animal, Kat began to chew at the only ligature she could reach, the strip of sheet wrapped around Luke's shoulder and neck that bound her to him. He was not dead, but he was dead weight.

Eli. She had to get free to save Luke and Eli. Clay had said Marnie had called him from jail. Maybe he was here for revenge against Kat for arresting his lover. Or this attack on Luke, her, or even Eli could have been planned before today. Marnie was covering for Clay and A.J. She must have made up the story about the two Cleveland guys.

Kat was enraged that the perverted demons who had tormented the Amish were going to win. They had set this up so that the gentle people would kill their own leader this time. She knew how terrible it was to bear such a burden of guilt....

Kat bucked against her bonds so hard that the ligatures cut into her flesh. All feeling drained from her hands below her wrist ties. Had they bound Paul to the windmill like this? Clay had access to portable generators. Clay had come out of Marnie's house that day with the self-satisfied look of a lover, and Kat had dismissed it. She wanted a lover, too, and to be loved...loved by Luke.

Her hip still hurt, in the same place where she'd been shot with the nail gun. Clay would know all about that. She should have seen it, should have known Clay was behind this. Clay and his son weren't estranged. They'd been in this together—with Marnie—from the first.

In the last moment before she knew the horses and combine would roar through here—through her—she pressed closer to Luke. She loved him. How had that happened so fast? So fast—

The pain in her hip—the knife was under her hip. She rocked to drag Luke down toward the knife, so she could reach it. She twisted her head to pick it up with her mouth, then managed to grasp it with her right hand. Once wounded and worthless, her hand did not betray her with the knife. Grab it, grip it. She sliced the wrist ties she'd stretched so taut that they flew apart.

She cut the other bindings, scrambled to her knees, her feet. Luke seemed as heavy as stone, but with her hands under his armpits, she heaved and tugged to drag him out, through two uncut rows of corn into the bare field that had been sliced to stubble. Even as the team of horses pulled the combine through the putting green area, they were in open field.

Stacking shocks, Mose stood down a ways. He came running with one of the young Miller cousins. She longed to tend Luke, but she had to find Eli.

"He's alive but hurt!" Kat shouted. "The sheriff's out of town, but call his deputies from Luke's office! Two men have taken Eli, and I've got to stop them."

"Two men?" the Miller boy said. "I didn't see Eli, but two men in black went toward Reuben's farm. But Reuben's here with us."

Still gripping her kitchen knife, hiking her skirt knee high, Kat ran. The newly cut field was hard to navigate with its erratic stubble. Clay and A.J. could have pulled into Reuben's, left their car there. One of them had probably ridden the motorbike to throw the fireworks and knew the exit roads down that way. They could have even dumped or hidden the bike in the silo to set up Reuben.

Kat darted into the third and only uncut Brand cornfield and ran down a row straight toward Reuben's. The windmill Luke had erected this morning grew larger as she ran. If she could just climb it, she could see all around, but there was no time. What did those bastards mean to do with—to—Eli? She hadn't saved little Jay or John, but she would die before she'd let anyone hurt Eli.

As Kat neared a road she'd walked with Luke that first day she was on the farm, she heard men's voices. Trying not to suck air so hard, she slowed and pressed her hand into the painful stitch in her side. If she had to take them on, her knife seemed so pitifully small.

"It's a long shot, thinking we can trade this kid for Marnie. If we can't, it'll still keep the Amish from making waves about the accidental deaths of Brand and our lady-cop friend. I owe Marnie something for not naming us."

"She's crazy about you, Dad, that's all I know."

"Just shut up and throw him behind our seats. I'll keep an eye on him while you drive. And we're gonna have to really cover all this up, because I'm not leaving my life here in Maplecreek."

Kat watched as A.J. obeyed his father, putting a limp, bound and gagged Eli into the narrow back seat of the same pickup truck that had stampeded the kids at the schoolhouse. Clay kept talking as he stripped off his ski mask and paintball goggles.

"We've got the Amish scum where we want them. They're not going to be underbidding good, solid Americans for union jobs anymore, I'll tell you that. They're either going to move out, or we'll give them some other little visits to think about. They tried to break my union, but I'm breaking theirs. Okay, let's go."

They got in and slammed both doors. She couldn't let them get away this time. Keeping low, Kat bolted from the field and approached the vehicle from behind. If they glanced back or looked in a rearview mirror, she was doomed. Thank God they had the tailgate down, maybe to show someone following that they had nothing to hide.

Cursing her long skirt, Kat dragged herself up onto the truck bed as A.J. turned the key in the ignition. She crouched behind the single window of the cab, then sprawled out to grip the ridged, hard rubber floor with her hands and feet as the vehicle accelerated. It bounced down the rutted lane, then turned out onto the road. The ride hurt her stomach; she thought she might throw up.

Luke had told her that Brooke and Dan's Jennifer had been abducted years ago and taken far from Amish country. Whatever else Kat had in common with Brooke, she wouldn't let that happen to Eli. The cycle of violence against the Amish had to stop, here and now.

So Kat held on, hoping someone would pull up behind them, praying they would go through town where she could scream for help. She fumbled for her cell phone to call the sheriff's deputies herself, in case the Amish hadn't. At least the dispatcher would send the medics. What if Luke was in a coma, like Melanie had been?

Her heart sank further when she realized her cell phone was gone. It was probably either trampled by the horses or lying in the fields she had run through. She had her knife, but Clay and A.J. had at least two guns—and Eli. But she wasn't letting terrorists and murderers get away this time.

"What the hell!" she heard Clay shout from inside.

He hit the brakes, banging Kat against the back of the truck bed. "Get out of the road!" A.J. shouted, rolling down his window.

Kat peeked through the rear window between the men's shoulders. Amish men, buggies and unhitched horses blocked the road while women and children lined the lane that led to the Brand farm.

"Turn around!" Clay ordered. "If you hit somebody, too damn bad."

Holding onto the side of the truck, Kat kneeled

so the Amish could see her. "They have Eli!" she shouted. "Get help!"

A.J. veered right, then left, sending her rolling. He jerked the truck to a stop, turned, gunned it. That sent her knife flying and nearly threw Kat out, but she held on. Clay stuck his handgun out the side window. At first she thought it was at her, but she saw Reuben had stepped calmly, stoically out into the road, so they didn't have the room they needed to turn.

Kat's cop instincts kicked in. "Gun!" she screamed. "Gun! Reuben, get back, get down!"

She leaned around the side of the truck and clawed at Clay's hand. His shot went low, into the pavement. She twisted his wrist, yanked his arm back and up. She slammed it twice against the back of his open window until the gun dropped and skidded away into the ditch.

Truck wheels squealing, A.J. managed to turn around. He floored it, knocking Kat off balance again. She grabbed the tailgate and, half on, half off the truck bed, held on for her life as they turned back toward Reuben's.

Clay's curses floated to her. A.J. hit the brakes again. Kat heard her deliverance before she saw it, the *bump-chug* of the Amish corn combine somewhere ahead. The truck swerved and skidded sideways against the old machine with a jolt and a *thud*. Kat got slammed into the side of the truck bed again.

"Bring the kid along!" Clay shouted, but he dragged Eli out himself. Kat was over to the passenger's door the minute Clay stepped down onto the road.

They must have thought they'd thrown her out, because they remained intent on the boy, on running into Mose's cornfield across the road on the other side of the water-filled ditch. Clay was slowed because he was carrying Eli, while A.J. led the way. Kat hurled herself onto Clay's back, reached around and pummeled his face, so that he dropped Eli on the asphalt.

Kat grabbed Clay's arm in a hold and flipped him over on his back so his head hit the car door. He slumped to the road, but pulled another gun from his jacket. A .45! She kicked it away before he could aim. She scrambled for the gun, retrieved it and lifted it toward him. Her hand shook holding the weapon after all this time. She knew she'd never have the hand strength to shoot it—but he didn't know that.

"Evidently Marnie told you I'm an undercover cop," she said, staring him down. "Actually I'm an ex-cop who's going to arrest a phony militia rookie and a corrupt union boss who can't even use a nail gun right. Still, everyone will know real soon you're very skilled at using portable generators in the rain. But abducting a child in front of a huge audience isn't very smart. You know, if they weren't the Amish you detest, Mr. Bigler, I imagine they would have lynched you and A.J. by now."

She held the gun stiff-armed despite the fact her hand trembled, and she heard the Amish gasp behind her. She wavered for a moment. She wanted only Clay to think she was berserk enough to shoot.

He went ashen. She thought he'd cry, but that's the way all cornered bullies were. His eyes darted wildly around. Whether he was staring at the Amish or looking for his son, she wasn't sure.

"Tell me—all of us—about your part in this," she demanded. "Now!"

For the Plain People had come from the direction of the dented combine and from down the road to make a circle around Kat and Clay. It was, Kat thought, a circle of safety. These gentle people, in their own way, had stopped these men just as surely as she had.

"Yes, I-I," Clay stammered, "I...Marnie wanted him gone too, Yoder. I took a generator from the worksite—but I didn't try to kill you in the Coblentz silo, I swear it. I was following you in the cornfield that day and saw it, but that was just a freak thing—Tyler's mistake."

"I want to hear about Bishop Paul Yoder!" she demanded. "A man who, with his hardworking crew, had labored side by side with you and your men to build Amish Acres—probably Marnie's own house. Did you kill him?"

"Yes," he whispered. "Yes."

"Then I'll let you tell that to the sheriff and the judge and jury," she said as she heard the distant siren that meant someone had called the sheriff's deputies. She raised her voice to the crowd behind her. "Did A.J. Bigler get away?"

"Ah, no," Reuben said. He sounded out of breath but close by. "Somehow he fell into the water in the ditch and a couple of the brothers took his clothes off so they could dry out. He's right over here—waiting for the officers."

"And Luke?" Kat asked, lowering her gun at last.

"He's got a bad headache," Ida said, coming up behind Kat and putting her trembling arm around her waist. "A concussion, but he's hardheaded. *Ja,* pretty worried about you and Eli, though. Took two men to hold him down in the backyard of the house during all this."

Kat almost collapsed with relief and joy. She hurried to Mose Susan and two others who were tending Eli. He had a goose egg on his head that was already turning a mottled purplish brown, but a boy had never looked so beautiful.

Kat knelt and hugged him. When she tried to sit back, he still held to her so hard that she stood with him in her arms as the crowd parted. The sheriff himself roared up with lights blazing and siren blaring. He jumped out of the car and hurried toward her.

"I see, thanks to you and your friends, Kat, we got the perps under control," he said, managing to look both angry and sheepish.

"Ready and waiting to be arrested," she said.

"Halfway to Cleveland, the officers there radioed me that Marnie gave a bogus address. I came back as fast as I could. I should have trusted you. Anything I can do for you, just—"

"Keep close to your son, Sheriff," she said as she shifted Eli in her arms to get a better hold on him. "Let's go see your *daad,* Eli." He wrapped his arms around her shoulders and his skinny legs around her waist as if he were a little child. The Plain People parted and several patted her on the back as she carried Eli through their midst.

"I'm so glad you saved *Daad,*" the boy said despite his sniffles. "If you'd just stay, Katie, I wouldn't have to try so hard to watch him, 'cause you could help, too."

As Kat kept walking toward the farm, she looked back to see Mose and Levi step forward to explain things to the sheriff. On her way up the lane, she saw Luke running toward them, holding a towel to his head.

It was over now, she told herself, really over. The terror and torment, the cruelty and killing. But her blessed days as an Amish woman—Luke Brand's betrothed—were over, too.

Luke met her halfway up the lane, where they held each other hard with Eli pressed between them.

Epilogue

Kat wished her CPD friends had picked anywhere but here to throw her a Welcome Back, Hero lunch, as the sign on one wall of the rented party room read. Schmidt's Restaurant was in a charming enclave near downtown Columbus called German Village. The food was great but the *bratwurst* sandwiches, hot potato salad, even the German chocolate cake reminded her so much of Amish gatherings, she could have cried.

Not that she needed a reminder of what and who she'd left behind. In the month since she'd been back in Columbus and in the two weeks she'd been working her new CPD dispatcher job, her love for Luke, his family and his people had not muted one bit.

It got worse daily—the memories sharper, stronger.

"Make sure that lime slice in your drink's not old Green Gill," Jim Lowe, the forensic chemist, kidded her as he clinked his glass to hers. "By the way, I just found out I'm going to be called to testify at the trials. They're moving the venue to Cleveland, since it's going to get so much press."

"I know. I'm going to be subpoenaed, too."

"It sounds pretty cut-and-dried against the woman, her union boss lover and his militia kid."

"I just hope it does some good to keep others from

committing hate crimes against the Amish or anyone else. And, for more than one reason, I'm glad it's not going to be held in Amish country.''

Kat moved on through the clusters of conversations. The guests were mostly cops she'd known on the force. Several had said this was a double celebration, for they claimed she'd just disappeared after her recovery from her shooting. Strange, she mused, that she didn't feel a part of these people anymore. She hoped the old sense of belonging would come back in time.

She looked around the room at about twenty cops in uniform, a few in civilian dress. The party was more or less an open house from noon to two, and those on duty who dropped by were supposed to stick to soft drinks instead of beer. As guest-of-honor, she'd been given her favorite old drink, a gin and tonic, but it tasted too sour to her, and she just carried it around. She wasn't on duty today, but she'd worn her uniform. It consisted of a medium-blue shirt and black pants. The shirt had the same patch the officers wore, but the dispatcher badge was much smaller. She was glad she wore a uniform. Somehow, deciding what garments to mix and match when she was off duty had become a real pain lately.

''Yo, Lindley!'' Mike Morelli said and threw an arm around her shoulders so hard he nearly sloshed ginger ale from his stein. A former alcoholic who was completely dry, Mike always drank his sodas from bar glasses. He might seem high but he was just in an ebullient mood, glad to have her back.

''I want you to meet my nephew,'' he told her, ''my brother's boy. See that guy over there.'' He pointed with the stein. The strikingly handsome, black-haired, tanned man was hardly a boy, Kat thought. ''Smart, a doctor, single and definitely feeling his oats,'' Mike added.

"Probably sowing a few wild ones, too,'' she countered.

"Come on, now. He's the best Italian-stallion catch of our entire family—'course, that's since Peg snagged me. I used to look just like that, by the way,'' he said and laughed.

"I may need fixing up, but not that kind,'' she said, elbowing Mike in the ribs.

"You're different since you been back, kiddo. And I don't just mean the fact you're really a hero, locking up those hate crimers. You're not focused and upbeat like you used to be—not that you were ever that much of a happy camper.''

"Morelli, I was too! I loved my job—and I'm glad to have this one.''

"Well,'' he said, shrugging as he took another swig of ginger ale, "you can't cuddle up to a job at night. Think about it.''

As he walked back toward some mutual friends, Kat saw the Italian stallion staring at her with a blindingly white grin. But she longed for a smile that hitched up on the right side first and carved a dimple in a chiseled cheek. And she wanted a family to go home to, one as big and convoluted as Mike and Peg Morelli's.

Columbus—the whole world—had changed for her. The sound of car horns and traffic made her jittery, and she hated the cramped feel of tall buildings pressing in on her. She missed hearing raccoons screech at night and watching Dilly's rhythmic sway on a slow buggy ride. More than that, she longed for Sarah's arms around her legs and Eli's mussed hair and the way the world shimmered when Luke was near.

She excused herself, left her drink on a table and

hurried into the bathroom. Wiping a wet paper towel under her eyes, she stared into the mirror until some friends came in trading stories about the police chief. After chatting with them briefly, she went back out.

It had suddenly become quiet in the room. Kat wondered if she was walking into some surprise—a gift or song or joke they'd set up for her.

When she saw the man standing in the doorway of the restaurant, she thought at first that someone had dressed Amish to kid her. Tall and wide-shouldered, the man took off his flat, broad-brimmed black hat. She gasped when she saw it was Luke.

Was she hallucinating? She felt faint.

Her feet froze for only a moment, then she hurried toward him. Someone had evidently invited him, perhaps to tell everyone what she'd done in Maplecreek or to thank her publicly. But that was so un-Amish.

Her heart thudded. The entire room seemed to tilt toward Luke as if no one else were here. His mere presence seemed to suck the air from the room; she almost couldn't breathe.

He saw her coming. His mouth tilted in that gradual smile as his eyes widened, going thoroughly up and down her. The impact of that was like a physical caress.

"Luke—hi! Did Brooke or Dan bring you in?"

They held hands like a double handshake, then let go. Only in his big, warm grasp did she realize her fingers were ice cold.

"Reuben's looking for a spot to park outside," he explained, "but his car's as shaky as usual."

She nodded. Luke was shaking as if he were still in that car. "It's so nice of you to come. Who contacted you?"

"I went to the main police station, and they sent me here."

"So you weren't invited?"

"We can be out of here in two seconds, if this is a closed party."

"I didn't mean that. I just didn't think... You came looking for me on your own?"

"I had to see you. I thought I should give you some time, but it's been a month. The day you left I had a concussion and figured you weren't thinking very straight either when you took off. I had to hear you say you don't want to live in Maplecreek, to be there with us—to let me court you."

"Court me. But you can't marry me when I'm not Amish—"

"I've got to admit, I'm not the only one hoping you'd consider becoming one of us. Kat, my barn, and Reuben's too, is half full of antique or country furniture that people have been donating for you to come back and start your resale furniture business. Eli and Sarah want you to come back, but the thing is, *I* need you, *I* want you, and *I* love you."

In the continued, curious hush in the room, he'd said those last words so quietly she'd almost had to read his lips. She stared at him now, his mouth taut, even trembling, as if he, too, could cry. His broken nose had healed a bit crooked. She could have happily drowned in the pools of his honest, passionate eyes.

Kat was amazed at the words that tumbled out of her mouth. "I know you don't see movies, Luke, but I saw one called *An Officer and a Gentleman*. At the end of it the hero came looking for the woman he loved with all her co-workers around. He carried her out and she was so happy he came for her and wanted her, and she left her old life behind because she'd loved him from the first."

"And after he carried her out...?"

"It just ended with everyone cheering. But I'm sure she was more than hap—"

His quick switch to loud German surprised her, but she thought he said, "Sweetheart, I've been waiting to touch you, to hold you and not let go!"

When Luke scooped her up, everyone clapped and cheered. Above the noise, she could pick out Morelli's raucous whoops. Luke's hat was crushed between them. She put it on her own head.

Whoever said the Amish were shy, gentle and proper was crazy, Kat thought, as Luke devoured her lips in a crushing kiss in the doorway between the party room and the public restaurant.

"I knew you were missing home," he said as he started for the front door, "especially when I heard I could find you in a place called German Village. Wait until we tell our family."

Home, he'd said. *Family. Our family.*

She laughed through tears of joy and held hard to him as he shouldered the restaurant door open and carried her out.

Author Note

I would like to thank the experts who advised me as I researched this book. Although I greatly appreciate their help, any mistakes or misinterpretations made in presenting facts are the author's and not those of my generous informants:
—Special thanks to former Columbus, Ohio Police Lieutenant Susan Lowe
—To Dr. William Barker for descriptions of Kat's gunshot injuries
—To Garrett Burkham, Physical Therapist, for advice on rehabilitating her wounds
—To Joe Armstrong for information on how the Department of Child and Family Services is organized
—To George W. Hime, Supervisor of the Toxicology Laboratory, Medical Examiner's Office, Miami, Florida
—To *Columbus Dispatch* reporter Holly Zachariah for her articles about Amish trade union difficulties

Also, I owe a debt of gratitude to the Amish of Holmes County, Ohio, for providing the inspiration and the setting for Roscoe County and Maplecreek, which is loosely based on Charm, Ohio, a town surrounded by outlying farms with big barns, silos, large farmhouses and *daadi hauses*.

Thanks too to my wonderful support team of Miranda Stecyk; Amy Moore-Benson; Meg Ruley, Annelise Robey and the Rotrosen Agency; and my proofreader, Amish-country companion and husband, Don Harper.

I hope that readers will enjoy the two other books in this series. Book 1, *Dark Road Home,* is Brooke and Dan's story. *Dark Harvest* is the middle book of the trilogy. Look for *Dark Angel,* Leah Kurtz and Dr. Morelli's story, next spring from Mira Books.

Karen Harper, Columbus, Ohio

Suggested reading group discussion questions for
DARK HARVEST

———————

1. The Amish value cooperation rather than the American ethic of competition. What are the pros and cons of bringing up children with each of these different ethics? Most of us would never choose to be Amish, but what can we learn from them?

2. Kat longs for a strong family unit. What are the advantages of a close-knit family as opposed to one that is more loosely constructed? Which kind of famly are you from and how has that shaped you as a person?

3. The Amish school system relies on rote learning and memory work of basics such as reading, spelling and math. Is this different from the emphasis in schools (up to eighth grade) today? What are the good and bad points of the structured basic education versus more independent, individualized learning?

4. Kat will no doubt give up many things if she becomes Amish, but will she gain things, too? If she marries Luke, do you think she'll regret sacrifices or think they were worth it? Have you seen marriages or relationships where the two people involved were extremely different? Too similar? Is a mix of backgrounds and personalities helpful or harmful?

5. Have you ever wanted to just chuck modern civilization for a simpler life? What would be the pros and cons of this for you and your loved ones?

6. Several key characters, including Kat, come from difficult family backgrounds. How has this affected them? Have you seen or experienced tough childhoods and how have those helped make people what they are today?

7. If you live near an Amish community, how do neighboring English people regard the Plain People? Have you seen negative feeling toward the Amish and why?

8. Hate crimes and terrorism are not just international threats but can include such ''minor'' incidents as elementary school or neighborhood bullying. How can we, as citizens, lessen or stop such everyday events before they reach the stage of crime and prosecution?

[There are many excellent Amish cookbooks. You might make some of the dishes and share them during this discussion.]